Praise for Diann Thor...

GANWOLD'S CHILD

"Thornley's highly respectable debut inaugurates yet another saga laid in a future universe, The Unified Worlds....Good, solid action SF."

—*Booklist*

"A very good first novel. In most ways, it seems to fall within that SF subgenre that can only be called military bildungsroman in which a youngster plunges into a demanding military environment and is forced to find out just how good he is. But Thornley subverts and transforms that subgenre at every turn.

"As for the military speak, the fact is that unlike most writers who toss that stuff in for fake authenticity, Thornley was career military and she uses that language because that's the way military people express their military ideas economically. This novel is exemplary for showing how the effective military mind really works— you'll find no romantic military nonsense here."

—Orson Scott Card writing in
The Magazine of Fantasy & Science Fiction

"Thornley's first novel begins a military SF series set in a far-future universe of alien slavers and bold fighting men and women....The author's skill in bringing space combat to life provides strong focus...well-written."

—*Library Journal*

"*Echoes of Issel* is a terrific book on many levels. Thornley has an unusual gift for creating characters that are immediately fascinating. Characters of great emotional depth whose conflicts are believable and individual.

"Then there is the action. Wow! Yes, she has a military background, which means she knows how combat happens....but some combat veterans convey nothing but tactics; others nothing but the spilled guts. Thornley handles action-adventure scenes with that rare mixture of poise and authority, grace and grittiness, which leaves a reader breathless, heart-pounding, wholly caught up in the story.

"There is a balance few writers achieve—she neither glorifies the violence nor denies the glory due to courage and honor. I have the feeling that Thornley is a writer still in the process of maturing—that we haven't seen anywhere near her best work yet—which means that this impressive and engaging book promises a very bright future."

—Elizabeth Moon

"Thornley's deft rendering of alien culture, battle strategy, and the subtle relations between the main characters should further her popularity with fans of military SF."

—*Booklist*

Tor Books by Diann Thornley
Ganwold's Child
Echoes of Issel

DIANN THORNLEY

ECHOES OF ISSEL

A TOM DOHERTY ASSOCIATES BOOK
NEW YORK

ECHOES OF ISSEL

Copyright © 1996 by Diann Thornley

Cover art by Bruce Jensen

Edited by David G. Hartwell

A Tor Book
Published by Tom Doherty Associates, Inc.
175 Fifth Avenue
New York, NY 10010

Tor Books on the World Wide Web:
http://www.tor.com

Tor® is a registered trademark of Tom Doherty Associates, Inc.

ISBN: 0-812-55097-8

First edition: March 1996
First mass market edition: April 1997

Printed in the United States of America

0 9 8 7 6 5 4 3 2 1

For my agent, Cherry Weiner,
for going the extra mile,
and my editor, David G. Hartwell,
for his faith in me.

ACKNOWLEDGMENTS

I owe a great deal of thanks to a large number of people for their patience and willingness to answer my endless stream of questions while I was writing this book. For the medical portions, I owe special thanks to Debbie Hatchett, R.N., and the other emergency-room nurses of Greene Memorial Hospital in Xenia, Ohio; Robert Rowe, R.N. and paramedic; Dr. Tom Geller, neurologist; Dr. Bill Breuerton and the staff of the Rehabilitation Center of Louisville, Kentucky; Cheryl Whitmore, R.N. and PsyD; and Elizabeth "Liz" Moosman, R.N. For their assistance with and critical review of the military aspects, I want to thank my fellow officers, Captain Joe Scioscia, Captain Dan Bartlett, Captain Gary Watson, Captain Barry Wardlaw, and Lieutenant Colonel Max Remley (Ret.), USAF, and Major David Stock, U.S. Army. I also owe a very special thanks to the Connolly family for all the free meals that accompanied the in-depth critiquing and proofreading of the manuscript through its various stages.

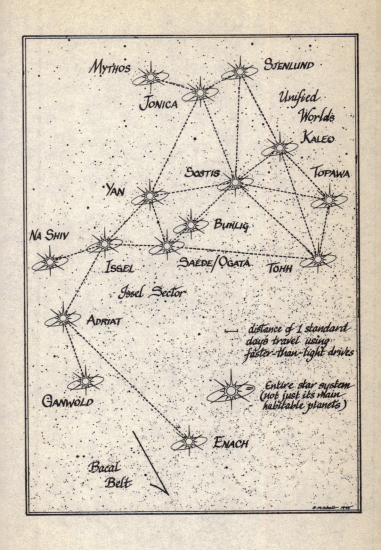

MYTHOS

JONICA

SJENLUND

Unified
Worlds

KALEO

SOSTIS

TOPAWA

YAN

BUHLIG

NA SHIV

ISSEL

SAEDE/OGATA

TOHH

Issel Sector

ADRIAT

— distance of 1 standard
days travel using
faster-than-light drives

GANWOLD

Entire star system
(not just its main
habitable planets)

ENACH

Bacal
Belt

PROLOGUE

Tristan started when a gloved hand closed on his wrist. Its grip drew him out of his dream as hands would pull a drowning swimmer from the water; he broke the surface of consciousness with a gasp. He was sweating.

"Nightmares again?" he heard.

He turned his head with an effort and stared up at the sterile-suited figure beside his bed. It was a moment before he recognized the face inside the head bubble as that of Doctor Libby Moses, the ship's surgeon. "Yes'm," he said, and raised a hand to touch his forehead in respect for her.

"Sit up and let your head clear," she said, and reached out to assist him, careful of the welts that crosshatched his back and shoulders, and the intravenous line that ran from his arm to the hemomanagement system built into the bulkhead. He turned over slowly and sat up—swayed in a sudden whirlpool of dizziness—but Doctor Moses steadied him. "You should try to take some water," she said, and moved away to fill a cup from the dispenser in the bulkhead.

Images from the nightmare flicked across his memory; he could still feel the crimson heat of blood on his hand. He tried to rub the feeling away—

"Tristan?" Doctor Moses said.

He jerked his head up, glimpsed her querying eyes, and his face heated with embarrassment. He ducked his head, touching his brow again.

"What's wrong with your hand?" Moses asked.

He didn't want to talk about it. "Nothing, ma'am," he said, shaking his head.

She held out a cup to him. He had to take it with both hands because they were still so shaky. He managed two or three sips, keeping his gaze lowered, but he could see her at his periphery, standing there watching him. His stomach knotted up. He clamped his teeth on the rim of the cup.

"What are your nightmares about?" Moses asked.

He shuddered. Nearly gagged on another sip of water. Hunching himself in the posture of petition, he said, "Please, I-I really don't want to talk about it right now."

Moses raised an eyebrow at that, but she didn't insist. Instead, she turned her attention to the monitor mounted above his headboard and studied its display.

Beneath the bedsheet, his mattress and pillow were covered with thousands of tiny white and black and silver beads. They were sensors, she had told him, which continuously monitored his temperature and respirations, his blood pressure and pulse—even his bowel sounds and restless activity—and relayed that information not only to the display above his bed but to the med techs' desk as well.

Moses pursed her mouth as she eyed the readouts. "Your blood pressure and temperature are still up," she said, "and I'm reading a lot of activity in your brain, like combat responses to an attack. Whatever that nightmare was about, it must've been pretty intense!"

Tristan barely heard her. The nightmare curled up at the back of his waking consciousness like a tendril of smoke. A shape—two shapes—solidified before his mind's eye.

"What did he do to my mother?" he demanded.

"What, Tris?" Moses turned away from the monitor. "Who did something to your mother?"

Tristan swallowed hard. He shouldn't have said anything, he thought; it only prompted questions. Questions about things he just wanted to forget.

"Your mother will be all right," Moses said. Her tone was

meant to reassure, to comfort him. "She's on bedrest but she's getting her appetite back."

He wondered if he dared to believe her. Wondered if she thought he was crazy.

"My biggest worry right now," she was saying, "is how *you're* feeling."

He ducked his head again, turned it away from her. Felt her watching him for a moment. "What *are* you feeling right now?" she asked gently.

Scared, he thought at once. He couldn't even say that. He shook his head.

Moses was studying him. Closely. But she changed the subject. "Do you still have much pain in your back or ribs?"

The half-healed lacerations throbbed across his back, and every time he moved, there were jabs from his cracked ribs, like a knife piercing his side—

The knife went in upward—

No! He fought the image down, shaking his head, blinking back tears.

The ache in his soul was the worst.

Moses pulled out the fold-down seat from the bulkhead beside his bed and sat down. Picked up his hand as if to count his pulse. "You're having a hard time getting any sleep between the nightmares, aren't you?" she said, looking into his face.

He didn't look back. He kept his head down, kept his teeth closed tight so he wouldn't say anything.

He'd stiffened when she first took his hand, but he didn't attempt to withdraw it; there was something comforting about the contact. His hand lay under her sterile-suit glove, and he realized how hot and dry his skin was.

She released his hand after a moment. Rose and unlocked the medications cabinet and returned to her seat with a packet in her hand. "These will help you relax," she said, tearing it open.

The tension, which had just begun to ebb, shot up again when she tipped the little discs into her palm. It tightened still more as she peeled the backing from one. His whole body was rigid when she looked up.

"What's wrong, Tris?" she asked.

"The patches." His mouth was so dry he could barely rasp out the word. He indicated the discs in her hand. "Please. I don't want them. I-I don't want to sleep again."

Moses shook her head. "These aren't sedation patches; they're electromagnetic buttons. They pick up your normal brain waves and stimulate the ones that cause you to feel relaxed; those are called alpha waves."

They looked like sedation patches. Tristan let his vision flick from the buttons to Moses's face, his eyes narrowed with suspicion.

"At least give them a try," she said. "If they don't help, I'll take them off when I come back later and we won't use them again."

He eyed the patches once more. Probed her gaze with his—cautiously. Finally nodded. "All right," he said. The words were barely audible even to himself.

But he couldn't keep himself from closing his eyes and clenching his teeth as she pressed the miniature transmitters to his temples and forehead.

Moses patted his hand when she finished. "You'll start feeling better in a few minutes," she said.

She paused then, frowning at the deck for a moment before she reached for the keypad above his headboard. "I'm going to put you on NonREM, too," she said. "It's a sleep inducer that keeps you from entering the REM, or dream state, of sleep; it'll prevent the nightmares. We can only use it for a couple of nights, but that should be enough to get you over the exhaustion so you can start to heal."

When the prescription appeared on the small screen beside his monitor, she looked it over and keyed in something else. "There. That won't kick in until tonight." She looked over at him. "How do you feel now?"

The tautness had left his muscles and stomach, he realized

at once. His hands had stopped shaking. The gnawing, guilty fear had subsided. "Better," he said.

"Good," said Moses. And then, "Your father would like to see you today, just for a couple of minutes."

Tristan swallowed reflexively. His guts knotted back up on themselves; his palms were suddenly damp. "Do I have to see him?" he asked.

Moses's face was a mask of neutrality. "Not right now, if that's what you want," she said. "But you'll have to deal with these things eventually—when you're ready to, of course—in order to really heal." She was studying him again. "What is it about your father that makes you feel so uneasy?"

He shook his head, let it droop. He wasn't even sure he knew—except that he didn't know his father. All he knew were the terms others used when they talked about him:

Admiral.

Assassin.

Hero.

Traitor.

Fighter pilot.

Brilliant strategist.

Religious fanatic.

The words tumbled around in his mind: memories of his mother's bedtime stories when he was a child mixed up with the things the governor had told him.

He shuddered.

Doctor Moses was watching him when he looked up. He couldn't meet her gaze; he ducked his head once more and made a resigned motion with one hand. "Let him come in," he said.

"Okay, Tris." She rose. "I'll see you this afternoon." And she squeezed his hand and left the room.

ONE

One glimpse of Darcie's eyes, one glimpse of the color that rose along her cheekbones when she roused and saw him sitting there, left Lujan feeling as awkward as a teenage boy alone with the prettiest girl in the class, incapable of putting one coherent word after another. He'd felt that way for the last several hours, sitting here watching her sleep. "Darcie?" he said.

She studied him for a full minute, sleepily. "I guess I wasn't just dreaming after all," she said at last. "You're still here."

His hands were sweaty inside the gloves of the sterile suit he wore, but he smiled. "I hope that's good."

The smile she responded with appeared uncertain. Her gaze held his for a second more—then slipped away. "You're an admiral now," she said. Sighed it. "And I'm a mess. My face feels like peimu leather, my hands are callused, and my hair—" She broke off, coughing, and turned away as she covered her mouth.

"I've never seen anyone with hair as long as yours," Lujan said. He hesitated, then added, "I—like it that way."

It tumbled loose and wavy around her shoulders, and when she'd gathered it up earlier and drawn it free of the bedcovers, he'd been startled to realize it would reach nearly to her knees if she stood up.

"It's all gone gray," she said.

"So has mine," Lujan countered.

"At least yours looks—dignified."

He laughed at that, but she lowered her attention to her hands, interlocked tightly in her lap; and he found himself once more at a loss for words.

Several silent seconds followed, each more strained than the last, and then Darcie looked up again and asked, "How is Tristan? Have you seen him yet?"

Lujan sighed, partly with relief at the change of subject and partly out of anxiety for their son. "Not yet," he said, and leaned forward on the fold-down seat to plant his elbows on his knees. "Doctor Moses says he's still running a fever and that he had nightmares all night." He glanced up from the deck, met her gaze. "Did she—tell you the rest of it?"

"She said he'd—been flogged," said Darcie. Her voice was little more than a shocked whisper, her face a mask of maternal anguish.

Lujan nodded. Returned his vision to his boots. "Mordan Renier did it to try to coerce me. He—sent me the holograms." He suppressed a shudder. But he couldn't keep his jaw from tightening, his eyes from narrowing with horror and fury at the memory of those images.

He could feel Darcie's stare. "Mordan beat Tris to coerce you? To do what?"

"To sell out Sostis," Lujan said, "the way he did during the War of Resistance. I wouldn't, of course, so he . . ." He couldn't finish. He shook his head, swallowed hard. Couldn't bring himself to look at her.

The silence after that seemed to stretch on forever, and then she finally said, very quietly, as if it were a eulogy, "He looks like you. He has your blue eyes, your mouth, and your sandy hair color. . . . He'll be nineteen in another few months."

He looked up at that. Studied her face—a shade paler now, he thought, than it had been when he came in. "I'm sorry," he said. "I did all I could."

"Libby had told me already."

"Then you didn't need to hear it again." He straightened

on the seat, rose to his feet. "I should probably just leave and let you rest."

She didn't say anything, but he felt her gaze follow him as he crossed to the door.

In the isolation lock between her room and the main corridor, he clenched his teeth as he stripped the sterile suit off from over his uniform. *Pretty lousy way to get reacquainted,* he berated himself. *Almost as bad as the first time.*

He was still scowling to himself as he headed up the corridor out of sickbay.

"Ladies and gentlemen," announced the spacer at the situation-room doorway, "the commander!"

The situation room had remained mostly empty for the briefings given earlier during the spacecraft carrier's simulated night, but every chair and holograph pad was occupied now. Every combatant in the Spherzah fleet was represented—and every officer, whether *Destrier's* own, present in the flesh, or the other ships' captains, attending via two-way holographic transmission from their vessels, came to attention as Admiral Lujan Ansellic Serege entered the room.

They formed a somber double-file down each side of the conference table's length, men and women clad in battle-dress uniforms marked only with name tape, rank, and shoulder patch. The patch bore the silhouette of a bird of prey with talons extended: the Kalese spherzah, from which the Unified Worlds' special operations force took its name.

"Please be seated," Lujan said, crossing to his place at the table's head. When everyone was, he nodded to the lieutenant standing at the podium. "Good morning, Petra."

" 'Morning, sir," the young woman said. "This situation update is classified Top Secret, releasable to the Unified Worlds."

She touched the cue on her podium and a map of a peninsula with several locations marked appeared in the holotank behind her. A key in a lower corner included the time-zone notation, to which the fleet's chronometers had been synchronized before its arrival in the Saede system.

"During the past night," she began, "Unified Worlds forces on the surface of Saede began cleanup operations throughout the militarized zone. Exchange of fire at the Assak surface-to-space transshipment depot on the Unkai Peninsula had ceased by seventeen-hundred local time yesterday, with the complex under the control of Unified Worlds forces.

"A POW facility has been set up inside Assak's main depot," she said, "and prisoner in-processing and interrogation are continuing at this time." An image of several enemy soldiers being searched by Spherzah captors filled the holotank. "Our troops report little resistance from human and umedo soldiers, but the masuki prefer suicide to surrender."

"No great loss," murmured someone at Lujan's left, and some of the others chuckled.

"They might have provided some useful intelligence information," Lujan said quietly.

A three-dimensional galactic map appeared in the holotank, showing Saede in relation to the Unified Worlds' protectorate planet, Yan, and the enemy homeworld, Issel. "The Cathana Range tracking station on Yan has confirmed that the last Isselan vessels departed the Yan system during the past twelve standard hours," the briefer said. "Their last known trajectory was toward the Yan-Issel lightskip point. Though Issel suffered heavy losses at Yan, the remaining ships could reinforce other fleets for another attack. Their most probable course of action is to attempt to retake Saede."

The lieutenant cued up an image of a middle-aged man in an Isselan general's uniform. "In other developments, sir, the Issel system has been placed under martial law. No reason was given for that action and the announcement made no mention of Sector General Mordan Renier, but a military coup seems the most likely explanation, particularly since the statement was signed by General Manua Ochakas, commander-in-chief of Intersystem Operations. We have no further information on that matter at this time."

A murmur ran up and down the table at that, taut voices

reined in to mutters. Lujan stroked his mustache with his forefinger and furrowed his brow at the implications of it.

"In conclusion, sir," the briefer said when the murmur had subsided, "the following charts provide the Isselan fleet status and battle-damage assessment to date." She touched the cue; the Isselan general was replaced by columns of numbers. "The charts show Isselan space and surface units by troop strength and equipment holdings and give numbers neutralized and forces remaining."

She paused to allow the command staff to study the charts, and Lujan spent a few moments on each. "What are our losses?" he asked.

"Lighter than expected, sir," replied the acting chief of operations, Lieutenant Commander Merrel. "We had fifty-two killed in action, two hundred nine wounded, and four are listed as missing. We also lost a troop shuttle and two fighters to surface fire. The shuttle had just finished unloading and was lifting off with a minimum crew of three aboard."

Silence hung over the conference table for several seconds, and Lujan turned back to the lieutenant at the podium. She said, "That's all I have, sir. Are there any questions?"

"Just a request, Petra." Lujan shifted forward in his chair. "Watch the message traffic for any mention of Sector General Renier. His status could be a factor in determining how Issel will carry out this conflict."

"Yes, sir." The briefer nodded. "Are there any others?"

"I have one." The hologram of Captain Kheyl of the destroyer *Hoved* raised its hand. "If Issel tries to retake Saede as you project, how much warning time will we have?"

"Five standard days from the time of launch, ma'am," the lieutenant said.

Kheyl's hologram nodded.

Lujan turned to his operations officer. "Have we received battle reports from our fleets at Yan?"

"They hadn't come in before I headed up here, sir," Merrel said.

"Marcus?" Lujan addressed his intelligence chief. "Any initial reports?"

"Not yet, sir." The commander shook his head.

"I'd like to see them when they do come," Lujan said. "I'd like to know what kind of impression Admiral Ne's people had of the masuki in the Isselan attack force. Did they appear to be assets? Or were they liabilities, as they were to the fleet we faced at Buhlig? That flagship had a bridge crew of better than fifty-percent masuki, and they killed Captain Mebius when we defeated them."

"Gutted the guy right there on the viewscreen," said *Destrier*'s executive officer, Commander O'Keaf, "and then they all committed suicide." He shook his head. "By the time our boarding party got over there, the bridge looked like a biorecycling plant! Smelled like one, too."

"I don't understand that," said the captain of the heavy cruiser *Asgarth*. "They killed the captain—a mutiny, basically—and then they killed *themselves?*" He sounded incredulous.

Commander Marcus Ullen, chief of *Destrier*'s intelligence section, motioned with one hand. "This is masuk mentality we're dealing with, remember. It was a mutiny, all right—the people we took off those ships as POWs confirmed that—but with some different implications than a mutiny by a human crew."

When *Asgarth*'s captain arched a questioning brow at that, Ullen explained, "The masuki are slave keepers. They prefer capture to killing because captives mean wealth, either as personal possessions or as profit from the slave market; the only prisoners they kill are those they consider unsalable." He spread his hands. "Worthless, in other words.

"On rare occasions, however, they've been known to use killing as a form of insult. It can go two ways, and I believe that's what we saw at Buhlig. They killed Mebius as an insult to their Isselan commanders, implying that they're worthless, and then they took their own lives to insult us—to deprive us of the wealth of slaves."

Asgarth's captain snorted. "They have an inflated estimation of their own value!"

"Masuki aren't subordinate," Lujan said, "particularly to a race they usually enslave." He tapped the tabletop briefly with his fingers. "Makes one wonder how long Issel's alliance with the Bacal Belt can be expected to last, or whether it just ended, with a coup." Several others along the table nodded thoughtfully at that, and Lujan leaned back in his chair and looked across at Ullen. "This is something we need to keep under a close watch. Monitor every signal coming out of the Issel system."

When the other nodded, Lujan turned to *Destrier*'s captain and more immediate concerns. "Ben, the rest of the staff meeting is yours."

Captain Benjamin Horsch nodded and looked around the situation room. "According to a communiqué we received during this past night," he said, "the Sostis Sixth Fleet out of East Odymis is on its way out to relieve us; it should arrive a few days behind our resupply and tender ships." Glancing down the table, he said, "I'll be glad to see the Sostish High Command take charge of its own conflict. Unless Issel or the masuki pop something new out of the ether, we should be able to head for homeport early next month."

Doctor Libby Moses must have returned from staff meeting only moments before his arrival, Lujan thought as he entered sickbay; she emerged from her office up the corridor ahead of him, pulling her lab coat back on over her uniform. Pausing to adjust it, she spotted him and waited for him to join her.

"Lujan, you look like a ghost!" she said as he drew up. "If you don't get some rest soon, you'll be in worse shape than your wounded!"

He responded with a dim smile beneath his mustache.

And Doctor Moses shook her head. "You're a hopeless cause!"

He ignored that; he just asked, "How *are* the wounded?"

"You can go in to see them today," she said. "Most are sufficiently stabilized now."

"Good," he said. "And my family?"

Libby Moses was an empathic specialist, trained to read every subtlety of posture, of gesture, of vocal inflection like words on a screen, but she probably could have sensed his unspoken questions without any of that, Lujan knew. They had known each other since he was an ensign in the Sostis Space Force, before he was even a candidate for the Spherzah, let alone that force's chief commander.

"Darcie's responding well," Libby said, "but I'll have to keep her in isolation for a few days. It took us a while to make the diagnosis. When the usual tests came up blank, we ran a battery of gene probes and enzyme studies, and ended up doing a complete immunoglobulin profile as well."

Lujan stiffened at that. "What is it?"

"It's a compound illness," Libby said. "It looks like she picked up some kind of virus somewhere along the way, probably from the natives she and Tristan lived with all those years. But she never knew she'd been exposed because she didn't develop any of the usual symptoms of a virus; it stayed dormant. What seems to have been the catalyst was contact with some kind of local fungal spores. Her body's attempt to fight off a fungal infection triggered the virus."

Lujan's heart contracted. "Can it be treated?"

Libby nodded. "Fortunately, yes. She received an injection with a gene-spliced bacillus just after you left for staff meeting. By the end of the week it will have reproduced enough to inactivate the virus, and the broad-spectrum antibiotics we're giving her will take care of the fungus. Beyond that, she'll just need a few weeks of bedrest and proper diet to regain her normal weight and put her back on her feet."

"Good," Lujan said again, and allowed himself a sigh of relief. Over the last twenty-four standard hours, he'd spent every moment he could spare away from command responsibilities sitting with Darcie or walking the corridor between the cubicles where the wounded troops, including his own son, lay. "What about Tristan?" he asked.

Libby drew a deep breath. "Physically," she told him, "he'll mend, too, once he gets over his exhaustion. He and Darcie are both on interferons to accelerate the healing. It's his mental cargo that concerns me most. Pretty rough stuff the kid's dealing with, Lujan—and not too successfully at this point. It may take hypnosis to help him talk it out." She sighed. "For now I'm using electromagnetic buttons to relieve his anxiety, and I'm giving him a sleep inducer for a couple of nights to block out the nightmares. But he's also been exposed to that Ganwold virus—and to a few other diseases I thought had been eradicated—so you'll have to wear a full-protection sterile suit in his cubicle, too, until I can be sure he's not a carrier. We can't risk either one of you infecting the other."

Everything in Lujan's chest constricted as he listened. "May I see him?" he asked.

"Yes," Libby said, and then hesitated, as if deliberating over adding something else. "Just keep it short," she told him.

Tristan looked up at him and swallowed hard—like a child expecting punishment, Lujan thought—when he paused in the doorway.

"Hello, son," he said. He found it difficult to speak, looking into the youth's face. There was no remnant of the childhood he'd missed, no trace left of the toddler he'd carried on his shoulders and hugged good-bye too many years ago, a few months before the War of Resistance ended.

His duties had detained him in the Enach system following the final battle there, so he'd persuaded Darcie to take some leave, bring Tristan, and come join him. Their transport had vanished several days out of port; search-and-rescue teams had never found a trace of it. But a few months ago his mate and son had suddenly reappeared—as hostages in the Issel system, held by Sector General Mordan Renier.

"Tristan," he said, crossing to the bedside, and felt his

throat tighten at glimpsing the youth's eyes, devoid of trust, and the welts across his broadening shoulders. He wanted to put his arms around his son, to pull him to himself, but that would doubtless cause pain, and Tristan had already had too much of that.

"Sir," his son said, and swallowed again.

Lujan tried to smile. "You don't have to call me that, Tris. 'Father' is fine with me."

Tristan's eyes searched his at that, a multitude of questions in them, and doubts, and Lujan wondered what to say. Nothing he thought of lent itself to being put into words. "I'm—very thankful—to have you back," he said at last.

Tristan ducked his head, turned his face away. "No you're not," he said. The words were barely audible but Lujan didn't miss their bitter edge.

He waited several moments but the youth said nothing more, offered no explanation. So he reached out, slowly, and placed a hand on his son's shoulder. "Yes, I am, son," he said.

The youth only studied him, his expression full of doubt, all the questions back in his eyes.

They were questions he would have to answer for himself, Lujan knew. But those answers wouldn't come easily, if they ever came at all. The hurt he saw in his son's face recalled his own grief when Darcie and Tristan were first lost. It had taken months to put it to rest and years to try to ease the emptiness.

Though Tristan's reconciliation with his recent experiences would have to come from within himself, he wouldn't have to deal with them alone, Lujan vowed. He gripped the youth's shoulder more tightly. "I'll be here when you need me, son," he said.

Tristan didn't answer.

Doctor Moses was waiting when he came out into the isolation lock. She activated ultraviolet lights to kill any virus on the sterile suit. Didn't speak until he'd removed his head bubble and turned to face her. Then she said, "When was the last time you got some real sleep, Lujan?"

He tried briefly to remember and couldn't.

"That's what I thought," she said. "You're spreading yourself too thin between your fleet and your family and what's happening down there on Saede. You can't keep going like this much longer."

He handed her the head bubble. "I'm all right," he said, and shrugged out of the sterile suit.

Libby looked him in the eye. "You're too tired. Your doctor's ordering you to your quarters for a few hours of sleep." She pressed a slip of paper into his hand before she bundled the suit into its sterilization chamber. "Take that to the techs' desk on your way out; they'll give you what you need. We don't need you joining your troops on the patient roster."

Her tone of voice provoked a smile. "Yes, ma'am," he said.

Entering the admiral's quarters a few minutes later, he strode across the compact living area and paused before one of the three observation panes in the far bulkhead. Each was nearly the height and width of a man, and at the moment they admitted the only light in the room, reflected from the blue and green world that turned beyond them.

The berth in his sleeping cabin resembled a small square cave, built into the bulkhead with stowage compartments for clothing and gear above and below it. Lujan peeled the backing from the sleeping patch Libby had prescribed and pressed it to his temple before he removed his boots and shirt and stretched out in the berth. He stared at its overhead, unable to get Tristan's haunted eyes out of his mind.

It was late morning when he woke. There was no residual drowsiness, just a fully rested feeling. With a glance over at the timepanel on the bulkhead, he sat up, peeled off the patch, and reached for his shirt.

He was tucking it in as he entered his quarters office. Activating the desk terminal, he said, "Access the ship's main library and list any items on masuk sociology and military history added in the last six standard months."

"Accessing," came the synthesized response. And after several seconds, "There are thirty-seven new items on the topics you requested, sir." The list ran down the right margin of the screen.

Lujan scanned it, selected half a dozen, and turned away to fill a mug with steaming shuk from the bulkhead dispenser as the first item appeared on the screen.

He had just taken the first swallow, had barely seated himself to begin reading, when the commset buzzed. "Open," he said. "Serege here."

It was the operations officer. "Lieutenant Commander Merrel, sir. Those battle reports have come in. No time-critical items. Do you want them forwarded to your desk screen?"

"No," Lujan said. "Notify Captain Horsch and the intelligence section. We'll come to the CIC."

When Commander Ullen had joined Lujan and Horsch in the Combat Information Center, Merrel said, "These reports are in audio only, gentlemen. We also received a log entry made by Admiral Ne, commander of the Sostis Eighth Fleet out of Ch'on-dok." He glanced at Lujan. "That may actually provide more information on the masuk question than the formal reports do, sir." He switched on the audicorder.

"Log entry made at twenty-two-eighteen ship's time, day thirteen of month two," it began. "This is Admiral Ne Chong-Son aboard the flagship *Aboji*, Ch'on-dok Eighth Space Fleet."

Ne's Standard was formal and accented with the inflections of his native language but that didn't interfere with understanding. "Exchange of fire ceased by twenty-thirty-two ship's time," he said. "Eighth Fleet has lost nine ships. Five more have sustained moderate battle damage and eighteen have light damage, but the Isselan attack fleet has been reduced by half, from sixty to approximately thirty ships. I consider it still a dangerous force.

"Our call for its surrender was answered with a statement to the effect of, 'We will not surrender. We will have our revenge.' The response was made in audio only and the speaker refused to identify either himself or his ship, despite our repeated order that he do so.

"Whereupon, we again ordered the Isselan fleet to surrender, this time with a warning that failure to do so would force us to continue the engagement. The refusal was repeated. At that point, I ordered the Eighth Fleet to reengage the enemy.

"Within two standard hours the remaining Isselan ships began to withdraw, still returning fire. Our forces continued pursuit to the limit of Yan's planetary defense zone.

"Most of my ship captains and command staff share my suspicion that the Isselan fleet is under masuk command. However, if that is the case, we are puzzled by the fleet's retreat from the Yan system, as that seems an unlikely course of action for a masuk commander. Therefore, we are holding our defensive positions in Yan's planetary space and maintaining our alert status until further notice. End of entry. Admiral Ne Chong-Son out."

Everyone exchanged glances, and Captain Horsch shook his head. "I've never heard of masuki retreating before, but the rest of the encounter sounds like what you'd expect from them." He glanced sideways at the intelligence chief. "What do you think, Marcus?"

"It sounds like masuki to me," Ullen said. "Above all else, they're unpredictable."

"How do you interpret their statement about getting revenge?" Horsch asked.

Ullen directed their attention to the holotable they sat around, which displayed a map of the Saede, Issel, and Yan star systems. "The most likely scenario," he said, "is that they'll return to Issel to reinforce other fleets for a second strike against Yan and Saede. As the lieutenant said in her briefing this morning, they appear to be heading for the Yan-Issel light-skip point.

"But—and this is where masuk unpredictability comes in"—he glanced around the circle—"we have no way of confirming right now whether or not they actually made the 'skip. Once outside the Yan system, they could have changed course. They could be regrouping for another attack on Yan, or"—he traced a flight path across the holotable with a blunt finger—

"they could even be heading toward Saede."

"What?" said Horsch.

Ullen tapped the holotable with his finger. "By the time they began their retreat from Yan, the Isselan fleet would have known the outcome of the battle at Buhlig; Admiral Ne did. Knowing that, they could have projected our final destination. For all we know, the masuki may intend to get revenge for their Buhlig fleet."

"That'd be just like a bunch of those hairballs," said Merrel. "What's their strength?"

"According to intelligence reports from Yan," said Ullen, "it's estimated between twenty-five and thirty ships, including three carriers."

"They're crazy enough to try it with only ten ships!" said Merrel.

It was an unlikely scenario, Lujan thought, except that the masuki had long ago proven themselves capable of irrational actions. They seemed to be driven only by emotion and the convoluted expectations of their culture, disregarding even the loss of their own lives. A masuk attack against Saede could not be discounted entirely.

"If that's what they're doing," said Horsch, "how soon should we expect the attack?"

"In less than seventy-two hours, sir," said Ullen.

TWO

Blood still stained the deck in the center of the *Adamaman's* bridge where the human captain had been killed. s'Agat Id Du'ul gave no thought to having it cleaned up, though it had been there for several days and had begun to smell. The scent was not offensive to masuk noses.

The bridge was not the only place on the spacecraft carrier that had been bloodied. Id Du'ul had given the word and humans had died—the ones most likely to oppose him, whose potential for trouble outweighed their worth. The rest, having been made to witness the example of their officers, had been herded into the spacers' open berthing areas, like the livestock he considered them, and masuk guards had been posted.

Id Du'ul had kept three humans on the bridge: the ones he needed to operate the navigation computers, the lightskip drives, and the communications console. All three of them were young, their faces hairless as an infant's, and their fear caused their bodies to give off an odor stronger than the scent of the blood on the deck.

They had value to him, he had told them. They should feel honored that he, a prince of Mi'ika, had selected them to serve him. He expected that they would be wise enough to recognize that and to perform their duties well, for he was in a position to honor them further by presenting them as gifts to the Pasha of Mi'ika.

They should also remember, he had said, that on Mi'ika

worthless slaves were neither given nor sold. And he had toyed with the handle of the knife in his sash, the knife he had used to dispose of their captain.

They were all at their posts now, their faces white and their bodies sweating under their uniforms. Id Du'ul paced the bridge, watching them. They would obey him, he knew. He had often been told how much humans feared death and how they would do anything to postpone it.

"Sire," said the one at the nav station, "we are now sixteen minutes from the lightskip window."

Id Du'ul acknowledged with a small gesture and addressed the human at the engineering station. "Begin acceleration to lightskip speed," he said in their language. They didn't speak his.

He didn't return to the command chair until the warning horns sounded, and even then he didn't secure its acceleration straps. They wouldn't have reached around his torso in any case. "Begin countdown to lightskip," he ordered.

An artificial human voice intoned human numbers over the intercom, and he felt the hair on the back of his neck rise with anticipation. The sensation of 'skip was like being torn apart in battle, as exhilarating as being in rut. He heard the roar of his pulse in his ears and answered with a roar of his own. Space ripped open all around him and he emerged from lightskip sweating and aroused.

He looked around the bridge, still panting.

The humans were unconscious at their consoles.

It didn't matter. They had served him well; they had given him their world. He would keep his promise to them.

Issel's star burned before him on the bridge viewscreen, only a little more prominent than the constellations beyond it in this view from the outskirts of its system. The blue planet that followed the second orbit out from that star wouldn't become visible for another day and a half, but he knew that it bore enough human wealth to satiate half the worlds in the Bacal Belt. He ran his tongue over his upper canines.

"Sire."

The human at the communications console had lifted his head. He was white and wet around the mouth and nose. He swallowed once, twice, and his hand shook as he touched his headset. "Sire," he said again, "we're receiving a signal. It's from the command post on Issel Two."

Id Du'ul considered that for a moment. His masuk subordinates studied him, silent, until he sat back in the command chair and smiled. "Answer their signal," he said. "Tell them, in your language, that we have battle damage and must enter the system at once for repairs."

"Yes, sire," said the young man.

Id Du'ul saw the way he set his jaw, the tremor of his hands as they moved over the console, selecting frequency and mode. He didn't see the moment's hesitation, or the sudden resolve in the young man's eyes despite the sweat that welled up on his forehead as he entered the message.

The silent signal was encrypted now, but it would be plainly understood when it came through Issel II's command-post receiver.

General Manua Ochakas glanced around the command post, a compact amphitheater hewn from stone two kilometers beneath the surface of one of Issel's two moons. The secure commsets placed at intervals along each tier of desks and the three viewscreens that faced them still weren't functioning despite numerous efforts to find and fix the problems.

"Are you sending on all hailing frequencies?" Ochakas asked the NCO at the comms console.

"Yes, sir," the tech sergeant said. "All channels are open." Adjusting his headset, he bent over the panel again.

It was an antiquated piece of equipment, pulled out of some storage room and dusted off, but it was the only back-up system available and right now Ochakas was grateful to have it.

He furrowed his brow. "Carry on, then," he told the sergeant. "Request acknowledgment."

"Yes, sir."

Ochakas was Isselan, a stocky man in his late fifties, with a receding hairline and a paunch that tested the clasps of his uniform jacket. He had never wanted to fight the war he was now involved in, had never wanted the position he now held. Both had fallen to him a few hours after the scan screens went blank, when Sector General Mordan Renier was found sprawled on the floor of his study with an energy pistol lying near his cold hand. Ochakas grimaced, remembering the scene.

Mordan Renier had not been a native Isselan. He was Sostish—had been the hereditary World Governor of Sostis—until the enemy Dominion appointed him Sector General over several star systems in exchange for his homeworld's allegiance during the War of Resistance.

Already devastated by the war, Issel had benefited under his rule as Sector General. In the twenty-six years since the Dominion's defeat by the Unified Worlds, Renier had taken on the task of rebuilding Issel's razed cities, industries, and agricultural areas. It had required patience and discipline and sacrifice from the people, but it had put roofs over heads and food on tables. And as Issel had reclaimed its lost glory, the success of their efforts had united the people in support of their Sector General.

Until he had become obsessed with regaining the homeworld he had ultimately lost.

The costs of building an arsenal had come from the civilian economy. Over the last two years Ochakas had seen the standard of living sag as emphasis was shifted from consumer to heavy industry. He had seen universities close as students were conscripted to fill industrial shock forces—and he'd seen those students marching and shouting through city streets until they were arrested and tried and sentenced to hard labor in Issel II's carmite mines.

Ochakas had never approved of either the student arrests or the effort to recapture Sostis.

Turning away from the empty screens, he began to pace the width of the command post. He resisted a shudder at the sensation of narrowed eyes following him. Forced himself not to glance back at their owners, who lounged against the command post's rear wall.

They were masuki.

Renier had signed a pact with the rulers of several masuk worlds despite all advice against it. Ochakas had never trusted them, but Renier had granted the masuki officer's billets in his attack fleets, had assigned them to his bridge crews, had even given one command over his base on Saede.

Two days ago Renier's bid to take Sostis had failed. The Unified Worlds had broken both prongs of the attack, at Buhlig and Yan, and then moved on to Saede.

There had been no masuk survivors at Buhlig; the masuki preferred death to capture. Ochakas suspected it was because, being slavers themselves, they had expected to be enslaved by their conquerors. He could understand that. What he couldn't understand was why they had slain the human captain as well. To prevent *him* from being captured? He doubted it. Masuki were not known for their compassion.

Half of Issel's second fleet had survived the battle at Yan; Ochakas had received its admiral's reports in this command post before the communications were disrupted and the scan screens went blank. That fleet had also been heavily manned with masuki.

The Yan fleet was limping home now; it had just cleared the Issel-Yan lightskip point. But with no response yet to the command post's hails, Ochakas still didn't know how many ships had made it through and how many survivors there were.

He needed those ships, those survivors, despite his dislike for masuki. His distrust of the Unified Worlds in general and of Sostis in particular ran twenty-six years deeper. He scowled at the floor. With both Yan and Saede now under their control, there was nothing to prevent the Unified Worlds from making a retaliatory attack against Issel.

At the moment, a third fleet was departing the docking arms of Issel's main space stations. Its original orders, to strengthen the forces launched against Sostis days before, had been canceled; its battle groups were now spreading out on early warning defense patrols of the star system. The Yan fleet would be needed to reinforce them.

Ochakas turned back to the knot of men standing around the communications console. "What's our Yan fleet's ETA here from the 'skip point?" he asked.

"Based on the time they were picked up by our early warning systems, a little over seventy-six hours, sir," said his operations officer.

Ochakas frowned. "They should be receiving our hails by now!" he said, mostly to himself. "They should be responding!"

"Maybe they can't, sir," said one of the younger men, a lieutenant named Siador. "Maybe they've got damage."

"To *every* ship's long-range communications systems?" Ochakas shook his head. "That's highly unlikely."

"They may be running silent intentionally," said someone else. "They may have good reason to out there."

Ochakas didn't want to imagine what that reason might be; his first few thoughts on it sent chills up his spine. "Keep trying to hail them," he said.

After straining for so long to pick up *anything*, the crackle through his headset was like a clap of thunder. Tech Sergeant Tradoc stiffened and shot a glance at his console. One amber panel in a column of twenty had begun to glow: The incoming message was encrypted. Tradoc toggled a couple of switches.

Words emerged from the static, rattling in his earphones: ". . . control! This is an attack! Issel II, this is *Adamaman*. Our ships are under masuk control! This is . . ."

As the message repeated itself, he slipped a surreptitious look over his shoulder and located the masuki, muttering to each other at the far side of the room. He caught his commander's eye with a slight motion of one hand.

"Sergeant?" said General Ochakas.

He scribbled the message on a notepad, as casually as if he

were doodling, in case the masuki were watching.

The general arched an eyebrow, and his mouth pursed almost imperceptibly as he met Tradoc's look. But he said nothing. He simply clasped his hands behind his back and moved away from the comms console.

He paced the command post for several minutes, his posture and stride as patient as those of a man who is willing to wait through eternity. Only his eyes, if they had been glimpsed up close, would have betrayed him with their fresh intensity.

When at last he returned to the comms console, he beckoned, and Tradoc pushed his headset back, letting it hang around his neck while he rubbed at the raw spots developing on his ears.

"Have we got two-way communications with the main comms center yet?" Ochakas asked.

"Should by now, sir," Tradoc said, "but I can't make any promises." He picked up the headset and placed its 'phones gingerly over his ears again.

He opened the direct line and hit SEND. Got nothing back but the hiss of static.

He shook his head. "Still dead, sir. Guess I'll have to try the patch again."

It was archaic, the long way around, but it was the only way that worked right now. He punched in the number to Operations Planning and said to the voice that answered, "This is Tradoc in the CP. Do you have your line to Communications back yet?"

A pause. "Sorry, still down," came the response.

Tradoc fidgeted, thought again. "How about to the Advanced Warning folks?"

"Don't know. Lemme try."

Another wait. A long one this time. And then, "You're in luck, Trad. I've got Warnings on, and they're back on line to Comms."

"Good," said Tradoc. He flashed a thumbs-up at the general, still standing behind him, and said to the voice, "I need you to patch me through. General's orders."

"Right away."

He heard a crackle then several seconds of static, and the general reached over his shoulder to lay a message on his console. He scanned it. Drummed the panel with his fingertips while he waited.

He'd nearly given up on getting through at all when a very faint voice, nearly lost in static, said, "This is Comms. Go ahead, CP."

Tradoc glanced across the room at the masuki. The muttering had stopped; one guard, arms folded on his chest, stood there watching him.

"It's coming encrypted," he said quietly.

"Say again, CP? I didn't copy." The voice seemed to be fading, breaking up in the static.

He didn't dare repeat himself. He switched over to encrypt mode, grabbed the general's note, and placed his hands on the keyboard. His fingers moved swiftly, tapping it out:

```
URGENT URGENT URGENT
172254L 2 3308SY
TO ALPHA STATION CMDR
    DELTA STATION CMDR
    3RD FLEET CMDR
FM CP ISSEL II
FOURTH FLEET ON APPROACH TO ISSEL UNDER MASUK
CONTROL AND THREATENING ATTACK. THIRD FLEET
VECTOR TO INTERCEPT. MAY ATTEMPT TO SEIZE
ALPHA AND DELTA STATIONS. BEGIN EVACUATION TO
PRIMARY AT ONCE. REPEAT, BEGIN EVACUATION AT
ONCE AND PREPARE TO DESTROY STATIONS, BY
ORDER GEN MANUA OCHAKAS.
```

Tradoc entered SEND, cleared his display, and then erased the memory record. He hoped and prayed the message had made it through. Hoped even harder that the faint voice on the other end had been a human's.

THREE

Darcie looked up with a start at the sound of Lujan's step at the doorway. She'd been sitting so still, staring with such concentration at the bedcovers over her legs, that he asked, "Are you all right?"

"Y-yes," she said at once. "I was—thinking about Tristan."

He waited in the doorway. "May I come in?"

She hesitated. "Yes," she said again.

He took the same fold-down chair beside her bed. "Libby says he's starting to show some improvement," he offered.

Darcie nodded. Muffled a cough. "Have you seen him today?"

"Briefly." Lujan shifted on the seat. "He always seems uncomfortable to have me there, so I don't stay very long."

"You're a stranger to him," Darcie said, "—even more so because you're his father."

Lujan drew his brows together. "I don't understand."

"He grew up in a matriarchal culture," she said. "Gan mothers run the clans, and they choose a new male every season. Nobody knows who his father is; it's not important. We'd been there four years before I even heard the gan word for father. The very idea of you telling him you're his father is strange to him."

Lujan considered that, his brow furrowing more deeply.

"Everything is going to be strange to him," Darcie said.

"Some things are strange to me right now. It's going to take time to get used to it."

That goes for all of us, Lujan thought.

He was about say it aloud when his pager chirped and its little electronic voice said, "Admiral Serege, please come to the Watch."

He switched the pager off. "I'm sorry," he said, rising. "I'll be back when I can."

She gave a slight nod in reply and watched him leave the room.

He blew out a full breath as he peeled off his sterile suit in the isolation lock, and started up the main corridor.

The Watch was up six decks, located just off the Combat Information Center. A startled petty officer began to call the area to attention when he came in, but Lujan made a negating motion with one hand and said, "As you were."

Captain Horsch and Commander Marcus Ullen were already there, their expressions grim, and Lujan said, "What've we got, Marcus?"

"We just received a message intercept from Issel, sir," said Commander Ullen. "The surviving ships from its Yan fleet cleared lightskip outside the Issel system a few hours ago. According to communications from its flagship, the fleet is under masuk control and has stated intent to attack the planet."

Lujan arched an eyebrow at that. "What's the possibility this message could be a deception? Could they be trying to divert our attention?"

"I wondered that myself, sir," said Ullen, "but I don't think it's very likely. The message was sent over military channels from the command post on Issel Two, to its orbital stations and to a fleet commander."

Captain Horsch was shaking his head, disbelief etched around his eyes and mouth. "They're attacking *Issel*? That's impossible! It doesn't even make sense!"

"Actually, sir, it does," said Ullen, "from a masuk point of view. I should've realized it the other day when we first played Admiral Ne's log." He said, "Masuki don't accept defeat. They're probably blaming their human counterparts for betraying them, so revenge is the natural recourse. Issel is, from their way of thinking, fair game."

Lujan didn't feel any surprise, hearing that—except, perhaps, that it had happened so soon. "How is Issel responding?" he asked.

"They're taking the threat seriously, sir," Ullen said. "They've initiated Attack Warning Alert and vectored several carrier groups from system-defense patrols to intercept. There's some indication that the main spacedocks are being evacuated as well."

"Are all of their returning ships accounted for?" Lujan asked next.

"We believe so, sir," said Ullen, and nodded toward Merrel. "The original estimate from Admiral Ne was about thirty surviving ships. This message gave a count of twenty-seven."

Captain Horsch, arms folded, still appeared skeptical. "Just how likely is it that they'll really attack?"

The intelligence chief made a wry face. "If they're under masuk control," he said, "it's highly probable."

"And what would be their most likely targets?"

"Probably the spacedocks or the command-post moon. Maybe both. The spacedocks certainly wouldn't be difficult to seize."

Horsch only nodded, and everyone stood silent for a moment, weighing the likely outcome of such attacks.

Then Lujan said, "If you haven't already, Marcus, relay this information to Sostis immediately. The situation has just entered a whole new dimension; we should probably expect some amendments to our current ops orders."

The commander nodded. "Yes, sir."

"At this point, though, all we can do is wait, repair, rearm, and keep watching," Lujan concluded. "I want a status report every twelve standard hours. Report any unusual signals, ships, or other activity."

"Of course, sir," said Ullen.

* * *

Lujan was still mulling it over as he pulled the sterile suit on again, but he put it from his mind when he reentered Darcie's cubicle.

She had fallen asleep in his absence. He crossed to the seat he had vacated earlier and sat down with a sigh. Picked up her nearest hand and began to examine it, turning it gently in his own.

In another few minutes he found himself fondling her fingers, twining them with his. He'd done that often during their intimate conversations before they were joined. He'd done it through most of the night that she lay in labor with Tristan.

Her hands had been smooth and immaculately clean then, he remembered. As a surgeon, she'd considered them her most important tools and had always taken good care of them. That obviously hadn't been possible on Ganwold. The calluses and cracked knuckles and small scars gave a mute account of what it had cost her to survive there.

His thoughts wandered while she slept, but they always came back to the masuki, and to how he'd lost her. The subject had troubled him through the years because it had never been resolved—in fact, had never even been confirmed.

Her hand tensed in his. He glanced up, and saw uneasy puzzlement in her eyes. She drew her hand away, folded it with the other one in her lap.

"I'm sorry," Lujan said. And then, "It must've been—a very difficult life."

"It wasn't easy," she said. After a little silence she indicated his pager and asked, "Did you get—whatever it was—taken care of?"

He managed a short smile. "For the moment . . . Did you have a good nap?"

"I suppose so."

Silence again. It always came back to the silence, the search for something to say.

The call to the Watch slipped back through Lujan's mind. He hesitated for some moments, searching her face, before he finally asked, "What really happened to your transport, Darcie? All we could ever find out was it'd been attacked en route to Enach."

She didn't seem startled by the question. She said, "It *was* attacked. By masuki."

He leaned forward on his chair. "Do you still remember anything about it?"

"I remember nearly all of it," she said.

"Can you tell me about it?"

Darcie drew a deep breath. "The masuki disabled and boarded the ship and killed most of the crew. I took Tris and hid in a maintenance locker, and a little while later I heard them going through the cabins and rounding up the passengers; I could hear people going up the passage outside the maintenance compartment."

"They were slavers?" said Lujan.

"Yes." She muffled a cough, nodded curtly.

He suddenly wondered how masuki defined revenge, and exactly what had driven them to seek it against Issel. Was it a matter of pride, of saving face after their defeats in battle? Was there some specific loss they hoped to recoup? The cost of their ships and troops, maybe?

Or was it the spoils of battle denied them by Issel's failure to take Sostis? What promised payment had motivated them to make such an alliance in the first place?

He didn't like the possible answers. He shifted on the seat, his jaw tightening, and Darcie said, "Is something wrong?"

"No. I'm sorry. Never mind." After a pause, he asked, "How did you escape?"

"They tried to make lightskip—several times," she said. She fisted her hands in her lap and fixed her vision on them. "They almost destroyed the ship doing it, but they finally came out near Ganwold. That's when the Dominion legionnaires came aboard; I think they were System Defense troops. They searched the ship then and—they found Tris and me in the maintenance locker." She had to stop to cough again.

He waited, wordless, patient, and when she caught her breath, she said, "They had knives—belts of boarding knives around their waists." He saw her shudder, saw how she began to gather up the edge of the sheet between her hands. "They marched me down the passage," she said. She never looked up. "I—ducked into the cross-corridor and fired the shield door—and then I grabbed Tristan and ran.

"I wanted to get to the lifepods." She was gripping the wadded sheet with both hands now. "That was all I could think of. The lift to the lower deck was all shot up, and there were bodies and smoke in all the passages, and the legionnaires were coming 'round the other way to head us off. So I took a—a pistol—from one of the dead soldiers.

"I had it—in my hand—when we got to the bottom of the—emergency stairs." Her words came in snatches as if she were running; the vital-signs monitor above her headboard showed her pulse had accelerated. "There was a masuk down there, too. He tried to grab me and—I shot him—point-blank. I didn't even think about it—I just did it.

"I had—no idea where we were until I launched the lifepod, and then all I could think of was—how was I ever going to take care of Tris?" Her hands, kneading the sheet, were white and pinched looking. "I knew I couldn't let the Dommie colonists find us—but I didn't know if I could trust the ganan either."

"Tell me about the ganan," said Lujan.

Darcie glanced up briefly. "They're Ganwold's native race," she said. "They're the people the planet was named for. They're hunter-gatherers. They're nocturnal, and they have—fangs—and fingernails that look like claws.

"They're really very—gentle—but they don't look like it. I was afraid of them at first."

She sat silent for a while, looking past the sheet wrinkled in her lap, apparently remembering. "I don't know why I finally went with them. I think it was because the legionnaires were looking for us, and I knew what would happen if they found us." She kneaded the sheet in her hands. Released a shaky breath. Never looked up. "At any rate, the ganan took us into their clan. They shared their food and played with Tris, and they taught us how to survive."

"And you lived out there with them all that time?" Lujan asked. His tone had softened.

She nodded. "Until Mordan's soldiers came through the camp and torched it, looking for us." She looked up at last. "There wasn't a way to escape that time."

Lujan didn't say anything to that. He couldn't. Searching her eyes, he saw the lingering terror in them, a sort of unfamiliar vulnerability, and he wondered if he should offer her the comfort of his arms.

"Twelve-point-two hours ago," said the lieutenant from Intelligence, "an Isselan spacecraft carrier group totaling ten warships intercepted the Yan fleet, which entered the Issel system about thirty-six standard hours ago."

There was complete silence in the situation room; all attention was fixed on the briefer.

"The Yan fleet responded by launching fighters against the defending vessels," she said. "Having broken the Isselan ships' outer fighter defense, the Yan fleet seems to have overwhelmed the Isselan main defenders." As she spoke, symbols of ships in the holotank behind her reenacted what was known of the battle.

The command staff followed the unfolding action through narrowed eyes. "The fighters were obviously masuk-flown or -commanded," murmured the tactical officer.

"Exchange of fire ceased within six hours," the briefer went on, "with the defending ships damaged and most of them destroyed. The Yan fleet also received severe damage, losing five ships, including one of its carriers. As of oh-six-thirty local time, the masuk-commandeered vessels were confirmed underway and moving farther into the Issel system. If they maintain their last known speed and heading, ETA in Issel's planetary space will be thirty-two standard hours from now."

Lujan nodded acknowledgment, and the lieutenant said, "In the Bacal Belt, Kalese sources have observed a nonmerchant fleet on-loading assault troops, heavy weapons, and short-range escort fighters at Mi'ika's three spacedocks. Kalese analysts believe this fleet was intended to reinforce Issel's attack forces, but on-loading has not halted nor slowed since Issel's defeats. Destination is unknown. We will continue to monitor this activity.

"Finally," she said, "the Isselan newsnets have announced the death by suicide of Sector General Mordan Renier."

A few people reacted to that with disbelieving snorts and muttered speculations on how much assistance the sector general might have had, but the lieutenant said, "This concludes my briefing, sir. May I answer any questions?"

"Yes," said the holographic figure of a frigate captain. "Why are the masuki attacking Issel? I thought they wanted revenge."

"I've thought about that," said Lujan. "I suspect Issel bought their assistance with a promise of payment in Sostish slaves, and having been denied them, they're returning to Issel to collect on the debt." He glanced over at the intelligence briefer.

She nodded confirmation. "That's our consensus, too, sir. It would fit their pattern."

"How great a threat are they, really?" asked the holofigure of a female cruiser captain. "They don't have much more than a task force."

Another holofigure shook its head. "They practically annihilated a whole carrier group, didn't they?"

"By force of numbers," said the cruiser captain. "They're down to twenty-two battle-damaged ships now. Unless the Isselan space fleet is considerably less capable than we've always been told, it'll stop them before they can cause much more trouble."

"If it can regroup in time," said a second frigate captain. "Right now it has battle groups scattered all over the Issel system, and they don't appear to have any long-range eyes or any central control."

"There *is* a potential threat," said the briefer. "The fleet being formed in the Bacal Belt could as easily reinforce the Yan fleet as it would have the Isselans. If it finishes on-loading and launches as expected, it could reach the Issel system within two months. Even if the Yan fleet has been completely annihilated by then, this new fleet would have more than enough strength to conquer Issel."

"Good," said a destroyer captain at the rear of the room. "If the Isselans have their hands full with the masuki, maybe they'll keep their reach out of Unified space for a while!"

Lujan swiveled his chair to face him. "For a while," he said. "And then what? Once the masuk worlds have expended Issel, what will be their next target? Adriat and Na Shiv? Or Sostis? They won't spend their limited resources exploring remote sectors of the galaxy when there are plenty of inhabited worlds to plunder in this one." His gaze touched each face down the length of the table. "We'd be very unwise," he said, "to lower our guard because the threat doesn't appear to be directed at Unified space right now. If anything, the threat has just become more complex."

FOUR

The shadowed side of Issel II filled the center of Id Du'ul's forward viewscreen, blotting out all but a bright sliver of the planet beyond in an artificial eclipse. The human at the navigation console had plotted a lead-pursuit intercept trajectory against the moon's orbital path; in less than seven standard hours, as the humans measured time, the spacecraft carrier *Adamaman* would enter orbit around it.

"Ship's computer," he said, "display a chart of Issel's planetary space on the forward viewscreen. Show the current position and orbital paths of all satellites."

The view of the moon vanished, replaced with computer-generated graphics of the planetary system. Id Du'ul ignored the world in the center, noting instead the two moons and better than twenty space stations drifting around it. The majority of them, clustered around Issel II, were small. Ore-smelting plants, he knew. Lacking defenses and inhabited by only a handful of personnel, they were of no concern to him.

Two large stations, designated Alpha and Delta on the graphics, circled the primary in low orbits. Those were Issel's main hubs for out-system commerce, where trade freighters and passenger liners docked to be serviced by fleets of surface-to-station shuttles. Control of those stations would be essential to his control of the system.

The eight outermost stations, posted like sentries around the perimeter, were planetary defense bases. Their early warning sensors were doubtless already tracking his fleet. They might even be scrambling their fighters. But it would do them no good, Id Du'ul vowed. The defense bases, particularly those that would be near enough to oppose his attack, would be the first to die.

He considered their symbols on the viewscreen for some minutes, estimating time against their orbits, before he shifted in the command chair and turned his gaze on his comm operator. "Hail the captains of our brother ships *Sanabria* and *Tulacana*."

"Aye, sire," the young man said. And, after a few seconds, "The captains of *Sanabria* and *Tulacana* are responding, sire."

"Put them on the forward viewscreen."

The screen split; they appeared in it together, n'Aseem Suliyal and r'Oban Id Sixhat, both disheveled and bloodied, both veiled with the static and poor resolution that indicated damage to comm systems and minimal power to support basic functions. The battle with the Isselan defenders had left both ships with hulls breached in two or three places and major sections sealed off against depressurization. Both had lost weapon systems and, between them, hundreds of personnel.

But both had sublight drives and guidance systems that still functioned, Id Du'ul knew. Those were all that would be required. They were not yet without value to him.

"There is a need," he said in the ceremonial language of the Bacal, "a task worthy of you and your vessels."

Both captains met and held his gaze. They waited, wordless, for his order.

"Two planetary defense bases lie between us and our objective," he said. "They will launch fighters to challenge our entry into the system. They must be destroyed. If the bases die, then the fighters will die also."

"Sire." Suliyal, the *Sanabria*'s captain, replied in the same ceremonial language. "My vessel is crippled. It no longer has weapon systems."

Id Du'ul narrowed his eyes at him. "Your vessel will be your weapon, Captain," he said. He flicked a glance at

Tulacana's captain before returning his look to Suliyal. "You will both initiate your ships' self-destruction sequences, and then you will enter the bases' docking berths. You will ram their gates if necessary, so that the explosion of your ships inside their docks will cause the greatest possible damage. Their elimination is vital to the success of our attack."

He paused, and both looked at him in silence, their own eyes narrowed. He bared his teeth a little, showing just the points of his canines, and said, "The glory of the Bacal is above all."

For another few moments there was nothing but the white noise of failing communications, and then n'Aseem Suliyal drew himself up. "For the glory of the Bacal," he said.

When he'd dismissed them, Id Du'ul motioned again at the comm officer. "I must speak with the captain of the carrier *Admiral Griset*."

The viewscreen flicked; another figure appeared in it. He raised one hand before his chest in greeting when he recognized Id Du'ul and said, "What is your word, sire?"

Id Du'ul continued in the formal tongue. "My word is this: You will take your portion of this fleet and move against the orbital station designated Delta. You will take possession of that station and your soldiers will occupy it, while the ships of my portion take and occupy the station called Alpha. They will be our bases of operation when our brother ships come from the Bacal."

The other bared his teeth in acknowledgment. "They are ours already."

The passageway echoed. Spacer Third Class Len Perris's bootfalls seemed to ring back at him from the very girders that formed the skeleton of Alpha Station. There had been no echoes topside despite the emptiness of the station crew's quarters; the circular passages were carpeted there. In the past, the most prominent noise had been the rush of air, like a ceaseless wind through the life-support vents. But life support had already been shut down; Perris wore an oxygen pack on his shoulders and its mask over his nose and mouth.

Alpha and Delta Stations had been evacuated over the past few standard days. Perris and his teammates were their last occupants, and they wouldn't be here much longer themselves. Only until they'd accomplished their task. There had been no explanation with the order, but even Perris knew it would be less costly to destroy and later rebuild both stations than to let them come under masuk control. Intact, they could be used to effectively hold Issel under siege.

The oxygen mask kept slipping down Perris's nose, a couple of millimeters at a time, and the cold sweat that caused the slippage made his skin itch. It plastered his hair to his forehead and made his palms clammy.

He thought it strange that he should be sweating when the station had grown so cold. When he pulled at his mask to adjust it, his breath escaped in a puff of vapor, and despite the dampness of his palms, his fingernails were blue. He noticed that when he glanced at his wrist chrono—and its reading made his heart skip a beat: two minutes left to make rendezvous. He broke into a trot.

The pumping section had already been dusted with frost when he'd entered. It was one of four aboard the station, each drawing from its own reservoir so that four ships could refuel at once. He'd played his palm light over the arching conduits that carried fuel to the docks where the merchant traders and passenger liners snugged in. Pale under the dim light and the hoarfrost, they had looked like the bleached bones of some immense beast.

Hands shaking less from the cold than from the enormity of his task, he'd taken each charge from its nest in the box at his feet and encoded it, whispering to himself all the while, "Don't blow, don't blow, don't blow!"—as if there were an actual possibility of the thing going off in his hands and that words alone would prevent it. Each charge weighed only a kilogram, but, properly placed, two or three would be enough to touch off the pumping sections and trigger a string of secondary explosions that would rip the station apart.

With less than one minute remaining now, Perris reached the hatch hanging open in the bulkhead to his left. He ducked through it into a frosty, echoing utility tunnel so low he nearly had to crawl. It still had emergency lighting though, enough that he could make out three shapes crouched close together around a hatch in its deck and a fourth lowering himself into it. Perris flashed his palm light at them. "Hey! Hey, I'm coming!" he called, and the ringing tunnel and his own shivering amplified the near panic in his voice.

One of the shapes looked up and waved an arm at him in urgent beckoning, and he recognized his squad leader's voice: "Move it, Perris! The timer's running!"

He scrambled. Only Tech Sergeant Soto was left outside the escape hatch when he reached it, and he had sweat beaded on his brow, too, above his oxygen mask. He glanced once at the display on the remote kit lying beside him and said, "Get down there! Move!"

Perris shoved his legs into the hatch, reached for its rungs, but someone grabbed his legs from below. "Just drop! I've got you."

He let go; arms caught him, shoved him toward an acceleration bench, and he sat down hard as Soto scrambled in behind him. He heard the slam of the escape craft's hatch, the sucking sound of it sealing, and the sergeant yelling, "Detach!" Perris fumbled for his straps—got them clasped just as the craft rolled sideways, thrown clear of its coupling with the station and the artificial gravity created by its rotation.

Thrusters fired. The craft stopped tumbling, banked around into its programmed heading, and began to accelerate rapidly. Perris swallowed down the bile burning the back of his throat and gulped at the oxygen hissing through his mask.

Beside him, someone kept urging the craft to "Go! Go! Go!" in a tense whisper. Perris glanced over.

Spacer Rick Meldon sat with eyes closed and hands knotted into fists. "It's not fast enough!" he hissed through clenched teeth. "We shouldn't have waited so long. We'll never get clear in time!"

"Cut it out, Ricky!" said Soto, who sat strapped in across from them.

But Len Perris knew that Ricky was right, and the expression in Soto's eyes said that he knew it, too.

"Our course is set and locked in, sire."

Captain n'Aseem Suliyal stood in the center of the *Sanabria*'s bridge, facing the forward viewscreen and the Isselan defense base displayed in its center. "Good," he said. There was no nod, no other suggestion of acknowledgment, just a single syllable more grunted than spoken.

He felt the narrowed gazes of his bridge crew on his back—those members of his crew who still lived—but he waited several minutes, standing motionless in front of the viewscreen, before he spoke again. Then he said, "Engine room, prepare to initiate self-destruction sequence."

Over the intraship comm came a grim "Aye, sire."

He waited, and his comm officer said, "Sire, we are being hailed by System Defense."

"You will not respond." He shot a look over his shoulder. "Helm, you will maintain present course and speed."

"Sire," a masuk voice said over the comm, "this is the engine room. We cannot initiate self-destruction."

Suliyal turned away from the viewscreen as if to face down the speaker. "For what reason, engineer?"

"The computer requires access authorization codes, sire. We do not have the necessary codes."

Suliyal curled his lips back from his teeth in a snarl. The Isselan Sector General, fool that he was, had trusted his masuk allies with much. But he was not fool enough to have entrusted them with the access codes to his ships' most deadly weapon systems, nor to their self-destruct sequences.

"Sire," said his scan officer, "the base has launched fighters. I read twenty-four contacts approaching at a rate of—"

"The fighters are not our concern," Suliyal said, cutting him off. "We have a mission to accomplish, and we will do so without the aid of human self-destruction devices. Engine room, you will bring the main reactor to one hundred ten percent of capacity and you will not allow it to drop below that level. Do you understand my order?"

"Yes, sire," the unseen engineer responded. "I understand." And his voice bore a note of awe.

As it rightly should, Suliyal decided, and resumed his position in the center of the bridge with his arms folded over his chest. It was so like the humans to complicate the process with their computers and their codes when all that was required were mass and momentum and reactors pushed too far past their capacity for too long. "Then execute," he said.

"Yes, sire."

The thrumming of the drives accelerated, gradually at first, like the heartbeats of a living creature. He could feel their pulse through the deck, through his boots.

In moments a ribbon of tracer fire flashed across the forward screen. A second followed swiftly behind it. Warning shots, Suliyal knew. The fighters that had launched them were not yet visible, and at such a range their weapons had no accuracy. But that would not remain so for long.

Sanabria was a dying vessel; that was accepted. But it must not die too soon. It must not die before its own death throes would take its enemy with it. Suliyal called for the distance from the defense base and for the ship's velocity, measured the time from those, and balanced the result in his mind. He said, "Activate the deflector field."

"Field activated, aye."

"Sire," said the scan operator, "we have the fighters on visual."

They were barely visible against the starfield, but as Suliyal watched, they closed like a cloud of Mi'ikan yellow gnats, careening, diving, banking, and stinging over and over again. Their fire shattered against the electromagnetic field, illuminating space and the forward viewscreen with bursts of deflected energy as *Sanabria* plowed through it.

The vessel rocked at a glancing hit; Suliyal, standing before the viewscreen, staggered to keep his balance.

"Sire," came a call over the intercom, "this is the engine room. The field is being drained by the enemy barrage. The generators require more power."

"Then give it," said Suliyal.

"Aye, sire," the engineer replied.

The Isselan defense base rotated on the forward screen. Suliyal could make out its communications towers, its radar transmitters, its solar panels, and sporadic flashes from its weapons emplacements: energy tracers reaching out to touch him with their deadly fingers.

"Sire," the engineer called, "the main reactor is approaching critical."

"Good." Suliyal bared his teeth. "Deactivate the deflector field. We do not need it any longer."

"Field deactivated, sire."

Energy tracers lit up space like a lightning storm, swept across the viewscreen, and burst into brilliant blossom upon it. Suliyal was still standing in the center of the bridge, arms still folded loosely over his chest, when the antispacecraft fire found its target.

The carrier *Adamaman* was entering orbit around Issel II when its comm operator stiffened in his seat. "Sire, Alpha Station just—exploded!" he said. "The destroyer *Caneb* reports damage from flying debris, and the cruisers *Haliphen* and *Friesey* are—lost! They were approaching to dock when it blew."

Id Du'ul, about to enter the lift off the bridge, stopped just short of its door and blocked it open with one hand. "On screen," he said, and turned to look over his shoulder.

Only a cloud of glittering particles remained, expanding from the point where Alpha Station had been minutes before. Id Du'ul narrowed his eyes and let his lips draw back. The loss of two, maybe three ships had been expected in this attack. But to have Alpha Station, his prize, snatched from him even as he closed his fist about it . . .

He said, "Order my surviving ships to assist the *Admiral Griset* at Delta Station on the far side of the planet. Then contact the command post on Issel Two. Tell them that my shuttle will arrive on the surface within—"

"Sire." The comm operator had gone pale. "Delta Station has blown up, too!"

The hair rose up on the back of Id Du'ul's neck. He snarled, the sound starting low in his throat and swelling to a howl of rage. The bridge crew sat paralyzed, silent, watching him. He saw their fear in white faces, smelled it in the odor of their bodies, and held them there for long minutes before he demanded, "Damage report!"

The comm operator gulped a breath. "Our task force hadn't cleared Issel, sire. None of those ships were damaged."

It was unlike the humans, Id Du'ul thought as the bridge lift carried him down to the shuttle bays, to sacrifice willingly what they knew they could not keep. The human way was more typically to waste weapons and soldiers, to hold the objective at all cost. This act, which had deprived him of the orbital stations, was worthy of a masuk commander.

His hackles were still raised when he emerged from the lift, and his subordinates, waiting there to join him, shrank back, watched him with wary eyes, and knew better than to ask what had displeased him.

He didn't speak through the flight to the surface, except to give terse directives to his crew. He felt for the dagger he wore in the sash of his tunic and ran his thumb along its blade, testing its edge.

A masuk guide was waiting outside the landing bay when the pressurization cycle finished, allowing him to disembark. He said only, "Take me to the command post."

His guide said, "This way, sire," and turned up the gray stone passage toward another lift, which descended deep into the maw of the moon.

Id Du'ul smelled human blood as soon as the lift doors opened. Wrinkling his nose at it, he strode down the corridor, past Communications and Operations Planning, with his entourage falling in behind.

The command post's battle cab was splashed with thick

crimson. Id Du'ul stepped over an eviscerated body sprawled at the doorway and spotted others within. "Remove these," he said first, and prodded the nearest corpse with his boot. "They're in my way."

The four most junior masuki left their posts to carry out his order, and Id Du'ul moved around them to the center of the battle cab, where a handful of humans stood close together under guard. One wore the silver epaulets of an Isselan general, one was a junior officer, the other three were enlisted. "Why do these still live?" he demanded.

k'Aram Qal'an, the masuk captain, came forward. "I would make them a present to you, sire." He bared his canines in a smile. "The command post is yours."

"But the orbital stations are not." Id Du'ul's bared fangs showed menace. "I wish to know who gave the order to destroy them."

"I gave the order," said one of the humans.

Id Du'ul wrenched around. Stared with narrowed eyes into the unflinching features of the general, the one called Ochakas. "You've denied me my objective," he said, drawing close to the man. The snarl had come back to his voice. "You've sacrificed your own to prevent me from seizing them." His thumb rode the blade of his dagger.

The others saw it: the humans, the other masuki. The general straightened, met his glower. "Better that than to let them fall into the hands of the enemy!"

In a single swift movement, the nearest masuk guard seized the man by the hair, jerked his head back, and pressed the point of his dagger to his throat. "Your words are an offense to your allies!" he snarled. "You'll die for that!"

"No." Id Du'ul knocked the other's blade away with a backhand stroke; it left a shallow cut across the base of the general's throat. "This one doesn't offend me; let go of him."

He waited until the guard moved back, returning his knife to his sash, and then he said, "This one has shown the cunning of a masuk warrior. I will keep him—but not here. You will take him and his soldiers to the place where the other slaves are held."

Ochakas had seen Issel II's subterranean maintenance passages only once, knew only that they connected the command and quarters areas with the terrarium caverns where oxygen-producing lichens were cultivated: the life-support system for the moon's populace.

The maintenance passages were low, bored into gray stone, and dimly illuminated. Ochakas strode between his subordinates and their masuk captors—who were forced to stoop to clear the ceiling—making mental notes of the luminous arrows and numbers painted at intersections and on heavy doors.

The masuki followed the arrows to Utility Plant Six, passed its darkened office and breached shield doors, switched on palm lights as they entered a metal stairwell. One shoved at Ochakas's shoulder when he hesitated on the top step. He reached for the rail and began to descend.

Another shield door closed off the stairwell at the bottom. Its cipher-lock panel had been destroyed, evidently with a few blasts from an energy pistol. It took two of the masuk guards, straining hard, to shove the door aside.

The squad leader said, "Go in," and Ochakas strode from the dark into what looked at first like a sunlit canyon with teal-green walls, half-filled with fog.

"This way," said the masuk, and gestured at a walkway of plastic grating.

They walked for some time in silence, except for the creak of the grating underfoot and the muted splashes of water droplets onto rock. And then Ochakas caught a glimmer of light in a side cave. As he turned his head to look, it flickered out, and he heard a scuff like a workboot on gravel.

FIVE

Tristan looked up from picking over his breakfast—
reached up to touch his forehead—when Doctor Moses entered his cubicle.

If she noticed his gesture of respect, she didn't acknowledge it. "You're never going to regain your proper weight at this rate," she said, indicating his barely touched biscuits and gravy.

He hunched himself, lowered his head in apology. "I don't like it," he said. He had dutifully taken a few bites, but the biscuits were dry enough to stick in his throat and the grayish gravy covering them was almost flavorless. He said, "It doesn't taste like anything."

"Well, goes to show you're normal," said Moses. "Right after 'Will this hurt?,' the question most often asked by hospital patients is 'What do I have to do to get some real food around here?'"

Tristan only pushed the tray away.

And Moses rolled her eyes. "So much for trying to get a smile out of you," she said. "What *would* you like to eat, Tris?"

"Meat," he said. He didn't look up. "*Real* meat that you cook over a fire and chew off the bones."

"Hmm. That's a pretty tall order aboard a ship on combat operations," Moses said, "but if you'll talk to me for a little while, I'll see what I can do."

Tristan lifted his head, feeling sudden suspicion. "Talk about what?"

"The things that are hurting you so much."

His stomach tightened up. The few bites of biscuit he had managed to swallow lay in a lump in his middle. He cringed. "Why, ma'am?"

"So you can start to heal."

He couldn't refuse her outright; she was a female, a "mother," after all. He ducked his head, began to chew at his lower lip.

"Tris, listen to me for a minute," said Moses. "I've been talking with your mother a lot lately, helping her to heal, too. She's told me how you helped in her medical practice on Ganwold—such as it was out there. Did you ever see a really dirty wound?"

He thought about the injuries he had seen on Ganwold: the lacerated faces of gan males after mating season, the old mother who had laid open her leg with a fleshing knife, a hunter gored by a peimu bull. "I saw a lot of dirty wounds," he said.

"What did you and your mother do for them?" Moses asked. "Did you just put some herbs or something in them and wrap them up?"

"No." He thought she should know better than that, but he didn't dare say so. Not to a mother. He said, "We had to clean them first."

"And how did your patients feel about having their wounds cleaned?"

He remembered holding yowling youngsters tight in his arms and having to restrain adults while his mother took care of their injuries. "I know it hurt," he said. "Sometimes they fought me."

"Did you ever stop before the wound was clean just because it hurt them?"

"No." He shook his head a little.

"Why not?" Moses asked.

"Because it would get infected," he said. "They could get

gangrene, or"—he shrugged—"they might even die from it."

"That's right." Moses paused. "It's the same with you, Tris, except that your worst injuries aren't the physical ones. They're emotional. But they're still dirty and they still need to be cleaned, before you end up with an 'infection' in your mind that could ruin the rest of your life."

He realized then what she had done, how she had manipulated him right to the spot where she wanted him. He dared to glower at her.

But she was right, he knew. He'd begun to feel the festering already over the past week: the nightmares, the bursts of anger, the terror of being alone with his thoughts, the desperate, guilty fear—

He tore his gaze away from her and lowered his head.

"Do you *want* to get rid of all the dirt?" Moses asked gently.

"Yes," he whispered, without looking up.

But the thought of talking about it made his heart and stomach and hands clench up, made his pulse race, made him break into a cold sweat.

She seemed to have expected that; she took his hand. "Do you know what hypnosis is, Tris?"

"Yes." He'd seen his mother use it from time to time, to ease her patients' pain or to help them relax.

"I can put you under hypnosis," Moses said. "That'll make it easier."

He thought about it for several moments, then looked her in the face. "All right," he said. It was a whisper; his mouth was dust dry.

"Wise kid." She gave his hand a comforting squeeze and turned to unfold the chair on the bulkhead. "It's easier if you lie down."

His spine and ribs were still too sore and his healing skin too sensitive for him to lie on his back. He grimaced, turning onto his belly, and reached around to pull up the sheet before he closed his eyes.

Doctor Moses's voice was quiet, calming. He could feel the

warmth she described, beginning at his toes and flowing gradually up his legs until it filled his whole body. He began to feel drowsy. Her voice seemed to come from across a great distance when she said, ". . . going down, deeper now . . ." And when he felt that he was floating, she said, "Find yourself in a place where you feel safe . . . place that's restful."

He was on Ganwold, lying in tall grass with the summer sun warming his back and the soil cool under his belly. He could hear his hunting companions snoring nearby, could smell the richness of the soil, could see clouds scooting across the turquoise sky.

Then Doctor Moses was saying, ". . . talk about your nightmares . . . always the same?"

Tristan's hands closed on the edge of the bed. He swallowed.

". . . dreams are in the past," he heard. "They can't hurt you. . . ."

His hands loosened a little; he let out a breath.

". . . same dream?" Doctor Moses asked again.

He nodded on his pillow. "Yes."

"Tell me about it," she said. "Where are you? What do you see?"

"I'm in a cave," he said. "It has—shield doors at the mouth. There's—smoke, I think, and dust; it's hard to see. There's a tunnel at the back."

". . . others in this cave?" he heard. "Tell me about them."

"My mother's there." He felt an anxious twinge at the remembered image of her pale shape in the shadows. He said, "She's—lying on the ground and—she's not moving."

"What's happened?" Doctor Moses asked.

"He—" Tristan gulped. "He was holding her—with a knife to her throat. When he pushed her away, she fell."

"Who is 'he'?"

Tristan held tightly to the mattress edge. "He's—a masuk. He has a knife."

"And?"

"We—we're fighting." His mouth felt dry, as if from the exertion, from panting.

"What are you feeling . . .?"

"I'm angry," he said, "and I'm worried, and—I'm scared!"

". . . angry?" said Doctor Moses.

Tristan's hands hardened like claws. "Because he took my mother!"

". . . doing now?"

"He's backing me up to the tunnel." He swallowed. "I-I don't want to go into it!"

"It's okay, Tris," he heard. "Go on."

He was panting, his hands shook, his legs felt weak with remembered fatigue. "I'm—going in," he said. "It's dark. I can't see where—it goes. I'm—feeling it—with my hand, and—it turns."

"And?" Doctor Moses asked when he stopped.

"I'm going—around the corner. I can hear him—following me." His palms were sweaty now; his heart was thudding hard against his ribs. "I'm—waiting for him in there—"

He shook his head. Shuddered. His heart beat even faster.

"Tristan," said Doctor Moses, "what are you feeling . . .?"

"Scared!" he managed to say. His mouth was so dry it came out as a rasp.

"Why . . . feel scared?"

"I—" He swallowed convulsively. "Because I—" He broke off.

". . . rest now," said Doctor Moses's voice, as if from far away. ". . . feel peaceful. This is all in the past. . . . can't hurt you now."

The tension ebbed gradually from his hands, his shoulders, his legs. The shaking subsided. He began to catch his breath. He had no sense of time.

Doctor Moses said, ". . . go back, Tris." She reached out and took his hand. "What is it that scares you?"

"Blood," he said. He swallowed. "Blood on my hands."

"Where did the blood come from?"

Tristan shuddered. His breath came in labored heaves; he couldn't speak.

"It's all over," he heard Moses say. ". . . in the past." She was still holding on to his hand. ". . . How did you get blood on your hands?"

"I—stabbed him," Tristan said. His breath caught in a sob. "I—I *killed* him! I got—his blood—on my hands!"

"How do you feel right now?"

"Sick." He choked on the word. "I feel—I feel horrible— like I've done something—*horrible*—"

". . . calm," Moses said. ". . . Feel at peace. It's all past." She was stroking his hand now. "Rest for a while where you're safe and at peace. . . ."

He was back on Ganwold, lying in the grass under only the sky. The sunshine eased his shaking, eased his sobs. Still, it seemed like a long time before he began to relax.

". . . something else we need to talk about now," said Doctor Moses's voice. ". . . need to talk about your father."

The morning on Ganwold melted into the morning when Admiral Serege had come to his cubicle the first time. He was wearing a sterile suit, and his face wasn't fully discernible inside its bubble. Tristan swallowed.

". . . are you feeling?" asked Moses.

"Angry," said Tristan, "and—afraid."

"Angry?" he heard.

"Because," Tristan said, "he didn't come help us—when Mum was sick or while the—the governor—was holding me hostage."

". . . mean Governor Renier?"

The name sent tension down his beaten back. He said, "Yes."

"What else makes you angry?"

Tristan knotted his hands into fists. "I was—beaten for what he did to—the governor."

"What did your father do . . . ?" Moses asked.

"He—betrayed him," said Tristan. "The—governor lost

his world—and his children—because of him. He's a—a Spherzah assassin."

"How do you know these things?"

"Because the—the governor—told me."

There was a pause, and then, "You said you feel afraid," Moses said.

Tristan kneaded the mattress edge with both hands. "I'm—afraid of—being locked in a room again. —I'm afraid he'll *beat* me again!"

". . . all over, Tris," Moses said. "It's all in the past. . . . safe here now . . ."

The sound of her voice assured him that he *was* safe, that it *was* over. He relaxed, a little at a time.

In another moment Moses asked, "Why do you think your father would do those things?"

"Because," Tristan said, "the governor did."

". . . you think your father would do the same things . . . ?"

"Yes." He rasped it.

"Because . . . ?"

"Because the governor said my—" He had to force himself to say it: "—my father—is no different from himself."

". . . you believe that?" Moses asked.

Her question puzzled him. "Yes," he said.

"Because?" she asked again.

His puzzlement increased. He wrinkled his brow. "Because he said so."

There was another pause, longer this time, before Moses said, "How did you feel when the governor told you those things?"

Tristan chewed his lower lip briefly, remembering. "I felt—hurt. I—felt confused. I didn't want them to be true."

". . . and you believed him?"

He shrugged, a gesture of helpless confusion. "I thought he knew better than I did. He said they were things my mother couldn't tell me because she didn't know."

". . . you still believe . . . ?"

He thought about that. "I don't know," he said. His throat felt pinched, tight.

". . . *want* to believe them?" Moses asked.

He opened his eyes and looked up at her. *Can I dare not to?* he asked her with his eyes. He couldn't say it; his throat was too constricted.

She touched his hand as she had earlier. "It's all right to not believe everything people tell you," she said. "It's all right to question them and decide for yourself whether you should believe them or not. Do you understand that?"

He thought about it. Nodded.

"Good," Moses said. "Rest for a while now."

He rested in the grass on Ganwold again, until Doctor Moses said, ". . . have one more thing to ask about."

Her voice was calm, soothing. He felt relaxed, waiting for her question.

". . . mother told me . . . friend who went with you . . . Tell me about your friend," said Moses.

"Pulou," Tristan said. "He's my brother."

"Your brother?" asked Moses.

"That's what he calls me," said Tristan.

"Tell me about him," said Moses.

"I'm running through the grass," said Tristan. "I'm little, and it's almost as tall as I am. Pulou's big. He's chasing me, and I'm laughing and running, and—I fall down and hurt my knee." He could almost feel the smart again.

"And? . . ." Doctor Moses said after a moment.

"Pulou's picking me up," he said, "and holding me, and licking away the blood on my knee. He's telling me it's all well, and now he's—" Tristan grimaced and turned his head— "he's licking my face dry, too, and making funny faces at me. . . ."

"Where is Pulou *now?*" asked Moses.

Tristan's heart suddenly constricted. "I don't know," he said.

". . . last time you saw him?" Moses said.

He drew a shaky breath. Gripped the edge of the mattress

to steady himself. "He's in the copilot seat. I'm opening the seat harness and he—he falls on me. There's—blood—in his mouth, and his eyes—just stare at me; they don't blink." He felt hot tears welling up in his own eyes, felt his throat tightening.

"Th-they're capturing our ship. They're coming in—all in space suits." He was panting again, his pulse racing; he could see their shapes through the smoke, could see himself shoving onto his feet to ward them off. "I'm trying—to fight them—but I fall and—they put me on a—a sled—and take me away from him—"

"That's over now," said Moses. ". . . in the past . . . You're safe in the present. . . . feel at rest, at peace, and listen to me. Can you do that?"

He nodded weakly against the pillow.

". . . going to bring you out of the hypnosis," he heard. ". . . remember what we talked about . . . won't cause so much anxiety now . . . be easier to talk about . . . I'll be here when you need me. . . ."

"All right." He sighed it.

". . . come to when I say your name," Moses said, and then, ". . . Wake up, Tristan."

He blinked a few times and looked over at her. Sucked in his lower lip between his teeth. He felt as if his soul had been gutted and its entrails laid out before her in all of their repulsiveness.

But she said, "The wounds have all been cleaned Tris," and she lay a hand over his. "Now we can start to help them heal."

Libby scrolled through the patient chart on the bulkhead monitor, noting the steady improvement in vital signs, sleeping patterns, appetite.

Interspersed with the usual records were holoscan stills, cross-section images of her patient's vital organs. The most recent had been made that morning, and Libby studied them closely for several moments before she said, "Well, Darcie, the 'scans we did this morning confirm the complete inactivation of the virus.''

Darcie released a breath in a rush of relief. "Thank you," she said.

Lujan, seated on the bulkhead chair near her bed, looked equally relieved.

"Your vital signs have been normal for four days now, and you're starting to regain some of the weight you lost," Libby said. "I can't see any reason to keep you in here past breakfast tomorrow."

"That sounds good to me," Darcie said.

"I'll still need to see you every few days for a while," Libby told her, "but we can set up a sick-call schedule and brief you on recovery management in the morning. We can wait until you've gotten your strength back to decide whether we'll need to regenerate any new tissue. Right now"—she looked from Darcie to Lujan and changed the tone of her voice—"I need to talk to you both about Tristan."

She saw their faces change, the relief of a moment before clouding over with fresh concern. She unfolded the facing bulkhead chair and sat down, close enough that she could touch either one of them if she reached out her hand.

"Over the last few days," she said, "I've picked up on a few things from Tris that I thought I should check into, so this morning I persuaded him to talk to me under hypnosis. We'll need to do more talking, of course, but I think we were able to uncover most of the things that are troubling him.

"For starters, he's lost a very close friend."

Darcie's eyes widened. "Pulou," she said. The name was barely more than a breath. "No! Oh, no! What happened?"

"There seems to have been a space battle," said Libby. "Tris found him dead in the copilot's seat. Did you know him, too?"

Darcie nodded, covering her face with her hands. "He—was the one—who found us," she said. "He was—almost like another son."

"I'm sorry," Libby said.

Lujan was clearly uncomfortable with watching Darcie weep. Libby saw his quandary in his face, in his restless shifting on the seat. Should he touch her, try to comfort her—or would she rather be left alone? He finally placed a tentative hand on her shoulder—

She shrugged away from it. "Don't touch me!" she said over her shoulder, through her teeth.

He locked his hands together, between his knees. Studied them in apparent consternation for several seconds before he looked up at Libby; and she read the smart mingled with the questions in his eyes.

"We need to talk—later," she mouthed to him, and when he nodded, she thought, *It's going to be a long, hard readjustment.* Such tumults of emotions had to be expected, she knew, but that didn't mean they weren't going to hurt.

It was some minutes before Darcie wiped away her tears with her hands. "I—I'm sorry," she said without looking up. "Please go on."

Libby nodded. "Tristan seems to be 'stuck' at the point in time when he found Pulou dead," she said. "He's still in denial. He may need some guidance to get through the grieving process, some encouragement to talk about his feelings and allow himself to cry—maybe even some kind of symbolic burial ritual if he feels a need for that kind of completion.

"But he's having an even harder time with having taken a life himself." She paused. "That's what his ongoing nightmares are about. He's feeling a great deal of guilt and shame about it, and all that guilt is terrifying to him."

"I don't understand that," said Darcie. "Tristan was a hunter on Ganwold. He started when he was twelve or so, and he never had problems with that."

Lujan straightened. "It's not the same, Darcie," he said. Quietly. "I used to hunt, too, as a kid. Killing a game creature to provide for your needs is totally different from killing another intelligent being in battle."

"It's not an unusual problem among young troops who've just seen their first combat," Libby said. "I'm meeting with a handful of others right now. I want to include Tris in their therapy group immediately."

When Lujan and Darcie both nodded consent, she paused again. The hardest part was still to come. Forcing herself to look the admiral in the face, she said, "Tristan's most serious problems, though, come from the things Governor Renier told him about you, Lujan: that you betrayed him and caused the loss of his family and homeworld, that the Spherzah are assassins, and that you're really no different from Renier. Tris seems to have taken it all literally, especially the last part. I don't understand the reasoning behind that, but—"

"I do," said Darcie. "The ganan are very"—she motioned with her hands, apparently searching for the right word— "*honest* people. They're very—straightforward. They don't know what a lie is; they don't even have a word for it in their language! They have no reason to question what anybody says and so they don't; they're very trusting. That's the way Tris grew up. He never learned how to tell truth from lies because he never had to on Ganwold."

Libby pondered that briefly. "Well, that fits," she said, and hesitated again. "The end result, Lujan, is that Tristan is terrified of you. He's honestly afraid that you'd beat him if you got angry with him. He's lost every shred of his ability to trust anybody."

Lujan had learned over the years she had known him— many of those years spent working in diplomatically sensitive positions—to mask his emotions. But he didn't do so now. He slumped forward, elbows on knees, face pressed into his hands. There were no tears, but his expression, his posture, even the tension in his hands—Libby could almost *feel* the searing ache of his sorrow just by looking at him.

Darcie, pale and biting her lower lip so hard that Libby was surprised it didn't bleed, sat motionless, staring at him.

"Will I ever really get my son back?" he asked at last. The question came in a voice so constricted it must have hurt.

"Yes," Libby said at once. "Yes, you will. But it'll take time and a *lot* of patience."

She sighed. "Over the long haul, his recovery is going to be a lot more dependent on you two than it is on me. I recommend that he spend most of his waking hours either in the patients' dayroom or in your quarters. You need to spend as much family time together as you can—not easy right now, I know—but you need to start drawing him in.

"He's going to be moody," she warned. "He'll seem angry a lot. He may be quiet, but he'll be absorbing everything you say and do, and weighing it and analyzing it and forming conclusions. When he finally does get around to saying something, it'll probably come out sounding brusque or mouthy—and it'll probably be exactly the opposite of what he really means or feels. You've got to remember, when he's rude, that it's a shield to conceal all the pain and confusion he's going through right now.

"And another thing," she said. "He may try to play you two off each other. *Don't* let him! One of the most important things you can do for him is to let him see your commitment to and support for each other.

"Lujan, he'll test you especially. He'll do everything in his power to push the limits of your patience and temper—but unless he does something genuinely dangerous or destructive, the best thing to do is ignore it. He won't pay attention to anything you say to him because he's learned the hard way that words don't mean much. It'll be your actions—how you treat him—that he'll use to make his judgments. Because of that, the more time you can spend with him, the better."

Lujan only nodded, and Libby knew he couldn't speak right then. "You won't go through this alone," she said, softening, and looked at Darcie, too. "Any of you. I'll be meeting with all three of you on a regular basis, individually and together, for as long as this takes to work out. You're *all* going through some major changes right now."

There was silence for a few moments, and then Darcie asked, "When are you going to release Tris from sickbay? You only talked about waking hours."

"It may be a while," Libby said. "His vital signs are

stable—have been for a few days now—and I removed the isolation restrictions after I saw him on rounds this evening. But he's not sleeping well—he's still having those nightmares—and I don't dare take him off the hemomanagement system; he's not eating well enough yet. We'll have to fix him up with a pump-pack to make him mobile."

Suddenly recalling something, she turned back to Lujan. "He told me this morning he'd like some real meat that he can chew off the bones, and I promised him I'd see what I could do."

"Contact Chief Wassman in the galley," said Lujan. "If there's any real meat in the ship's stores, she'll know about it."

Darcie tried to smile. "He'll want it practically raw, you know, even after all the times I told him not to eat it that way. I hope you've checked him for parasites!"

"I have, and they've been taken care of," Libby told her. "Right now I don't care *how* he wants his meat as long as he'll eat it!"

After a moment she continued, "I'd also like to start the repairs on his back as soon as possible. It'll probably take three procedures to remove all the scar tissue and patch him up properly, and he'll need to stay down and quiet for a few days after each one. I'd just as soon have my med techs keeping an eye on him, since you should still be on bedrest yourself."

Darcie nodded. "When can I see him?"

"Tomorrow," said Libby, and forced a smile. "I've let you stay up too long past your bedtime as it is." She rose—and then paused, glancing once more from Darcie to Lujan. "Do either of you have any more questions?"

There was no response, but the pain she saw in their eyes suggested they had more than enough to deal with already. The questions would come later, she knew.

SIX

Tristan lay huddled on his side, his face toward the bulkhead, the scars across his back plainly visible. Darcie's throat constricted at the sight of them. Setting down her travel kit, she said, "Trisser?" and touched his shoulder.

She hadn't used that nickname since he was a small child, she realized at once. She wasn't sure why she'd used it now, except that somehow he seemed small and vulnerable again, curled up that way.

Her son jumped at her touch. Turned his head to peer up at her over his shoulder. He seemed to see only her borrowed medic's uniform at first, but in the next instant his eyes widened. "Mum!" he said, and pushed himself over to sit up, raising a hand to touch his forehead.

Darcie took him in her arms and gave in to tears.

For a long while she could only hug him and cry with relief. But as the tears passed and her breathing steadied, she relaxed her embrace. Taking his head between her hands—as a gan mother would have, she realized—she said, "It's so good to see you, Tris! When you left, out on Ganwold, I was so afraid I'd never see you again!"

He kept his eyes lowered. "It was *jwa'lai*," he said. His voice was husky. "I had to do it for you."

Jwa'lai. It was a gan word that meant a task carried out for or a promise made to one's mother. She should have guessed it, she supposed. Even before he'd reached his teens, Tristan had become, culturally, more gan than human. She'd also been keenly aware of his distress at her illness. And she knew he'd had no idea what he was taking on when he left the gan camp, without her knowledge, to venture into a human colony to seek help for her. She studied his down-turned face. "What an awful price you've paid for my life!" she said, a realization put into words. "Tris, I love you so much!"

He didn't respond to that; he wouldn't meet her eyes.

She took both of his hands. Paused when her throat tightened again. "I—heard about Pulou," she said at last. "I'm so sorry."

He looked at her then, his face pinched, his eyes full of hopelessness. "He—really is dead—isn't he?" he asked in a choked whisper.

His eyes, his question, stabbed at her heart. She nodded, unable to speak at first. "Yes, he is," she said at last, and sighed. "I've been thinking about him ever since Libby told me last night. I remembered the time he brought the flints and showed you how to make your first knife. I thought about all the times when you were small that you two would wrestle and he'd let you win—and how he always called you 'little brother' even after you grew so much taller than him."

"He shouldn't be dead!" Tristan pulled his hands from hers and turned his face away. "I should've known he was hurt! I should've done something to help him!"

"What happened, Tris?" she asked.

"I don't know! I don't know!" He shook his head. "He fell once, when we were running to the shuttle. There were soldiers shooting at us—maybe that's when it happened. But he got up and kept running! I didn't think—" His voice cracked. He stopped, swallowed, shook his head again.

"Even if you'd known he was hurt," Darcie said, "there might not have been anything you could've done for him. It's not your fault. It's the way things happen in battle."

Tristan didn't say anything. He was swallowing, blinking—fighting back tears, Darcie knew. She gathered him into her arms again, aching for him. "It's all right to cry," she said.

He held out for another few seconds. But then she heard his breath catch, close to her ear, and his sobs came freely.

They came for a long time, seeming to dredge the core of his soul, and she wept with him, mingling her own grief with his.

When the sobs finally ceased, he seemed drained of both strength and emotion; he sagged against her shoulder.

She had just gotten him a damp cloth to wash his face with when the door slid open behind her. At its telltale hiss, Tristan glanced up around her shoulder—and stiffened. Startled, she turned.

It was Lujan.

He hesitated in the doorway, glancing from her to Tristan, and back. "Am I intruding?" he asked.

"No," Darcie said. "You can come in."

At the edge of her vision, Tristan sucked in his lower lip and closed his teeth on it. She put her hand over his.

Lujan joined them at the bedside. "How are you doing, son?" he asked.

Tristan ducked his head. Shrugged. Didn't speak. He couldn't, Darcie knew, for fear his voice would break.

Lujan appeared to recognize his difficulty. "It's all right," he said quietly. After a little pause he gestured at the holovid on the facing bulkhead and added, "I thought you might like something to help pass the time." He withdrew a vid chip from his front uniform pocket, imprinted with the title *Hasama*. "It's a Kalese story that dates back almost five millennia," he said, "but it's still one of the most imaginative works in the known galaxy. I think you'll like it." He held out the chip.

Tristan eyed it for a long moment, glanced up, finally took it from his father's hand. "Yes, sir," he said.

"I have something for you, too, Darcie," Lujan said. He fished through his pocket again and brought out a pair of gold pins. "Your promotions continued during the years you were missing. Two years ago you were made a captain in the Sostish

Space Force. I didn't think about it until I saw you in that uniform this morning, and then I thought you should have the proper rank to wear on it.''

"Then you should do the honors," Darcie said.

She watched as he secured the captain's pins to her uniform's empty epaulets; and when he finished and stepped back, she came to attention and offered a solemn salute.

He smiled at that. "You don't have to salute me, Darcie," he said. "Especially not in here."

She questioned him with her eyes, not sure how to respond to that.

They were still standing there, still facing each other in awkward silence, when the door sighed open.

It was a med tech, a young man scarcely older than his patient. He paused at the threshold when he saw the admiral and said, "Excuse me, sir."

"It's all right," Lujan said. "Come in."

Darcie turned back to Tristan.

He had hunched himself up, sitting there in the bed. His jaw was taut, his eyes narrowed and focused on his hands, which were fisted hard in his lap.

"Tris?" she said.

He waited several seconds before he lifted his head, and then he fixed her with a look so full of rage it was like a blow to the face. Darcie nearly recoiled. But in the next instant she recognized the feelings he was trying to conceal. "I need both of you to leave," she said over her shoulder to the others. "We need a few minutes alone."

Tristan didn't relax when Lujan and the med tech left the room. He just stared up at her, his jaw still tight.

Darcie sat down on the edge of his bed, facing him. "What is it, Tris?"

"He doesn't show you enough respect," Tristan said. "He should be showing *jwa'lai* to you''—he lifted a hand to touch his brow—"not you to him!"

Darcie shook her head a little, caught his hand. "I wasn't showing *jwa'lai* to him," she said, "I was saluting him; it's—

not quite the same. And it's proper in a promotion ceremony."

In the next moment she remembered something. Couldn't remember where she'd heard it, but she said, "Someone told me you spent some time at a military academy while you were on Issel. Didn't you have to salute the instructors and other cadets there?"

"Yeah." He nodded, ducked his head. "It felt wrong there, too: males touching their foreheads for other males!" And he grimaced.

Darcie managed a smile at that. "I know it's different," she said. "A lot of things are different to me, too." She paused. Sighed. "It's going to take some time to get used to."

Tristan didn't answer.

And Darcie said, "It doesn't really have anything to do with the salute, does it?"

"No," Tristan said.

"What is it, then?"

He let his gaze fall to his lap. "It's—him."

"Him?" Puzzled, Darcie said, "Do you mean your father?"

Tristan nodded. "He acts like he's chosen you. I don't like that."

The comparison to gan mating practices startled her, until she realized it was the only comparison he knew to make. On Ganwold, the females—the mothers—did the choosing.

Darcie sighed. "Among humans," she said, "men and women both take part in the choosing. Your father and I chose each other. We're—still mates—even though that was a long time ago." That realization made her pause, sent her thoughts tumbling over each other. It was some seconds before she said, "We're—a whole family again, Tris. We all have to get used to that."

Tristan didn't answer, but after a few moments he nodded. So Darcie rose and collected her travel kit. Pressed a kiss to his forehead. "I'll come back tomorrow and spend the morning with you," she said.

Stepping into the corridor, she told the medic, "You can go in now," and when he did, she met Lujan's look.

"What was it?" he asked.

"Just some of the things Libby told us about last night," she said. "Tris is—" She looked down, away from him. "He's uncomfortable about—us."

Lujan didn't answer for a long minute. Then he asked, "How do *you* feel—about us?"

The question jerked her vision up. She swallowed, meeting his look. "I—I don't know—right now," she whispered. It was the simple truth. "It's—been so long, and—you're an admiral now. . . ."

And she was terrified, she realized. Terrified at the thought that he might still want her—more terrified that he might not. Her heart was racing, her mouth was dry.

"I understand," he said. His voice was quiet, kind, as if he were speaking to a child. "I didn't think it'd be appropriate to ask you to share my quarters, so I arranged for a cabin for you in the women officers' section. Let me show you where it is." He guided her away from Tristan's door.

Not appropriate? A pang of near panic shot through Darcie's heart as she followed him into the main passage out of sickbay. *What's not appropriate about it?* she thought, *We are still joined—aren't we?*

Or has our joining been dissolved? Is there someone else in your life now?

She kept her vision fixed on the curving deck as she strode beside him. Kept her hands tight on the handle straps of her travel kit and her teeth tight on her lower lip. Kept trying to swallow down the ache that swelled in her heart. It was some time before she even became aware of the ship sounds, the distant throb of engines and rush of ventilation, which had been muffled in sickbay.

Those sounds, and the curving stretch of corridor before her, prodded awake memories still nightmarish despite the distance of time: smoke in the transport's passages, bodies on the deck, the thunder of legionnaires' boots as they pursued her. She tightened her hold on the kit handles.

She actually jumped when Lujan took her by the arm and

drew her to the side. She looked up—and saw a handful of crewers coming along the corridor from the opposite direction. They pressed themselves to the bulkhead to let their admiral pass. Lujan returned their nodded greetings, and released Darcie's arm.

They stopped at a bank of lifts. When the first car opened and its passengers emerged, he motioned Darcie inside. "Women officers' quarters," he said.

She swayed a little as the lift started upward. Reached for its rail to steady herself.

"Are you all right?" Lujan asked.

She buried her ache beneath brusqueness. "I'm fine," she said. "I'm just—tired."

The lift moved swiftly, soundlessly up eleven decks. When it halted and she stepped out into the passageway, Lujan directed her to the right.

The door he stopped in front of lay near the end of the passage. It was unlocked. "I'll have someone from Security come up today and program the lock for your hand scan," he said as he slid the door open.

The cabin she strode into was only slightly larger than her cubicle in sickbay had been. At least this one had carpeting, and it didn't smell of disinfectant. She surveyed its stowage compartments, above and below the berth, noted the commset on the bulkhead, opened the door in the rear corner to find a compact head complete with a hygiene booth.

Lujan, standing just inside the door, watched as she looked everything over. "Will this be all right?" he asked at last.

Teeth still tight on her lower lip—and her throat so tight inside that it hurt—she only nodded in reply.

He released a full breath. "I'd better go, then," he said, and turned toward the door. "I shouldn't be keeping you from resting. I'll come by later."

She found her voice just as his boot touched the threshold. "Is that appropriate?" she asked.

She saw how he froze in the doorway for two or three heartbeats. Watched him turn on his heel to face her. When his vision met hers, his brows were drawn together in unmistakable bewilderment. "Darcie?" he said.

She felt suddenly weak, her legs too shaky to support her; she sat down—dropped, actually—onto the edge of the berth. "Lujan," she said in a rush, "you don't have to keep coming in to see me if you're just doing it to be kind. If that's the only reason you're doing it, I wish you'd stop."

His bewilderment took on a shade of shock. "What do you mean?"

She couldn't bear to look at him any longer; she lowered her gaze, shook her head. "If it's not appropriate for you to take me to your quarters," she said, "if I'm that unattractive to you now, or if—if you've dissolved our joining and taken someone else or something—then it's really not appropriate for you to come by later, either." Her throat was tightening again; she feared her voice would break.

He didn't move so much as a finger, standing there. She could feel his stare burning into the top of her head. Finally, he reached back and closed the cabin door. Unfolded the chair on the bulkhead. Sat down facing her. "I've never dissolved our joining," he said, "and I haven't taken anybody else. There's never been anyone else. I brought you here instead of taking you to my quarters because I thought you wanted it this way."

"*Me?*" She blinked at him. "How could you think that?"

He seemed surprised at her question. "Darcie," he said—and she didn't miss the strain in his voice—"every time I've tried to—to reach out to you over the past several days, you've rebuffed me. You've pulled back your hand, shrugged away from me. What was I supposed to think?"

"I don't know." Darcie shook her head, made a helpless gesture with both hands. Lowered her gaze to them as she interlocked them in her lap. "I don't know! All I know right now is that I need some time and space to sort all of this out. Everything has changed so much! I'm just feeling so confused and overwhelmed and lost right now."

"Lost?" said Lujan.

"I don't know you anymore," Darcie said. "We're practically strangers to each other. We can't even talk anymore! We used to talk to each other about everything, but all we've done these last few days is polish the tabletop—and as soon as we run out of polite, easy things to say and the silence starts to get uncomfortable, you find some excuse to get up and walk out."

He considered that for several seconds. "I have done that, haven't I?" he said at last. "I hadn't even thought about it, but you're right." He looked into her face. "What would you like to talk about?"

She had no idea what she'd expected him to say, but it wasn't that. Caught off her guard, she simply eyed him back for a moment. Then she said, "Tell me about you. Tell me about what you've done all these years."

That appeared to catch him off guard, but he said, "Fair enough. I just hope I can remember everything." Furrowing his brow, he fixed his attention on the deck.

And his pager sounded. "Admiral Serege, please come to the bridge," its electronic voice said.

He lifted his head. Met her eyes.

She locked her vision on his. *There you go*, she thought. *You're going to walk out again, aren't you?*

He didn't even leave his seat. Still holding her gaze, he reached past her and punched a couple of buttons on the bulkhead commset. "Serege here," he said.

"Sir, Commander O'Keaf," Darcie heard. "Admiral Duphar sends his compliments and asks that we inform you of the Sostis Sixth Fleet's arrival in the Saede system. The flagship *Pascinian* and its escorts should enter planetary orbit within twenty-four standard hours from now."

"Thank you, Commander," Lujan said. "Return my compliments to Admiral Duphar and request that he contact us when he's established in orbit. Serege out." His eyes touched Darcie's once more.

She didn't say anything. Just continued to hold his look.

He shifted on the chair, as if settling in, and then he said, "We were working out the details of the Enach Accords when your transport was lost. Because of that, a provision was added which allowed each side to send search-and-rescue teams to any opposing world suspected of holding missing personnel. The searches could last up to a year in each star system." He glanced up briefly. "I asked to be assigned to the team that went to Ganwold.

"We spent the next year scouring the whole star system; we didn't leave an asteroid unturned."

He paused then, his expression pensive. Didn't look up again. "Leaving at the end of the year without finding you and Tris was the hardest thing I've ever done in my life."

"We hadn't even arrived there yet," Darcie said. "The masuk pirates messed up their lightskip navigation and took us through a timeskip instead. We lost about nine years, I think."

Lujan nodded. "I know that now. I figured it out when Mordan sent his ransom message a few months ago."

He sighed, then said, "I was assigned to a Spherzah unit on Jonica on returning from Ganwold. It was rough for a while; there were times when"— he shook his head—"I felt like my life was over. Flying was about the only thing that filled the emptiness. Sometimes I'd just head out away from everything and do high-G aerobatics until I was so exhausted I could barely climb out of my spacecraft when I landed."

Darcie felt no surprise at that. She'd worked long enough as a flight surgeon to know how cathartic flying was for pilots. She didn't speak, just waited for him to continue.

"From Jonica," he said, "I went to the Spherzah school on Kaleo, as an instructor. I couldn't fly as much there, so I took up *ba'gua* and *iaijutsu* in my off-duty hours."

"*Iaijutsu?*" Darcie wrinkled her nose. "What's that?"

"It's a Kalese martial-art form that uses long swords," Lujan said. "It takes a high level of self-discipline and concentration. It can also be a little dangerous. But it was the kind of outlet I needed. I still practice it from time to time."

Darcie cocked her head, trying to imagine the man sitting across from her wielding a sword.

"I went back to Jonica after the Kaleo tour," he said. "I

studied the Holthe language some during my first assignment, and that helped me get an education billet at Fullener-Thieme University. I spent a couple of years there writing a dissertation on executive-level leadership between human and nonhuman species.

"I was promoted to captain when I graduated, and offered my first operational command. They gave me a choice of five or six Spherzah units. I took the Anchenko detachment on Topawa."

Darcie remembered Topawa's Anchenko region; she'd been stationed at a military hospital there for a few months during the War of Resistance, while Lujan was stationed forward on Tohh. She remembered the arid heat, the relentless sun. Even the night winds had been hot! Anchenko was Lujan's home region, but—

"Why?" she asked.

He offered a dim smile. "It was the detachment that needed the most work."

"That sounds a little arrogant," she said.

"Maybe it was," he conceded. "But I learned a great deal about being a commander during the years I spent out there. . . .

"I held a couple of headquarters staff positions after that," he said, "and then the Triune and Defense Directorate appointed me to this job. That was about four years ago."

Darcie studied him for a long minute. "How does it feel to be an admiral?" she asked at last.

Lujan chuckled first, deepening the tiny creases about his eyes. But then his features turned somber. "At times like these," he said, "it feels like a weight on my shoulders—so many lives in my hands. It's not a position I'd wish on anybody."

He said it with a solemnity she'd seen in him only once or twice before. He didn't lift his vision from his boots for a long space. Finally he said, "I think it's time to move on."

"What's left to move on to?" she asked.

He looked up at that. Smiled. "Retirement," he said. "I've

been in uniform for thirty years now—more than half my life. I think that's long enough."

She thought so, too. "What will you do then?" she asked.

"Go home to Topawa," he said at once, "back to the homestead." His gaze went back to the deck; his tone turned contemplative. "The history department at the regional college has expressed interest in having me create a curriculum that covers the Resistance period; I've thought a lot about doing that. Or maybe I'll just turn the homestead back into a functional farm."

He fell silent then, still studying the deck. Sat that way for some time before he raised his head and looked her in the face. "I hope that you and Tris will want to go there with me," he said.

Darcie didn't answer.

SEVEN

"**With the destruction of both main space stations** and probably two of the orbital defense bases," said the intelligence officer, "the masuk-controlled remnant of Issel's Yan fleet has effectively placed the planet under a blockade.

"A few hours after the stations were destroyed," he said, "the spacecraft carrier *Adamaman* was observed in close orbit around Issel Two. Ship-to-surface communications noted at that time indicated that a party from the orbiting vessel had shuttled to the moon base. Shortly thereafter, communications from Issel Two ceased entirely and have not resumed since." The briefer glanced up from his podium. "That was better than seventy-five standard hours ago, sir. We expect that masuki have taken control of the Issel Two command post. The status of the human personnel believed to have been there is unknown."

Admiral Aryn Duphar, seated next to Lujan in a conference room within the Assak transshipment depot, acknowledged with a nod, and the lieutenant went on:

"Over the past three days, Issel's defending fleet has returned to the planetary defense zone from its wider-ranging system patrols. Two skirmishes noted during that time resulted in the destruction of one and possibly two masuk-controlled ships. The surviving masuk ships, now numbering sixteen or seventeen, have withdrawn from the planetary defense zone. Their present position is unknown, but we believe they are awaiting reinforcement by a fleet forming in the Bacal Belt.

"Although Issel's defense forces are capable of hunting down and destroying the masuk-controlled ships, they appear reluctant to do so," he continued. "Reasons for this may include conservation of fuel and supplies, as the loss of the main space stations will make replenishment difficult, or fear of their task forces being ambushed by masuk ships in remote parts of the system, or of leaving Issel undefended. At any rate, no efforts have been made thus far to pursue the masuk-controlled ships beyond the planetary defense zone. We believe there are three carrier groups, a total of about thirty ships, in close patrols around the planet at this time."

The briefer switched off the holotank with its diagram of the Issel system and faced his audience. "This concludes the situation summary and update, gentlemen. Are there any questions?"

Admiral Duphar leaned back in his chair, brow furrowed. "You said that Issel is effectively under a blockade, Lieutenant. How is the loss of out-system trade going to affect its population, and how soon?"

"Actually, sir," the young man said, "sustaining the population wouldn't be of great concern even if the blockade went on forever—as long as it never escalated into anything else. Issel has a strong worldwide agriculture industry and good distribution networks. The problems will come with hostilities, which are almost certain to occur eventually. In that case, the difficulty will be keeping its combat forces refueled and supplied with only the remaining defense bases. We doubt the Isselans will be able to keep up during a high-intensity conflict. That's when they'll need the support from their allies, primarily Na Shiv, and that support probably won't get through."

"What kind of time window are you looking at for the arrival of the fleet from the Bacal Belt," Duphar asked next, "and do you expect hostilities to begin at that time?"

"The Bacalli fleet could arrive any time within the next two to three standard months," the lieutenant said. "And yes, sir, hostilities will most likely start then."

The older admiral nodded.

There were no more questions after that. The lieutenant excused himself and left the conference room, and Duphar glanced over at Lujan. "Quite a situation they've got on their hands," he said, shaking his head. He glanced around the table, filled with his own staff and Lujan's. "But we've got our own situation to deal with right now. How's everything shaping up for this transition?"

"Very well." Lujan tapped the folder lying on the table before him, identical to those placed before everyone else. "We'll spend this afternoon going over the tentative rotation schedule in detail and making whatever adjustments are necessary; this morning, Aryn, I'd like to take you and your staff on an inspection tour of the facilities here at this depot." He pushed his chair back from the table and rose, and the others stood, too, at attention.

Outside the conference room, several security troops and a handful of newsnet personnel fell in with the admirals' party. Lujan and Duphar, flanked by security, strode through the dim corridor toward the cavernous main entrance, and the rest strung out behind them.

"We're in the process of removing all human equipment and operations from this complex in order to return it to the native race, the umedos," Lujan said. "According to their local leaders, Issel has had bases here on Saede for some time. Assak, however, is a recent acquisition. An entire umedo community was apparently displaced when Mordan's people moved in here."

Emerging from the underground facility was like stepping into a sauna. Sunlight filtering down through the leaves of the jungle trees made illuminated columns of mist, and Lujan saw how his counterpart squinted against the sudden brightness. "I can understand why the umedos want their buildings back!" Duphar said.

A trio of troop carriers waited near the entrance, the lead

one bearing admiral's flags. The soldier at its door gave a crisp salute and said, "Good morning, gentlemen," as Lujan and Duphar approached.

" 'Morning, Brion." Lujan returned the salute and mounted the carrier; Duphar and the security troops followed. When they were settled in, Lujan said, "We're building a new command post at one of the dozen or so landing complexes the Isselan engineers cleared out of the forest. We'll see that on the way back. Right now we're going out to the POW compound, which we relocated from the underground facilities to another landing area."

"With the situation currently developing in the Issel system," said Duphar, "repatriating those POWs could turn out to be a real problem."

"I know. I've thought about that." Lujan watched over the driver's shoulder as the carrier lumbered down a jungle track. "They may not have much of a homeworld to return to by the time an armistice is accomplished."

"Assuming we can even pin down whoever's in charge of Issel now to begin negotiations," Duphar said. He shook his head. "I don't know, Lujan. I just don't like this. It's the kind of thing that could get way out of control at the twitch of a gnat's whisker."

Lujan nodded. "Pray that it doesn't," he said.

There was barely enough illumination to distinguish the other prisoners, huddled together in knots between the wire partitions, from their own shadows or those of the guards who paced outside the cage and up and down the catwalk overhead. Not enough illumination at all to discern their faces, but Ochakas could feel them watching him. At best their eyes smoldered with distrust; at worst they burned with hatred.

They had very nearly killed him when he had first been brought here.

He wasn't even certain now how long ago that had been. His masuk captors had marched him and his surviving staffers for some distance through the bright terrarium caverns, once natural formations that ran for kilometers below the moon's surface. Isselan laborers had developed them, in order to cultivate the oxygen-producing lichens and to make them safely passable for maintenance crews, by widening natural cracks and building paths.

In the areas where carmite ore showed through in russet veins, the caverns had been mined. The carmite ore was what had brought humans here in the first place, what had necessitated the life-supporting lichens. Areas where ore was found became hubs from which up to half a dozen shafts might extend. The hubs had eventually become independent mine complexes, each with its own control office, utilities plant, ore transport shuttles on the surface above, and its own lines of miners.

Malin Point was typical, Ochakas supposed. When the mines had become penal colonies, they had been sealed off from the cave system; they were accessible now only by manmade tunnels.

Ochakas and his people had been herded through one of these dim tunnels and made to wait while its shield doors groaned open. Prodded through, they found themselves standing in a subterranean vault that appeared larger than Issel's Chamber of Ministries in the capital city of Sanabria. In actuality its size wasn't wholly discernible; its only lighting shot in harsh yellow streams from the windows and doorway of a control shack built up on gantries next to the ceiling.

The shack's windows were shattered and its door battered in, Ochakas saw, looking up. Its placement had afforded its occupants little defense when the power failed several days before. When the containment field had been disrupted, two hundred prisoners were suddenly set free. While some had attempted to escape, others had scaled the structure and rammed the door. The personnel inside were cudgeled with tools and fists and finally hurled to their death over the walkway railing.

Most of those prisoners had been tracked down and rounded up by heavily armed security personnel shortly before the masuki arrived. But some remained at large in the caverns and tunnels. Mostly criminals with lengthy résumés of violence, Ochakas recalled.

The cell block stood in the cavern's center. It resembled a vast cage of wire mesh, divided up inside into cells, and its outer barrier stood more than twice the height of its occupants.

The containment field still was not functional, so the prisoners were not confined to the individual cells. When the masuki approached the mesh gate, every inmate drew up around it, leaving just enough space for it to swing inward. The masuki shoved Ochakas and his staffers inside, and suddenly that space around the gate looked like an arena.

The prisoners just stood there studying him and his people at first, and in the random movement of the guards' palm lights, as they tugged and rattled the gate closed, Ochakas glimpsed several of their faces. All were haggard, whiskered, filthy, and most were twisted into sneers.

The man who finally spoke was nearly a head taller than Ochakas, almost as tall as a masuk. He wore the gray coverall of a convict, worn through at the elbows and knees, with faded characters stamped on the right chest that spelled out the name FOROS. "Well, well, General-sir," he said, "how nice of you to join us in the Government's Home for Unhappy Citizens. We feel we'd be truly remiss if we neglected to express our appreciation for having this wonderful place"—he spread his arms wide in an all-encompassing gesture—"to call our own." And he made the slightest motion with one hand.

The human noose closed. A jungle of hands, hard as claws, seized Ochakas by his arms, pinned them, tore off his shirt. The weight of the mob forced him backward onto the mesh and held him there, hard enough that the wire pressed into his flesh.

Some of the mob moved back when the ringleader strode closer, and Ochakas tried to look around for his subordinates. He found them only after craning his neck, forced to their knees on the wet stone and held in restraint by a handful of prisoners.

Foros planted himself in front of Ochakas. "Now then," he said, "what shall it be for our dear Sector General's top military man? How shall we execute him?"

"I say we beat 'im t' death," growled someone near Ochakas's left ear, "the way we did the guards in the control shack."

"Nah, that'd take too long," another shape muttered. "Too much fat."

"We could hang 'im. Hang 'im on the cage." Hands fumbled for Ochakas's belt, unclasped it, pulled it loose. "He's got one of them military-issue web belts; that'd take 'is weight."

Someone else produced a blade, filed down from part of a metal ration plate. "I like how the masuki do it." He lay the crude point at the base of Ochakas's throat, where the masuk guard's scratch still smarted. "They start here and . . ."

Ochakas didn't stiffen, didn't even swallow. He felt as if he were smothering in the stench of the mob's bodies, a mingling of sweat and urine and rancid breath, but he held the gaze of their leader.

And Foros eyed him back, almost contemplatively. "I'm curious," he said. "I can't help wondering how the Commander of Intersystem Operations—one of the Sector General's chief henchmen—fell out of favor so far as to land down here."

"The Sector General is dead," said Ochakas.

Foros arched his brows. "But you didn't do it," he said after a moment. "If you had, you'd still be up there, running the show yourself." He leaned closer. "So who did, General? Who *is* in charge up there now?"

"Masuki," said Ochakas.

It wasn't the answer Foros seemed to be expecting. He straightened, his crooked smirk displaying disbelief.

"They want human slaves," Ochakas said. "We have reason to believe they're preparing to enslave Issel."

The other turned away, throwing back his head in a bitter laugh. "Did you tell them they're too late, General? Did you tell them that Issel has already been enslaved for the last thirty years?"

Ochakas said nothing, and Foros turned back to study him through narrowed eyes. "Let them go," he said abruptly; and then, when his people hesitated: "I said, *let them go!*"

He waited until they obeyed, reluctantly, to address Ochakas again. "Welcome to slavery, General," he said. "I think that's more fitting than killing you outright. This way you'll get to see what it's like. You'll die with all of us, a little bit at a time."

EIGHT

Tristan turned his head, grimacing, when a hand closed gently about his wrist. "Still having a lot of pain?" Doctor Moses asked.

"Yes," he said.

She sighed. "I was afraid of that. We did a lot more work this time than we did in the first procedure. We removed a lot more scar tissue and did some pretty massive patching up. Some soreness has to be expected. Have you been using the morphesyne infuser?"

"Yeah."

She didn't have to remove the sheet to examine his back; he'd already pushed it down around his waist because even its touch on his skin caused irritation. He locked his teeth, pressing his lips tight, as her cool fingers probed at his shoulder blades and along his right side, where the lacerations had been most severe.

"The soreness will probably last a couple more days," she said, "but it'll pass once you start to move around and stretch these artiskin patches a little. The third procedure won't be this bad."

She stepped back. "You're healing properly," she told him. "Your temperature is coming down and your other vital signs look good." She met his look as she washed her hands. "How does your stomach feel? Would you like to try something solid for dinner tonight?"

He considered. "All right."

"How about some real meat that you can chew off the bones?"

He stared. It had been almost three weeks since he'd told her of that want, and never expecting it to be met, he'd practically forgotten about it. He wondered if she was teasing him. He questioned her with his eyes.

She was smiling. "You didn't think I'd come through, did you? Well, some people do keep their promises, even if it takes a while. I'm just sorry it took so long. Need some help sitting up?" She reached out to assist him, then touched the tray-table button on the bed rail.

As it slid up from beside the mattress on its mechanical arm, pivoted, and lowered itself across his lap, she said, "Next time I won't mess with all the bureaucracy of galley chiefs, resupply ships, and mixed-up shipping containers—I'll just go big-game hunting! That's *got* to be less complicated!"

She turned and picked up a covered dish from the bedside cabinet. "Your mother says you like your meat on the rare side." She set the dish on the tray table before him and lifted its lid. "How's this?"

The slab of meat, two fingers thick and with a bone through the center, practically covered the plate. It had been browned on top and bottom but the rest of it was as red as a freshly killed peimu and oozing with juice. Tristan stared at it, mouth watering.

He glanced up at Doctor Moses, wordless.

"You may or may not want these," she said, unrolling a set of utensils from a handcloth onto the tray. "I figured you wouldn't care for seasonings. Anything else?"

"No." Tristan eyed the meat again for a long minute. "Thank you," he said quietly.

"Thank me by eating it," Doctor Moses said. "I want to find that plate empty when I come back for it!"

He waited until she left to take up the meat with both hands. The juice ran down between his fingers, blood hot, and he licked it away before he tore into the flesh. He chewed with his eyes closed, giving his whole attention to texture and flavor, savoring every bite of it.

It wasn't peimu meat. The flavor was different, bland by comparison, and he hardly had to chew it at all before he could swallow it.

Close to the bone the meat was virtually raw. He gnawed it off, growling in his throat as Pulou and the other gan hunters had done over their kills.

He didn't see the stains on his hands, the smears on his palms and between his fingers, or the marrow caked under his fingernails, until he returned the stripped bone to the plate. By then his hands looked as they had after—

The blade went in upward, under the masuk's breastbone. Tristan felt him stiffen and stagger back. Hot blood coursed over his hand—

He recoiled, suddenly cold. Tried to rub the stains off, but they were practically dry already. "No!" he said, shaking his head. "No!"

The masuk's face burned in his mind as it did in his nightmares: He saw the gaping mouth, the eyes staring at him, wide with shock. The darkness of the tunnel hadn't hidden those images, hadn't muffled the death rattle as his enemy slumped back against the wall.

"No!" Tristan shoved the tray table away. His hand was shaking. He gripped it in the other one, trying to control it.

He had to wash. He swung his legs around, jerking at the sheet that tangled around them, pushed himself out of the bed and nearly buckled at the pain. He staggered. His hand left a smear on the bed rail when he caught it to steady himself.

The IV line was just long enough for him to reach the basin in the cubicle's head. He almost bumped into the door frame on the way in. Fumbled with the faucet for a moment, forgetting until it switched on that it was automatic. Then he scrubbed his hands hard with its soap and hot water.

A chance glimpse of himself in the reflector nearly made him gag: There was blood all around his mouth. He scrubbed at his face until it smarted.

He was still washing, still shaking, his stomach still in knots, when Doctor Moses came back. He didn't hear her come in—didn't even know she was there until he saw her in the reflector, standing in the head doorway behind him. He twisted around.

She said, "Sorry, Tris, I didn't mean to—good crikey, you're as white as the sheets! What's wrong? Did you get sick to your stomach?"

"No." He shook his head. He could barely make himself stammer, "I got—blood on my hands."

"You're having a flashback," said Moses. She drew him away from the basin, flicked on the hot-air blower. "We need to talk about it."

He swallowed hard. Ducked his head and wouldn't meet her eyes. "It's gone now," he said. He forced himself not to look at his hands as he held them out to the blower. "I'm all right now."

The way she studied him, brow furrowed, warned him that she knew better. She stood there watching while he dried his hands, and he concentrated on controlling their shaking and avoiding her gaze.

He hesitated when the blower shut off, half expecting her to block his way out of the head, but she moved back when he turned. He gestured toward the tray table, attempting to distract her. "I emptied the plate."

"You're welcome," said Doctor Moses. "If you keep that up, I can relieve you of the IV line."

He sat on the bed, settling himself carefully cross-legged.

"If you were willing to talk about it," she added, "maybe we could relieve you of the nightmares, too."

He touched his brow, keeping his head bowed. "Please, ma'am, I'm all right."

She didn't counter him; she just unfolded the bulkhead chair and sat down. "Tris," she said, "what are you feeling right now?"

It was an hour before she left. Only then did he pull his knotted hands from his lap and examine them for traces of blood. And during the night, the dreams woke him, shaking and sweating, four times.

He was still in bed the next morning, his breakfast untouched and cold on the tray table, when his mother came in. She placed a gray bundle on the cabinet and drew up by the bed to study his monitor, and he pushed himself up, raising his hand to touch his forehead.

She caught his hand, squeezed it. "You don't have to do that here," she said.

He sighed. "When are we going back to Ganwold?"

"We—won't be going back, Tris." She paused. "Even if we could, it wouldn't be the same. Not now. Too many things have happened to us—especially to you."

He wasn't sure what she meant by that. But before he could ask, she said, "Libby told me that you had a bad night."

He ducked his head. "Just a lot of dreams."

"Tell me about them," she said.

"No, Mum." He didn't look up. "I-I can't."

"You might feel better if you had some breakfast," she said.

His vision flicked to the bowl of cooked cereal on the tray table, and he made a face. "Not that! It's too slimy!"

She smiled. "That isn't what I meant." She reached up to switch off the hemomanagement system, clamped off the IV line, detached it as she spoke. "Libby says you haven't left this room since your surgery three days ago and it's high time you did, so I'm taking you up to your father's quarters. He'd like for us to have breakfast together." She attached a heparin lock to the intracath set near his collarbone. "There. Go wash up." And she put the gray bundle into his hands.

A vague sense of dread made his stomach tighten up. He didn't move, just sat kneading the gray bundle in his lap. "I don't want to go up to his quarters," he said, almost inaudibly.

There was a long pause. "Because of what Renier said about him?" she asked.

The tension in his stomach increased, thinking about the

things Governor Renier had told him. He squeezed the bundle harder and said, "Yes."

His mother sighed. "I know you're—uncomfortable about him, Tris, but you're not even giving him a chance. You need to give him that."

Tristan didn't answer.

"If you wait too long," she said, "breakfast will be cold before we get up there."

He sighed, resigned, and pushed himself out of the bed.

His shoulders and back were still sensitive enough that the hygiene booth's spray made him wince, but the warm air afterward soothed the smarting. The gray bundle, when he unrolled it, was an athletic warm-up suit: lightweight, loose, and fleecy on the inside, with a black stripe down each leg and sleeve and the Spherzah insignia in black on the upper left chest. He grimaced, pulling the shirt on over his head, but then he could barely feel it across his shoulders.

His mother gave him an approving look when he came out of the head. "That looks better. How does it feel?"

He shrugged. "It's all right."

She took his arm as they left sickbay. The tautness in her grip startled him, and he glanced down at her. "Mum?"

"It's still hard to walk these passages," she said. "They're too much like the ones in that transport."

He didn't have to ask her what transport; he still had memories of his own. "But you've come here—by yourself—almost every day," he said.

"I knew it was the only way I'd get over being afraid," she told him. "I had to force myself to take every step at first, but it's not that hard now." She smiled. "At least I don't have to keep myself from running every time there's a gravity shift or a change in the engines' pitch." She looked at him pointedly. "Sometimes you have to look your fears right in the eye."

He knew very well what she meant by that; he felt a little pang of guilt for his animosity toward the admiral. He lowered his head and stayed silent.

* * *

A servo from the galley arrived at the admiral's quarters just as he and his mother did. It whirred across the carpet and circled the low octagonal table in the center of the living area to set places for three, laying out plates and cups and utensils with the precision of a practiced human steward. Then it unloaded a tray of fresh fruit of half a dozen shapes and colors and sizes, cut and cored and artistically arranged. There were loaves of hot whole-grain bread, too, wrapped in white cloth and stacked in a basket, and a bowl of red preserves and a steaming pot of shuk. Tristan hadn't felt hungry before but the sight of the food made his stomach rumble. He glanced across at his mother.

"We'll wait to eat until your father comes," she said. "His staff meeting should be over soon."

Restless, Tristan paced the circumference of the living area. He trailed his hand along the gray fabric covering three of the bulkheads, to feel if the weave was as coarse as it looked. He tried a closed door at one side simply because it was there, and wasn't surprised when it didn't open for him: Most of the doors in the governor's residence on Issel hadn't opened for him either. He paused at one of the observation panes and stood looking out for some time. Then he moved around to examine a veritable fleet of model ships mounted on the fourth bulkhead, which was paneled with dark wood.

Some of the represented ships were ancient, some were modern. All were crafted by some artisan from bits and pieces of amber metal. Tristan went from one to another, touching, looking. His breath caught when he realized he could identify some of them.

A one-man craft set almost at eye level caught his attention. Held it. He'd seen images of such ships in academic history vids, clips made with nosecone recorders mounted on Dominion warbirds. The clips usually ended with the Unified ship disintegrating in a fireball under bursts from Dominion plasma cannon. He leaned close, shifting back and forth to scrutinize the model from all angles.

"That's the kind of fighter your father flew in the War of Resistance," his mother said beside him.

He lifted it from its bracket to turn it carefully in his hands—just as the door hissed open behind him. He wrenched around, hands tightening on the model, as Admiral Serege strode into the room.

His mother didn't seem concerned. "Breakfast is waiting," she said.

"Good! I'm starving!" Joining them beside the bulkhead display, the admiral said, "It's good to see you back on your feet, Tris. How are you feeling?"

Every muscle in his body had gone taut, Tristan realized. "I'm fine," he said. Clipped the words.

The admiral didn't miss the sharpness of his tone; Tristan saw it in his eyes. But Serege chose to ignore it—this time. "I'm glad," he said, and then, "What have you got there?"

Tristan glanced down at his hands—still cradling the fighter model. His vision jerked back up; he braced himself. "I just wanted to look at it!"

"That's all right." The admiral studied him for a moment. "Do you know what it is?"

Tristan said, "It's a Cettan-Trevaska 45 *Solar Arrow* interceptor."

The admiral looked mildly surprised. "That's right! What do you know about it?"

A display from a spacecraft-recognition handbook came into focus in Tristan's memory. "The CT-45 was designed by Cettan-Trevaska on Sostis to counter the Dominion Space Force's Ap-202," he recited. "It was also produced on Kaleo, Jonica, and Topawa. A highly maneuverable and exceptionally fast transatmospheric craft, it was capable of carrying up to twelve missiles in four internal wing racks and also featured a plasma cannon for turning combat. Its lethality in such encounters earned it the nickname 'shark of the stars.' By the end of the War of Resistance, over seven thousand CT-45s had been produced." Tristan hesitated, then added, "You flew a CT-45 in the attack on Dominion Station, sir."

"Yes, I did!" The admiral actually grinned. "And at Adriat and Issel and Tohh, and every battle in between. Where did you learn all of that?"

Tristan's hands were damp, holding the model. "At the Aeire City Academy, sir."

The admiral arched an eyebrow. "I heard that you did very well at Aeire City. It's quite an honor to make Alpha Flight." He paused. "If you'd like to continue your schooling, I'd be willing to sponsor your application to the Sostis Aerospace Institute. No special favors, you understand. Just a chance to complete what you've started."

Tristan's gut clenched up; the taunts of a former classmate echoed through his mind: *"So, how much did your old man pay for your slot in Alpha Flight? Aw, c'mon, everybody knows you're the Spherzah commander's brat. That's the only reason you haven't washed out of here yet!"*

"N-no, sir," he said. He could still see the other cadet's leer. His humiliation heated up his face even now. He bowed his head. "I-I didn't really make Alpha Flight."

There was a little silence, and then the admiral said, "It doesn't matter, Tris. I never made Alpha Flight, either." He appeared to think briefly, then he said, "I'm still a licensed instructor pilot. I could finish teaching you myself, if you'd prefer that."

Another memory flashed up from pilot training at Aeire City: He knelt on a landing bay's hot tarmac with his instructor towering over him. *"And you're Lujan Serege's brat,"* the captain said, his voice laden with disgust. *"He'd probably disown you if he saw you puking all over the deck like that!"*

Tristan's face heated again, and his stomach knotted up. He shook his head. "No!" he said, and realizing that he still held the model, he turned about abruptly and replaced it on its mount. He couldn't meet the admiral's eyes.

But he could feel the other's perplexity. For a moment Admiral Serege seemed about to add something else, but then he just released a full breath. "Let's see what the galley sent up for breakfast," he said instead.

Surveying the table, he gave a mischievous smile. "No eggs," he said. "Good."

Darcie was already pouring the shuk, and the table was enveloped with its spicy aroma. She looked up at the admiral's comment and gave a small smile. "Well, one thing hasn't changed!" she said. "You've never learned to like eggs!" Indicating the place at her left, she added, "Tris, you sit here."

They offered thanks before they touched the food. The small ritual wasn't new to Tristan. His mother had always done it on Ganwold, had taught him even before he could talk to fold his hands together while she said the words. But it startled him to see the admiral with head bowed and hands clasped on the table. He remembered a former classmate telling him that all Topawaks were religious fanatics, and he stared, oblivious of what was being said, until the admiral raised his head.

The table was too low and the deep-cushioned chairs too far away from it to be practical for eating. Tristan wanted to sit on his heels on the carpet, where the table would be within easy reach. But after a glance at his mother, balancing her plate on her knees, he settled for loading his own with bread and fruit and sitting cross-legged in the chair, where he could place the plate in his lap.

"The reps from the newsnets are pressuring me for interviews with you two," the admiral said, looking at Darcie and Tristan in turn as he filled his own plate. "They're saying that our reunion after all these years is the biggest human-interest story since World Governor Kedar Gisha gave birth to her first son—and he's sixteen now!"

Darcie smiled over the cup of shuk she held with both hands. "I doubt we'd be such a big story if we weren't your family, Lujan. All the newscasts I've seen lately call you the most widely respected military leader in twenty years."

Admiral Serege rolled his eyes. "That's just the Sostish media," he said. "They're even worse than the general population when it comes to hero-worship. You'd be a big story with or without me." He reached for the bread and the dish of preserves and grinned at her. "Better start getting used to it."

The glint of his knife caught Tristan's eye; the dark red of the preserves being spread on the bread held it. Something about the color, the texture, made his stomach clench up. He put his own bread back on his plate, watched the admiral take a bite, studied his face as he chewed.

"How many people did you have to assassinate to make admiral?" he asked.

Through the corner of his eye he saw his mother stiffen. She set down her cup, so sharply that its amber contents sloshed over the rim, and stared at him.

Admiral Serege looked shocked, too, but only for a moment. He deliberately finished chewing. Swallowed. Looked Tristan squarely in the eye. "I've never assassinated anyone, Tristan," he said, and there was a grimness to his tone that held Tristan's attention as if with an armored fist. "Contrary to what you've been told, the Spherzah are not assassins." He paused then, and his voice was quieter when he spoke again. "I did have to kill sometimes, in order to accomplish a mission. But I'm not proud of any of those times."

Silence followed. Tristan searched the admiral's face for several seconds, letting his doubts smolder in plain sight in his own eyes.

A chirping sound startled him out of his glower.

The admiral reached for the pager in his front pocket. "Admiral Serege, please contact the Watch," it said. He sighed, turned an apologetic look to Darcie, and stood. "Excuse me."

Tristan studied his back as he crossed to his office, more puzzled now than he had been before.

Lujan shut the office door firmly behind him and crossed to the secure commset on his desk. It had a direct line to the Watch. He touched its green button and the monitor lit up with the image of Commander Ullen, who said, "This will be a conference call, sir. We're connecting with Admiral Duphar and his ship's intelligence center as I speak."

Lujan nodded acknowledgment.

With a blink, the monitor divided into three segments, one still showing Ullen, the others filled by Duphar and his intelligence chief. Duphar nodded a curt greeting. "Well, Lujan, what's come up now?"

"I'll let Commander Ullen explain," Lujan said.

"Gentlemen," said the commander, "we've just received a message from a Mythosian ship patrolling the Bacal Belt. It was transmitted nearly twenty-six standard hours ago. They've detected the departure of several major vessels from the spacedocks of At'tawab, one of Mi'ika's strongest allies. After tracking the vessels for some time, it was determined that they were heading for a central region within Bacalli space, probably an assembly area."

"The masuk reinforcement fleet?" asked Lujan.

"That's what the Mythosians believe, sir. They estimate thirty-five ships, mostly combatants."

Duphar's intelligence chief wrinkled his brow. "That's about half the strength of a normal masuk slaving fleet, but it could still pose a substantial threat, considering Issel's military capability right now."

Admiral Duphar scowled at his monitor. "What's their ETA in the Issel system, Commander?"

"A little over a month, sir," said Ullen.

Duphar appeared to consider that for a moment. Then he blew out a breath and looked directly at Lujan through the monitor. "If you get back to Sostis in time for Cheeveh's Day," he said, "hang out a prayer ribbon for us. We're going to need it."

NINE

Shinchang Military Station drifted above the sunlit globe of Sostis as languidly as a carnivorous plant Tristan had once observed, growing submerged in the reedy, muddy water near the edge of a lake on Ganwold. Innocent as a flower it had appeared, swaying on its stalk as the water rolled gently up to lap the shore and then retreat. Until a curious minnow had poked its nose into the blossom. Then it had contracted, enveloping all but the fish's tail, which had flipped frantically for several seconds afterward.

Shinchang Station had no tethering stalk, but it had several docking bays that gaped like mouths, each large enough to engulf an entire spacecraft carrier. Tristan's hands, spread on the observation pane, tensed as the station blocked out more and more of the planet turning beyond it, and he abruptly realized that he was trying to push the ship back.

But *Destrier* glided through the space gate as smoothly as the fish the ganan had caught for food, and was guided to its berth by a pair of tugcraft flashing signals to the helmsman with an array of colored lights. Tristan became aware that the carrier had stopped moving only when a voice came over its general address system: "Docking is complete. Welcome home, *Destrier!*"

Behind him, Admiral Serege gave Darcie a smile, and she returned it, somewhat shyly. Tristan saw it as a reflection in the observation pane; glowering, he fixed his attention outward again.

He was still looking out when the door buzzer sounded. He started, but the admiral turned and said, "Come in."

A pair of young spacers stood at stiff attention in the doorway. "Your gear, sir?" said one.

"Right there by the door." Serege nodded toward a couple of canvas duffles, one of them his own, the other containing Tristan's and Darcie's few belongings.

The young men each shouldered a bag and pivoted out through the doorway, nearly colliding with the flagship's first officer and several members of the admiral's staff, who had arrived in their wake. Stepping aside to let the spacers pass, the first officer said, "Your shuttle to the surface is standing by, sir."

Serege nodded. "Thank you, Commander. Tris"—he beckoned—"let's go." Turning, he offered his arm to Darcie. She hesitated, giving him a quizzical glance before she tucked her hand around it.

Tristan followed, his teeth set tight.

The admiral's party was met in the passage to the gangway tube by *Destrier*'s captain and bridge crew: a line of officers in gray service dress who came to attention as their fleet commander drew up.

"As you were," Serege said. Then he started down the line, exchanging a few words and a handclasp with each of them.

Tristan watched them. Saw earnestness in their smiles, in their nods, and admiration in their eyes. Not fear. He wondered at that.

Serege paused once to look back along the line. His face was solemn, but his eyes bore an intensity Tristan couldn't read. "I salute you all," he said. "You've served your home-worlds with distinction."

Side boys stood at the airlock: four on either side, at attention. As the admiral approached, the boatswain's mate sounded his pipe and they snapped, as one, to a salute. Serege returned it as he passed through them into the gangway.

More people crowded the boarding area at the end of the tube, held back by a line of Sostish security troops. Most were station personnel in various military uniforms, craning their necks and jostling one another.

But there were people from the media, too, wearing ear receivers and voice pickups and carrying compact holocorders. They pressed against the security line, leaning forward with their holocorders, and Tristan froze up.

His mother must have seen it; she twined her free arm through his and gripped his hand. Her own features had grown taut, he saw.

The admiral maneuvered them through the cordon, acknowledging with curt nods the newsnetters who pressed close after them.

Security troops escorted them through the curving corridor to a lift, rode down with them several levels, conducted them to another gangway tube. Only the shuttle's cockpit crew waited there, but they snapped off salutes and the captain said, "Welcome home, sir."

It was an official flag officer's shuttle: The forward bulkhead of the passenger cabin was blazoned with an admiral's crest. The rest of it resembled a command office, furnished with acceleration seats as high-backed as conference chairs, and console desks with commsets. Admiral Serege shook his head as his party settled in. "These seats feel softer every time I have to travel in this thing!"

"You've just gotten too used to camp chairs lately, sir!" his executive officer said with a grin.

Serege chuckled. "You're probably right, Jiron."

A chime sounded over a hidden intercom, followed by the pilot's voice. "Welcome aboard, ladies and gentlemen. We'll be departing Shinchang Station in two minutes. Please ensure that all acceleration harnesses are secure."

Tristan fastened his and listened as the throb of idling engines swelled to a muffled scream. He felt the push as the craft slid back from its berth. Once clear, it rolled out and banked around, and he watched through the viewport as another space gate opened, like interlocked fingers drawing apart to let a bird fly free. The shuttle burst through into space so brightly lit by Sostis's sun that it made him blink.

The pilot came back on the intercom. "Sir, our flight time from Shinchang Station to Ramiscal City will be approximately one hour and thirty-five minutes, standard. ETA at Herbrun Field will be sixteen-hundred-eighteen, Ramiscal City time."

"Just in time for the review and dismissal of the troops," Serege said. He turned to his exec. "What else have we got on the agenda for the next few days, Jiron?"

The captain drew a microwriter from his front pocket and flicked it on. "The review and dismissal are all for this evening, sir. Tomorrow there's the preliminary report to World Governor Gisha and the Triune at zero-eight-hundred hours in the governor's private conference room. Also at zero-eight-hundred tomorrow, Captain Dartmuth"—he nodded at Darcie—"and Tristan are scheduled for transition assistance sessions at Winthancom Military Medical Center, followed by meetings with representatives of the MIC at ten-hundred."

Darcie looked up at that last. "Why are they starting the debriefings so soon? Tris needs time to get well first. I don't think—"

The exec looked uncomfortable. "Actually, ma'am," he said, "all the debriefings would've been done before we left the Saede system if there hadn't been medical restrictions."

Tristan felt his stomach contract into an unstable lump of dread. Hands curling around the arms of his chair, he searched the admiral's face.

"That's the normal procedure," Serege said, "but I want you to contact Doctor Moses first; I'm not sure those restrictions have been lifted yet. Even if she feels it's all right to go ahead, I want her to provide monitors." He met Tristan's look, and then Darcie's, with one that said he understood.

"Yes, sir." Jiron tapped briefly at the 'writer's keypad before he went on. "Tomorrow is also the memorial service for the war dead, thirteen-hundred hours in the Hall of Heroes. You're slated to speak, sir."

The admiral acknowledged with a nod.

"Then there's a meeting with a Jonican public-defense delegation at fifteen-hundred—an info package will be on your desk by tomorrow morning, sir—and a small informal dinner at the Governor's Mansion at nineteen-hundred. That's for your whole family." Jiron glanced over at Darcie and Tristan again as he thumbed the scroll button.

"The weekly staff meeting will be at its usual time on the morning of the twenty-fourth, followed by the command-level intelligence update at zero-nine-thirty. On the twenty-fifth, Captain Dartmuth and Tristan are scheduled for medical follow-ups with Doctor Moses, at ten-hundred and ten-thirty. Your war report to the full Assembly, sir, is set for the same day, starting at zero-nine-hundred." Jiron looked up. "That will probably fill most of the day."

"No rest for the weary," Serege sighed, and tapped the arm of his chair with his knuckles. "Guess I'd better enjoy this soft seat while I can!"

Approaching the planet, the shuttle entered a deceleration orbit, and Tristan pressed his forehead to the viewport. A massive polar ice cap, gleaming under the sun's light, caught his attention first; in another moment he could make out the outlines of continents, partly obscured by clouds. The shuttle passed over the nighttime hemisphere, where cities were marked with a glitter of lights, then circled into daylight a few minutes later, and topographic features became discernible.

A short time afterward the pilot's voice came over the intercom again. "Ladies and gentlemen, we are now entering Sostis's atmosphere. As there may be some turbulence during our descent, please be sure that all safety harnesses are secured."

Wisps of clouds began to blow past the viewport. Tristan looked out into a bright blue sky and down at sunlight flashing off a blue-green ocean. The shuttle dropped, dropped, until vessels became visible, trailing V-shaped wakes over the water, and land came into view far ahead.

Land that seemed to jut straight up out of the ocean like a row of canine teeth! Tristan's breath caught.

The coast was a ragged fringe of fjords and islets, and snowpack still covered the mountains. Ramiscal City lay at the mouth of one fjord, tucked into every crevice and cranny of available space between the water and the sheer slopes until it seemed to be stacked up on itself. The shuttle banked around, skimming over the structures.

Darcie leaned forward to share Tristan's viewport, her lips pursed, her eyes intent. "I'd almost forgotten what cities look like," she said after several seconds.

"I met your mother in Ramiscal City, Tristan," Serege said. He turned to Darcie. "Do you remember that?"

"Yes." She reflected for a moment and then said, "Berg took me with him to attend your graduation from the Sostis Aerospace Institute. After the speeches and swearing-in, we pinned on your ensign's marks." She seemed to grow suddenly solemn. "It was only a few days before we shipped out for Yan."

Tristan's attention returned to the viewport when a roar erupted from beneath the shuttle. Its forward motion slowed, stopped; it hovered for a moment and then began a vertical descent. Tristan could imagine the plumes of its thruster fire reaching down like legs for the surface, letting the craft down slowly, slowly, until it settled with a final *whoosh,* and a billow of vapor and dust that filled the viewports.

At the shuttle's hatch and the docking bay's entrance there were more security troops, more salutes. Three skimmers were waiting, one bearing admiral's flags. Admiral Serege guided Darcie and Tristan to that one; his staff boarded the others.

Herbrun Field lay on a rugged jut of land, outside the city and surrounded on three sides by the North Beloje Sea. Its tarmac made Tristan think of the parade ground at the Aeire City Academy, except that this one was several times larger. And it was filled with people.

The returning troops stood in formation, company after company in precise human blocks. Their commanders called them to attention as the admiral's skimmer came up the tarmac toward the reviewing stand, sending a ripple effect the length of the field. But Tristan had never seen so many people as crowded the barriers at the field's borders! Thousands of people: a sea of faces shouting cheers and hands waving amber ribbons. The sight sent a shiver down his spine.

Banner-sized amber streamers snapped in the afternoon breeze at the tops of flagpoles overlooking the field; smaller ones fluttered in bunches along the rail of the reviewing stand.

"Is this one of their religious holidays?" Tristan heard his mother ask.

"Looks like it," Serege said, and gave a wry smile. "Or it could just be part of welcoming the troops home. Amber prayer ribbons are for their warrior god—Cheeveh, I think."

There were twenty or more dignitaries on the reviewing platform, a few of them military, most civilian—and at least as many newsnetters and journalists. Those last closed in as Admiral Serege dismounted the skimmer and escorted his family up to the platform. They made Tristan uncomfortable; he jerked his head away when someone thrust a holocorder into his face.

The woman who received them at the podium was about his mother's age and build. She clasped the admiral's hands in both of hers and kissed him on each side of his face. "On behalf of the government and the people of Sostis," she said, "I offer you, Admiral Serege, our deepest gratitude for your preservation of our world in safety and peace. Your name and your deeds will be immortalized among those of the heroes of Sostis for all time. We wish you welcome home, both you and your family!"

The crowd behind the barriers exploded into cheers as she released Admiral Serege's hands and turned to Darcie, gripped her hands briefly, then took Tristan's. She gave them a little squeeze, gave him a little smile before she let him go, and then she motioned Admiral Serege to the podium.

He took that place with some reluctance, Tristan saw: He gripped the podium so hard with both hands that his knuckles turned white. A glance at his face revealed nervous tension along his jaw as he looked out over the crowd. He waited uneasily while the cheering died, settling into the silence of anticipation.

"Thank you, Governor Gisha, people of Sostis and the Unified Worlds," he said, and the pickups boomed his quiet words across the whole expanse of Herbrun Field. He stood very still. "If there are heroes to be honored here today, they are the men and women who stand before you on this field— and those who do *not* stand here, who are remembered by their comrades-in-arms with empty places in the ranks."

He ducked his head at that, and Tristan saw him swallow once, then twice. He felt a sudden urge to swallow, too. Found he couldn't tear his vision from the admiral's face.

"It was *their* discipline," Serege said, "*their* dedication, and *their* courage that kept Sostis safe. Hail your sons and daughters as your heroes."

He paused to clear his throat before he looked out over the field again, and the intensity Tristan had glimpsed earlier was back in his eyes. "To you, my troops," he said, "you have my admiration and my deepest regard. I'm privileged to be your commander.

"But"—and he suddenly smiled—"you have better things to do than stand here in formation listening to speeches! You have families and friends waiting who haven't seen you for a while. So . . ." He released the podium and straightened to attention. ". . . Spherzah force, dis-*missed!*"

On the tarmac, the tidy blocks of soldiers burst and scattered like wildlace seeds on a wind, surging for the sidelines and merging with the mass of humanity that flowed over the barriers.

On the platform, Admiral Serege stepped back from the podium and wrapped his arms around Darcie and Tristan, pulling them close in a three-way hug. The holocorders hummed and the onlookers applauded but the admiral seemed oblivious to it all. "Let's go home," he said quietly.

The Flag Officers' Residential Complex was a quintet of towers planted at the foot of a mountain and surrounded by a park. It lay a little distance up the fjord, away from the business and governmental districts of the city. "It's practically a self-contained community," Serege said, setting the skimmer down on a rooftop landing pad. "And it's quiet—the city noise doesn't carry up this far." He shut down the engines and popped the hatch.

They stood for several minutes on the roof, studying the glaciered peaks that enclosed them. The range that rose up ridge after ridge to the west was already streaked with purple shadows, in stark contrast with the floes of ice. To the east was a view of the ocean, wedge-shaped through the mouth of the fjord and as dark as the spring storm clouds rolling in over it.

Tristan turned his face to the breeze, testing it as Pulou had taught him to do. He recognized the salty tang of the sea—the same scent that the wind had borne over Aeire City—but the predominant smell was of the pine forest that covered the lower slopes like a peimu robe.

"We're far enough north that the sun won't set for another hour or two," the admiral said, "but it's still early spring here; it'll start getting chilly in a little while. Let's go inside."

They rode a lift down two or three stories, past parking and maintenance levels, and stepped out into a carpeted entry. Admiral Serege smiled as he touched the door's scanpad. "Welcome home, Darcie, Tristan."

The first thing Tristan saw, looking across the living area as he stepped inside, was another view of the mountains. Either the entire wall was transparent or it was the largest holo-screen he had ever seen.

The second thing he saw was the dog. It was lying on the floor near the middle of the room, lying partly in shadow. It lifted its head at the sound of the admiral's voice, and when it did, Tristan heard his mother gasp.

"Kazak!" said Serege. He slapped his thigh and the dog came to its feet and trotted up to him, tongue lolling, tail wagging. Its head reached nearly to his hip, but he crouched to rub its ears and talk to it. "Hello, old boy!" he said, and laughed as he turned his face away from its repeated attempts to lick him. "I didn't expect to find you back here already! I thought Jiron's kids'd try to keep you as long as they could!"

Every muscle in Tristan's body turned taut. His teeth locked in a hiss; his hands curled like claws. He retreated a step, feeling as if he were reliving a nightmare.

The dogs shoved up around him, their tails beating his legs. A black nose touched his palm, cold as a fish, and it butted and sniffed him from belly to boots until the governor called it back. "He's identified you now," the governor said, smiling. "Abattoir never forgets a scent."

When the dog turned away from Serege to thrust its nose toward him, Tristan interposed himself between it and his mother and bared his teeth at it. "Get away from her!" he said. His heartbeat shook his whole body. He brought his hands up, curled hard. "Don't try to smell us!"

Serege caught the dog by its collar and pulled it back. "What's wrong, Tristan?"

He turned his look on the admiral, narrowing his eyes with accusation. "*He* had dogs—big ones, like that!" His words came in bursts, between gulps. "He let them get our scent, and then—" He swallowed, chilled at the memory of the hounds baying through the forest behind him, his back to a tree, the steamy breath and flash of fangs as one sprang for his throat. He was shaking. "—he used them to chase us—like jous on Ganwold—when we tried to escape."

"Kazak won't chase you," Serege said. He made the dog lie down, rumpled its ears again. "He may be big, but he's really pretty harmless."

Tristan didn't reply, didn't relax. His vision flicked from

the admiral to the dog and back. He kept his hands tense, his stance ready.

Serege studied him. After a long moment he said, "It isn't just the dog, is it, Tris? It's as much about me having one, isn't it?"

"He *told* me you were no different from him!" Tristan said. His tone was accusing.

His mother put her hand on his arm, but when he glanced back, he saw that she was biting her lip.

Serege eyed them both for several seconds. "Maybe Mordan was right," he said at last. "Maybe, in some ways, we *are* alike. Both of us were pilots during the war. Both of us came into positions of authority. Both of us keep large dogs. I truly hope that's where the similarities end, son, but you'll have to make that judgment for yourself."

Tristan glowered at him, jaw tight, for several seconds, but Serege only said, "Let me show you the rest of our quarters now, so you and your mother can start settling in. Stay, Kazak."

Still wary, still shaky, Tristan made a wide circle around the dog. It lay with its head on its front paws and watched him with eyes like a jou's.

The bedrooms were at the far end of the residence. "This one will be ours, Darcie," Serege said. He motioned toward a room nearly as large as the living area. "The middle room is my office. This over here will be yours, Tris. I kept it as a guest room but it wasn't used very often."

The room was larger than the one Tristan had been forced to live in on Issel, and this one had a window. He crossed to that at once, ignoring everything else.

It faced west, looking up the darkening fjord and over the park, higher than the tops of the trees. He probed along its frame with one hand. "How does this open?" he asked.

"There's a switch to the left," Serege said.

Tristan found it, pressed it, and the pane split into several slats, each as wide as his hand, which rotated inward. A curious breeze slipped through the openings and caught at his hair. It already bore an early evening crispness, but he stood there for a long time, breathing deeply and squinting at the golden brilliance gathering over the mountaintops.

He stood until he thought the admiral had gone. Actually started when he turned around and found him still leaning in the doorway. "Why are you still there?" he demanded.

Serege arched an eyebrow at the question. "I wanted to be sure this would be all right with you," he said.

Tristan cast a cursory glance over bed, desk, chair, the storage compartments in one wall. "It's fine," he said brusquely.

But he felt as if the walls were closing in. Felt as confined as he had in that room on Issel.

"Good," Serege was saying. "The lighting is voice activated, but the door has a manual switch like the window's." He reached out. "It's over—"

"No!" Tristan's hand shot out as if to stop the door. His muscles were suddenly tense again. Memories of trying to force his fingers into a closed door's seam, of straining to pull back a panel secured from outside, left him shaking. "Leave that door open!"

"All right." Serge drew back his hand. His voice was even but his eyes searched Tristan's. "What's wrong?" he asked.

Tristan locked his teeth and lowered his head and didn't answer.

When Serege left, he looked around the room again. He had no use for the bed. He stripped off the bedcovers with a few tugs and shook them out on the floor below the window, arranging them to imitate the peimu robe he'd slept in on Ganwold. Then he pulled off boots and shirt and trousers and tossed them onto the bare mattress. Clad only in his shorts, he sat on his heels and stared out through the open window.

"Tris?" he heard from behind him. He twisted around.

His mother stood in the doorway now. She said, "The servos are setting out dinner."

His stomach was in knots under his ribs. He turned back toward the window. "I'm not hungry," he said.

She came in fully then, came around the stripped bed and sat down beside him on the bedroll. "You're homesick, aren't you?"

He only shrugged.

She put an arm around him. "I am, too," she said. She was silent for a minute, then she sighed. "I would never have thought, when we first landed on Ganwold, that I'd have ever missed it. It was all so different from everything I'd ever known. It was so—so primitive—and I was so scared and lonely." She stroked the back of his head. "There were a lot of times at first, especially when the rain was leaking through the lodge roof and the floor was one big mud puddle, that I'd huddle up in whatever dry corner I could find and just hold you and cry."

Tristan looked over at her, surprised. He could remember, as a small child, watching her dig little trenches with a bone scraper to channel the rainwater out of the lodge. And when the rain stopped, he'd watched her tug sodden peimu hides off the dome-shaped frame to let the sun dry the inside. Knowing how heavy those hides must have been with even the hair on the underside soaked through, he marveled now that she could have handled them at all, small as she was. He'd seen her weary, he'd seen her sunburned, he'd seen her hands bleeding, but—"I never saw you cry," he said.

"Well, I did. Plenty of times." She sighed once more. "But we learned to live there, didn't we?"

He nodded, reluctantly.

"We'll learn to live here, too," she said. She ruffled his hair and planted a kiss on his forehead and rose to her feet. "Come and eat now."

"Later," he said, and watched her leave the room.

It seemed darker when she had gone.

He turned back to the window.

The lowering sun shot fire across the clouding sky. Sent deepening shadows down the peaks until all detail was lost and they were no more than silhouettes, strange as an alien cityscape.

An Isselan skyline loomed up in Tristan's memory, seen from a room near the top of a round tower. Sick and alone and afraid, he had watched that sky turn bloody, then black, from a room with a sealed door.

He peered over his shoulder through the dimness to be sure that this room's door hadn't closed.

It still stood open. But he was every bit as afraid as he had been that first night on Issel.

TEN

The debriefing room was small, furnished with only a table and four chairs. It was carpeted and well lit but it had no windows. Tristan glanced around it and then at Doctor Moses. His palms were damp; his stomach felt as if it were full of buzzing, careening grass beetles.

"I'll be here with you the whole time," Doctor Moses said. "I'll call a halt if it looks like it's going to be too hard for you."

He only nodded, too dry-mouthed, too nervous to speak.

He jumped, twisting around, when the door opened behind him and a young man in uniform stepped through it. He had red hair and freckles, and carried a sealed pouch tucked under his arm. "Tristan Serege?" he said, placing the pouch on the table. "I'm Ensign Rolly Beekes, Sostish Space Force. Go ahead and have a seat, make yourself comfortable." He motioned toward the chairs. "This isn't going to be an interrogation, just sort of a conversation."

Tristan pulled out the nearest one, glancing at Doctor Moses again, and felt a measure of relief when she drew her chair around to his side of the table. She touched his hand as she sat down beside him.

Ensign Beekes sat down at his other side, at the table's end, so his knee almost touched Tristan's. He took a microwriter out of the pouch. "I know this will probably be hard for you," he said. "Maybe it'll be a little easier if I tell you why we need to do it." He leaned forward on the table, interlacing his hands, and looked Tristan in the face. "The situation out in the Issel system is pretty dangerous right now, and it's getting more dangerous to us all the time. While you were being held on Issel, you may have seen or heard things that could be very important in helping us to deal with that threat. A lot of people's lives on a lot of worlds are at stake. What you can tell us may help us save their lives. Okay?"

Tristan met his look. Studied it for a long space. "Okay," he said at last.

"Good." Beekes leaned back in his chair. "First, Tristan, let's establish a few things about your situation. Were you imprisoned in one room all the time, or did you have any freedom of movement?"

Tristan remembered the circular hallway of the tower in Sanabria, the underground corridors of the moon residence. His palms were damp again; he rubbed them on his pant legs. "I wasn't locked up all the time," he said. "There were a few other rooms I could go into, like the big room where he ate—"

"Who is 'he'?" said Beekes.

Tristan's stomach lurched; he glanced at Libby and swallowed. "The governor," he said.

"Okay." Beekes nodded and tapped a note into his microwriter. "Go on."

"I couldn't open some of the rooms," Tristan said. "He—said I didn't have any business in them. But sometimes he took me with him when he went to different places."

"Where were some of those places, Tristan?"

It came back to him as clearly as if it had been yesterday. "To inspect the mines on Issel's moon," he said, "and the—caves, and the command post—"

"Governor Renier actually took you with him to the *command post*?" Beekes asked. He looked incredulous.

Tristan nodded. "Yes."

"Do you remember much about that? How it was laid out? How to get there from, say, the surface?"

"Yes," Tristan said again. Using his finger, he began to draw on the tabletop.

"Wait, wait!" said Beekes. He fished in his pouch, pulled out a pad and stylus and put them before Tristan. "There. Draw me a map of everything you can remember about the governor's complex on the moon—and tell me about it as you draw it."

Tristan shifted the stylus in his hand and leaned over the pad. There was the shuttle bay on the surface, the gray corridor to the lift that went down, down for two kilometers, rattling and squeaking the whole way. There was the diagram on the lift's wall that showed every level: flightline and shuttle maintenance, supply and storage, personnel maintenance and quarters, mine and life-support offices. Tristan labeled them all with careful characters.

The ensign, leaning close to watch, tapped the drawing with his finger. "What's this over here?"

"Emergency stairs," said Tristan. He shuddered, remembering clanging metal steps that spiraled down to a dizzying depth. "They go up to the shuttle bay and down to the caves."

"What about this part?"

"Those are the rooms where he lives." Tristan pointed out each one. "That's his office, and that's where we ate, and then you go through the lift and out the other side to the command post, over here."

"What are these lines, the ones that look like a river with all the twists and and turns?" Beekes drew his finger along it. "And what are the dots you've drawn on it?"

"Those are the caves," Tristan said. "That's where they grow the blue—lichens?"—he cocked his head—"to make the oxygen. The caves go everywhere under the ground between the mines—that's what the dots are. That one"—he pointed—"is Firnis. That one is Malin Point."

He paused, remembering the heat and the noise, and the pain in his side that had hunched him over as he walked. He wiped a sweaty hand down his trouser leg.

"All right, Tris?" Moses asked.

"Yeah," he said, shakily.

She looked at the ensign. "I think we'd better take a break."

"Sure, ma'am," said Beekes.

Moses pushed her chair back from the table and stood. "Let's go for a walk, Tris."

He released a breath in a rush of relief, stepping out into the corridor. He hadn't realized until that moment how tense he was. He let Doctor Moses guide him up the hall, back to the building's main lobby, where two rows of pillars drew his vision up to a vaulted ceiling. He wandered around and between the pillars, drawing a hand over their polished surfaces, sliding his fingers up and down their fluting.

"What are you feeling?" Moses asked, following him.

Relieved to be out of that room, he thought. He was uncomfortable at all the memories the questions prodded up. Anxious to have all the questions over with so he could leave this cold stone building.

He answered Moses's question with only a shrug.

Beekes was still studying Tristan's drawings and shaking his head when Moses steered Tristan back to the room. Beekes folded the papers when they came in, tucked them into his pouch, and said, "Ready to go on?"

Tristan just shrugged again.

"From those drawings, it looks like you saw quite a bit of Issel Two," said Beekes. "Did you see many people besides the governor's immediate household?"

"Yes," Tristan said.

"Were any of them masuki?"

Tristan stiffened, his vision flashing up to meet the ensign's.

Beekes hesitated. "Do you know what masuki look like?" he asked.

"Yes," said Tristan. His jaw tightened.

"Did you see any on Issel Two?"

Tristan knotted his hands on the table. "Yes."

"How many did you see there?" Beekes asked. "Were they in the command post?"

"Some of them were," Tristan said with an effort. "There were—ten of them."

"Do you have any idea how they got along with the humans?"

Tristan thought about that for a few moments, head bowed. "They were rude," he said. "They acted like—like they thought *they* were the governors."

Beekes raised an eyebrow at that. "How did they act toward Governor Renier?"

Tristan spread taut hands on the tabletop. "I think he was afraid of them," he said. "I—heard them arguing once." *Just outside my bedroom door—about what to do with me and my mother.* The memory made him sweat all over again. He curled up his hands.

". . . think the masuki would obey the governor's orders?" Beekes was asking. His eyes bore an intent expression.

Tristan had to think about that, too. "I don't know," he said, shaking his head. And then, "I don't think so."

"Hmm." Beekes moved in his chair. "If the governor wasn't there, do you think the masuki could run the command post by themselves?"

"Maybe," Tristan said. "But—they're kind of stupid."

Beekes was punching things into his microwriter. "Did the governor ever mention anything about plans or schedules within your hearing?"

Tristan furrowed his brow, thinking. "I don't think so."

"Do you know if Governor Renier might have put a masuk commander in charge of his command post?"

"I don't know," Tristan said. "But he had one on Saede."

"You know that for a fact?"

"Yes," Tristan said. His jaw muscles were tight again.

"How do you know that? Did you hear someone talk about it?"

"No." Tristan glanced down. His hands, still lying on the table, were quivering. He spread them out again, pressed them hard to the surface to still them. He said, "I saw him."

He had done more than that. He had *fought* him, had—

He could feel sweat welling up on his forehead, and even pressing his hands as hard as he could to the tabletop didn't stop their shaking. He slipped a desperate look at Doctor Moses.

She caught it, placed her hand over his. "That's enough for today, Ensign," she said.

He put out his hand and touched stone: The passage turned. He shot a glance over his shoulder. The masuk nearly blocked out the light of the doorway behind him. Tristan slipped around the turn in the tunnel and crouched down.

A step scuffed on stone. He looked up. The masuk's shadow fell on the facing wall. Tristan gathered himself, shifting his knife in his hand. The masuk came around the corner with his knife extended, and Tristan lunged.

The blade went in upward. Tristan felt the masuk stiffen and stagger back, felt hot blood coursing over his hand and spattering his face—

"No!" He recoiled, gasping. "No! No-o-o!"

He woke in a sweat with his scream still dying in his throat. He pushed himself up in a tangle of blankets and raised his hands to examine them in the moonlight that fell through the window. They were shaking.

"Tristan?" he heard.

He thrust his hands under the blanket, jerked his head up.

Admiral Serege was just a silhouette in the bedroom's open doorway. "Are you all right, son?" he asked.

Tristan swallowed. "I'm fine," he said.

Serege stood there for another moment, then came fully into the room, and Tristan felt his heart, which had just begun to slow, accelerate again. He pushed himself back against the wall and gathered himself.

Serege sat down on the foot of the stripped bed. The moonlight from the window fell across his lap, but his face remained in shadow. He said, "I'm here to listen if you want to talk about it."

"No!" Tristan said at once.

"All right." Serege nodded.

He didn't move for several seconds. Then he shifted, and Tristan waited for him to get to his feet and leave the room.

He did neither.

Tristan felt a surge of anger. "Why are you still sitting there?" he demanded.

"I was thinking." Serege's voice was quiet, contemplative. He was silent for another space, and then he turned to face Tristan. "Your mother told me you were a hunter on Ganwold." It was more a question than a statement.

"Yeah," Tristan said. "What about it?"

Serege shrugged. "I used to hunt, too." In another moment he said, "Your mother also told me that gan hunters always go out in pairs—they even have a proverb about it, something to the effect of 'Hunters who go by themselves don't bring back any peimus.'"

"Yeah," Tristan said again.

"Why is that?" Serege asked.

Tristan wasn't expecting the question. He hesitated. "Because it takes two hunters to kill a peimu and carry it," he said.

"One hunter can't carry it by himself?"

"No."

"Why not?" Serege asked next.

Tristan cocked his head, wondering why the admiral should be interested in how the ganan hunted. But he said, "Peimus are too big to carry by yourself."

"Hmm." Serege nodded. "Sounds like the ganan are a very wise people." He looked away, stroking his mustache, apparently thinking again.

It was some time before he drew a deep breath and straightened. "I think, son," he said, as if weighing each word, "that you're trying to carry a peimu by yourself—except that this one doesn't have horns and hooves. This one is all the guilt you're living with."

Tristan turned rigid. Glanced down and saw that his

hands were knotted. The emotion boiling in his gut was a mixture of fury and fear and humiliation. "What do you know about guilt?" he demanded.

Admiral Serege leaned forward, planting his elbows on his knees. "More than I want to," he said. Sighed it. He turned his face back toward Tristan's. "I know it can be a good thing if it drives you to resolve the reasons for it. And I know that one of the first steps of resolving it is sharing it—letting someone else help you carry it, like a peimu."

Tristan didn't answer. He couldn't.

"I'm here, son," Serege said. "I'm willing to carry it with you." He stretched out a hand, as if to place it on Tristan's shoulder.

Tristan cringed away from it.

But he sat there for a long time after the admiral finally rose and left the room. Sat staring at the open doorway through which the admiral had disappeared.

ELEVEN

"All right. Thanks for the information, Marcus. Good night." Lujan switched off the commset and leaned back in his chair, rubbing his eyes and forehead with one hand. His head ached. He squinted at the timepanel on the wall. Past midnight. He'd been cloistered in here for over three hours. No wonder he was tired!

Emerging from the office, he paused to peer into Tristan's room.

The youth lay on his belly on the floor, half swathed in blankets and the moonlight that slanted through his open window. Its cool glow highlighted the artiskin patches along his ribs where the scars had been. Lujan grimaced.

He was about to turn away when Tristan stirred, groaning and curling up on his side. His face showed pain; his mouth was open. Lujan started toward him, bracing himself for the screams that always accompanied Tristan's nightmares.

They didn't come. After a few moments Tristan's face relaxed and the hand that had closed on a fold of blanket went slack. Lujan waited, crouched beside him, until his breathing was steady again. Then he touched Tristan's head, stood a bit stiffly, and left the room, being careful to leave the door open.

There was still a light on in the master bedroom: the reading light set in the bed's headboard. Darcie appeared to be asleep, lying with her back to him, her loose hair spilling over her shoulders and the sheet. He crossed quietly toward the adjoining bathroom, hoping to find something for his headache, but the carpet scuffed under his bootless foot.

Darcie turned onto her back. "Lujan?"

"Yes. Did I wake you?"

"No." She sat up, wrapping her arms loosely about her blanket-covered knees. "I've been waiting for you."

He stopped. He couldn't see her face clearly with the reading light on behind her, but there was distress in her voice. He asked, "What's wrong, Darcie?"

"Everything," she said.

He stood still for a moment. Released a full breath, slowly. Then he sat down on his side of the bed. "Tell me about 'everything,' " he said.

Darcie hugged her knees tighter. "I feel as if in the last few days Tristan and I have gone from being prisoners on Issel to being prisoners on Sostis, except this time we're being kept in transparent boxes with holes just big enough for people to poke sticks through."

"What do you mean?" Lujan asked.

"The debriefings," said Darcie. "They make me feel more like a captured spy than a returned hostage!"

"It's standard procedure," Lujan said. "Former hostages and POWs can often provide—"

"I *know* that, Lujan! I even know the reasons for it! But that doesn't make it any easier, especially for Tris. He's not eating well, his nightmares have come back—"

"I know, Darce." The throb in Lujan's head was growing sharper. He kneaded his scalp.

"—and when they finally let us come home, you're never here. We might as well be back on Ganwold for all we see of you! If it weren't for your exec's mate, Heazel, coming 'round every day or so, I'd go completely crazy in here!

"And then there's the visiphone!" Darcie looked up from her knees. "I thought you said there was an office downstairs to screen all the calls coming up here."

"There's a concierge—"

"Well, they're not doing a very good job, or somebody's

learned how to get 'round it! Some twit from some newsnet keeps calling and asking for an interview. He's starting to remind me of a peimu fly! Today I told him so and disconnected him!''

Lujan could imagine her doing it. It might have been funny under other circumstances. "I'll take care of it," he said.

Darcie rested her chin on her knees. Rocked a little. "If only Tris and I could get out of here once in a while, besides for the debriefings." She sighed. "We could go anywhere we wanted on Ganwold, but the only way out of here seems to be in a skimmer off the roof—and even if there were an extra one, I don't have a permit to fly one right now. We can't go into the city, we can't go up into the mountains—we're stuck here!''

"There's the subterranean transit system," Lujan said. "It goes into the city. The route maps and schedules are in the house computer.''

"If I could access them," said Darcie. "It wouldn't all be so bad if I understood how everything in this flat works, but it's a completely different technology than what I remember." She laced her hands over her head in obvious frustration. "I *still* haven't figured out half the appliances in the kitchen—there aren't any buttons!—and the tech manuals are useless!''

"Everything in the kitchen operates on voice commands," Lujan said.

"I've tried that," Darcie said, "but they all keep telling me 'Insufficient instructions.' ''

"Well, the tech manuals won't be any help for that," said Lujan. "They're useless even if you haven't been away for twenty-five years." His tone betrayed annoyance. "I think they were written by mechanicals. I can show you everything you need to know.''

"You don't have to do that," said Darcie. "I'm figuring it out—little by little.''

The way she said it was more puzzling than the statement itself. Lujan blinked. "Darcie, you just said you wished you knew how everything worked. I just offered to help you!''

"I know." She straightened. "But I don't need your help. I

managed all those years out on Ganwold without it."

She made it sound as if it were *his* fault she hadn't had his help on Ganwold. He didn't understand that one; he wasn't certain he really wanted to. "Forgive me for trying," he said, and rose. Clenching his teeth against the pounding inside his skull, he crossed to the bathroom.

The very thought of putting on the bathroom light made his eyes hurt, too, so he stood there in the near dark before the cabinet. "Extra-strength analgesic patches, two," he said, and they slid from their dispenser into his hand. He applied them to his temples and then just stood there, waiting for them to take effect and hoping Darcie would be asleep by the time he came out.

She wasn't. She was still huddled there, arms wrapped around her knees again. "Lujan?" she said when she saw him.

He detected a quiver in her voice. He resisted the impulse to look up. Kept his attention fixed on unfastening his shirt instead. "What?" he said. It sounded gruffer than he intended.

"I'm sorry."

He did look up at that.

"I just feel so overwhelmed right now!" Darcie said. "I feel so—so out of place! I've got hundreds of questions and no one to answer them. I don't know the first thing about current local politics or social customs. I spent all of last evening at the Governor's Mansion concentrating on not offending everyone and not embarrassing you. I still catch myself wanting to eat with my hands and sit on the floor!"

The headache hadn't faded entirely yet. Lujan winced. "You didn't embarrass me," he said. "But I can get you a protocol consultant if it would make you feel better."

"No!" Darcie said. "No consultants! I'd just prefer to be left out of it. All I want is to be a mate and a mother—*just* a mate and a mother! And eventually, to go back to medical school."

Lujan sighed at that, and sat down on the bed again. "I'd like some time to be a father, too," he said. "I probably know less about that than you do about protocol—especially when it comes to trying to reach a troubled teenager who sits there, nearly naked, staring out his bedroom window all day, and cringes every time he sees me. I'm not getting much time to spend with him—or you—between running this blasted war and giving eulogies for the people I've lost in it and"—he grimaced—"preparing that report for the Assembly tomorrow!"

There was a long silence before Darcie said very quietly from behind him, "I'm sorry, Lujan. I—hadn't thought about everything you're dealing with."

He gave a sort of humorless chuckle. "That makes two of us, then. I hadn't really thought about all the readjustments you're going through, either." He looked over his shoulder at her. Sitting this close, he could see the pain in her face. "I'm sorry, too," he said.

Darcie finally slept, held close in the circle of his arms, her head cradled on his shoulder. But Lujan was still awake, still staring at the ceiling, when the timepanel buzzed at zero-five-hundred.

The Assembly chamber was a half circle with a spectators' gallery suspended between the frescoed dome ceiling and the 460 seats of the Unified Worlds' representatives, which filled the floor. The podium was centered against the flat wall, on an elevated platform bearing three chairs for the Triune and the banners of the nine member worlds. Every seat on the floor was occupied today, and the gallery was filled past capacity with both civilian officials and members of various military services of every rank—anyone who could show the guards at the doors proof of the necessary clearances for admittance, Lujan surmised.

The report itself, accompanied by maps and diagrams and holographic stills projected in two huge holotanks behind him, had taken only two hours to present. It was the question-and-answer session afterward that had taken all day, broken only by an hour recess at midday. Lujan had spent that time in a secure office with several members of his staff, reviewing documents from a number of computerized files in preparation for the afternoon's round.

There had been questions about casualties, about refugees, about the Isselan fleet's remaining strength and the current situation in the Issel system, questions that would have been more appropriate to ask of his intelligence or operations people. There had also been extensive debate over the effect of the Issel situation on the Unified Worlds. Should the military presence in the Yan and Saede systems be increased? What action might have to be taken in the months to come?

"While Issel's attack was repulsed and its war-making capability severely damaged," Lujan said in conclusion, "we cannot consider this conflict over yet. The masuki started out as Issel's allies. They're now proving themselves to be a greater threat than Issel. The current conflict will not be resolved until the masuki have been driven out of this sector of the galaxy." He scanned the faces filling the chamber. "We who serve in the defense forces of the Unified Worlds ask for your continued support until we have accomplished our mission. Thank you."

He stepped back from the podium, switching off its prompter screen—and the audience rose to its feet in a standing ovation.

He hadn't been expecting that. He simply stood there for a moment, head bowed, before he nodded acknowledgment and glanced over at Jiron and Marcus Ullen. They followed as he left the platform, flanking him as he crossed to the nearest exit.

Doctor Moses was waiting in the vast marble lobby when he emerged from the chamber with the thunder of the applause following him through the double doors. He caught her I-need-to-talk-to-you look at the same moment a clutch of newsnetters surrounded him.

It was well past seventeen-thirty. He was hungry, he was tired, the headache had come back; he wanted to be on his way home. But he paused.

"Admiral Serege!" said one, pushing a voice pickup toward him. "For the benefit of the people of the Unified Worlds, could you briefly repeat what was said in today's report to the Assembly? Has the Isselan threat been put down once and for all?"

Lujan selected his words with care. "Issel's ability to wage war has been severely degraded," he said. "We consider them incapable of attempting another attack any time in the near future, though we believe they still have at least one numbered fleet. It will be some time before they can reconstitute a force capable of another major offensive."

"Sir," said someone else, "what of the rumors that the Isselans are having trouble with their alien allies? Can you tell us anything about that?"

Lujan glanced at Ullen. "There does appear to be a conflict developing," he answered. "At this time all we can do is watch and wait as events unfold."

"And could this become a concern to the Unified Worlds, sir, enough that we might have to take some kind of action?"

"Yes," Lujan said, "it very well could."

That caused a brief lull, but then someone at the rear of the group put up his hand. "Rumor has it, Admiral, that you're planning to retire as soon as this conflict is over. Have you ever considered going into politics?"

The question was so unexpected that Lujan actually laughed. He shook his head. "Absolutely not! I've had more than my fill of politics over the last several years. Besides"—he smiled—"I *hate* public speaking!" Catching Moses's look from across the lobby once more—she was leaning against a column with her arms crossed over a brown folder—he added, "You'll have to excuse me now. I have an appointment."

She pushed away from the pillar as he approached her. "How'd the report go?"

"Well enough," Lujan said, and allowed himself a sigh of relief. "I'm just glad it's over." He studied her. "But that's not what you've been waiting to talk to me about, is it?"

"No." Moses glanced over her shoulder at the flood of people beginning to spill out of the Assembly chamber. "Is there someplace in this building that's suitable for a private talk?''

There were a number of conference and committee rooms on the second floor, some large, some small. Lujan led her to a small one at the end of a wing and activated lighting. "Will this do?"

Moses looked around. "Fine."

They sat facing each other on the same side of the conference table, and Moses began, "I met with Darcie and Tristan today, after their debriefing sessions." Her tone was grim. "I canceled the rest of them. Tristan can't take any more."

"That's why I asked that you monitor those sessions!" Lujan said. "I asked you to tell me if they were going to be too hard on him!"

"So I'm telling you," said Moses, "and I've stopped them. They're setting back his recovery. He's having nightmares again, his blood pressure's way up, he's stopped regaining weight—and you don't have to be an empathic specialist to see the fear in his eyes.

"He has a near-perfect holographic memory," she said. "I ran a couple of tests the other day after he produced some minutely detailed drawings to answer some of the debriefer's questions." She opened her folder, which was stamped SE-CRET, and removed a couple sheets of paper. "This is the layout of the command post on Issel Two," she said, placing the first page on the table. "I suspect it's drawn to scale. Everything's labeled; spelling's even correct." She laid the second sheet over it. "This one's the layout of the shipping level of the Malin Point mine complex on Issel Two, showing the cargo shuttle bays. Same excruciating detail."

Lujan picked up the sketches and studied first one and then the other with increasing amazement. "You don't even get this kind of detail with most covert holographic equipment!" he said.

"That's right." Moses nodded. "And he's done the same thing with the campus of the Aeire City Academy and a view from his room in Sanabria on Issel. In fact, the analysts took a long look at that one and were able to determine exactly what building Tris had been held in, based on recognizable landmarks on the skyline!

"His ability may eventually become a valuable asset to him," she said, "but right now it's more of a curse. He *can't* forget what he's seen and heard, much as he'd like to. And having to deliberately dig it all up this way is just too painful for him right now."

"I understand," Lujan said.

"But it isn't just Tristan," Moses went on. She returned the drawings to the folder and sealed it before she looked up. "Darcie's having a hard time, too. Some of it's the pressure of the debriefings, but she's also having difficulty getting oriented to her new surroundings. And then, of course, there are her concerns about Tris, about her relationship with you, and about the fact that her recovery isn't progressing as it should—mostly because she's not getting nearly enough rest. At any rate, she's feeling a lot of frustration."

"I know," Lujan said, and ducked his head. "We—had an argument about it last night."

"So much for the honeymoon, eh?" said Moses.

Lujan lifted his head just enough to give her a black look.

And Moses shook her head and sighed. "You have to expect disagreements, Lujan. You're two completely different people now than you were when Darcie was lost. The life experiences you've each had over the past several years couldn't have been more different if they'd been planned. They've shaped the way you perceive yourselves, your respective places in the universe, and your memories of each other. You can't expect to have the same kind of relationship now that you had before."

"I realize that," Lujan said. He leaned forward in his chair, his elbows on his knees, and studied the floor.

Doctor Moses touched his hand. "The relationship you're beginning now," she said, "has the potential to be even better, if you're both willing to work hard at it. You're both several years more mature now, your separation has given you a deeper appreciation for the things you valued in each other before, and you both want to fall in love with each other again.''

He glanced up at her.

She was smiling. ''It doesn't take an empathic specialist to see that, either,'' she said. She paused. ''One of the biggest points I always felt you two had going for you, from the beginning of your first relationship, was your ability to talk things through. That's going to be even more important now—and you certainly don't have a shortage of things to talk about!

''The trouble is, you're not taking enough time to *do* it.'' Moses's features grew serious. ''You no longer have a reason to be a workaholic, Lujan—in fact, you can't afford to be now! What you need is to get Darcie and Tristan out of here. Take them home to Topawa and just spend as much time with them as you possibly can.''

Lujan spread out his hands on the tabletop before him. ''That's exactly what I'd like to do, Libby, but I'm running this war—''

''But we're not in the middle of hostilities right now, and you're every bit as entitled to take leave as your troops are.'' She looked into his eyes. ''You *need* to take some leave, Lujan. It's written all over you. How long have you had that headache?''

''Since last night,'' he said with some irritation. ''A couple of pain patches will take care of it.''

''So will a little R and R,'' said Moses, and sighed again. ''If you won't do it for yourself, do it for your family.'' She locked her vision on his. ''It may be Tristan's only hope for recovery.''

TWELVE

"Who is this 'Chief Minister' Remarq who's calling a short-notice meeting, Hamp?"

Hampton Istvan, Issel's minister of interplanetary relations, turned away from the tinted viewpane of the government skimmer long enough to glance at his counterpart. "Seulemont Remarq was the chief minister in Governor Renier's cabinet until a few years ago," he said. "Then they had a falling-out and the governor dismissed him. I had thought Remarq had died since then; he's well over a standard century old now."

"A *former* chief minister?" Nioro Enn Borith, minister of planetary defense, arched a scant eyebrow. "What position does he hold now? I don't understand your sense of urgency to keep an unscheduled meeting with a *former* chief minister."

"Remarq was Governor Renier's mentor at the outset of his governorship," said Istvan. "In fact, Nioro, he's held one office or another in various world governments for more years than you've been alive." He gave a grim smile. "When Minister Remarq makes a request, wise men don't ask questions; they simply comply."

Borith remembered having heard that statement before. Burdened with the sudden sense that he knew something about this Remarq after all, he pursed his mouth and turned his gaze to his own viewpane, trying to remember what it was.

There wasn't much to look at beyond the viewpane's reflection of his own dark-skinned features. Sanabria was a city of cylindrical gray towers, the majority of which seemed to have been built from the same materials following the same plans. Only the student protesters, parading through the streets with their banners and their chants, lent any color or variation. But the protesters were known to hurl rocks and debris as well as invective, so the skimmer operator had selected a roundabout course, bypassing the city's three major universities and two parks, to deliver himself and Istvan to the World Government Building.

Minister Borith was personally surprised that the protesters were still at it, given the threat now hanging over the planet. There had been two or three days of silence in the streets when the warning sirens first sounded; even the students had run for the nearest civil-defense shelters. But when the horns died down, everyone had emerged from the shelters and returned to business as usual.

The skimmer turned off the city street where the gray towers gave way to an elevated plaza. It dipped down a ramp to the parking levels beneath the World Government Building, whose chambers and halls were pillared and porticoed to resemble an ancient temple. Constructed of pale gold marble, the government building gleamed among the gray towers like sunlight breaking through storm clouds.

A scanner at the end of the ramp identified the skimmer and raised the barrier, and the operator pulled in and around to a bank of lifts. Borith and Istvan climbed out and entered the nearest lift without speaking, except to state their destination. The lift hummed upward. They exchanged grim glances when it came to a stop.

It opened into an antechamber with gold carpet, gold-veined marble walls, and a pair of high double doors: the World Governor's own private office. Borith shot his companion a questioning look from beneath a raised brow, but Istvan didn't acknowledge him.

A steward posted before the doors took their names and touched a button on his console. "My lord, the ministers of interplanetary relations and planetary defense have arrived."

There was a pause, and then the doors hissed apart. "You may enter," the steward said.

Chief Minister Seulemont Remarq sat in the governor's high-backed chair behind the vast expanse of the governor's desk. Though his hair was sparse and white and his face was a maze of wrinkles, his eyes were piercing and as black as obsidian. "Gentlemen," he said. "Come in. Please be seated." He gestured at two chairs to his right, beside the desk. "I'm impressed that you responded to my request for a meeting so quickly. It suggests that you do understand the gravity of the situation our motherworld is now facing."

"Of course, my lord," said Istvan. Borith noted the obsequious dip of his head as he accepted the proffered chair; he followed Istvan's example.

Minister Remarq leaned back, pressing his withered fingertips together, and surveyed them both for a long moment. "It has come to my attention," he said, "that there've been no communications from the military command post on Issel Two for at least a month."

Istvan dipped his head again. "Yes, my lord, that's correct. All communications ended a few hours after the masuki arrived there, and they've never resumed."

"Then you've had no information as to the status of the martial government there in all that time?"

"No, my lord," said Istvan. "We're forced to assume that General Ochakas and the others were killed when the masuki took over the command post."

Remarq arched a scraggly brow. "And you're quite certain that the masuki *did* take over the command post, Minister Istvan?"

The other looked startled. "Certainly, my lord. What else could have happened?"

The chief minister offered a sardonic smile. "A collusion, perhaps, between the masuki and the good general."

"My lord." Borith straightened in his chair. "General Ochakas was one of the most adamant opponents to Governor

Renier's alliance with the masuki. I don't think—"

"Ochakas was a wise man," Remarq said. "You're probably correct in your assessment, Minister. But he had no especial regard for most of the late governor's other recent programs, either." His smile darkened still more. "Had you considered the possibility that Governor Renier's death might not have been a suicide at all?"

Borith hesitated. Glanced over at Istvan, who sat rubbing his hands on his thighs. "That possibility had crossed my mind," he admitted.

"Well, then," Remarq said. But after a moment he sighed and spread his hands. "Exactly what transpired doesn't matter now. What does matter is that the result is the same—the one I expected and warned the governor against." He scowled. "Mordan Renier was a fool from his earliest days in the governorship. Worse, he was unteachable and impatient. He received what he deserved.

"He filled his cabinet with fools, too. Or cowards." Remarq's vision flicked from Istvan's face to Borith's. "Issel is in mortal danger, and it has no government to lead it—not a stable central one, at least—because its ministers have scattered."

Istvan and Borith both moved uneasily in their chairs, but Istvan said, "My lord, it was at the direction of the martial government. Ochakas felt that, in the event of a masuk attack, there was a greater possibility of some members of the cabinet surviving if we weren't all cloistered here together in one location. He also felt that order would be better maintained throughout the planet if the ministers were able to provide direct guidance to the people of their home regions."

"Order!" Remarq snorted. "There are national factions—even provincial ones—trying to claim power all over the planet! None of them are capable of dealing with the threat independently and few of them are likely to join forces. What we have, gentlemen, is chaos!

"But that will end very soon." He glowered first at Borith, then Istvan. "As the last chief minister to serve under the now deceased World Governor, I have exercised my authority to summon the rest of the cabinet back to Sanabria. They should all have arrived by tomorrow, and then we'll take whatever steps are necessary to restore Issel's central government."

Istvan and Borith exchanged covert glances, and Borith felt a growing urgency to remember what he had once heard about the chief minister.

"In the meantime," Remarq was saying, "there's another matter which must be discussed, the reason I specifically requested the attendance of the ministers of interplanetary relations and planetary defense." He paused to touch each of their looks with his own. "Due to our losses in the Buhlig, Yan, and Saede systems, Issel no longer has the military strength it will need to counter the masuk threat. It's essential that we have assistance if we're to turn the masuki back."

"But, my lord," said Minister Istvan, "Na Shiv's military power is even more limited than our own, and Adriat has—"

"I'm aware of those things, Minister." Remarq's tone was even, but it suggested a forced patience. "That's why we'll seek our assistance from the Unified Worlds."

Borith shot to his feet. "Are you mad, sir? We're still at war with the Unified Worlds!"

Remarq only lifted one hand. "And did you approve of this war, Minister of Planetary Defense? Is it a war you'd have chosen to enter?"

"No, my lord." Borith subsided, shaking his head. "It most certainly is not!"

"And what of your assessment of our military power? Do you have knowledge of a hidden force that I do not?"

"No, my lord," Borith said again. "We have barely one-third of our prehostilities' strength remaining, in my estimation."

"Then the need and the logic are both clear," said Remarq. "As the representatives of what remains of Issel's civilian government, you and Minister Istvan will bear our official apologies to the Unified Worlds, along with assurances that the recent actions against them were by Mordan Renier's design, that he is now dead, and that the people of Issel have no hostile intentions. I give you authority to negotiate the cessation of the current hostilities as well as the request for assistance. You may promise whatever reparations the Unified Worlds may demand."

Istvan said, "Humph! That should give them a good laugh—just before they throw us out of the Assembly!"

Borith shook his head. "To go crawling to the Unified Worlds *now*," he said, "after we attacked them without so much as a declaration of war . . ."

"The fact that they destroyed most of our ability to defend ourselves when they countered that attack should only serve to increase their sense of responsibility," said Remarq. "It may also be helpful to point out to them that if they don't assist Issel against the masuki now, they're likely to find themselves driving masuki out of their own systems later. It's in the best interest of the whole galactic community to stop the masuk incursion here; we now have a common enemy."

Istvan and Borith exchanged looks at that, and Istvan cleared his throat and shifted forward in his chair. "Your proposal might work but for one major factor, my lord. All intersystem communications have been shut down, and this system is full of masuk-controlled ships which would certainly intercept any vessel attempting to leave. Getting a message—or messenger—through to any of the Unified Worlds is virtually impossible."

Remarq turned a stiff smile on him. "That 'major factor,' Minister Istvan, was the first one I took into consideration when I began to develop this strategy." His fingertips came together again; his eyes narrowed. "There are five ships on this planet which are capable of escaping this system unnoticed by the masuki. They are cloakable, lightskip-capable, and the locations of all five are now—since Mordan Renier's demise—known only to myself. One of them is being prepared for flight at this time; it will launch at oh-seven-hundred tomorrow, and both of you will be aboard."

"*What?*" said Borith. "This is such short notice!"

Remarq turned those obsidian eyes on him. "It will take nearly a standard month for you to reach your destination," he said. "There is no time to lose."

Borith met his look, wondering if his skepticism showed in his face as plainly as he felt it. The plan seemed to be an act of desperation. And yet if they did not act at all, the outcome was inevitable. With a sideways glance at Istvan, he sighed and said, "Yes, my lord."

"You will arrive here no later than oh-four-hundred tomorrow morning," Remarq said. "A skimmer will be waiting to take you to the ship. You will take it to Na Shiv, where you will board a commercial liner for Mythos. All of the necessary diplomatic papers for passage are being prepared as we speak.

"Upon your arrival on Mythos, you will go directly to our embassy in the capital city of Bigornia—the only Isselan embassy in all of the Unified Worlds which wasn't forced to close when the hostilities began. Ambassador Pegaush will accompany you to the headquarters of the Mythosian delegation to the Unified Worlds Assembly, and"—Remarq paused to draw a flat package from a compartment in the desk—"you will deliver this to Seamus Trosvig, the senior member of that delegation." He handed the packet over the table to Istvan, and his expression hardened. "This must be given *only* to Delegate Trosvig, Minister; he will know how to proceed."

"Of course, my lord," said Istvan.

"Good." Remarq looked from Istvan to Borith. "Do either of you have any questions?"

Borith had too many to know where to begin. He hesitated, but then he said, "No, my lord."

Remarq nodded, and touched a panel on the desktop. The double doors to the antechamber slid open. "Then that is all, gentlemen."

They were emerging from the lift into the cool of the underground parking level when the missing detail about the chief minister abruptly coalesced in Borith's mind:

During the War of Resistance, Seulemont Remarq had

been known as the Kingmaker, the Empire Builder, the Left Hand of the Dominion.

Sliding into the waiting skimmer, Borith silently wondered if the masuki were the chief minister's only motivation for this mission to Mythos.

THIRTEEN

From the spacedock observation lounge, Topawa appeared mostly brown and beige with several broad stretches of green. Its oceans and polar ice caps were smaller than those of Sostis, Tristan saw, though the planet itself was somewhat larger. He wondered if its size had anything to do with it taking nearly twenty-seven standard hours to make each rotation.

Beside him, Admiral Serege tapped the viewpane with his finger. "The continent we can see from here," he said, "is called North Eusera. That's where we're going. My family lives in the southwestern part, the Anchenko region. Looks like it's all under cloud cover right now."

When he paused, Tristan glanced up and saw that his mouth was pursed.

His mother saw it, too. "What is it?" she asked over the tinkling music that spilled from a café across the concourse.

Serege gave her a half smile. "Bad timing," he said. "We're arriving in the middle of the rainy season."

"As long as I don't have to dig little ditches in the floor to drain the water out of that old farmhouse," she said, "I won't complain. We did enough of that on Ganwold!"

They took a commercial shuttle to the Anchenko Regional Spaceport. It was a heavy craft, designed for stability in all weather conditions, but the wind still snatched at it as it pierced the thunderhead on its final approach. The turbulence made Tristan's stomach roll under his ribs. He pressed himself into his acceleration seat, head back, eyes closed, and teeth clenched, hands locked hard on the arms.

He felt someone watching him. He opened his eyes and looked up—directly into the admiral's face.

"He'd probably disown you if he saw you puking all over the deck like that," his instructor had said.

Tristan made himself let go of the chair arms and took his lower lip between his teeth, mortified at being caught in his discomfort.

But Serege said, "I had to make a landing in a storm like this once, while we were out on Tohh. The inspector general came through for an operational-readiness exercise right after we set up the base out there. The weather office kept posting storm warnings, but we still had to fly ninety-plus sorties every day.

"Sure enough, on the fifth or sixth day some of us got caught out in a storm. Our alternate field was socked in and we were too low on fuel to go for another one. The only operational tanker was heading in the opposite direction to refuel some guys who were in worse shape than we were, so we didn't have any choice but to go on in." Serege shook his head. "The wind took our fighters and threw them around like toys. I'd been sick in the cockpit a couple of times before, but that was absolutely the worst!"

Darcie was listening, too, her expression hovering on the edge of amusement. "You never told me about that!" she said.

"I didn't think you needed to know," Serege said, grinning at her. "After all, I had an image to maintain!"

She smiled. "You and all the rest of those hot-stick fighter jocks!"

Tristan just stared at him, incredulous. "Did you have to— clean up—your own cockpit?" he asked.

"I sure did." Serege's smile was sheepish. "And my crew chief was standing by the whole time, chewing me up one side and down the other for messing up *his* bird!"

Tristan met his gaze. Searched it, head cocked, for some

seconds. He couldn't picture the admiral puking in his cockpit, but realizing that he had actually done it erased some of his own mortification; he felt an unexpected relief.

The shuttle set down a few minutes later, its thrusters flaring against the wind. Even in the passenger cabin, Tristan could feel its tug.

Tunnels from the landing bay provided dry passage into the spaceport. Entering the milling activity of the terminal, Tristan heard someone shout, "Hey, it's the war hero of Sostis! Over here, Lujan!"

Serege looked in the direction of the shout, and then laughed out loud. "What is this, the whole family?" he said, and opened his arms to the small crowd waiting at one side.

They rushed him: four sisters and a younger brother, their mates, and all of their children. The hugging and back-thumping and greetings went on for several minutes, and the women embraced Darcie as well. Overwhelmed, and fearing that they might thump his back too, Tristan edged away. But Admiral Serege put an arm about his shoulders and drew him forward. ". . . And this is Tristan," he said.

He felt as if he'd been put on display. The whole clan studied him, their faces full of curiosity, as Serege introduced them one by one, by name and relationship. No one tried to hug or thump him, but a couple of the women remarked that he'd been only a baby the last time he'd been on Topawa and that he'd grown up into a copy of his father. He couldn't think of a response for that, so he didn't say anything at all.

They all stood there and talked for what seemed like some time before the admiral's brother, Siljan, finally said, "I imagine you three would probably like to get home and get some rest. I'll go get the skimmer while you pick up your baggage, and we can get on our way."

There wasn't much to pick up—just three duffles and the shipping kennel to which Serege's dog had been confined for the trip to the surface—and a handful of young cousins retrieved those while their parents kept talking. Tristan watched, wary, as the youngsters let the dog out of the kennel, attached its leash, and took turns walking it around the concourse.

Emerging from the spaceport's parking ramp several minutes later, Siljan switched on the skimmer's headlights and rainsweepers. The storm had swallowed up both spaceport and city in its drenching pall.

Siljan kept the skimmer in repulsor mode, close to the ground, until the storm was several kilometers behind them. When the rain slacked off after a few minutes and the cloud ceiling was higher, he extended the skimmer's delta wings, cut in its thrusters, and took it airborne. Tristan leaned to look out through the canopy.

For most of Topawa's seventeen-month year, Admiral Serege had told him, the Anchenko region was desert: all russet rock and dust, arid, and scorched by a sun slightly larger and hotter than Sostis's. But during the three months of its rainy season, Anchenko was green. Rocky gullies became channels for churning torrents, stands of scrubby trees unfurled narrow leaves and stretched for another few millimeters of growth, shriveled succulents sent out surface roots and swelled themselves almost to bursting, and grass sprang up everywhere, punctuated with patches of wildflowers.

Tristan spotted occasional human structures, usually three or four clustered together like gan lodges, but they were separated by kilometers of countryside. All of the untouched openness reminded him of the prairie that had been home on Ganwold. A pang of homesickness stabbed through his soul as he looked out over it.

A handful of blocky structures built of stone came into view a short while later. They were gathered around a windpump with a well-house at its base. The pump's blades spun so fast they seemed nearly a blur.

"The house looks so small!" Darcie said from the seat behind Tristan.

"The whole thing would fit inside that suite we have on Sostis," said Serege, "but it's more than big enough for the three of us. It doesn't have the automated housekeeping or pneumatic-tube delivery system we have there, but we won't have to wash our clothes in a creek or build fires to do our cooking, either. It still has the kitchen and laundry systems my father installed when I was growing up, and the original house computer. Technologically, this place is about halfway back to Ganwold."

Darcie smiled. "That's fine with me!"

Siljan nosed the skimmer down, banked around, and settled it lightly in the farmhouse yard. "Home at last," he said, grinning, and popped the canopy.

The rain had ended here, but the wind coming off the mesas far to the west drove another storm before it; distant lightning was already visible as erratic illuminations of the thunderhead. The wind was laden with moisture and the scents of wet soil and vegetation, and Tristan knew it would turn cold by nightfall.

He barely noticed the chill, however, as he climbed out of the skimmer. As if pushed by the wind, he moved off to a small rise, where he stopped and turned his face into it. It slapped at his hair, tugged at his loose shirt, but he didn't mind its pummeling. It was familiar, something he had missed on Sostis. A hesitant hope nudged at the homesickness. He put back his head and stretched out his arms.

He didn't go into the house until Siljan had gone and the rain began to fall again.

The rain went on for several more days, nearly nonstop. There had been a rainy season on Ganwold, too, so it didn't bother him at first. At least the old farmhouse was a bigger place to be holed up in than a gan lodge! Its kitchen alone was the size of a gan lodge, in fact, and there were five bedrooms, two bathrooms, and a living area the size of *two* lodges.

"Why are there so many bedrooms?" he asked.

"Because my great-grandfather, who built this house, had a large family," said Serege. "My grandfather and my father and I all grew up here."

The house had timber ceiling beams but the rest of it, floor and walls, were blocks of cut stone—the building material most readily available to the first settlers, Serege had said. It seemed more solid and immovable than even the Flag Officers' Complex in Ramiscal City, and it smelled of wood and soil and the dust of old stone. Smells that were familiar and comfortable, that put Tristan at ease.

Still, by the fourth day he'd grown restless, and halfway through the morning he found himself pacing. "It never rained *this* much on Ganwold!" he said once, pacing through the kitchen, where the downpour drummed a numbing roar on the roof's solar panels

His mother looked up from the display on the kitchen computer and said, "Where's your microreader, Tris? Why don't you go sit down and read for a while?"

"Mum, I read all the way out here from Sostis," he said. "I've had enough sitting and reading for a while!"

"I can use some help with this," said Serege. He motioned with a grimy hand at a piece of equipment disassembled on a tarp on the kitchen table.

Tristan eyed it, nose wrinkled. "What is it?"

"It's a spare head for the windpump. I thought I'd better make sure it was in working order because the one on the pump is taking a real beating, and the pump is our main source of power and water out here."

Tristan studied commutators and slip rings, tiny brushes and cloths, containers of cleaning solvent and lubricating compounds. "I don't know how to do that," he said.

"I'll show you how,' said Serege. "It's not as hard as it looks."

Tristan hesitated, uncertain, but there was nothing else to do. He sat down on the bench with a resigned sigh.

The admiral showed him how to clean grit and old lubricant out of the gear teeth with a brush, how to examine the teeth and cams for wear, how to apply fresh lubricant. He watched, nodded when Serege asked if he understood, and picked up a gear and a brush.

The rain let up late in the afternoon and the dog, which

had been lying on the floor near the admiral's feet, rose and went to the side door and whined. The door slid open. The dog trotted out, lifted a leg to water the nearest rock, and then stood for a moment, snuffling at the wind. Then it sprang forward, heading out across the desert at a gallop.

Tristan watched through a kitchen window as it disappeared. "I'm going to go out and run, too," he said, rising.

"Good idea," Serege said. But then he set down his cleaning brush. "You don't have any running shoes, do you, Tris?"

"I don't need shoes to run," Tristan said. His mother had bought him shoes through the on-line catalog in their quarters on Sostis, as alternatives to the military boots he'd been issued aboard *Destrier*, but he avoided wearing any of them. They were too stiff, too confining. "I run better barefooted," he said.

"You'll need shoes here," Serege said. "There's ripweed and sharp rock out there." He sized Tristan up as he wiped grease off his hands with a rag. "My running shoes would probably fit you. Want to use them?"

The offer was the last thing Tristan had expected. He stared. "Me—wear *your* shoes?"

Serege seemed puzzled by his reaction. "Why not?" he asked.

"I didn't think—" Tristan started, but then he shrugged. "Okay," he said after a moment.

The shoes were scuffed and scraped, the tread on the soles well worn. Tristan pushed a foot into one and fastened the bands that hugged instep and ankle. It was snug but flexible, and there was still room to move his toes; it was almost as comfortable as a peimu-hide moccasin. Surprised, he put on the other one. Paused at the doorway to shed his shirt.

He was jogging across the yard in the direction the dog had gone when it reappeared, still galloping, over the lip of a ravine. Coming straight at him! He froze in midstride. But when the dog saw him, it wagged its tail, romped in front of him, and wheeled away, looking over its shoulder as if to be sure he was following.

"Jou!" he yelled after it.

To the east and north, the desert floor stretched as far as he could see, punctuated with occasional hills and hollows, as the plain on Ganwold had been. The air was rich with the scent of wet brush, as he remembered it being on Ganwold after a rain. Tristan felt a little thrill of familiarity. He broke from a jog into a run.

Grass and brush swished past his legs, soaking his pants to the knees. Where the plant growth was thin, the puddled mud sucked at his feet. He ignored the cold grip of wet trouser legs and the tug at his shoes. It had been too long since he'd last run this way.

He could almost believe he was back on Ganwold. If he didn't look to the side, he could almost imagine Pulou at his elbow, could almost catch the quick amber glance of his eye. Resisting the urge to look back, he pushed up his pace.

He couldn't stay with it. Within minutes his lungs seemed about to explode, his legs about to give out. His injuries and his months as a hostage had robbed him of more than he'd thought. He staggered to a stop and stood still for several minutes, one hand pressed to the pain in his side while he panted and shook and wondered if he would ever be able to run again the way he had on Ganwold.

Catching his breath at last, he ventured a glance over his shoulder.

Pulou wasn't there.

He hadn't really expected him to be, but his very absence produced a pang sharper than the one in his side. Closing his eyes, he began to shift his weight from foot to foot, to sway from side to side and to keen, from deep in his throat, as the ganan did around their funeral pyres.

He hadn't been able to mourn Pulou at the time of his death. Hadn't been able to vent his grief and loss. He could now, here. He poured out all his ache with his keening, poured it out from every part of his soul, until at last the ache ebbed, and then finally ran dry.

He stood for a long time in silence afterward, before he turned back to the farmhouse.

FOURTEEN

The storm moved on two nights later. "According to this morning's report," Admiral Serege said over breakfast, "we're supposed to have three or four days of clear weather before the next front blows in. Why don't we go camping, Tris?"

Tristan cocked his head. "What's camping?"

Serege chuckled. "That's living outdoors for a few days, the way you did on Ganwold." He turned to Darcie. "How about you, Darce? Want to come with us?"

"No, thank you!" She shook her head. "I've done more than enough camping for one lifetime!"

They spent that day preparing, while the wet land steamed under the heat of the sun. The admiral brought backpacks and sleeping cocoons in from a shed and dug a couple pairs of worn hiking boots out of a closet. He helped Tristan adjust one pack to fit his shoulders, then showed him how to load sleeping cocoon and extra clothes, poncho and ration packs, first-aid kit and fire kit in order to balance the weight.

"We didn't take this much stuff when we went hunting!" Tristan said, hefting the pack. "All we took was a gut canteen and a hunting knife!"

"You'll carry your knife and canteen on your belt," said Serege. "Where did you sleep?"

"In the grass, during the day," Tristan said. "We hunted at night when it was cool."

Serege paused to consider that, but then he shook his head. "We'd need more gear if we did it that way: a shelter to keep the sun off while we slept, and winter clothes for nighttime."

"We didn't use a shelter on Ganwold," said Tristan.

"This sun is larger and hotter than Ganwold's," Serege said. "We'd get badly sunburned if we slept in the open. And at night the temperature often drops to the freezing point, even during the hottest time of the year. I think we'd better stick with the sleeping cocoons this time. . . . We'll also need long-sleeved shirts and something to protect our heads and faces from the sun."

"This is stupid!" Tristan said, and turned a pleading look on his mother.

She didn't intercede as he'd thought she would. She only smiled at his expression and said, "Go on, Tris. You'll have a good time."

They ate an early breakfast the following morning and set out as the sun shot its first silver rays over the horizon. Tristan squinted at it as he stepped outdoors, and reached to pull his burnoose over his face the way the admiral had shown him.

"You won't have to do that this morning," Serege said. "We'll have the sun to our backs or over our heads most of the day." He made a quick survey of the countryside in all directions and then beckoned. "Let's go."

To the west, beyond several kilometers of desert, lay hills, a plateau, and in the far distance, still blue with predawn shadow, a wall of flat-topped mountains. Serege set out in that direction.

There was no trail, and Serege didn't leave one. He moved as easily as a gan hunter, making his way around brush and boulders, barely leaving a bootprint in the damp soil. Following him, Tristan couldn't help being impressed. But the idea that the admiral might actually know something about living on the land only increased his vigilance, made Tristan more determined to catch him in some mistake a gan hunter would never make.

"That's ripweed," Serege said once, pointing at a cluster of broad leaves. They seemed to grow right out of the ground without a common root or stalk, and their edges were serrated. "You can cut yourself as badly on that as you can with a knife. Siljan's still got a scar on his hand from falling on one when he was a kid.

"And those are sunhawks." Serege pointed out a pair of birds drifting lazily on an air current. "Once in a while when they're flying, you'll see a gold flash in the sky. It happens when the sunlight strikes their feathers at just the right angle."

A brown blur of motion around the base of a rock caught Tristan's eye. It caught the admiral's as well; he stopped short.

"What was that?" Tristan asked.

"A borbik." Serege surveyed the area where the creature had disappeared. "The whole desert is overrun with them; I can see four or five of their burrows from here." Then he added, "They're good eating. We'll snare a couple for supper tonight."

The sun seemed to burn all color from the sky as it climbed, leaving a void of bright white overhead. It evaporated the morning cool and the dew that had darkened Tristan's trouser legs, and made him sweat under his long-sleeved shirt. The sweat ran in trickles down his ribs and spine, and he couldn't relieve the itching it caused because of the pack. "This is stupid!" he muttered under his breath.

By the time Admiral Serege stopped in a stand of scrub trees and said, "We'll eat lunch here," Tristan was more than ready for it. He wrestled the pack off, dropping it unceremoniously into the grass before he plopped down as well and swept off his burnoose. His hair was plastered to his head with sweat; he ruffled it up with both hands.

Serege leaned his own pack against a tree, retrieved a ration pack from it, and dropped to a squat facing Tristan. "How are you doing?" he asked.

Tristan eyed him over a food bar. "I'm fine."

"Any soreness in your shoulders from the pack straps?"

There was some, but Tristan wasn't about to admit it. "No," he said.

"How about your feet? Any blisters?"

"They're fine."

"What about your water supply?" Serege persisted.

Tristan glanced at his canteen. "It's still half full."

Serege nodded. "That's about right. Go ahead and finish it if you need to; there's a seasonal spring where we're going. We're about halfway there."

They finished eating without further talk, relaxing in the patchy shade of the scrub trees. At least Tristan relaxed; the admiral kept sweeping their surroundings with his gaze the whole time, as if he were standing guard. When he stood, he took a minute or two to stretch his arms and back and shoulders, surveying the open country beyond the stand of trees as he did so. Then he shrugged his pack on again. With a resigned sigh, Tristan gained his feet and reached for his pack straps, too.

"Want a hand with that?" Serege asked.

"I've got it," Tristan said. He turned his back as he pulled it on so the admiral wouldn't see him wince when the straps settled over his collarbones.

The sun had begun its descent by the time they reached their campsite, a kilometer into the foothills. Admiral Serege chose a spot about two-thirds up the side of a hill, screened by trees and partially sheltered by a rock overhang. A muddy stream ran around the base of the hill.

"The first order of business is catching some dinner," he said, opening his pack. "We can make camp once we have the snares set." He brought out a roll of wire and a pair of small pliers. "Borbiks generally stick to paths, or runs, so those are the best places to—"

"I *know* how to set snares!" said Tristan. He didn't try to keep his annoyance out of his voice.

Serege looked up, his expression unperturbed. "Good" was all he said, and he held out a length of coiled wire.

Tristan didn't take it. "A lomo could break that, and they're not as big as borbiks!"

"It's stronger than it looks," Serege said. "It's also about the only thing a borbik can't chew through."

Tristan gave him a skeptical look.

"I noticed a spot a few meters over there where two runs cross," Serege added. He indicated the direction with a nod of his head. "You might want to set one there."

A snare set where two runs crossed doubled one's chances of catching something, Tristan knew. But it had been the admiral's suggestion. Taking the piece of wire, he headed off around the hillside in a different direction.

Within a few minutes he found a heavily traveled run that passed under a large stand of brush. It would easily conceal a snare.

The wire was actually easier to work with than the leather thongs he'd used on Ganwold, Tristan had to admit. He didn't have to prop the noose open, and it would certainly be taut enough. But he doubted it would take the weight of a kicking borbik. Rising, he wondered what else he could find for supper if the snare broke.

The stream tumbling around the base of the hill caught his ear with its gurgling melody. The water was muddier than any he'd ever seen fish in before but he decided it wouldn't hurt to look. He made his way down the hillside.

The flattened vegetation, matted with plant debris and soil, showed that the water level had been much higher a day or two before. A limb torn from a tree lay caught between a pair of boulders. Half submerged, its branches dammed the water's flow just enough to form a shallow pool. Tristan squatted at the water's edge and peered in.

Within seconds, a dorsal fin breaking through the water sent a ripple over the calmer surface of the pool. Something gray slid past one of the boulders.

Tristan sucked in a breath. "Fish!" he whispered in gan. "Big one!"

He tugged off boots and socks, shucked off his pants, left his canteen, belt, and burnoose piled on top of them on the bank. Practically holding his breath, he stretched one foot into the water. It wasn't as cold as he'd expected. His foot found the bottom and he slipped in without a splash.

The current rushed around his knees. Rolling up his shirt-sleeves, he waded into the area where the fish had touched the surface. There he crouched, just low enough to trail his hands in the water without soaking the seat of his shorts. All he needed now was patience.

"Tristan?" he heard. He looked up.

Admiral Serege stood on the bank.

Drawing one hand out of the water, Tristan made the gan hunting signal for *"Quiet."*

Serege either didn't see it or didn't understand. "What are you doing?" he asked.

"Fishing," Tristan said. "Be quiet!"

"There aren't—"

Tristan glared at him. "Sh-hh-hh!"

"All right," Serege said, and stood back, folding his arms over his chest.

It was several minutes before the ripple of gray circled the pool again. It slipped around the base of the boulder—actually brushed Tristan's leg! He forced himself not to jump, not to stiffen. Fixing his whole attention on it, he waited.

A couple of minutes later, it made another circle of the pool. Flickered past the boulder. Slid right between Tristan's ankles. Hands drifting in imitation of a water plant closed like claws—

—and something thicker than his wrists whipped around both his arms, pinning them together.

Reflex jerked him up straight, but the creature was wrapped around one of his legs, too. It cost him his balance, threw him backward into the water.

He couldn't catch himself with his arms pinned together. Submerged, he twisted over, trying to get his legs under him. One shin struck a rock; his toes sank into silt on the streambed. Half kneeling, he shoved himself up and broke the surface, gasping, while his attacker's tail thrashed the water into froth.

For the next few moments he was aware of nothing but the

water in his nose and mouth and throat, of coughing on grit and straining to drag in a breath of air, of tugging against coils that only tightened about his arms. Still spluttering, still blinking beneath dripping strands of hair, he got his first look at the creature that held him.

Its head and neck, writhing in the air just beyond the grasp of his hands, belonged neither to fish nor to snake but to something in between. Its mouth gaped, its gills fluttered frantically, and after another few seconds, its coils went slack.

Tristan shoved it away from himself, into the water, and scrambled to his feet as it settled into the murk. Several seconds passed before it wriggled. Its tail brushed his leg. He jumped, staggered back, but it slithered off into the current and vanished.

Only then, standing there catching his breath, did he remember that he was being watched.

He wrenched around.

Admiral Serege still stood on the bank, his face expressionless, his arms still folded over his chest.

Tristan stiffened. "That thing—almost drowned me!" he said. His voice was a rasp. Trying to speak made him cough again. "Why—didn't you—come help me?"

"Because you were doing fine on your own," Serege said. "You had the situation under control; you didn't need my help."

Tristan wondered if the admiral were mocking him. His tone was even, without any suggestion of sarcasm, but . . .

"Come on," Serege said, extending a hand to him. "Get out of the water and get that shirt off. The sun's almost down and in a little while it'll start to get cold."

Tristan stood still in the water for another long minute, holding Serege's gaze and defying it with his own. Then, disregarding the outstretched hand, he climbed up onto the bank.

One shin was bruised and scraped, one elbow was skinned. They smarted, but not so badly that he couldn't ignore them. His shirt clung like a second skin, its chill already making him shiver. He peeled it off with an effort and wrung it out. Used the burnoose like a towel to dry himself before pulling on trousers and boots.

As he started up the hill, Admiral Serege lay a hand on his shoulder. He tried to jerk away from it, shooting a glare back at him.

"You did handle that well," Serege said, "but you could've avoided it altogether if you had let me warn you."

His voice was calm, firm, without condemnation, but Tristan resented it anyway—mostly because he knew the admiral was right. He tried again to shrug out from under the hand—

It tightened. "This isn't Ganwold, son," Serege said. "Despite the similarities, you must never assume that something new is like something you're familiar with. You were lucky, just catching a stream salamander instead of a fish. A lot of people have died from making assumptions. Whether you're setting foot on a new world or meeting new people, the safest policy is always to expect the unexpected."

Tristan glowered at the ground.

But Admiral Serege squeezed his shoulder. "Go check your snare," he said. "I'll get a fire started."

Dusk was settling as Tristan started up the hill. The whole countryside lay in shadow and the breeze had turned chilly enough to bring up gooseflesh on his bare arms. Rubbing them, he paused to draw a deep breath.

The breeze was laden with moisture. He scanned the sky in the direction it blew from. There were no clouds visible yet but the scent on the air was unmistakable.

He found a borbik in his snare, rotating slowly at the end of the wire, so newly dead that it was still warm. It seemed to be mostly hindquarters and legs, well-muscled for jumping and running, but the small size of its chest cavity made it plain that those runs would only be short sprints. It also had little flat ears pressed close to its skull, a stumpy tail about as long as one of his fingers, and massive incisors. Tristan remembered what the admiral had said about borbiks chewing through things.

He removed it from the snare, pulled the knife from his belt and cut its throat. Warm blood spilled over his hand.

He stiffened, staring at it. Felt his heart accelerate. "No!" he said under his breath. He tried to shake the blood off. Tried to rub it off with a handful of damp soil. And then he sat, shaking and making himself take long, slow, deep breaths, until he'd pushed the images back, and his pulse and his hands had steadied.

He dressed out the borbik quickly then, tucking its rolled hide into his belt and burying the offal in a hole scooped out of the soil with a stick.

It was dark by the time he reached the campsite. Admiral Serege had a small fire burning under the overhang and forked sticks planted in the ground on either side of it. He was peeling bark from another stick to use as a spit when Tristan drew up and swung the borbik down off his shoulder.

Serege looked up. "Good catch!" he said. "If you're as hungry as I am, we won't have any trouble finishing off both of them!" He jerked a thumb toward another skinned and gutted borbik lying stretched on a piece of tarp.

But dinner was still some time away. While the fire burned down, settling into coals for cooking, Tristan unloaded his pack.

Tucked in beside the sleeping cocoon was a waterproof military poncho. He shook it out. It had a hood in the center, metal snaps at intervals along two sides, eyelets at the corners. He'd need only a handful of stakes and maybe some rope. He rose and crossed toward the trees that screened the camp.

They were stunted, twisted, and their foliage was scanty, but there would be broken branches on the ground that would suit his purpose. Tristan dropped to his heels. Without any moonlight, he worked more by feel than by sight, poking through the ground cover with his hands. It was still soggy from earlier rains but it yielded what he was seeking.

Squatting by the fire again, he drew his knife and began to whittle a point at one end of each stick.

Serege watched him for a couple of minutes before he asked, "What are you doing, Tris?"

He didn't glance up. "Making stakes," he said.

"What for?"

"To put up a shelter."

"I thought you preferred sleeping in the open."

Tristan set down one stake and picked up another. "It's going to rain."

Serege searched the sky. "I can't see even a scrap of a cloud. How can you tell?"

"I can smell it," Tristan said.

Serege arched an eyebrow. But he turned his face to the breeze and inhaled, slowly and deeply. "You're right," he said after a moment. "I hadn't given it any notice. What have you got in mind for making your shelter?"

Tristan stopped whittling and looked up in surprise.

"What's wrong?" Serege asked.

Tristan hesitated. "You mean—you actually believe me? Even after—?" He gestured toward his wet shirt, spread over a boulder.

Serege sighed. "Yes, I believe you, Tris," he said. "This may not be Ganwold, but some weather indications are pretty universal." He paused, then said, "What can I give you a hand with?"

Doubly surprised, Tristan handed him a couple of the sticks. "Whittle points on those," he said. "They're to hold that down with." He indicated his poncho. "It'll make a lean-to." He waved with one hand from the overhang to the ground.

Serege followed his motion and nodded. "Good idea," he said.

There were enough large rocks on the hill above the overhang to anchor the upper end of the poncho there. Then, armed with stones the size of their fists, Tristan and Admiral Serege staked down the lower end with their whittled sticks.

There wasn't any room to spare, but both sleeping cocoons did fit under the lean-to. "Pretty good, Tris!" Serege said.

A bank of clouds had blown into view over the plateau by

the time the roasted borbiks had been reduced to piles of bones. The breeze had grown stiffer and its chill sharper with the moisture it carried. "Smell that?" Tristan said. "Rain's coming."

Serege reached for the camp shovel. "Let's put out this fire and turn in before the storm breaks on us."

The sleeping cocoon lacked the fur and weight of a peimu hide, but it didn't lack the warmth, Tristan found. Only after he'd settled in did he realize how much his legs and feet and shoulders ached and how very weary he was. The last time he'd felt that way had been after a hunting trip on Ganwold. He sighed as he burrowed into the cocoon.

He woke with a hand shaking him by the shoulder and a voice calling his name. "Go 'way!" he said. Eyes still closed, he made an awkward swipe at the hand's owner.

Admiral Serege chuckled and shook his shoulder again. "Come on, Tris! It's time to get moving."

Tristan forced his eyes open.

Serege crouched beside him, grinning. "You slept through your whole rainstorm!" he said. "You didn't even stir for the thunder and lightning!"

Glancing skyward, he turned serious. "It finally stopped a little while ago, but I don't think that'll last long. We need to break camp and head out before it starts up again."

The angle of the watery sunlight said it was late morning. Tristan pushed himself up with a groan and crawled out of his cocoon.

The misty chill made his teeth chatter as he reached for his pack and his extra clothes. The pants he'd worn yesterday were all right, but his shirt, draped over the boulder, had spent the night in the rain. Tristan wrung it out and then tied it, open, to his pack frame to dry.

In another few minutes the lean-to had been taken down as well and Tristan was wearing the poncho. As he followed the admiral down the hill, the rain began to fall again, a chilling gray drizzle that he knew could go on all day. He shivered under the poncho.

Breakfast was a couple of food bars and a squeeze-bag of shuk, all swallowed on the move. They provided energy and some warmth but they barely took the edge off his hunger.

It was late afternoon when they reached the trees where they had stopped for lunch the day before. The drizzle had never let up and the cloud cover would bring darkness early, but Serege said, "We need to eat and rest; we've got several more kilometers to go."

Sinking to the ground, Tristan barely kept himself from groaning.

"Is your poncho keeping you dry?" Serege asked while they ate.

He nodded, his mouth full of food bar.

"Is it warm enough?"

It was. Nearly warm enough to make him sweat. He nodded again.

"How are your feet?"

"Wet," Tristan said between bites, "and tired."

"So are mine," said Serege, "but we've made good time in spite of the mud underfoot. We may get home before the storm really breaks."

They didn't. Darkness was gathering as they set out once more, and as it deepened, the wind came up and the daylong drizzle turned to a pounding rain. It pelted their ponchos and slapped their faces with cold water. Admiral Serege stopped to take a palm light from his pack and swept the ground with its beam to find their footing.

"How—do you know—where we're going?" Tristan yelled at him over the wind. He was panting, and the damp cold had begun to bite through his poncho, making his teeth chatter.

Serege pointed toward the rim of the valley, where a single light was dimly visible. "That light's at the top of our windpump," he said. His teeth were chattering, too. "We're not far from home now!"

They were coming around one of the sheds when a light came on at the house's side door and a figure stepped out into the storm. Clad in a slicker and clutching a bundle close to her chest, she bowed her head against the rain and started toward the skimmer shelter.

"Darcie!" the admiral shouted, and flashed the palm light at her.

She stopped, looked up, and came toward them at once. "Thank heaven!" she said. "Are you both all right? I was about to go looking for you." She touched Tristan's face, and then the admiral's, and said, "You both must be bordering on hypothermia! Get inside right now!"

The entry was warm with yellow light from the kitchen and the aroma of fresh soup. Tristan peeled off his dripping poncho, shrugged off his pack, and wiped water from his face with one hand.

"Warm showers for both of you!" his mother said. "Tris, right here." She opened the bathroom door. "Just leave your wet things on the floor; I'll bring you some dry ones. Luj—" She pointed Admiral Serege toward the bath off their bedroom. "Stay in the shower until you've stopped shivering and then come have some soup."

The steaming downpour in the hygiene booth eased Tristan's shivering and washed away the soreness of the last two days' activities, relaxing him and leaving him with a sense of well-being he hadn't felt since he'd left Ganwold. Still, it was another few minutes before he realized he was smiling.

Darcie was bundling a second load of wet clothes into the laundry system when Lujan came back out to the kitchen. She glanced up at him, taking in his still damp hair and heavy robe, and asked, "Feeling better now?"

"Much!" he said.

"Good." She gave him a mischievous smile. "You smell better, too!" Pointing toward the kitchen, she said, "The soup's in the canister on the counter. I've put out bowls and utensils and bread. Go ahead and help yourself."

Lujan did, and sat down stiffly at the kitchen table to offer silent thanks before he began to eat.

Darcie joined him once the laundry was started, sitting down opposite him and folding her arms on the tabletop. "How did it go?" she asked.

"With Tristan?" He stirred his soup briefly and sighed, considering. "I'm not sure. . . . I think we broke some ground." He was about to continue when the bathroom door clicked and slid open. He touched her gaze with his and said instead, "I'll tell you about it later."

Tristan padded out to the kitchen on bare feet and Darcie motioned him to the bench beside her. "So, Tris," she said, "how was the camping trip?"

Their son gave a noncommittal shrug, not looking at either of them, and reached for a bowl. He filled it and sat down to eat without speaking.

Lujan was finishing his second helping when Darcie reached across the table and touched his arm. "You had a call from the Spherzah detachment in Anchenko City early this afternoon," she said. "The Watch would like you to call back."

He stiffened. "Why didn't you tell me that when we first got in? Was it urgent?"

"No, it wasn't," said Darcie. "When I told the lieutenant I didn't expect you back until this evening, he just asked for you to call at your convenience. I thought if it could wait until you got home, it could wait until you'd gotten into dry clothes and had something to eat—especially if it means you'll be going in to the city tonight."

Lujan relaxed. "All right," he said, and pushed himself away from the table.

Entering his office, he closed the door behind himself, reached for the secure commset on the desk, and punched in the direct line to the Watch.

It was answered by a woman lieutenant. "A message came in from Saede today, sir," she said. "That reinforcement fleet from the Bacal Belt has arrived in the Issel system."

FIFTEEN

The scream of the sirens ripped the morning air as if it were a fabric. Everyone on the street stopped short, looked up, and searched the hazy sky.

It was reflex, Wenese Feirmont supposed. The attack-warning sirens had sounded nearly every day—and sometimes two or three times a day—for the last two months, ever since the main space stations had been blown up. The newsnets had run clips of the explosions over and over, accompanied by warnings of imminent masuk attack and terse directives to head for the nearest civil-defense shelter whenever the sirens sounded.

People had run at first, had tumbled into the shelters and huddled there, wondering what was happening outside and fearing for family and friends, often for hours, until "All Clear" was signaled by the sirens' winding down.

But nothing had ever happened. No attack had ever come, and people had begun to feel foolish, running from a threat that never materialized. The warnings and directives still interrupted every program on the air, but lately the newsnets had turned their attention to the labor strikes in Rauen Province and the establishment of an independent national government in Meilene. There had been no mention of masuki for a couple of weeks now—but the sirens still went off at every hour of the day and night.

People still jumped when the sirens began. Still looked up.

But few of them ran anymore. Hunching her shoulders as if that could block out the ongoing scream, Wenese continued up the street.

She was crossing through Memorial Park in the center of Sanabria when a flash through the overcast sky caught her eye. She glanced up—in time to see a second, then a third flash, like meteors crossing a clear night sky. She stopped walking again.

—And a muffled explosion shook the ground under her feet.

The second and third followed like echoes.

Wenese stood frozen, shocked with the realization that this time it wasn't a drill.

A man in a corporate uniform, a few meters ahead of her on the path, apparently realized it at the same moment she did. He turned around, white-faced, stumbling into a run. "Those were bombs!" he said. "Bombs!" He waved his arms. "Run! Run!" The sound of his voice was lost under the sirens but there was no mistaking the words his mouth shaped.

Feeling as if she were moving in slow motion, Wenese stared around.

Everyone else was already running, heading in the direction of the park's gate. There was a transit tunnel bearing a civil-defense sign just outside it. Wenese had glanced at it, cursing the sirens, as she'd entered the park. It was half a kilometer away.

The smell of burning came in on the breeze: smoke with a bittersweet bite. It hung on the air, heavier than the haze. It made Wenese dizzy. She staggered against a man who brushed past her, and lost her shoe. The man caught at her arm, pulled her on. But in the next moment he stumbled, too, and when he fell, Wenese went headlong over him.

She pushed herself up with hands that smarted, winced at the burn of a badly skinned knee. She rolled away from the man she'd fallen over, a middle-aged man with graying hair, and she sat up.

Her head spun. The whole park seemed to be tilting. She tried to get to her feet but the lawn suddenly tilted the other way and she found herself back on her knees. In front of her, the gray-haired man was sitting in the path, clutching his head with both hands. She couldn't see his face because everything was blurry.

And for some reason that seemed funny. Funny the way everything was when she got a little drunk and her boyfriend, Nally, would crack those one-liners that were only dumb when she was sober. She sat in the grass and watched the park sway back and forth as if it were drunk. Watched the graying man hold on to his head as if he were trying to twist it off. The thought of that made her giggle.

She noticed that her uniform slacks were torn, gaping open around her bloodied knee, and she giggled at that. She tried two or three more times to stand up but she had absolutely no sense of balance—and every time she fell down, she giggled again.

She was on her hands and knees when two pairs of feet paused in front of her. They were large feet with black hair on them and black toenails, shod in heavy leather sandals that might have been borrowed from the Museum of Ancient History. "Where'd you guys get th' killer beash—beash—*beach* shoes?" she said, "and what in th' two moons've you done t' your toenails?" She looked up, laughing.

The owners of the feet were half a meter taller than Nally. Her breath caught for a moment as she studied them from head to foot, and then she doubled over with another snort of helpless laughter.

Their headgear had probably been borrowed from the costume department of some cheap holovid company, she thought. Rubbery black hoods reached down to their shoulders, concealing their heads completely. They had transparent bubbles for eyes and more bulges with vents where their noses and mouths should have been. Except for a lack of mandibles, they looked like giant insects.

Besides the bug masks, they wore tunics as antiquated as the sandals, made of shiny black material with red sashes and red fringe around the hem. The whole effect was so incongruent that when Wenese glanced up, she burst out laughing again.

The nearest bugman took her by the arm and pulled her to her feet. "Get up!" he said, and the voice that came through his mask sounded artificial.

Wenese swayed, still dizzy, and caught herself with a hand on his chest. On his hot, hairy chest, where his tunic hung open. "Whatever you want, big boy!" she giggled.

He shrugged himself free of her and kicked at the gray-haired man. "Get up!" he said again, and the man climbed awkwardly to his feet, shaking his head and laughing. His shirt had pulled out of the back of his uniform trousers and his hair was disheveled so that it stuck straight out in several directions. Wenese giggled at that. But the bugman pointed across the park and said, "Walk."

Still unsteady, she grabbed on to the gray-haired man and she walked.

There were others in the park, all giggly, all tipsy. The bugmen rounded them up as well, hauling some to their feet, pushing at others with their hands. They ended up on the plaza at the park's center, where the monument to the war dead stood, and Wenese's eyes widened at the sight of all the people milling around: thousands of them—maybe even tens of thousands for all she knew! And there were more bugmen in red-fringed tunics.

"Some party!" said the gray-haired man beside her, and Wenese giggled.

One bugman pushed them toward the vehicles parked on the plaza, vehicles that looked like giant gray beetles squatting on jointed legs.

"Oh! Where're we going?" Wenese asked, and gave the bugman her best come-on look. "Are you coming, too?"

"Get in!" he said, and shoved her up the ramp of the nearest vehicle. "Go to the front."

There were four rows of web seating inside, all running the length of the vehicle, the same kind of seating that Wenese had once seen in a troop transport on display at a military show.

She made her way forward, chose to sit in one of the back-to-back center rows, and found herself opposite a woman in household livery who was tending to a little girl. Watching the woman help the child with shoulder and lap belts, Wenese found and fastened her own.

"Get on, get on!" the bugmen kept saying from the vehicle's rear, and they shoved people aboard, pressing them close together on the web bench. The gray-haired man bumped into Wenese as he sat down; she looked over at him and snickered.

By the time the vehicle was full, it had grown warm. There weren't any viewports, any visible vents. The closeness made Wenese feel sleepy, then queasy, then made her head begin to ache—and none of it was quite so funny anymore. She winced, her fingers going to her temples, when the hatch at the rear banged closed, but the light it had admitted had begun to seem like a glare and she was grateful for the sudden darkness.

She waited. The close heat brought up sweat across her forehead. Her skinned knee throbbed. She looked down. In the dimness, the blood that had dribbled down her shin appeared black.

She started at the roar of engines; they seemed to be right underneath her. They shook the deck and the partial bulkhead she leaned against as they cycled up. When their roar sounded like the scream of the sirens, their sudden thrust shoved her down into her seat—nearly made her pass out.

"Nanna?" The child across from her clung to the woman's sleeve. "Nanna, where are we going?"

The nanny opened her mouth as if to answer—then abruptly shut it again. Her head came up, her eyes flicked over the faces of the people packed in around her, and Wenese saw that they were as wide and frightened and confused as those of the child.

The masuki brought the newcomers down to the cavern in groups of twenty or so, via the lift to the shuttle level. They huddled together, staring through the wire mesh at the prisoners already inside, while the masuk guards opened up the gate. A few of them tried to resist when their captors began to prod them through, but the masuki struck them with their rifle butts, gashing one man's forehead and bloodying someone else's nose.

They looked as if they had been snatched out of business meetings, out of schools, from the merchant districts. There were men and women in the uniforms of various corporations, their faces grim and angry; youths in collegiate uniforms, their eyes belying the fearlessness of their swaggers; a few mothers, or maybe nannies, clutching tear-streaked children. They all shuffled through the gate and clumped together again just inside it.

"So it's begun," Ochakas said to Sergeant Tradoc, who stood at his shoulder. He waited until the gate had rattled shut, then pushed himself away from the mesh and approached a pair of middle-aged businessmen standing at the edge of the huddle. Strain showed in their faces, but that tightened to revulsion as they eyed Ochakas, taking in his beard and uncut hair, his torn and soiled clothing, the odor of his body. "Forgive my appearance," he said. "I just want to know what happened. Where have you come from?"

The men exchanged glances—as if they suspected he might be crazy, Ochakas thought. Their distaste creased their faces. But one of them said, a little stiffly, "We're from Sanabria. What's this place?"

"It's the Malin Point mine complex on Issel Two," said Ochakas. He looked from one to the other. "You came from the capital? Wasn't there any warning? What's happened to the air and near-space defenses?"

A few more newcomers were studying him from behind the two businessmen by now. The men exchanged another glance, shifted uneasily, and the first said, "When a warning horn sounds every day for two months without any apparent reason, it soon begins to lose its credibility. No one pays attention to it anymore."

"I understand that most of the orbital defenses have been destroyed," the second added.

"So they just marched into Sanabria and rounded up anyone they spotted?" Ochakas asked. "Wasn't there any resistance?"

"None at all," said the first man. "They used some kind of gas. The—invaders—were wearing what appeared to be gas masks."

"I remember thinking that the smoke from the explosions smelled strange," said his companion. "It was a sort of sickly sweet smell. It induced a—euphoria."

"Made everybody act like they were drunk," put in a young man standing behind them.

Gas. The same gas that had been developed in Issel's military labs to subdue the Sostish populace. Ochakas felt no surprise: He had feared just such an irony ever since Governor Renier first proposed his Cooperation Pact.

"Why have they brought us here?" asked someone else, a young woman with red hair, a bloodied knee, and only one shoe. "What do they want us for?"

"Slaves," said someone at Ochakas's shoulder.

He turned.

Foros stood there, looking smug. "As if being slaves to the Sector General wasn't bad enough," he added with a pointed look at Ochakas. "Even our dear commander-in-chief of intersystem operations is now a slave!"

The newcomers stared from Foros to Ochakas, all wordless. Someone cleared his throat. A woman pressed her cheek to the head of the toddler she carried and began to cry.

An expensive skimmer with the Isselan Embassy's seal gleaming on its hatch was waiting for them at the Bigornia Spaceport on Mythos, along with the Isselan ambassador himself and a number of his staff and security personnel.

"My lords!" Ambassador Pegaush reached out in formal greeting, first to Istvan, the senior, and then to Borith. But a suggestion of urgency lay beneath the formalities, and once they were all seated in the skimmer's passenger compartment, sealed off even from the driver's cockpit, Borith inquired about it.

"I had planned to brief you fully once we reached the embassy," Pegaush said, "but this compartment is sufficiently secure." He leaned forward and lowered his voice nonetheless. "A new matter has come up which you must be made aware of before tomorrow's meetings with the Unified Worlds' representatives." He focused his vision hard on Borith's and lowered his voice still more. "Yesterday Issel came under masuk attack."

"*What?*" Borith stiffened in his seat.

"It was a most unusual attack," Pegaush said, "conducted only against Sanabria. Almost no physical damage was done, and there were few injuries and no deaths, but thousands of people are missing." He opened the pouch that lay on his lap and removed a folded printout, which he handed over to Borith. "By ten-hundred this morning the list had exceeded thirty-six thousand names, and they're still coming in."

Borith flipped through the pages, noting that the individuals were listed both by name and citizen ID number. "This looks like a slaving raid," he said, and looked up. "How did you learn of this, Ambassador? And where did you get this list? We"—he indicated Istvan with a glance—"were told that all communications out of Issel had been cut off."

"All official communications, yes," Pegaush said, "but some newsnets are still operating. That list was published by the Intersystem Broadcast Corporation."

Borith pursed his mouth for a moment. "Are there any indications as to where these missing people might be now?" He tapped the printout.

"It's fairly certain that they were taken off-world," Pegaush said. "There were sightings of what appeared to be several alien shuttles lifting away from the city after the attack. We expect they were taken to the masuk ships which have entered the system." He paused. Looked from Borith to Istvan. "Your arrival at this time, my lords, is truly providential."

Nioro Borith could only hope that statement would prove more prophetic than premature; but at this point, he knew, providence for Issel lay in the hands of the Unified Worlds, not in those of its own cabinet ministers.

SIXTEEN

Lujan flung his robe over the foot of the bed and sat down on its side, his jaw tight, his vision fixed on the wall. *Of all the unmitigated gall!* he thought for what seemed the six thousandth time.

Behind him, Darcie closed her microreader with a soft slap. "Lujan, you've done nothing but glower ever since you got back from the detachment this afternoon," she said, "and you've barely said two words to Tris or me all evening. What's gnawing at you?"

"Issel," he said. He practically growled the word.

"Oh?" said Darcie. "What now? Or aren't you at liberty to talk about it?"

"There's nothing classified about it," he said. "Those two cabinet ministers who showed up on Mythos the other day didn't just come to negotiate a peace settlement. They're also requesting military assistance from the Unified Worlds to help them put down the masuk threat!"

"I saw that on the midday newscast," said Darcie.

Lujan glanced at her over his shoulder and gave a humorless chuckle. "Takes some kind of nerve, doesn't it? Two months ago they were launching a full-scale assault against us!" He turned to face her. "What I want to know is why they think the Unified Worlds should even consider assisting them right now—why they think we should trust them in any kind of alliance—and how they expect to justify the cost of it to us, especially in lives."

"But I've heard you say several times," said Darcie, "that you'd rather deal with the masuki in the Issel Sector than wait until they move into Unified space."

"I would." He released a full breath in a sigh of exasperation, shoved himself to his feet, and began to pace out his agitation. "But I don't want to do it in an alliance with Issel. I don't trust them."

Darcie sat still in the bed, watching him as he paced. "There's still so much of this I don't understand," she said. "I thought Issel petitioned to come back into the Unified Worlds after the War of Resistance. Weren't they accepted after all?"

"They were," Lujan said, "Sostis, Issel, and Na Shiv were all allowed to petition for reentry. But when Mordan refused to step down as World Governor, which was one of the conditions for Sostis, his people forced him into exile.

"Issel accepted his request for asylum—which was allowable under the Accords—but the next thing we knew, he'd been reinstated to his wartime position of Sector General over Issel and all of its colony worlds!" He shook his head. "No one's sure how he managed that, but it got Issel permanently expelled from the Unified Worlds.

"Two years later," he said, "Isselan forces swept down on Na Shiv and took power, and three years after that, they did the same thing to Adriat." He looked over at Darcie when she uttered a small gasp; Adriat was her homeworld. "By the time the Unified Worlds uncovered what was going on," he said, "it was a fait accompli; there was nothing we could do but impose a few sanctions.

"There've been other crises, too. We've spent the last twenty-plus years expecting and preparing for exactly what happened two months ago."

"But wasn't Mordan behind most of that?" said Darcie. "He's dead now, isn't he?"

"Maybe," Lujan said. "But there's still his cabinet. He tended to surround himself with like-minded people." He let his jaw tighten. "I'd really like to know who sent those two ministers."

"As members of the cabinet," said Darcie, "could they have authorized it themselves?"

"Not unless they were the only members still living," said Lujan, "and if that were the case, it's highly unlikely that they'd actually leave Issel. No, it had to be either by the consent of the whole body or by the order of the chief minister."

"It must be terribly humiliating for them," Darcie said, "coming to us for help after we beat them so badly. They must be desperate."

" 'Cunning' would probably be a more accurate word than 'desperate,' " Lujan muttered.

But Darcie said, as if she hadn't heard him, "The midday newscast also said that the number of people reported missing since the slave raid has reached nearly forty thousand."

Forty thousand people!

The words seared across Lujan's mind like a laser, jolting him awake.

Forty thousand people.

More lives than that probably ended every day on worlds like Issel, whose populations numbered in the billions. Lives that were never even known, and certainly never missed by their planetary governments. But Lujan couldn't banish the thought from his mind.

He looked over at Darcie, curled in sleep beside him. Took up a strand of her hair and twined it around his fingers to be sure, even now, that he wasn't just imagining her there.

There had been only five hundred people on the transport the masuki had seized years ago, and he had personally known only two on its passenger list. But he would have taken on the whole Bacal Belt by himself to get those two back.

How many of those missing forty thousand were other men's mates and children? he wondered. How many on Issel knew the same despair now that he had known then?

And how many more families would be torn apart, how

many more cities terrorized, how many more worlds violated this way if Issel were left to repel the masuki alone and failed?

The more he thought about it, the more he knew there was no hope of sleeping again. He glanced at the chrono on the cabinet by the bed. 0432. Half an hour until he'd be getting up anyway. He sighed heavily and sat up.

Kazak, sprawled on the floor near the foot of the bed, lifted his head and pricked up his ears when Lujan rose to put on shoes and wrap his robe about himself against the early morning chill. When he opened the bedroom door and said, "C'mon, boy," the dog stood and stretched and trotted after him.

He paused on the doorstep for a moment, studying the sky and watching as Kazak galloped off into the thinning dark. It had rained during the night. The air was crisp with it, the ground puddled, and the narrow scarlet border of sky that touched the eastern horizon promised more rain to come. He inhaled deeply, let the breath out in a sigh, and turned toward the dojo.

The low structure had been a barn originally, built the same time as the house, but there had been no livestock under its roof since Lujan was in his late teens. On returning to Topawa to take command of the Anchenko Spherzah detachment, he had put part of his pay and much of his spare time toward converting it into a dojo.

Cabinets constructed for the purpose held clothing and swords. Shedding his shoes and robe, he reached for the short jacket and *hakama*, the traditional split skirt of the *iaijutsu* student. He fixed his full attention on his preparations: the proper snugness of the jacket; the position of the sheathed sword, or *katana*, in his sash.

Clothed, he knelt in the center of the floor to draw on that state of concentration and awareness that his instructors had called *zanshin*.

He was beginning his fourth practice sequence, or *kata*, when the dojo's door opened. Darcie, he knew without looking. She stood just inside the door, watching without a sound while he completed the *kata* and sheathed the sword. Only then did he turn around to look at her. "You're up early," he said.

"So are you." She huddled deeper into her robe, and he saw her gaze flick from his face to the sheathed *katana* and back. "You have something on your mind, don't you?" she said.

"Yes." He sighed, and crossed to her. "I spent a lot of time last night thinking about the people who were taken in that raid. Then I thought about the members of their families who were left behind, and I remembered . . ."

He couldn't continue. He wrapped an arm about her and pulled her close. So close that he could kiss her hair without ducking his head. He put his other arm around her, too, and just held her to himself for some time. And when she tipped up her face to search his, he said, "Thank you, Darce, for keeping me straight on what's really at stake here."

"There's a message coming in marked 'Personal for the Commander,' sir," his acting exec said over the intercom. "I'm sending it into your mailbox."

"Thanks, Reg." Lujan cleared his monitor of the detachment's daily briefing file and called up the mailbox.

An asterisk blinked in the Top Priority box. He touched READ, and the message unfurled itself down the monitor's face:

TOP PRIORITY
260918L 4 3308SY
PERSONAL FOR ADM LUJAN SEREGE, CINC SPHERZAH
FM NEOL BALTHROP, CHMN, UW DEF DIR
UNCLASSIFIED
1. THE PEACE TALKS BETWEEN THE UNIFIED WORLDS
AND THE REPRESENTATIVES OF THE ISSEL SECTOR ARE
NEARING A SETTLEMENT. HOWEVER, THE FINAL DRAFT
OF THE TREATY MUST BE APPROVED BY THE MEMBER-
SHIP OF THE DEFENSE DIRECTORATE BEFORE IT CAN BE

SEALED. AS A MEMBER OF THE DIRECTORATE, YOUR
ATTENDANCE IS REQUIRED AT THE APPROVAL SES-
SIONS, WHICH ARE EXPECTED TO BEGIN NOT LATER
THAN 8/5/3308 SY.
2. FURTHER, THE MYTHOSIAN DELEGATION HAS COM-
PLETED A DRAFT PROPOSAL FOR MILITARY ASSIS-
TANCE TO THE ISSEL SECTOR, WHICH IS TO BE
BROUGHT BEFORE THE FULL ASSEMBLY AS SOON AS
PEACE FORMALITIES ARE CONCLUDED. ALL MEMBERS
OF THE DEFENSE DIRECTORATE ARE ADVISED TO AT-
TEND THE HEARINGS AND TO PARTICIPATE IN THE
NEGOTIATIONS.
END OF MESSAGE

Lujan allowed himself a wry smile at the last paragraph. If the
Mythosian delegation was sponsoring the assistance proposal,
he'd *better* be there for the negotiations! Knowing their historic
softness toward Issel, they were likely to offer basing rights on
Yan and Saede, or to grant access to Unified Worlds' military
intelligence!

It had already taken two days for the message to reach
him, he saw by its transmission date, and travel time between
Topawa and Sostis would be another seven standard days.
With the limited amount of ship traffic through the Topawa
system, he'd be lucky to reach Sostis by the eighth. He tapped
the intercom to the exec's desk, and when the young man answered, he said, "Reg, I need reservations on the next flight
out to Sostis."

"Yes, sir," Reg said.

The exec called him back a few minutes later. "Sir, the first
flight to Sostis is day after tomorrow; the shuttle lifts at
thirteen-forty-five. You have seat number fifty-three, and
cabin two-thirty-two on the starliner."

"I received a message from the Defense Directorate today,"
Lujan said over dinner that evening. "I've got to go back to
Sostis for a while, probably for a couple of months. I'll have to
leave day after tomorrow."

Darcie paused with her utensil halfway to her mouth. Slowly lowered it to her plate again. "A *couple* of months?" she said. "We haven't even been here on Topawa for *one* month yet!"

"I know." Lujan sighed it. "We should probably be glad that I had this much leave. I have a feeling this will be just the first of several trips I'll have to make back there."

"It's about military assistance for Issel, isn't it?" said Darcie.

Tristan's head jerked up at that. "For *Issel?* The Unified Worlds is going to help *Issel,* after . . ."

Lujan and Darcie exchanged glances, and Darcie laid her hand over their son's. "You've seen the newscasts, Tris," she said. "You know what the masuki are doing and how many people have been captured—"

"They captured *us!*" said Tristan. "They—they *tortured* me! They deserve it!"

"No, Tris." Darcie's voice was quiet but firm. "Governor Renier did those things to us; the people of Issel didn't. And Governor Renier is dead now."

"He's dead?" Tristan looked from Darcie to Lujan, as if for a confirmation, and when Lujan nodded, he asked, "Who killed him?"

"The Isselan newsnets said that he killed himself," Lujan said, "but some of us have wondered about that; we know he hadn't enjoyed a great deal of loyalty from his people lately."

"Everybody was afraid of him," Tristan said, and Lujan didn't miss the quaver in his voice. He nodded.

"With good cause. The people of Issel haven't been much better off as citizens under Renier during the last couple of years than you were as a hostage; he imprisoned and tortured them, too."

"They're victims as much as we were," said Darcie, "except that they didn't have any hope of being rescued."

Tristan's vision fixed on the tabletop, his whole face taut and pale as if he were recalling the horrors he'd seen. "I know that," he said at last, and the words were little more than a whisper.

"They're victims even more, now," Darcie said, "thanks to Renier's alliance with the masuki. They've come and asked for our help and, given the alternative of slavery for so many innocent people, I think we should give it—with our guard up, of course." She touched Lujan's gaze with hers.

Tristan didn't say anything to that, but Lujan saw how he shuddered; and in another couple of minutes he rose and left the table without eating any more.

Jiron was waiting with a staff skimmer when Lujan emerged from the Herbrun Field shuttleport into a late spring sea wind.

"Good to see you, sir," Jiron said, saluting. "How was Topawa?"

"Wet, mostly—at least in Anchenko," said Lujan. He swung his duffle off his shoulder when the driver stepped forward to take it. "Tris and I did get in one night of camping between storms, though. Hopefully, the rainy season will be over by the time I get home so we can go again."

As they seated themselves in the skimmer, Jiron said, "When Heazel learned what time your flight was coming in, sir, she suggested that I invite you to join us for dinner. Unless you need to go somewhere else first, we'll go directly to the Flag Officers' Complex."

"Sounds good to me," Lujan said. "I appreciate the invitation." Leaning back in his seat, he asked, "What's the latest on the Issel situation?"

Jiron grew serious. "There was a second slaving raid three days ago, on the city of Bronwyn in the southern hemisphere. According to the newscasts, people headed for the civil-defense shelters this time, so the masuki did, too. Just battered in the shield doors and threw in the gas canisters. There were also some attempts at resistance, but they were mostly futile; just resulted in a larger number of casualties."

"Organized resistance?" Lujan asked.

"Local militia," said Jiron. "They're apparently equipped

with gas masks." He paused, then added, "Our sources have observed something else of interest lately, too. The spacecraft plants at Sanabria, Narcessa, and Ednilao have accelerated their fighter production, and the central government has issued a recall of former combat pilots from retirement, instructor posts—wherever they can get them."

Lujan gave that some thought. He would have been surprised if Issel hadn't made some effort to defend itself, but he wondered how long it would take the masuki to start targeting the spacecraft plants for destruction when their slaving raids began to meet with resistance. "Any indications of warships under construction?" he asked.

"No, sir. Those spacedocks have either been destroyed or fallen under masuk control," Jiron said. "They're just building transatmospheric fighters."

"That could still complicate an assistance effort."

"Certainly could, sir." Jiron's nod of agreement was grim.

Lujan returned to the original topic. "How many people are missing this time?"

"The count stands at a little over thirty-three thousand right now," Jiron said.

Thoughts of the lost transport rose up in Lujan's mind. "Blast!" he said through clenched teeth. "Any indications yet of where they're being taken?"

"Intelligence thinks to Issel Two. Our sources have observed quite a bit of activity out there—and they've confirmed that there were no slave transports in the reinforcement fleet, just combatants and shuttle carriers."

"That fits," Lujan said. "The masuki usually keep their transports well out of harm's way, so they were probably only concerned about sending replacements for the ships most likely to be lost. . . . Has there been any response from what's left of Issel's space fleet?"

"There was when the masuki first returned to the planetary defense zone," said Jiron. "There were a couple of engagements, but the Isselan space force has been pretty well destroyed by now."

Lujan smoothed the corner of his mustache as he considered it all. After some moments he asked, "What about the peace talks?"

"Approval sessions start tomorrow," said Jiron. "Before I forget, sir—" He reached for his front uniform pocket, pulled out a data chip in a plastic envelope, and handed it to Lujan. "Defense Director Balthrop has requested that you be one of the Def Dir witnesses at the assistance proposal's initial hearing. The chip contains the full transcripts of both that and the peace agreement. I knew you'd want to review them ahead of time."

"Thanks, Jiron." Lujan slipped the envelope into his pocket. "I'll go through them tonight."

But not until after dinner.

Entering Jiron's residence, they were greeted by his ten-year-old son, who yelled, "Mom, they're here!" and leapfrogged toward them over a footstool. The boy gave his father a quick hug, and then turned to Lujan to ask, "Did you bring Kazak back with you, sir?"

Lujan chuckled. "Not this time, Heazon." When the boy's mother appeared and sent him off to wash his hands, Lujan said, "I see you're still setting out an extra plate for every wandering waif Jiron brings home, Heazel!"

She laughed. "You're hardly a waif, Admiral! More like family." She took both his hands in the customary greeting and said, "Welcome back, sir. Did you have a good flight? Come in and sit down; we'll eat in just a minute."

She waited until after dinner, when Heazon had plopped down in front of the hologlobe in the living room with his headset and keypad, and her teenage son and daughter had been shooed back to their studies, and the servo emerged from the kitchen bearing cups and a fresh pot of shuk. Then she said, "I had hoped Darcie and Tristan would come back with you. Are they all right?"

"They're doing quite well," Lujan said, and added, "Thank you," when she offered him a cup of shuk. "They're beginning to feel at home on Topawa," he explained, "and I didn't think it'd do them any good to come back here with me."

"That's probably true," Heazel said, and passed the next cup to Jiron. "I remember that Darcie had been quite sick. Is she doing better now?"

"Fully recovered," Lujan said. He took a swallow. "She's been talking about going back to medical school, and I've been encouraging her, but she hasn't decided yet which university to apply to."

"SAI has an outstanding medical school," Heazel said, and sipped from her cup. "How is she readjusting to human culture and all the new technology? I remember dropping by several times and showing her how this or that worked."

"She's getting more comfortable with it," Lujan said. "Of course, that old house on Topawa has about the same level of technology as what she grew up with. She was actually surprised that everything out there still works!"

Heazel smiled. "What about Tristan?" she asked. "Wasn't he—injured or something?"

Lujan nodded. "Tortured, actually. Physically and psychologically." He took another drink and began to swirl the shuk gently around in his cup. He kept his vision focused on the vortex it formed. "He still has nightmares occasionally," he said, "and half the time he still acts as if he's afraid of me. The other half of the time he's testing my patience!"

"That's normal," said Jiron. "Jirrel is nearly seventeen and he's been an expert at that for a long time!"

Lujan smiled at that. "We've gotten Tris into an on-line tutoring program," he said after a moment. "He's doing pretty well with it. Except for that stint at Aeire City while he was a hostage, he's never had any formal education. Darcie said she taught him the Standard character system and numbers when he was a child but it didn't go much farther than that." He sighed, still looking into the cup. "Tris has a lot of catching up to do."

There was a pause, and then Heazel asked, "And what

about you, Admiral? How are you coping with all of this?"

He looked up. She was years younger than himself—younger even than Darcie—but her expression and the tone of her voice were almost maternal. He smiled, a little self-consciously. "Better now," he said. "It was pretty rough at first; there were a lot of misunderstandings and a few arguments. It's taken a lot of patience—especially with Tris. . . . I've also had to give up a few things." He grinned. "Like working overtime, and leaving my boots lying wherever I take them off!"

His solemnity returned almost at once. "I'd have given up the admiralty for Darcie, though, if that had been necessary. It would've been worth it. We're still going through readjustments—probably will be for quite a while—but I can honestly say that I'm happier now than I've been since we were first joined, and—I think she is, too."

"I'm glad," Heazel said. "Send her our love."

"I will," Lujan said.

His suite, when he entered it a short time later, was dark and chilly, and seemed emptier now than it had before Darcie and Tristan were found.

Entering the kitchen to reset the house computer's environment controls, he found its message light blinking. Official dispatches, most likely about the upcoming hearings, he thought. "Transfer the messages to my desk screen," he said, and filled the shukmaker before turning toward his office.

Only one of the messages was official, a reminder that the treaty approval sessions were to begin the next day. The other four were letters from Darcie. Each began with, "My dear Luj," gave a cheery account of the day's events, and closed with, "I love you. I miss you."

They were like the audicorded letters she had sent out to him on Tohh when the War of Resistance was going so badly. Those letters had offered encouragement, had often made him laugh, had helped to fill his emptiness. These had the same effect. He hit the PRINT button.

Only two months, he reminded himself, watching the pages slide into the catcher tray, and wondered how he'd made it through twenty-six years without her.

He sat down and wrote a long letter back before he brought the fresh pot of shuk from the kitchen, poured himself a cup, and slipped Jiron's data chip into the reader.

"The Assembly of the Unified Worlds will come to order," the officiator announced from the podium, "and hearings will proceed on Mythosian bill number six-thousand-four-hundred-one, a proposal for providing military assistance to Issel."

Those still conversing in the aisles or at the rear of the chamber moved quickly to take their seats as the officiator introduced the Honorable Seamus Trosvig, senior member of the Mythosian delegation and author of the bill. Trosvig, a stocky man with thinning red hair and a bulbous nose, lumbered to the podium and leaned heavily upon it as he launched into his obligatory introduction speech.

Familiar by now with the content of the proposal, Lujan gave the speech only partial attention. His initial suspicions about it had not been greatly exaggerated: The proposal called for the sale of state-of-the-art combat vessels and weapon systems to Issel, and joint Unified-Isselan command of all forces marshaled against the masuki. *Over my dead body!* he'd thought when he first read it.

The reactions of the rest of the Defense Directorate had been virtually identical, he'd learned. Their sessions over the past few days had been animated, vehement, and frequently stormy.

Not as stormy, however, as the demonstrations currently going on outside the Unified Worlds Tower. The protesters were mostly military veterans who had spent their careers deterring Isselan aggression against the Unified Worlds, and their chants of "No aid for Issel!" and "Let Issel pay!" continued nearly nonstop, day and night. Though Lujan understood their concerns only too well, he didn't approve of the way they chose to vent them.

The chants didn't penetrate into the Assembly chamber though, and Trosvig droned on, undisturbed, from the dais.

Lujan reached for his microwriter, which lay on the table before him, and scrolled through the document in its memory, reviewing its major points.

The first witness to follow the Mythosian delegate was the Isselan minister of planetary defense, a distinguished black man named Nioro Enn Borith. Lujan closed the microwriter and sat back in his chair as Borith scanned the full chamber from the podium.

"Men and women of the Unified Worlds Assembly and Defense Directorate," he said, "I wish first to express my personal regrets, as well as those of Issel's present government, for the events which have brought us to this point. This conflict, which we have now resolved, was not the will of the people of Issel, nor of most of those in her circles of power.

"Nor was the formation of an alliance with the Bacal Belt. In fact," he said, "many officials, both in civilian positions and in the military, warned the late World Governor of the potential for exactly the situation which we now face. Their warnings were not heeded; in some cases, they were punished.

"During the late World Governor's recent adventurism against the Unified Worlds, Issel's defense forces were reduced to one-third of their former strength. Since the masuk invasion of the Issel system, the surviving forces have been decimated even further. Simply put, we no longer have the military capability to drive the masuki out of our sector."

Borith looked out over his audience again. "In only two raids," he said, "masuk slavers have seized more than seventy-three thousand men, women, and children. Of those children listed among the missing, approximately eight thousand are under the age of ten standard years. The location and conditions of these people are not known."

Listening, Lujan felt a tightness in the pit of his stomach, a tension that moved through his spine and shoulders and neck until he realized his teeth were clenched and his hands, lying on the table, were knotted into fists.

". . . The fate of my motherworld hangs on the decision you will make," Borith concluded. "But remember that that decision may determine the fate of your own worlds as well." He paused. "I thank you most deeply for allowing me to participate in this hearing. I will now respond to your questions."

There were several, and the minister answered them all with the same urgency and persuasiveness that had characterized his testimony.

Four more witnesses followed before Lujan mounted the platform. He cued the prompt screen on the podium and placed his hands flat on either side of it to keep himself from gripping its edges.

"Ladies and gentlemen of the Assembly," he said, "the Defense Directorate of the Unified Worlds submits the recommendation for the swift approval of military assistance to Issel in order to eliminate the masuk threat. However, it is the opinion of this Directorate that the bill proposed by the Mythosian delegation far exceeds the bounds of what is necessary to meet that threat, and that it would actually serve to delay rather than to expedite the liberation of Issel.

"Of particular concern," he said, "is the proposed sale of advanced ships and weapon systems to Issel. Though the intent is sound—to encourage Issel to carry some of the burden of its liberation—its history of aggression over the past twenty-six years makes weapon sales of any kind out of the question.

"Even if that were not the case, the proposal overlooks the risks of attempting to deliver weapons to a world under enemy blockade, the unavailability of personnel trained to operate such systems, and the length of time required to recruit and train new personnel—assuming that a pool of recruits is even available. The amount of time which would be needed for training them certainly is not.

"The proposed joint command of combat forces is equally untenable, as our Isselan petitioners have already informed us that the status and whereabouts of their high command is unknown."

Lujan shifted slightly behind the podium, glanced down at its prompt screen, and realized that his hands had closed on its sides. He left them there when he looked up again.

"Therefore," he said, "it is the proposal of this Directorate that an expeditionary force be formed from the space fleets and surface forces of the Unified Worlds, and that this force, under the command of officers selected by this Directorate and the civilian Triune of the Unified Worlds Assembly, enter the Issel system, block all possible escape routes, and destroy the masuk fleet within that system."

A gasp of protest came from the bench where the Isselans sat. Borith was bolt upright in his seat, his face taut with shock and fury, his hands locked on the edge of the table as if he were about to pull himself to his feet.

Lujan acknowledged him with a look and continued. "It is also the proposal of this Directorate that Ministers Hampton Istvan and Nioro Enn Borith, as the representatives of the Isselan world government in its request for our assistance, be invited to submit their opinions, concerns, and any materials which may assist the planners in the development of their campaign against the masuki, and further, that Ministers Istvan and Borith be kept apprised, via regular briefings, of the status and direction of that planning, and be allowed to voice their approval or disapproval of such plans."

He looked out over the chamber once more. "The Defense Directorate requests that the Assembly give serious consideration to all aspects of both this proposal and Mythosian bill six-thousand-four-hundred-one in reaching a final decision. As previously stated by Minister Borith, the future of our worlds will rest upon it. . . . Thank you. I will now take questions."

Borith was on his feet in an instant. "Admiral Serege," he said, "the proposal you have just described amounts to nothing less than an invasion of Isselan space by Unified Worlds forces! That is absolutely unacceptable! What is there to guarantee that your proposed expeditionary force wouldn't simply sweep down on Issel and finish what the masuki have begun?''

Lujan met and held his look. ''At this time, Minister,'' he said, ''the only guarantee we can offer you is our word.''

Borith snorted at that, and Lujan said, ''Your mistrust of our motives is understandable, Minister, but by your own admission, Issel has little choice in the matter right now: The masuki are already in your system enslaving your people and you don't have the means to stop them. We have no desire to see the same thing happen to our own worlds, but if we don't take decisive action now, that possibility would become very real.''

He paused. When he spoke again, he had lowered his voice a little. ''I know from personal experience, Minister, how it feels to lose loved ones to the masuki. My own mate and son were passengers on a transport which was seized over twenty-five years ago. I was fortunate—we were recently reunited—but no one from *any* world should have to experience something like that.''

Borith had nothing more to say after that. He stood still for a moment in the utter silence that filled the chamber before he lowered himself back into his seat. But he was still scowling when Lujan left the platform.

SEVENTEEN

When the dog, stretched on the floor outside his bedroom, lifted its head from its paws and pricked up its ears,
Tristan looked up from his monitor and tilted his head to
listen.

"Tris?" said his mother.

"He hears something," said Tristan.

His mother listened, too, her lips pursed with concentration, but it was another minute or so before either one of them
could hear the skimmer. By then the dog had gotten up and
trotted toward the side door, wagging its tail and whining.

"It's probably your father," Darcie said, and she pushed
back her chair and followed the dog out to the kitchen.

Tristan sat still, chewing at his lower lip. His palms were
suddenly damp. He rubbed them on the legs of his trousers.

In a couple more minutes he heard the skimmer setting
down outside, and his mother opening the door as its engines
died. "Lujan!" she said. "We weren't expecting you home
until tonight!"

Tristan heard Admiral Serege's chuckle at that, heard his
bootfalls in the entry and his reply, muffled by their hug. It
was several seconds before he heard Serege ask, "Where's
Tristan?"

He curled up his hands in his lap.

"He's finishing his studies," his mother said. "We were

just reviewing the sciences section when Kazak heard the skimmer."

There was a bootstep at Tristan's bedroom doorway. He jerked his head up.

Admiral Serege stood there. "Hello, Tris," he said. "How are you doing?"

Tristan's mouth was suddenly dry—as dry as it had been when the admiral had come to see him in sickbay the first time, when he had been a complete stranger. Two months had nearly made him a stranger again. He answered only, "Fine, sir."

He spent most of dinner listening as his mother and the admiral talked about the negotiations with Issel, the people involved, and their major concerns; about the last rainstorm three weeks earlier, which had flooded part of Siljan's farm, and summer in East Odymis, with the snow melting off its mountains and daylight lasting until well past midnight; about the nest of iggles Kazak had dug up under the storage shed, and the medical schools his mother had transmitted her applications to. He looked up, startled, when the admiral said, "Tris, your mother mentioned in several of her letters that you've been putting in a lot of time at your studies. How are you doing with the second level?"

He swallowed the mouthful he'd been chewing. "I'm—almost finished with it—sir."

"Already?" Serege seemed surprised. "You were just starting on it when I left!"

"Yes, sir," said Tristan.

"Sounds like it's about time for a break!" Serege said, and looked over at Darcie. "When I stopped by the detachment on the way home, I learned that they've moved up the training at Lost Prospector Canyon they had scheduled for next month; they're going to conduct it next week instead. I'll need to be there to observe, and"—he turned back to Tristan—"I thought you might like to go with me, Tris. We could go out a day or two early and camp in the canyon, then join the troops for their training."

Tristan remembered their last camping trip: the familiar, wild flavor of the borbik he'd caught and cooked over the fire, the scent of damp soil under his sleeping cocoon, and how Serege had trusted him about the coming rain in spite of the incident in the creek. It hadn't been as bad as he had feared; it had actually eased his homesickness for Ganwold.

He met Serege's eyes and nodded. "All right," he said.

They took the skimmer this time. Lost Prospector Canyon was a half-day's flight to the southwest, and the farther they went, the more rugged the terrain became. The flat floor of the desert seemed at first to have been crumpled, then torn open. Tristan looked down into shadowed chasms and saw rivers running white at their bottoms like lifeblood flowing freely from a wound.

He was startled out of his study of the landscape by the admiral asking, "Want to take the controls for a while, Tris?"

He jerked around, gaping. "Me, sir?"

"Why not? I hear you're a pretty good pilot."

The offer, and the trust it implied, amazed Tristan. But the thought of actually taking the controls made his stomach clench up, made his palms sweaty. "No thanks," he said, and shook his head. "I've had enough of piloting for a while."

"All right." Serege shrugged. "Just thought I'd ask."

Tristan was still marveling over the invitation a good while later when a shaded block appeared on the skimmer's naviscreen. It straddled part of a side canyon. The key identified it as a military training area.

"That's where we're going," Serege said. "We'd better let them know we're coming in." He flicked the radio switch and said, "Canyon base, this is lima sierra one-two-niner requesting clearance to land."

"Lima sierra one-two-niner," a voice crackled back at them, "please transmit identification sequence."

"Transmitting now," said Serege, and touched another switch.

The response came back almost at once: "Base to lima

sierra one-two-niner, ID sequence cleared, sir. Your landing pattern should be appearing on your naviscreen. Welcome to the base."

"Roger that," said Serege, and nudged the skimmer around into a gradual descent.

He set it down in a landing area bordered on two sides by low buildings, and by the time he'd shut down the engines and popped the hatch, a squad of troops had marched out to meet them.

Tristan left the greetings to the admiral. Climbing out of the skimmer's other side, he squinted across the red and orange abyss. The wind that swept over from the far rim was cool, and spicy with the scent of desert pines. He inhaled deeply, filling his lungs with it again and again.

When the squad headed back toward the buildings, Serege turned to Tristan. "Let's break out a couple of ration packs and have lunch before we start down into the canyon. We won't get to the bottom until about dinnertime."

Tristan opened the package the admiral tossed over to him and eyed its contents: three different kinds of food bars and a squeeze-bag of fruit juice. He made a face. "Are there borbiks in this canyon?" he asked.

"Plenty of them." Serege smiled. "What's wrong, Tris? Getting tired of ration packs already?"

"Yes," he said.

They put on burnooses before they shouldered their backpacks, wrapping the pale cloth close about their faces so that only their eyes showed. "Don't hold back from drinking," Serege said, indicating his canteen. "It's a lot hotter today than it was for our first hike."

The trail into the canyon twisted its way like a snake along the contours of the wall. It was dusty, well-worn, and its slope was gradual, but Tristan wished it was wider. Following Admiral Serege, he kept his left shoulder to the wall and tried to avoid looking over the half-kilometer drop to his right.

It was late afternoon by the time they reached the canyon floor. The ocher walls were turning purple with shadow, and the wind that chased the river down the chasm was almost chilly. Tristan pulled off his burnoose and turned his face into the wind, raking his fingers through hair that stuck to his head in sweaty tendrils.

Admiral Serege led the way along the riverbank, around rapids where the water lashed itself to foam over a bed of boulders and its roar reverberated from the canyon walls. It was too loud to shout over, so Serege mouthed words and motioned him to turn around. Brow wrinkled with puzzlement, he did.

Slanting sunlight caught the rapids' spray and turned it into rainbows over the water. Tristan stopped and stared, his breath taken away by the sight.

A little distance below the rapids, the river tumbled around a bend, still swiftly but with less violence. The turn had once swept the water against the wall and over time it had carved out a cave, a pocket that lay two or three meters above the river now. "That's where we'll sleep tonight," Serege said.

It was a short scramble up the incline to the cave's mouth. Tristan paused at its lip to shrug off his backpack and discovered that he had to duck when he stepped inside. It was only about three meters deep but it was at least twice that wide, and the floor was dry and fairly level. It could have sheltered a whole hunting party of ganan, he thought.

Admiral Serege was already opening his own pack. "If you'll set a couple of snares," he said, producing a coil of wire, "I'll gather up some driftwood and get a fire started."

Beyond the bend, the canyon expanded into what was almost a valley. The river widened, too, and ran so shallow that Tristan could have waded across it. The banks on either side were meadows, green with grass and brush that hadn't yet succumbed to the summer heat, and crisscrossed with a maze of borbik runs.

Snares set, Tristan squatted at the water's edge and looked out over it. Clear and fast, with occasional pools and the roots of grassy hummocks to hide under, the river seemed an ideal place for fish. Tristan sat motionless and watched, and as the last shafts of sunlight vanished behind the canyon's rim, a dark torpedo shape caused a ripple on the surface—

—a dark shape with glowing red eyes!

A second joined it, and then a third, like demons emerging from dormancy in the mud. Tristan moved back from the bank, feeling gooseflesh rising on his arms and the skin crawling at the nape of his neck.

He didn't bother to dress out the borbiks he found in his snares before he took them back to the cave.

"What's in the river out there?" he asked the admiral. "The things with the red eyes?"

"They're fish with red markings on their gills." Admiral Serege placed a handful of small driftwood on the fire and looked up, smiling. "They're called evil-eye trout. Pretty startling, aren't they?"

"Yes!" Tristan said.

"A few of them would be great for breakfast, though," Serege said. "The best time to catch them is just before sunrise, when they'll feed again. I brought some fishing gear, if you'd like to try it."

Tristan remembered his last attempt at fishing. "Maybe," he said.

He took the borbiks back down by the water to clean them. Took nearly as much time after he finished to make sure he'd gotten all the blood off his hands and out from under his fingernails. The memory of it running hot across his palm and between his fingers still made him shudder.

The memory of the blood still shocked him awake with his own screams sometimes.

He was sitting up by the time he got his eyes open, but the image of the bloodied masuk lingered in his mind like a mist. He blinked and shook his head to disperse it. Gulped in a few breaths. It was some moments before he was even certain of his surroundings.

He sat in a cave, half swaddled in a sleeping cocoon, with the canyon wind cold against his bare chest and the roar of the river in the background. He had come here with . . .

He looked over his shoulder.

Admiral Serege was propped up on one elbow in his own cocoon, watching him. "Tris?" he said. The creases of concern across his brow appeared even deeper in the starlight.

Tristan wrenched away from him. "I'm all right!" he said.

There was no response to that at first, but then he heard Serege stir in his sleeping cocoon. Another silence followed, a long one this time, before Serege said quietly from behind him, "My first Spherzah mission was a rescue. Our team was assigned to penetrate an enemy space base, locate the POWs held there, and get them all out—and we had a limited amount of time to do it in. If we hadn't completed the mission when the time window closed, we could expect to die along with the prisoners when the Unified Worlds attacked.

"I'd drawn sentry duty. While the others located our POWs and broke them out of their cells, I guarded the gate tunnel between the control area and the cell blocks.

"Only about half of the POWs were out when a Dommie guard came into the tunnel. He walked right past me, heading for the block where my teammates were, so I jumped him. It wasn't a clean takedown. He struggled, and when he tried to yell for help, I used a bar arm choke on him and—broke his neck.

"He—didn't die instantly. He lay there and—gasped—for what seemed like forever. It was so loud I had to keep my hand over his mouth—and he just lay there and stared up at me while he gasped, until finally he . . ."

Serege's voice trailed off, the sentence unfinished. There was no sound but the river for a couple of minutes, and then he said, in a voice that broke under the weight of his emotion, "I—still see his eyes—in my sleep—sometimes."

Tristan turned around slowly at that—and saw the admiral's tears, turned by the starlight to glinting trails down his face.

He swallowed hard at the sight of those tears, at the depth of the sorrow in the admiral's face. He felt that same sorrow himself; it made everything inside of him ache. "I know—how it feels," he said. Whispered it. It was all he could manage, but he couldn't keep it in anymore. "I—killed somebody, too." His hands shook. He locked them together in his lap and ducked his head. "He was a masuk. We were fighting in the cave, and when he came around the corner, I—I stabbed him—with my knife—and—his blood got all over my hands."

He choked. His eyes blurred over with tears.

A hand closed on his shoulder. An arm lay across his back and pulled him around. Pulled him close.

Tristan pressed his face to his father's shoulder and sobbed.

They were sobs of torment, of terror, and they came unchecked for some time, tearing at his very soul.

But with the tearing came a release, like a logjam giving way in a river. It eased the guilt and the fear, and Tristan sagged, weak with relief.

When his sobs gave way to shaky breaths, his father loosened the arm he'd wrapped about his shoulders. "Sharing the load is always the hardest part," he said. He sighed, and his hand stayed on Tristan's shoulder. "These things take time to get through—sometimes a long time—but the ache won't last forever. The peace *will* come, son. Until then, you don't have to bear it alone. I'm always here for you to turn to."

Tristan lifted his head and looked into his father's face. He explored the expression in those eyes for several moments.

He had seen that expression many times before but he'd never trusted it until now. He hadn't dared to. Hadn't even dared to accept it. But now he understood, and he knew he would never fear his father again.

He woke when the first shaft of sunlight reached over the canyon's crest and tickled his face. He turned his head, wrinkling his nose at it, and opened his eyes.

He was alone in the cave. His father's sleeping cocoon was empty, his boots gone. Tristan lay still for a few minutes, studying that empty cocoon and reflecting on what had hap-pened during the night.

Wondering where his father was, he pushed himself up on one elbow and looked out toward the river.

Shirtless in the dawn's chill, Admiral Serege stood motion-less on the riverbank, his feet planted far apart, his knees slightly bent. He seemed to be holding something in his hands at chest level, and Tristan cocked his head at the sight of the massive scars twisting around his upper right arm. He stood with his back to Tristan, his face unreadable, but he appeared to be completely at ease.

Tristan watched for some time, but Serege never moved so much as a finger. Curious, he crawled out of his own cocoon and got quietly to his feet. Planted them as wide as he could and bent his knees.

He hadn't stood that way for even a minute before the insides and backs of his thighs began to burn with the strain, and then to quiver. He locked his teeth, tried to control the quivering—but after another few seconds he couldn't hold the stance any longer. He straightened his knees, releasing his breath in a rush, and bounced a little to relieve the burning in his legs.

"Not easy, is it?" he heard.

Tristan looked up abruptly, but Admiral Serege hadn't glanced around. "Was that you, sir?" he asked.

"Yes." His father straightened and turned toward him, closing the microreader he wore on a long cord around his neck.

"How did you know I was trying that?" Tristan asked.

"I was just—aware that you were." Serege smiled, and reached for the shirt he'd draped over a rock. He must have seen Tristan's puzzlement as he pulled it on because he said, "It's hard to explain. It's—a kind of higher awareness that comes with training in the martial arts. It's kind of like gaining an extra sense."

Tristan cocked his head. "Why were you standing like that, anyway?" he asked.

"That's called the horseback stance." Serege fastened up his shirt. "It's basic to most of the martial arts, and once your body gets used to it"—he smiled again—"it's actually relaxing. I use it for meditation when I finish working out." Coming up to the cave, he studied Tristan for a moment. "How are you feeling this morning, son?"

Tristan released a shaky sigh. Met his father's gaze and held it. "Better, sir," he said, and this time he meant it.

The cliff jutted out from the canyon wall, a sort of promontory caused by a change in the river's course thousands of years before. It was only twenty meters high but from its top, looking down, it seemed twice that. Tristan stayed well back from the edge.

But Commander Amion, detachment operations and training officer, strode right along the rim. "We've got some good solid anchors here for setting up rappels," he said. "I know most of you are old hands at this but we've got some new troops in the unit who may need belays, so set up for them. Let's move!"

The team leaders said, "Yes sir!" almost together, and began to give orders—more with hand signals than with words, Tristan noticed. Armed with coils of rope, flat webbing, and racks of metal rings, the troops snapped into action.

"Rappelling is one of the most basic Spherzah skills, Tris," his father said. "It's often used for infiltration into target areas, and sometimes for exfiltration out; the idea is to come and go as quickly and quietly as possible. There are several systems and techniques for use in different circumstances. You'll probably see most of them before we're done today."

The setups were simple: a sturdy tree or horn of rock around which a rope had been passed and both its ends thrown over the edge. "That's the preferred method for our purposes," Admiral Serege said. "Once your team is down, you can retrieve your rope quickly and leave no evidence of having been there."

Commander Amion jerked a thumb toward one of the four rappels. "Looks like Sladsky's ready to go, sir."

A stocky young man stood at the edge of the cliff, his back to the drop. As Tristan watched, he attached himself to the doubled rope with metal rings, put on helmet and gloves, passed the rope behind his back and down his right side. Almost as one, his buddies leaned forward to watch as he went backward over the lip. Six seconds later he was on the canyon floor. He freed himself from the rope with a single motion and called, "Off rappel!" and someone else stepped up to the edge.

"We'll be working on rescue techniques today," Amion said, "but I want everyone to make a few practice rappels first; some of our new troops are still pretty green at it."

Standing back with his father and the commander, Tristan watched as one soldier after another disappeared over the edge, and then came bounding back up the trail from the cliff's foot to do it again. Everyone had made two or three rappels when one of the team leaders said, "Admiral Serege! Would you like to take a turn, sir?"

Troops at every rappel point turned to look at Admiral Serege, and Tristan saw eagerness in their faces. Heard it in their voices, too:

"Let's see you do it, sir!"

"Come on, sir, show us how it's done!"

"You can use my helmet and gloves, sir!"

Serege grinned, glancing across at Amion and Tristan. "Why not?" he said.

The whole detachment gathered around as he pulled on a seat sling, attached carabiners, and snapped himself onto the rope. Pausing to recheck rope and equipment, he said, "Always double-check everything, no matter how many years you've been doing this."

Hands held out helmets and gloves. "Thanks," he said,

and accepted a helmet from one soldier and gloves from another.

"I'll time you, sir," said a young man standing next to Tristan.

"I'd rather you didn't." Serege gave him a sheepish smile. "It's been a few years since I last did this for time."

"How does that line go, sir?" said Amion. " 'Old Spherzah never die, they just kind of drop out of sight'?"

Admiral Serege grinned at him. "Thanks a lot, Commander." Drawing the rope around his waist, he shot Tristan a split-second look before he said, "On rappel!" and leaned back off the ledge.

Tristan swallowed hard and looked over.

Serege dropped as swiftly and smoothly as a spider on a web, touched bottom, detached, and stepped back to call out, "Off rappel!"

"Yipes!" It was the guy with the timer. "Three seconds flat! That even beats Sladsky's best time!"

"The Old Man hasn't lost it!" someone else said over the cheers, and Tristan didn't miss the note of awe behind the words.

He turned when someone touched his arm. It was one of the female troops, a girl with green eyes and close-cropped dark hair barely visible under her helmet. Her name patch said KERSCE. "What about you, Tristan?" she said. "Want to try it?"

"I've never done it before," he said.

"We'll teach you," she said, "and you can use a belay—a safety rope."

Tristan glanced around the circle of Spherzah, all of them a few years older than himself. He hesitated, then said, "Okay."

There were more cheers, more grins, and several slaps on the shoulder.

"Get him a swami belt and a sling," said Kersce, "and we'll need a belayer."

With the whole detachment watching him, Tristan fastened the belt around his waist, and Kersce attached the belay rope. "A wide belt spreads out the jolt around your middle and prevents injuries if you fall," she explained. "Now, where's that seat sling?"

Someone handed it over: leg loops attached to another waistband. "Make sure it's snug," Kersce said, and eyed him. "That looks good. Okay, let's get you on the rappel line." Taking him by the arm, she maneuvered him into the space between the anchor tree and the lip of the cliff.

It was less than two meters wide. Tristan forced himself not to look back; he gave Kersce his full attention.

"Always attach the carabiners with the gate up," she said, "this way, so they don't get pushed open. Same thing with the brake bar." She showed him a thick cylinder with a hooklike indentation at one end. "Lock it in like this, so the rope pulling through the carabiner holds it in place. If you put the brake bar in backward, the rope will push it out and you'll bust the admiral's time to the bottom." She gave him a mischievous smile. "Free-fall down twenty meters only takes *two* seconds."

Tristan tried to return the smile, but his heart was beating too hard and too fast.

"Now the rope," she said. "Take it around your back and hold on to it like this. That's your braking hand. If you want to slow down, bring your hand forward; if you want to speed up, swing it back. The most important thing is never, *never* let go with this hand! The other hand is just for balance; hold it loosely around the rope up here. Got that?"

Tristan nodded. His hands were sweaty.

"You need gloves," Kersce said, "and mine won't be big enough for you." She looked up. "Anybody got some gloves?"

Several pairs were offered. Tristan took the nearest and managed a dry-mouthed "Thanks" as he pulled them on, and Kersce pushed her own helmet onto his head.

"This is the tricky part," she said. "If you just step off, you'll smack into the wall, so keep your body perpendicular and put your weight in the sling. Just *sit* in it; it'll hold you."

"It's easier if you crouch a little as you go backward," someone else offered.

Tristan nodded. His knees felt weak.

"On belay?" Kersce called over the cliff.

"Belay on," the call came back up.

It was Admiral Serege's voice. Tristan looked over his shoulder.

His father stood on the canyon floor, the belay line wrapped tightly behind his own body. "I've got you, Tris," he said.

Those words, Tristan realized, were as much a guarantee as the safety line itself. He said, "On rappel," and sat back in the sling, and pushed off.

It wasn't as smooth as most of the starts he had seen, but he didn't crash into the wall—and he didn't plummet straight to the canyon floor. He hung for a moment, a couple of meters beneath the lip, and released a breath he didn't even know he'd been holding.

"That was good!" Kersce called down. "Now let up the brake line a little and go for it!"

It was effortless—*almost like running in low gravity*, Tristan thought. And it didn't last long enough. He was grinning when he touched the ground, so broadly that the corners of his mouth hurt, and his shout of "Off rappel!" was almost a laugh.

Admiral Serege was grinning, too, when he turned around. He flung an arm about Tristan's shoulders and said, "Well done, son!"

Tristan settled down in the skimmer's seat and leaned sideways to rest his head against its canopy. The desert slid by below, fiery red in the late afternoon light, but he was only peripherally aware of it; his mind was replaying the day's events.

"Tired?" his father asked, glancing over at him.

"Yeah," he sighed. But it was the same kind of tired that he'd felt after peimu hunts on Ganwold. The kind of tired that came with a sense of accomplishment. "But it feels good," he added.

His father smiled at that. "I know what you mean."

He shifted a little then, just enough to study his father's

profile. Studied it for some minutes before he finally asked, "What do you have to do to become a Spherzah?"

Admiral Serege looked over at him, eyebrows arched with mild surprise. "Think you might be interested in doing that?"

He answered with a shrug.

"Well, this is the time to start preparing, if you are," his father said. "The best way to do that right now is to keep at your studies. Most of the Unified Worlds require their officers to have at least a basic university certificate and the enlisted personnel to have finished a tenth-level equivalent."

Tristan furrowed his brow. "What does that have to do with being a Spherzah?"

"Candidates are selected from the active-duty forces," Admiral Serege said. "After three years of service you can take the qualification tests and submit an application package. That includes your regular evaluations, your commander's recommendation, and a detailed description of every skill you have that would make you an asset to the Spherzah; the more skills you have, and the more varied they are, the better.

"If you're selected, you go through six months of basic training and indoctrination at Dengau Sanctuary on Kaleo, and if you make it through that, you're assigned to a unit.

"It's not as simple as it may sound," his father cautioned. "There's stiff competition for every slot. Only one applicant out of ten is accepted, and only five or six percent of those make it all the way through Spherzah indoctrination."

"Oh." Tristan sank back in his seat, pressed down by an unexpected surge of discouragement.

But his father gave him a meaningful look. "It's not beyond your reach if that's what you really want, Tris," he said. "I think you have a lot to offer the Spherzah."

"Using the principles which I have just demonstrated," said the tutor's synthesized voice, "find the areas of the following figures."

The first shape to appear on his monitor was a simple parallelogram. Tristan tapped its dimensions and his answer into the keypad, and the tutor's voice said, "That's correct. Go on to the next problem."

The figures grew increasingly complex; the sixth was three-dimensional. Tristan turned it over and around on the monitor, tracing it with a lightstylus to measure each side.

He looked up when someone paused at his bedroom doorway. He'd expected it to be his mother, so he was a little surprised to see his father standing there instead. Especially when it was still early in the afternoon. "Uh, hello, sir," he said. "I didn't know you were home."

"I just got in," his father said. And then, "May I come in for a minute?"

There was something serious, something urgent about his tone. Tristan set down the lightstylus and said, "Yes, sir."

His father came in and sat down in the chair his mother usually used and leaned forward to rest his elbows on his knees. His features were serious, too, Tristan saw. Almost grim. It was enough of a premonition to make him swallow.

His father saw that. Saw the questions in his eyes as well, and gave a pensive sigh. "A couple members of the Defense Directorate arrived here in Anchenko a few days ago," he said. "They've spent most of their time in meetings with the detachment command, but"—he looked Tristan in the face—"they want to talk with you, too."

"With *me*? What for?" Tristan stiffened. "They don't want to debrief me again, do they?"

"No." His father's tone made that definite. "No more debriefings. They want your help with—a project."

"A project?" Tristan cocked his head. "What is it?"

"I'd better let them explain it to you," Admiral Serege said. "But there are a couple of things I think you should know before you talk to them." His eyes burned into Tristan's. "Whether or not you choose to participate in this will be completely up to you, son. I've told them that, so don't let them pressure you. Take as much time as you need to think it through from all sides. If you have questions, don't hesitate to ask them; get as much information as they're allowed to give you.

"You also need to know that no matter what you decide, you'll have my full support in it. All right?"

Tristan only nodded.

"Good." His father gripped his shoulder and rose. "Let's go into my office, then. It's secure enough for this kind of discussion."

The visitors sat in the living area, two men with sparse gray hair wearing the military uniforms of two different worlds. They stopped sipping from the glasses of chilled fruit juice Darcie had brought them, set their glasses down and stood when Admiral Serege and Tristan came into the room.

"Gentlemen," the admiral said, "this is my son, Tristan. Tris, this is General Ande Pitesson, Mythos's commander-in-chief of surface forces, and General Choe Pak-Sung, chief of planetary defense for Sostis."

Tristan exchanged solemn handclasps with each of them, and then his father motioned them toward his office.

They pulled chairs into a circle in front of the desk, and General Pitesson, at a nod from the admiral, did the talking.

"No doubt you're aware, Tristan," he said, "of the situation unfolding on Issel with masuk slavers seizing people out of its cities."

"Yes, sir," said Tristan.

"And you're probably also aware that the Unified Worlds and Issel are working out an agreement on military assistance to help drive the masuki out of the Issel system."

Tristan let his hands curl into fists on his thighs. He nodded stiffly. "Yes, sir."

General Pitesson shifted in his chair. "A war plan is taking shape on the strategists' tables right now," he said. "I can't go into any detail, you must understand, except to say that its successful execution will require the participation of someone who knows Issel Two intimately, who knows where everything is and can go directly from one place to another without maps or other assistance. General Choe"—he nodded toward the other—"myself, and several members of the Plans department have studied the reports which were compiled from your debriefings, Tristan, and we feel that your experience makes you the best qualified person for that role."

Tristan's hands curled up so tightly that they hurt. "What do you want me to do, sir?" he asked.

Pitesson and Choe looked at each other and then at Admiral Serege, and Pitesson changed position again, as if his chair were too hard. "We need you to act as a guide for a number of Spherzah teams."

"On Issel Two?" Tristan's question was a dry-throated whisper.

When the general nodded, he felt suddenly weak. He didn't even have to close his eyes to see the gray maintenance tunnels again, or the caverns full of lichens, or the clanging metal stairs that spiraled down into bottomless darkness. He felt chilled and shaky, as if he were going into shock.

Both generals were watching him. His first impulse was to shake his head, to tell them he couldn't do it.

But his father was watching him, too. He touched Admiral Serege's look with his own and saw his promise in it, of support no matter what he decided. Take as much time as you need to think it through, he had said. And ask questions.

"What will Spherzah teams be doing on Issel Two?" Tristan asked.

"I'm afraid I can't tell you that," said Pitesson.

Tristan cocked his head. "What, sir?"

Pitesson said, "All information on the subject is classified."

"How can I decide if I want to do this if you can't tell me anything about it?" Tristan said.

Pitesson sighed and moved in his chair again. "I understand your concern, Tristan," he said. "I assure you that if you choose to do this, you will be fully briefed at the appropriate time." Exchanging a glance with General Choe, he said, "All I can tell you at this point is that this mission will be one of the most important parts of the operation. All you'll have to do is guide the Spherzah to specific places; the rest will be up to them.''

Tristan looked at the floor. Shuddered at the thought of going back to Issel II. Rubbed clammy hands up and down his trouser legs. "How soon?" he asked.

Pitesson shook his head. "I can't tell you that, either."

And Tristan glanced at his father once more. "I—want some time to think about it," he said.

"We can give you tonight," said Choe. "We'll be returning to Sostis tomorrow and we'll need to have your answer before we leave."

He went directly outdoors from the office. "Tris?" his mother called, looking up from her studies, but he went on outside without answering.

It was the hottest part of the day; the air shimmered with the heat. Tristan padded between the farm buildings and around the dojo, where there was a strip of shade. He dropped to his heels, pressing his back to the structure's stone wall, and squinted out at the desert.

His mind was in turmoil. Fragments of memories whirled and tumbled, as random and fleeting as images in a kaleidoscope: illuminated maps in the Issel II Mine Control Center, the pain in his side that nearly doubled him over, the ceaseless steady sound of dripping water. Hazy periods of consciousness as nightmarish as his fevered sleeps on the cavern floor. Weil's anxious eyes and Nemec's anxious voice and Pulou's anxious stroking of his hair . . .

He was sweating, and it had nothing to do with the heat. It was a cold sweat.

His strip of shade stretched slowly across the farmyard, but he didn't even notice until it was lost altogether in the twilight. The heat dissipated in an evening breeze and the breeze grew chilly. When gooseflesh rose on his arms, Tristan drew his knees up close to his chest and wrapped his arms around them for warmth.

He could still see the patrol monitors in the Mine Control Center, the monitors that showed gray figures in coveralls shuffling through a tunnel, and more figures in wire cages. He saw haggard faces—not those of prisoners this time, but of people on the newscasts from Issel, people whose children or parents or mates had been taken by the masuki. And he remembered masuk faces, grinning with bared teeth. . . .

He shivered, and it had nothing to do with the evening chill.

They're victims as much as we were, his mother had said of the Isselans, except that they don't have any hope of being rescued.

He remembered two children he'd seen on a newscast, faces streaked with tears, showing the newsman a holo of their missing mother.

He remembered Saede: two figures emerging from a tunnel, one small and wrapped in a pale robe, the other as large and dark as the cavern in which he stood, holding a blade to his hostage's throat.

His heartbeat shook his whole body when he finally gained his feet. He put out a hand to the wall to steady himself and stood still for a long moment. Then he drew a deep breath and turned toward the house.

A dim light was still on in the kitchen, a plate and utensils still laid out at his place at the table. Tristan glanced at the kitchen chrono: past twenty-three hundred.

Another light showed across the dark living area, slanting through the half-open door of his father's office. Tristan made his way toward it and peered inside.

Admiral Serege sat behind his desk, brows drawn together as he studied something on its monitor. But he looked up when Tristan paused outside the door. "Tris!" he said, and motioned. "Come in."

Tristan did—and only then saw the two generals, still seated before the desk as if they hadn't moved since he left. He hesitated, feeling their eyes on him. He swallowed.

"What is it, Tris?" his father said.

Tristan drew himself up. Clenched his hands at his sides to quell their shaking. "I'll do it, sir," he said.

Pitesson and Choe both visibly relaxed. Shoving themselves from their chairs, they each clasped his hand and gripped his shoulder, and General Choe said, "Well then, Tristan, you'll need to start packing. You'll be spending the next few months on Kaleo, getting ready."

EIGHTEEN

Tristan accepted his duffle bag and ID plate from the Customs scanners and started down the corridor. "Welcome to Onomichi Station, gateway to Kaleo," a female voice said over hidden speakers. "Please proceed into the main concourse for starliner and shuttle connections."

The voice went on, advising new arrivals that Kaleo's rotation time was twenty-two-point-nine standard hours and providing local times and weather reports for several major cities, but Tristan wasn't listening.

Onomichi Station's main concourse was three or four times the size of the concourse on Topawa's space station—and three or four times as crowded. Tristan hesitated as he stepped through the boarding gate, his fingers tightening on the duffle's cord as he moved out into the throng. Not even at Aeire City Academy had he seen such diversity. Humans of every build and skin color, and many nonhumans as well, brushed past and around him as he crossed the concourse to a waiting area.

All of its seats were occupied, but Tristan had no desire to do any more sitting. He moved closer to the viewpanes and set his duffle down between his feet. *Don't worry about finding him*, he'd been told. *He'll find you.* But he glanced around anyway before he turned to look out on Kaleo.

Since that second camping trip with his father, since that day on the cliff with the Spherzah, since the conversation on the way home, he'd been determined that someday he would come to Kaleo as a Spherzah candidate. But he hadn't expected it to happen so soon. That camping trip had been barely three weeks ago.

It felt more like three months ago, Tristan thought.

He started at a deep, quiet voice near his ear. "Tristan Serege," it said. He jerked his head around.

The man who stood at his shoulder was about ten years younger than his father, he guessed, but nine or ten centimeters taller. His shoulders were as broad as a bull peimu's and his skin as black as a starless night sky. He wore civilian clothes, not a uniform; there was nothing that distinguished him from any other traveler in the concourse. Tristan tilted his head. "Fathi Tonaso?" he queried doubtfully.

The other answered with a slight nod and said, "This way." Then he turned, and in another moment he'd become part of the crowd.

Tristan snatched up his duffle and followed.

He had to duck around pedestrians, had to jog through the open spaces to keep the other in sight; Tonaso moved, with long, even strides, like a fish through water, and he never looked back.

Tristan caught up to him, halfway around the station it seemed, only when Tonaso stopped before a bank of lifts. Tristan was practically panting by then, and Tonaso eyed him without speaking as he pressed the call button.

They rode the lift down several levels, emerged into a smaller concourse, and Tonaso motioned him to the right, toward a shuttle in a private bay. "Stow your bag in the back and strap in," he said.

Tristan obeyed without answering.

He waited until the shuttle had cleared the space station and locked onto its flight profile to ask "What—?"

"Be quiet!" Tonaso cut him off sharply.

Tristan blinked. Hesitated. "But—" he said.

"Be *quiet!*" Tonaso repeated. He didn't raise his voice; he didn't have to. His tone and the expression of his narrowed eyes were enough to make Tristan close his mouth and swallow.

Tonaso held him with that look for a long minute. "If you learn nothing else while you're with me," he said, "you'll learn immediate, unquestioning obedience, and you'll begin to learn it right now. I have few rules, so they'll be easily remembered. Punishment for breaking them, or for disobedience of any kind, will be swift and painful.

"The first rule is, you will not speak unless told you may do so.

"The second rule is, you will address me at all times as *ishku*, which means 'master' in the Shiotan language, and you will answer to *yatsu*, which means 'pupil.' If you have something to say, you will ask permission with the request '*Ishku, may I speak?*' and then you'll wait until that permission is granted." Tonaso's vision burned into Tristan's. "Is that understood?"

Tristan nodded his response.

"Answer me, *yatsu!*" Tonaso ordered.

Tristan said, "Yes—*ishku.*"

He studied the other after Tonaso turned back to the shuttle's forward viewport. Noted the hard set of his jaw, the hard glint in his eyes. It was several minutes before he dared to ask, "*Ishku, may I speak?*"

"You may," said Tonaso.

"What are the other rules?"

Tonaso looked over at him. Hard. "You'll learn them as the need arises for them," he said.

Shiota was an island nation, a line of extinct volcanoes lying off the east coast of Kaleo's largest continent and straddling its equator. The crumbling cones were now carpeted with forest, and cities hugged the lower slopes and sand beaches. Their towers gleamed in the morning light, catching Tristan's eye as the shuttle arced out of Kaleo's nightside shadow.

Dengau Sanctuary lay inside the crater at the top of Wasika Ok, the Widow's Head, the highest peak on the island. The sun's light hadn't yet reached into the crater and its floor was still blanketed with mist and shadow, so the shuttle was well into its descent before Tristan could make out tiled roofs among the tangle of trees and fog. Then the whole sanctuary appeared: a maze of low buildings connected by cloisters and enclosed within a wall.

There were landing pads inside the compound, two of them occupied by other shuttles. Tonaso settled his shuttle down beside them. "Get your bag," he said as he shut down the engines, "and wait for me here." Dismounting, he strode off toward the nearest building, an ancient timber-framed structure with carvings at each corner of its roof.

Tristan brought his bag out of the cargo compartment and bounced a little on his heels to loosen up his legs.

He watched the sun rise over the crater, touching the west wall with its light first and then sweeping across the valley floor. Watched it melt the mist to wisps and then to nothing, and heard the chorus of birds in the forest gradually grow quiet.

He grew restless after a while, and a little bit impatient, so he began to pace around the shuttle pad, pausing every two or three laps to look in the direction Tonaso had gone.

As the sun continued to climb, it grew too hot to pace. It was a humid heat, and it made Tristan's clothing feel heavy. Made him sweat itchy rivulets under his shirt. He scratched, but it didn't do any good.

And then his stomach growled. He'd had only a light meal on the starliner before it docked at Onomichi Station, and that had been several hours ago now. Annoyed at being left to wait for so long, he leaned up against the shady side of one shuttle, arms folded over his chest, and scowled at the building into which Tonaso had disappeared.

The sun was approaching its zenith when Tonaso finally came out again, wearing a backpack and carrying a ration pack and a canteen. "These are yours," he said, thrusting canteen and ration pack at Tristan. "Let's go." And he turned toward the compound gate.

"Go *where?*" Tristan asked. "Isn't this—?"

The blow came out of nowhere, snapping his head to the side, sending him sprawling. The landing pad's tarmac bit into his hip and the hand he flung out to catch himself. His lower lip throbbed where the back of Tonaso's fist had smashed it into a tooth, and he could taste blood in his mouth. Smarting but angry, he rolled onto his back and shoved himself up on his elbows.

Tonaso towered over him. "What's the first rule, *yatsu?*"

For one furious moment as he picked himself up, Tristan considered tackling the other about the knees, throwing him to the ground, and—

"Tell me, *yatsu!*" Tonaso curled his fist.

Tristan met his look. Held it for a moment, defiant, before he said, "You will not speak unless told you may do so."

Tonaso gave a stiff nod. "Don't forget again," he said. "Now pick up your gear and get moving."

By the time he'd found the ration pack, flung into tall grass two or three meters away, and slung the canteen's strap and duffle's cord over his shoulder, Tonaso was nearly through the gate. Teeth gritted, Tristan followed.

The forest beyond the wall was ancient, the trees so gnarled and scarred that they seemed stunted, their roots as twisted and entwined as the branches overhead. It was dim enough under the leaf canopy that Tristan had to pause to let his eyes adjust, and it was noisy with the whir and clicks of insects. The air was laden with unevaporated moisture, and it actually felt cool after his long wait in the sun.

"Stay with me," said Tonaso, and he started away through the trees the same way he'd started off through the crowd on Onomichi Station.

Following him here was harder than following him on the station had been. Insects flew into Tristan's face, whined around his ears, got caught in his hair. He swatted at them with one hand and fought his duffle with the other. Tangled branches kept snagging at it, rolling its cord off his shoulder or nearly yanking it from his hand. He tried bundling it under one arm for a while but that proved to be even more awkward, especially when every root on the forest floor seemed to be lying in wait for his feet. He hadn't had to carry a duffle when he'd gone hunting on Ganwold. Its ungainliness made him feel even clumsier than he'd been when Pulou had first started teaching him to hunt. When he saw Tonaso moving effortlessly through the trees far ahead, he felt a fresh wave of anger.

The humidity made it all worse. After the first few minutes the air no longer felt cool; in fact, it made Tristan sweat harder, plastering his shirt to his back and sides and soaking his hair about his face and neck. It made the air wet and heavy as well. Made drawing each breath an effort. It puzzled him that being enveloped in so much moisture could make him so thirsty, but he didn't hesitate to drink from his canteen.

They were two or three kilometers into the forest when its floor became a gradual incline. The ground became rockier, too, and over the next several minutes, as the incline grew steeper and walking turned to climbing, the trees began to thin out. Tonaso was leading him up the crater wall, Tristan realized.

He stopped in his tracks and stood panting when he got a glimpse of its slope through a break in the trees. Above him, only occasionally visible between the branches, Tonaso was still moving steadily. Tristan raked sweaty hair out of his eyes with his fingers. Rubbed at an insect bite on his neck. "Jou's whelp!" he said through his teeth.

Tonaso was waiting for him when he reached a level area in the shadow of a jutting rock. "We'll eat here, *yatsu*," he said.

Tristan released a breath in a rush of relief. His knees felt rubbery and his calves and thighs burned from the climb. Swinging his duffle off his shoulder, he winced at a twinge through his elbow and wrist. Had to flex his cramped fingers for a few moments before he could untie its cord and retrieve the ration pack from its top. Then he sat down on it, as if it were a log or a rock, and pulled his canteen strap off over his head.

He had just removed the cap, was just lifting the canteen to his mouth, when Tonaso kicked the duffle out from under him. He hit the ground with a bump, losing the canteen as he flung out his hands to catch himself, and it rolled, spilling its contents. Glaring up at his tormentor, Tristan scrambled after it—but Tonaso put his boot on it first.

"The third rule," he said, "is, you will never sit down. You will keep your feet under yourself at all times so you can move quickly if you have to. Do you understand, *yatsu?*"

Tristan glanced at his canteen, at its ebbing flow of water. "Yes, *ishku,*" he said.

Tonaso said, "Hmph," and nodded and took his boot off the canteen, and Tristan grabbed it up.

It was practically empty. He drank all the water that was left.

He sat on his heels, gan-style, while he ate. It was the posture he normally preferred—when his legs weren't quivering with fatigue—so he thought Tonaso's third rule was unnecessary. And thinking about the spilled canteen sent a new rush of anger through him. He glowered at Tonaso over his food bars.

The rest lasted no longer than it took Tonaso to eat. Tristan hadn't finished his last food bar or his squeeze-bag of juice when the other straightened to his feet, shifted his pack on his shoulders, and said, "Let's go, *yatsu.*" He stuffed the rest of the food bar into his mouth, shoved the empty canteen into his duffle, and glared at Tonaso's back as he started after him.

Tonaso led him up and around the curving inner wall of the crater until the sun's last yellow rays shot over the rim above and the valley below was blue with shadow. Then he stopped and pointed and said, "There."

It was a moment before Tristan spotted the square stone gateway, nearly lost among the shadows and trees and so low that he had to duck when he followed the other through it.

He found himself standing in a flagstoned courtyard enclosed on four sides by a cloister and on the fifth by a structure much like those within the Dengau Sanctuary compound. Except this one was built of stone, built right into the volcanic wall: a carved façade sheltering a grotto. A small stream of water flowed from the grotto, poured over its single worn step into a shallow pool like a basin, then spilled into a ditch that crossed the courtyard and emptied noisily into a drain beneath the cloister. In the early twilight the place appeared to be little more than a ruin. "*Ishku*, may I speak?" Tristan said.

Tonaso eyed him over his shoulder. "You may."

"What is this place?" he asked. "Why have we come here?"

"It used to be a temple to some Shiotan idol," said Tonaso. "Now it's going to be your school."

Tristan cocked his head, puzzled by that, and the other said, "You're not a real Spherzah candidate, so you can't be trained in the real school. You won't be getting the full curriculum, either. Just enough to keep you from being a liability to your team and to keep you alive. Understand, *yatsu?*"

"Yes, *ishku*," Tristan said.

"Good." Tonaso gestured toward the cloisters. "Choose a cell; it'll be your quarters for the next few months. Then get some water from the pool and wash up."

Tristan nodded and turned away, fanning at the cloud of gnats that hovered about his head.

The cells were all exactly the same: stone rectangles only slightly larger than the cabin he'd had on the starliner, each with a square window in the back wall that let in the last fading light, and a shelf below it just large enough to unroll a sleeping cocoon on. They all smelled musty, damp, and Tristan remembered his room on Issel II with its vent to the lichen caverns below. He shivered despite the heat.

Plopping his duffle down on the bed shelf in the cell he selected, he pulled out his tightly rolled sleeping cocoon, shook it out, and spread it on the stone floor.

There was no basin or pail to get water with so he took his canteen out to the pool. The courtyard was blue with dusk, and empty; Tonaso seemed to be nowhere within its walls. Puzzled, Tristan glanced about himself as he stripped and crouched by the pool to fill his canteen.

He poured the water over his head first. Gasped at its chilliness as it ran down his shoulder blades and spine. And jerked around, clapping a hand to his side at a sudden smart there, like the sting of a tsigi.

A pebble lay on the pavement near his bare foot, a pebble that hadn't been there a moment before. He picked it up and glanced around.

There was no sign of Tonaso, but Tristan knew he was there somewhere, studying him from the shadows, waiting for him to let down his guard. He peered hard into the corner from which the pebble had probably come before he poured water from the canteen over his shirt, using it to scrub the day's sweat from his body.

He was washing his shirt and shorts and trousers, scrubbing them on the flagstones by the pool, when the next pebble struck, stinging the middle of his back. He wrenched around, shooting to his feet.

Tonaso stood no more than four meters behind him, holding something in one hand. "The fourth rule," he said, "is, you will be vigilant at all times. At *all* times, do you understand?"

"Yes, *ishku*," said Tristan.

Tonaso tossed a ration pack at him. "Supper," he said as Tristan caught it. "Eat it and then go to bed."

"Yes, *ishku*." Tristan scooped up his damp clothes and started away.

"*Yatsu!*" said Tonaso.

He froze. Turned.

A dark object, larger than his fist, came hurtling toward his face. He reached out to intercept it, dropping his clothes.

It was a plastic pouch full of black capsules. He questioned the other with his eyes.

"Insect repellent," said Tonaso. "Take one with every meal. It makes you smell bad to the bugs."

Wearing only his shorts, Tristan squatted in his cell's doorway while he ate. He had hoped there might be a little breeze, but the air was still and heavy and hadn't cooled at all with the sun's setting.

After finishing the food bars and juice bag, he stretched out on top of his sleeping cocoon. It offered him only scant padding on the flagstone. He couldn't even scoop out hollows for his shoulders and hips in the stone as he had in the soil beneath his peimu robe on Ganwold. He shifted, trying to get comfortable, but the heat was even worse than his bed's hardness. Exhausted though he was, it was some time before he slept.

He sat up in the dark when someone shouted, *"Yatsu!"* He blinked, briefly disoriented, and glimpsed a splinter of moon through the square window over his head. The shout came again, over a swelling chorus of bird calls, and he shoved himself to his feet, stiff in the legs and sweaty again.

Something slid off his body as he rose, and landed lightly about his feet: a length of dark cloth. Wrinkling his brow with puzzlement, he bundled it up and stumbled out of his cell.

In the next instant he was nearly jerked off his feet. Thick arms looped under his own from behind; hands like claws locked onto his collarbones. The sudden pain snatched a scream from his throat.

"What is the fourth rule, *yatsu?"* Tonaso hissed close to his ear.

His answer came out in gasps: "You will—be vigilant—at all times!"

"But you weren't being vigilant just now, were you?" Tonaso dug his fingers in harder around Tristan's collarbones.

He writhed, helpless in the other's grip. "N-no, *ishku!"*

"And you weren't vigilant during the night, either."

"No, *ishku!"*

Tonaso let go of him. Pointed at the wad of dark cloth, which Tristan had dropped in the scuffle. It was crimson in the predawn light. "Pick that up," he said.

Tristan's arms were limp, as if they'd both been dislocated. It was all he could do to make his fingers close on the folds.

"Do you know what that is?" Tonaso asked.

"No, *ishku,"* said Tristan.

"It represents blood," said Tonaso. "*Your* blood. It means I 'killed' you in the night." He took the cloth from Tristan's hand, wrapped it loosely around his own. "Vigilance, *yatsu*," he said.

Tristan didn't answer. He only met Tonaso's eyes and swallowed.

"The stones of the courtyard need to be washed," Tonaso said as Tristan finished his ration-pack breakfast. "You've got until sunset to do it. Begin at that corner"—he pointed—"and scrub one flagstone at a time, using your right hand to do the first one, your left hand to do the second, right hand for the third, and so on. There are a bucket and brush inside the sanctuary. Draw your water from the pool, not from the ditch. After every third stone, empty your bucket into the ditch and get fresh water. You'll report to me when you're finished."

Tristan stared. Barely kept himself from blurting out a protest. "*Ishku*, may I speak?" he said instead.

Tonaso eyed him. "You may."

"Why?" he demanded. "What does scrubbing the courtyard have to do with learning about the Spherzah?"

Tonaso raised an eyebrow. "Maybe a great deal," he said. "Maybe nothing at all. That's not important, *yatsu*. You'll do it because I told you to. Is that understood?"

Tristan met his gaze, saw in it a wordless warning, and nodded. "Yes, *ishku*," he said.

He filled the bucket at the pool and crossed to the corner Tonaso had indicated. Shot a quick glare in the other's direction as he got down on hands and knees. His collarbones still ached where Tonaso had grabbed him earlier; he winced as he reached out with the brush.

He hadn't even finished the first flagstone when something stung him at the seat of his pants. He jerked around. A pebble lay on the pavement behind him, and Tonaso stood in the shadows of the cloister.

"What is the third rule, *yatsu*?" he asked.

Tristan glowered. Drew his feet under himself so that he

sat on his heels. "You will always keep your feet under you," he said.

Tonaso held him with his look. "Don't forget again."

Tristan stayed in a crouch after that. Kept a weather eye on the other's whereabouts, too, as he washed the flagstones. The smart of a pebble striking his back or his sides snatched his attention up each time he relaxed his guard.

"What is the fourth rule, *yatsu?*" Tonaso asked him the first time.

Jaw taut, he answered, "You will remain vigilant at all times."

"Remember that," Tonaso said.

But by the time he finished, his back and sides were dotted with small welts raised by pebbles, and the sweat that ran in rivulets along his ribs smarted on them like salt. Straightening from dumping his last pail of water, he found that every muscle in his back and chest was in knots, and he could barely move his arms. He stretched carefully, grimacing at the shocks through his shoulders, and glanced around.

Tonaso squatted on a grass mat in the shade of the sanctuary, apparently in meditation. Gathering up bucket and brush, Tristan crossed to him. "*Ishku*, I'm finished," he said.

The other looked up, his features as expressionless as the flagstones. He gave a slight nod and then said, "Tomorrow you'll wash the courtyard again, except this time you'll begin in *that* corner." And he turned his head in its direction.

Tristan could barely push the brush the second day; every movement shot fire through his torso. He glared at the stones, at the concealing shadows of the cloister from which he knew Tonaso watched him, and clenched his teeth more with fury than with pain.

"*Ishku*, may I speak?" he said over supper that evening.

Tonaso took another bite of his food bar and chewed it slowly before he said, "You may."

"When am I going to start learning about the Spherzah?" he demanded. "All this scrubbing the courtyard is just—stupid!"

Tonaso arched both eyebrows at that. "Is that what you think, *yatsu?*" he said. "Then tomorrow you will scrub the courtyard again."

He scrubbed the courtyard ten days in a row.

On the tenth evening Tonaso asked over supper, "What have you learned so far, *yatsu*, about becoming a Spherzah?"

Ten days of scrubbing flagstones had given Tristan a lot of time to think, in spite of the threat of stinging pebbles. "I've learned to follow orders," he said, "even if I don't know the reason they were given."

"What else?" said Tonaso.

He hesitated, feeling a little sheepish. "I've learned that—getting angry about things—only makes them worse."

"What else?"

Tristan looked up. Looked his instructor in the face. "I've learned that being a Spherzah takes a lot of hard work—and a lot of patience and self-control."

Tonaso nodded at that. "Now you are ready to begin," he said.

"Your body and your mind are your weapons and shield," Tonaso said, "but you must learn to use them properly if they are to serve you."

He talked of leading force and turning force and demonstrated what they meant in hand-to-hand combat. He talked of balance and maneuver and battle awareness.

"You must be alert to *everything* that is going on around you," he said. "Keep your eyes centered on your opponent's chest and use your wide-field vision. If you watch only his eyes or his hands, he may feint with his fist and you won't see him attack with his foot or his knee."

He started with a basic fighting stance: one arm held horizontally to protect the body, the other raised vertically to shield the face, feet planted wide apart and knees slightly bent. "From this position," he said, "you can block almost any attack. Go ahead and hit me in the face."

Tristan put all his strength behind his fist.

Tonaso's upright arm deflected it, sent it shooting harmlessly past his shoulder so that Tristan staggered with his own momentum. And in that moment of unsteadiness, as he flailed to regain his balance, he realized how open, how vulnerable, he would be to his opponent's counterattack.

He spent the next fifteen minutes in the on-guard position, parrying his instructor's rapid punches. "Deflect! Deflect! Deflect!" Tonaso said, fists flying. "Inside! Outside! Inside! Outside! Again! Again! Again!"

The same principle was used to block body punches, uppercuts, and backfist blows. Tonaso drilled him in all of them, over and over again, until Tristan thought he could block blows in his sleep.

"You'd better be able to," Tonaso said. "I may test you at any time, and there won't be any warnings."

The first test came barely three minutes later, in the middle of a lecture on aiming through the target. Tristan didn't even see the sudden punch until it smashed into his nose. It sent him reeling, blood coursing hot down his upper lip. He stared at his instructor through a veil of pained shock.

Tonaso held his look. "You failed that test, *yatsu*," he said. "Your enemy won't warn you before he attacks. And he won't pull his punches the way I just did. Your defense must be *reflexive!* It's useless if you have to think about it. An instant's hesitation gives your adversary time to kill you."

Tonaso added something new to each day's workout: a countermove against kicks or strikes, another way to escape from a hold or a choke, an unarmed defense against knife- or club-wielding opponents.

"Every one of these tactics is defensive," he said. "Your duty is first to protect yourself and then to subdue your attacker. You must be willing to use as much force as is necessary in a given situation but wise enough to know how much that is and to use no more than that; to do otherwise wastes your energy, time, resources, and is morally wrong. There is no room among the Spherzah for wanton aggressors. All use of force must be disciplined and measured."

He drilled Tristan on each new tactic, drilled him until the movements no longer felt awkward to his unaccustomed muscles, until they came swiftly, smoothly, without hesitation.

"Block, catch, counterjab!" Tonaso shouted at him. "Faster, *yatsu!* Do it again. Block, catch, counterjab! Again! Again!"

They finished each workout by facing off. Bodies gleaming with sweat, shirtless under the tropical sun, they lunged, blocked, kicked, and threw each other to the ancient grass mats spread out on the courtyard's flags, until their breaths came in ragged gulps and grunts, and sometimes in gasps of pain.

As Tristan's skill with a number of tactics increased, so did the frequency and complexity of Tonaso's tests. He found himself living in a state of constant alert, always making sure of his instructor's location and movements as he went about his chores, always aware of the slightest shifts of his hands or his feet as they ate or trained together.

He even found himself sleeping on alert. A footfall outside his cell, a sudden change in the forest sounds outside his window, would bring him to his feet in the fighting stance. The crimson cloth that he'd found in his cell every morning at first began to appear less frequently then, though his instructor might strike two or three times during a single sleeping period.

Tonaso ambushed him once during their daily endurance run. One moment he was a few meters ahead, jogging effortlessly up a mountain goats' trail, the next he was gone, hidden behind a lava ridge that jutted out into the path. Tristan recognized the setup just as he rounded the ridge himself—

—and swayed back, out of the path of a club improvised from a broken branch. As it whistled past, he dove in, taking Tonaso down with a tackle before he could reverse his swing.

Regaining his feet, he assumed the on-guard stance. Watched, wary, as his instructor picked himself up. But Tonaso didn't pursue the scrimmage. Not then. "Hmph," he said, arching an eyebrow. "Keep up with me, *yatsu.*"

Two days later, Tonaso attacked him in the latrine, a cell in the corner of the cloister under which the ditch drained. It had three holes in its floor along one wall. Its single square window admitted little light, leaving it mostly in shadow, and the gurgle of the water below the holes masked the sound of footsteps outside.

Tristan knew he was being watched when he entered. He hesitated in the doorway, searching the corners, before he stepped to the third hole. There he could at least put his back to the corner.

He was just pushing his pants off when a dark shape filled the doorway. He straightened, yanking at his pants, but there was no time to fasten them: The other had already lunged.

Tristan sidestepped, blocked the blow with one arm, caught the other's wrist. Only then did he see the wooden practice knife in Tonaso's hand.

Pivoting under the other's arm, he applied an elbow lock and pulled down. Tonaso hit the floor on his back—but his free hand suddenly closed on Tristan's shirt, near his shoulder, and jerked hard.

It broke his hold on Tonaso's knife hand, sent him headfirst over his opponent. He tucked his head, took the fall as a roll—and Tonaso was on top of him, practice knife poised over his chest.

Tristan seized the weapon arm at elbow and wrist, pulled down and across. Tonaso rolled over and off of him, grimacing with the strain on his elbow, and Tristan used his momentum to pull himself up. He gained his feet, backed off, and assumed the on-guard stance, still panting.

Tonaso rose more slowly. "As you were, *yatsu*," he said, and left the latrine.

His training wasn't limited to combat skills. Over supper each day, Tonaso filled his head with theory and Spherzah doctrine. It was also the one time of day when Tristan was allowed to speak without asking permission. He was expected to speak, in fact, and to ask questions.

"The ideal mission," Tonaso said once, "is the one in which a team enters its target area, accomplishes its objective, and departs without ever being observed, allowing the enemy to see nothing. Contact is to be avoided at all times because it reveals your destination and purpose, increases the chances of taking casualties, and reduces your chances for successful mission completion. Stopping to fight slows your progress. And yet, if you should be detected and attacked, your response must be reflexive and perfect. There are no second-place winners in combat."

Another time he emphasized, "Your task is to help your team accomplish the mission, no more and no less. Above all, you must not be a liability. You must learn to think the way the other team members think and to act as they act. There is no room for independent action on a mission—unless the others' lives are in immediate danger or you are the only team member still living."

Sometimes he would stop in midsentence, making a quick cutoff motion with one hand, and demand in a whisper, "What is it, where is it, and how long has it been there?"

"It's over there," Tristan said the first time Tonaso did that, and pointed off to his left, "just outside the wall. It's been there about two minutes."

Tonaso's eyebrows raised ever so slightly, his only manifestation of surprise. "And how do you know that, *yatsu*?"

"I heard the jungle noises go quiet," Tristan said.

Tonaso nodded, approving. "Where did you learn to listen that way?"

"On Ganwold, *ishku*," Tristan said. "My gan brother, Pulou, taught me that while he was teaching me to hunt."

"In the field, that could save your life," said Tonaso. "On a mission, as in hunting, you must be constantly aware of your surroundings. A change—a sudden silence in the forest, for example—could mean the approach of an enemy. You must always divide your attention between what you're doing and the background noises around you."

It took a while to learn to pinpoint distance as well as direction, but Tristan was never caught off guard. One evening a flurry of wings above the courtyard wall caught his eye, a flurry followed by stillness. He cut off Tonaso with a hand motion of his own. "Birds just flew up," he whispered. "It's probably a Cormor's constrictor."

He didn't miss his instructor's suggestion of a smile.

There were other skills, too: use and handling of energy rifles, explosives, and specialized weapons; fundamentals of electronic communications systems and sensors; specialized languages and hand signals; team responsibilities and procedures; and emergency field medicine. "This training isn't enough to make you an expert in any of these fields," Tonaso told him. "We don't have enough time for that. But you need to be able to step in and assist should that ever become necessary."

Tonaso's regimen never followed the same schedule from one day to the next. Sometimes the day began with the endurance run, sometimes it ended that way. Calisthenics and combat drills, instruction and daily chores were never accomplished in any set order. Some days were spent outside the compound walls, some days they never left at all, and sometimes they came and went from one task to another. Meals didn't come at regular intervals, either; sometimes they ate only once or twice in a day. Even rising and retiring times were shifted, so that sometimes a full day's training was conducted at night and dawn was approaching when they withdrew to their cells.

"Why do we do everything in a different order each day?" Tristan asked once over supper.

"When you were a hunter on Ganwold," said Tonaso, "how did you know where to find the game?"

Tristan thought for a moment about scouting the peimu herds. "We watched them," he said, "until we knew where they went for water, and when, and where they sheltered at night—" He cut himself off, startled with a sudden understanding.

Tonaso gave a single slow nod. "Their behavior was predictable. *You* must never become predictable to the enemy who may be stalking you."

Never be predictable. The words echoed at the back of Tristan's mind through the rest of that training day. Later, crouched in the dark of the empty cell next to his own, he locked his teeth, annoyed with himself for having been so predictable for so long. He wouldn't be predictable tonight, he vowed. He'd never be predictable again!

He strained to pick up any indications of movement within the courtyard but heard only the trill of the insects in the trees outside the compound. Heard the eerie cry of a spherzah on the wing, the nocturnal hunter from which the special-operations force had taken its name. A shiver raced up his spine.

Over the last three and a half months—had it been that long already?—Tonaso had lengthened his sixteen-hour training day to seventeen hours, and then to eighteen. Though his body no longer ached as it had at the beginning, Tristan knew he should be exhausted. But he wasn't. Knew he should be sleeping. But he couldn't. Not tonight. It was too hot to sleep. Too sticky. And he was too taut with anticipation.

The moon slipped over its zenith, began to sink toward the horizon. Tristan silently shifted in his crouch, easing his legs. And then he froze, aware without sound or sight that someone was coming.

A shadow moved past his doorway: Tonaso, armed with the crimson cloth that marked his "death" whenever he wasn't vigilant. Tristan rose in one fluid motion and waited.

Tonaso was halfway into Tristan's usual cell when he stopped and suddenly twisted around, already in a combat stance, as if he were expecting an attack.

He stood motionless for a moment, searching his surroundings. Then, silent as a shadow, he checked the next cell down, two cells down from the one where Tristan waited.

Tristan got a glimpse of his face in the moonlight when he emerged from that cell. It was a mask of concentration, and something about his eyes told Tristan that he knew he was being watched. Tristan held his breath, trying to flatten himself right into the wall as Tonaso turned toward his hiding place.

When Tonaso's shadow fell across the threshold, Tristan grabbed him in a shoulder throw.

The next several seconds were a melee of blows and blocks and holds and throws, which ended only when Tonaso seized Tristan by the shoulders, hauled him to his feet—and slammed him backward into the wall.

It was like taking a fall. Tristan tucked his head and broke the impact with a slap of out-flung arms, as Tonaso had taught him to do.

His feet dangled, toes just off the floor. Tonaso pinned him there, suspended, leaning into him so hard that Tristan couldn't even knee him in the groin. Tonaso's teeth were clenched, his chest heaving; his eyes fixed Tristan's with a murderous fire.

Tristan glared back, his own teeth gritted against the realization that he was helpless.

Tonaso held him eye to eye for several heartbeats. Then his scowl broke. He chuckled. Let go of Tristan's shoulders and let him slide down the wall. As Tristan stared, still catching his breath, Tonaso caught up the banner of crimson cloth. "Not bad, *yatsu*," he said, wrapping the cloth around his hand; and he turned on his heel and left the cell.

NINETEEN

"**I think Foros is up to something, sir,**" said Tech Sergeant Tradoc. He jerked a thumb over his shoulder. "Looks like he's got half the people in the cell block gathered around him over there."

"Any idea what it's about?" Ochakas asked.

"No, sir," said Tradoc, "but it doesn't look good."

"Well, then." Ochakas glanced around at his staff. "Maybe we'd better see what's going on."

He tugged at his pants as he gained his feet. The scant rations of the past several months had reduced his girth by half, so that his belt gathered his pants' waistband like the mouth of a drawstring bag. His salt-and-pepper beard touched his chest and in the back his hair hung to his shoulders, but somehow he had managed to retain his military bearing.

Tradoc's estimation hadn't been an exaggeration. Besides Foros's usual gang of convicts, the group seated around him included a large number of citizen captives. Mostly young people, Ochakas saw, but he spotted two or three middle-aged corporate types in the gathering, and several of the women with children as well.

Foros looked up, smirking, as Ochakas and his people worked their way toward him through the crowd. "Well, it's the Long Arm of the Martial Law himself," he said. He didn't stand, just tipped his head back to meet Ochakas's look.

" 'Evening, General-sir. Going to take away our right to assemble along with our right to eat?"

"Your right to fight over and steal other people's rations, you mean," said Ochakas. "No one gets any more than you do, Foros. At least everybody *gets* to eat now." He turned slightly to look over the assemblage and said, "I was just curious as to how you've managed to draw such a crowd. It didn't seem very likely to me that you'd taken up evangelism."

Foros laughed at that, but then he said, smiling, "Actually, General-sir, you're not too far off the mark. We were talking about freeing ourselves—our corporeal selves, that is, not our souls."

Ochakas raised a skeptical eyebrow. "How do you intend to do that?"

"Why should I tell you, General?" Foros cocked his head.

"So that I can be assured," said Ochakas, "that you're not going to further endanger the lives of these people with some half-planned action."

Foros seemed about to reply when bootfalls rang along the catwalk overhead. Ochakas cut him off with a motion of his hand and looked up.

A masuk guard paused on the walkway, energy rifle cradled in one arm, a palm light in the other. He played the beam over the gathering, then grunted to himself and strode on.

And Foros shot to his feet and leaned nearly into Ochakas's face. "So you want to offer your strategic expertise?" he said. "No thank you, General. I want to keep this simple." He sneered it. "By the time you finished reworking my plan, it'd take the whole Isselan Space Fleet to carry it off!" He made a grandiose gesture with both arms.

Ochakas ignored the sarcasm. "How much thought have you given to this? Have you ever commanded two thousand people before? That's basically what you'll be doing, you know." When the other hesitated, he asked, "What's your objective?"

"To get back to Issel," said Foros.

"Fine." Ochakas nodded. "Let's go through it one step at a

time, then. How do you plan to get out of here?" He twirled his finger, indicating the mesh enclosure.

"Simple," said Foros. "The next time the guards open the gate, we rush it."

Ochakas opened his mouth, but Foros said, "There are a grand total of ten masuk guards at this site, General—I've been watching them—and there are almost two thousand people in this cage. We outnumber them by about two hundred to one! The next closest mine is over two kilometers away, so it'll take the masuki a few minutes to get reinforcements here, and a few minutes is all we'll need."

Around them, members of Foros's audience were getting to their feet and pressing closer in order to hear. Ochakas glimpsed pale faces at his periphery and over Foros's shoulders. "If you rush the gate," Ochakas said, "the masuki will fire into the crowd—I can promise you that—and a lot of these people will be killed or wounded."

"So we'll lose a few." Foros shrugged. "You have to expect a certain number of casualties in combat, don't you, General?"

"This isn't combat," said Ochakas. "What you're purporting is a liberation operation, and that comes with the inherent objective of getting *everybody* out safely. But I don't see any concern for *everybody* in this, Foros. All I can see is you conning your fellow prisoners into acting as rifle fodder to cover your own escape. That's what rushing the gate would amount to."

"That's—" Foros began.

Ochakas cut him off. "Let's assume for a minute that you do get everybody out of the cell block. What do you plan to do then?"

"Enter the terrarium caves," said Foros.

"You tried that when the containment field first went down," Ochakas said. "We can all see how successful that was. What makes you think it'll be any different this time?"

"This time we're dealing with masuki," said Foros, "not the Sector General's elite security force. They knew the caverns. I doubt the masuki do."

"How well do *you* know them?" asked Ochakas.

"General, I've spent the last fifteen years of my life down here," Foros said. "This isn't the first mine I've worked in. I know my way around."

"Then you know how you'll feed two thousand people while you're traveling through the caves? What about water for them?"

"When we've taken out the guards here," Foros said, "we'll raid the ration stores, take those with us."

"Those will last you two or three days at the most," said Ochakas. "Where are you going to go? How fast and how far do you think two thousand hunger-weakened people can travel?

"What if the masuki send patrols out through the cave system to hunt for you? How long do you think that many people will be able to elude them? How will you conceal a group that size—or, when the pursuers get too close, will you just abandon them and make a run for it?"

Foros brought up clenched fists, but Lieutenant Siador glanced across at the sergeants and they all moved closer, all watching Foros, all ready.

Ochakas looked him in the eye. "Personally, Foros," he said, "I wouldn't trust you to lead me out of a duffle bag."

"Then you can sit here and rot," said Foros. "The rest of us will head for the main shuttle bays. It'll take us three days at the most to reach them."

"And how do you know there will be shuttles in those bays?" Ochakas persisted. "What if there aren't? Do you have an alternate plan? How will you decide who goes and who's left behind if there aren't enough shuttles to evacuate everyone? There won't be any return trips, you know.

"And who will fly the shuttles, Foros? Are you a pilot? Are there *any* pilots in here? Or are you going to commandeer a masuk pilot? Do you know what kind of system defense the masuki are using? What will you do if they pursue? Have you thought about any of those things?"

Foros's fists were knotted again, his eyes flashing. "You're surrendering before you've even fought the battle!" he said, and his words were laced with accusation.

"This isn't surrender," Ochakas said. "This is war-planning. A wise commander doesn't embark on a campaign without taking into account every possible contingency, and frankly, you don't have viable answers for any of the contingencies I've mentioned. A certain amount of risk is unavoidable, but this—particularly with civilian hostages involved—is absolutely mad! A better alternative must be found."

"The only alternative," Foros said, "will be to rot in here until the masuki herd us onto their slave ships and haul us off to the Bacal Belt! I don't consider slavery a viable answer, General! I've spent too much of my life in it already—to people like you! Nothing was ever achieved in this universe without taking risks!"

"But not uncalculated risks," said Ochakas.

Foros snorted. "You're just a coward, General!"

"That may be," Ochakas said, "but you're a fool."

Foros set his jaw, tightened his fists, and Ochakas saw how his staff edged closer again. "I think it should be the people's decision," he said. "After all, they're the ones whose lives you're so willing to risk."

"Fair enough." Foros swept his gaze around the enclosing circle. "All right, then," he said, "what will it be? Do you all want to sit here and rot with the Sector General's chief coward, or do you have enough guts to take a chance on freedom?"

Ochakas looked around the circle, too, and saw hesitation in most of the faces. And doubts. Saw genuine suspicion in some. No one said anything.

Foros stared around at them a moment longer and then threw up his hands. "You're all cowards!" he said. "You'll all rot!"

A masuk shout and the thunder of boots on the catwalk overhead jarred Ochakas out of restless sleep. He shoved himself to a sitting position, flung up an arm to shield his eyes as searchlights suddenly lit up the cavern.

Two of his staff were already on their feet. "What is it?" he asked them.

His question was lost under two quick bursts of rifle fire, a scream, a third shot. He hit the ground—saw his men dive, too.

The shots had been fired from the far end of the catwalk into the rear corner of the cell block. Looking up, he saw three masuk guards shifting about on the walkway, weapons still poised. There were two or three guards on the cave floor outside the cell block as well, moving around near that back corner, and their exchanged remarks, mostly grunted monosyllables, carried through the cavern.

The stench of seared flesh drifted across the cell block. Ochakas nearly gagged on it. He glanced around at the other prisoners.

They were huddled together in the cells or corners where they'd been trying to sleep, every face turned toward the activity, every face turned pale.

The masuki took some time to conclude their search; it was almost an hour before one of them shouted toward the control room on the gantries and waved a hand. The searchlights shut off, leaving the cavern briefly in blackness.

As his eyes readjusted to the near dark, Ochakas reached out for the wire wall of the cell he and his staffers had claimed and pulled himself to his feet. A few moments later, the two who had gone to investigate slipped up to join him. "What was it?" he asked.

"Escape attempt, sir," said Sergeant Tradoc.

"Foros," Ochakas said.

Tradoc nodded. "Probably, sir. I saw him with three or four others right after the last ration dump. Looked like they were having a pretty serious conversation. A couple of 'em were college kids."

"And?" said Ochakas.

"They went under the fence, sir," said Lieutenant Siador, "through the gap back in the latrine area."

There had been a row of latrine stalls in that back corner at one time, but they had been destroyed before Ochakas arrived here, probably during the riot following the containment field's failure. Now there was only an expanding pool of raw sewage.

The fact that the cave floor sloped down and away at the fence line had kept most of the pool outside the cell block. But it had also left an opening at the bottom of the wire mesh, an opening just large enough for a man to crawl under—if he were desperate enough to crawl through three or four meters of human waste as well.

Apparently, Foros and his compatriots had been desperate enough.

"How many dead?" Ochakas asked.

"Two, sir," said Tradoc. "Both college kids. Looks like one of 'em got stuck and the other, who was already out, was trying to pull him through when the masuki got 'em. They just left the bodies there."

"We finished pushing them under the fence, sir," said Siador. His boots were caked, and his trousers were smeared with sewage where he'd wiped his filthied hands.

Ochakas grimaced. "Any sign of Foros?"

"None at all, sir."

He shook his head. "The man's a fool!"

"This is completely unacceptable, Admiral Serege!" Minister Borith, striding swiftly through the corridor, scowled at Lujan over his shoulder. " 'Planetary envelopment' indeed! That's nothing more than a euphemism for putting Issel in a stranglehold!" He shook his head. "We're down to three weeks before the launch window and the closer we come, the more I dislike the whole idea—particularly since we're not hearing anything new in these supposed update briefings. I don't think your people are telling us everything, Admiral. I think they're keeping a great deal to themselves. I'd sooner trust my life to the rabble out there shouting death threats in your streets than I'd trust the protection of my motherworld to you and the rest of your warmongers!"

The cabinet minister's ceaseless stream of protests were growing more worn than his own patience, Lujan thought, but he managed to keep his voice level when he said, "Perhaps I should remind you, Minister, that it was you who came to the Unified Worlds asking for help—the epitome of audacity, in my opinion. I think it's only fair to point out that I don't trust the ulterior motives of your government any more than you trust mine."

"Of *my* government?" Borith flung out his hands. "Admiral, the only motive *my* government has is to prevent Issel from becoming a masuk slave market!"

"Are you sure of that, Minister?" Lujan let his tone turn deadly serious. "If you truly believe that's the only reason for Chief Minister Remarq's sending you here, then you don't know him as well as I do."

Borith stopped short, spun around, stared at him, and a stream of emotions ranging from shock to panic to indignation crossed his face in a handful of heartbeats. "That is an utter outrage, Admiral!" he said at last.

But it wasn't exactly a denial, Lujan observed. His own accusation had been little more than a shot in the dark, based on gut feelings and history, but the cabinet minister's reaction to it confirmed everything he had suspected since the Isselans first arrived. He kept his vision fixed on the other's face until Borith turned and stormed up the corridor.

Rahm Guavis paused in the entry of the Subcellar Lounge in the heart of Ramiscal City and looked across its dim expanse. There were few patrons here this time of the afternoon; he could have taken almost any table with little chance of having his solitude disturbed. But he crossed to the booth in the farthest corner, where he could sit with his back to the wall and watch others come and go without being noticed.

The booth's table was mushroom-shaped, with a round top and a single thick support in the center. Rahm slid onto the bench behind it, drew his ID plate from his jacket's inside pocket, fed it into a slot near the table's edge. The drink list lit up but he didn't bother to look it over; he just tapped the third entry from the bottom. Its display blinked THANK YOU and showed the amount subtracted from his credit account.

Waiting for his drink to arrive, Rahm scanned the lounge again. The holovid above the bar was on, and right now it was filled with shots of the demonstrators in the streets. With a snort of disgust, he leaned forward and punched the patron-assistance button on the table. "Shut down the stinkin' vid, Maury," he said to its condenser mike.

"Rahm! Is that you?" the bartender's voice came back over the table's speaker. "Had enough of the news business for one day, eh?"

"Had enough of the *Issel* business," Rahm growled.

He heard Maury chuckle at that, but across the room the holovid switched to a sports program. "Listen," Maury said through the speaker, "I'll be out in a few minutes. Have a couple on me while you wait. It's been a while, buddy!"

Rahm grunted an acknowledgment and sat back.

His drink arrived a couple of minutes later, through the vacuwaiter in the center of the table. He retrieved it and took a couple of long, slow pulls.

He was well into his third glass before Maury showed up and settled into the booth facing him. Interlacing broad black hands on the tabletop, Maury said, "So what's new, my man? I take it you've been covering all the ruckus out there?"

Rahm gave a single nod. "Lot of useless noise," he said. "Nothing but noise. Nobody in the Tower's even paying attention."

"Their death threats have gotten a few people's attention," said Maury. "So have their bomb threats."

"Yeah, the Security Department's," Rahm said. "Not the Assembly's or the Defense Directorate's." He shook his head. "They haven't stopped the whole business yet—haven't even slowed it down. It's still just noise, and that's all it'll ever be. Some of 'em actually confessed that there were never really any bombs." He shrugged. "They'll never do anything."

He felt the other studying him. "You make it sound as if they should," Maury said.

He lifted his head, looked Maury in the face. "Providing aid and comfort to the enemy is treason," he said, "and there's only one penalty for treason."

Maury shoved himself back in his seat. "Wait a minute! There was a peace treaty a few months back, remember? Issel's *not* the enemy anymore—"

"Maybe not to you," said Rahm, "or to Sostis, or even to the Unified Worlds. But it is to me! Issel still has my mother-world under its heel."

"Na Shiv?" Maury furrowed his brow.

Rahm nodded, took another swallow, fixed his gaze on the bottom of his glass. "When Gov'nor Renier sent his troops in all those years ago, he promised t' rebuild the cities that'd been destroyed in the War of Resistance. He promised protection from Unified aggression, too.

"Well, he rebuilt, a' right. But th' only aggression Na Shiv ever saw was from Isselans. They kept telling us how *grateful* we should be that we weren't livin' like rodents in burned-out cities anymore. But they expected that—gratitude—t' be expressed in certain ways."

Rahm interrupted himself to take another bolstering swallow and let it burn its way down his throat before he went on.

"A couple Isselan officers came into m' mother's accounting firm one evening, jus' as she an' my sister were closin' up. They said they wanted t' make sure th' lease for th' office space was in order. They finished by raping 'em both."

"You never told me that before," said Maury.

Rahm flicked a glance up at him. Ran his hand up and down the ribbed sides of his glass. "I was fifteen," he said. "The only 'man' in th' family. All I could think about was gettin' revenge. Some Isselan soldiers were gonna pay, I didn't care which ones. I started waitin' around outside th' drinkin' halls where they went, an' one night I got real lucky. This guy with silver crescents on 'is shoulders came out by himself, so blitzed he could barely stand up."

He raised his glass again, but it was empty. He shoved it aside, punched the drink-list button for another.

"I offered t' help 'im to 'is shim—skimmer. When we got there, I knocked 'im over the head, tied 'im up, an' pulled out m' street knife—"

Maury moved uneasily in his seat. "I don't think I want to hear this, man."

"I never killed anybody," Rahm said, waving him off with a pale hand. "I jus' made sure he'd never rape anybody else's ma an' sister. I was jus' finishin' with 'im when he woke up an' started screaming."

Maury was shaking his head, his expression a cross between disbelief and horror, and Rahm felt a peculiar kind of satisfaction in that. He swept up his refill when it appeared from the vacuwaiter and said with some smugness, "Turns out th' guy was a full colonel in th' Isselan Planetary Assault Force." He took a long pull from the glass. "I thought they'd jus' vaporize me on sight when they caught me, but they didn't. D'ported me instead. Never even got to say g'bye t' Ma an' Jebbie. Don't know if they even know wha' happened."

Rahm gave an ironic smile and tossed back another swallow. "I came here," he said when he could, "b'cause I knew th' Unified Worlds weren't any friends of Issel."

"Things change," said Maury, shrugging.

Rahm ignored him. Rotated the glass until its contents swished halfway up its sides. "I was on th' news crew that covered th' sealing of th' peace treaty," he said. "I had to stand there an' watch while th' Unified Worlds betrayed my trust, Maury. Not only watch, but record that betrayal for all posh—posterity.

"I spent th' whole ceremony wishin' that that holocorder in m' hands was a weapon. Every time I focused on somebody's face, all I could see was th' red beam of a laser sight between their eyes."

He stopped twirling the glass and looked Maury in the eye. Lowered his voice. "Nex' time it *will* be a weapon," he said. "I can promise you that. This Assistance Agreement is treason, plain an' simple, an' there's only one sentence for traitors."

TWENTY

Dawn was still more than an hour away when they approached the temple compound at the end of their night march. Not even a faint paling of the eastern sky heralded its arrival yet. The trill of crickets and the clickety cadence of drummer beetles still filled the steamy air, their unvaried rhythms offering assurance that all was well. But, following his instructor silently through the trees, Tristan felt his heart accelerate with a sudden sense that something was about to happen.

A few strides ahead of him, Tonaso slipped around the tree that sheltered the temple gate—and abruptly froze. Tristan froze, too.

For several seconds he could see nothing, but then, as he watched around Tonaso's shoulder, a slight movement in the temple courtyard caught his eye. A shadow separated itself from the dark to stand in the open, the silhouette of a man holding empty hands away from his body in a demonstration of nonhostile intent. "Come into the courtyard, *Yatsu* Tonaso," he said, "and tell *Yatsu* Serege to come with you."

Tonaso flashed Tristan a hand signal as he emerged from his concealment, and Tristan, still wary, followed him.

The figure standing in the courtyard was his father.

"It's time," Admiral Serege told Tonaso. "A ship is waiting to take Tristan and me back to Sostis." He paused, then asked, "Is he ready?"

Tonaso looked his chief commander in the eye. "I've taught him all I can in the time we've had," he said. "Whether or not he is ready, *ishku*, is now up to him."

Serege turned to Tristan then. "Son?"

Tristan held his gaze. "I'm ready, sir."

A shuttle was waiting when they reached Dengau Sanctuary at midmorning, but they didn't take it back to Onomichi Station. Admiral Serege set an arcing course around Kaleo instead, crossing the terminus from daylight back to night. Within an hour they were approaching a ship in parking orbit, a long-range courier craft with Unified Worlds markings. Tristan watched as a docking bay slid open in the courier's aft section. Watched as the admiral oriented the shuttle over the bay and lowered it inside with brief bursts of directional thrusters.

A gentle bump, almost a small bounce, confirmed contact with the deck. Admiral Serege pulled back the manual locking lever and said into his pickup, "Flight deck, shuttle locked down in docking bay one."

"Roger that, sir," a voice responded over the speaker. "Bay doors closing. Stand by for pressurization and departure from orbit."

Admiral Serege removed his ear receiver and unfastened his acceleration harness as the bay began to repressurize. "There'll be about fifteen standard hours before we make our first lightskip, Tris," he said. "General Pitesson wants to wait until after that to in-brief you, so you'll have plenty of time to wash up, get something to eat, and get some sleep." He glanced out through the forward viewport when a green light on the docking bay's bulkhead lit up, and pushed himself out of his seat. "Let me show you where your cabin is."

The courier ship was smaller than Tristan remembered Renier's private voyager being. Its main passage was so narrow that his shoulders almost brushed the bulkheads on either side as he moved along it, and the cabin Admiral Serege guided him to seemed barely half the size of his cell on Kaleo.

"My cabin is right across the corridor," the admiral said,

"and the galley and common area are forward." He jerked a thumb in their direction. "Feel free to use them."

"Yes, sir," said Tristan.

He examined the cabin more carefully once his father had gone, starting with the stowage locker beneath the berth. He yanked it open, half expecting someone to be lying in wait for him there. He didn't let his breath out when he found it empty, just stowed his duffle and secured it. Then, flattening himself to the bulkhead, he punched the latch on the panel marked HEAD.

The door swung open, revealing a corner barely big enough to stand in—also empty, except for a toilet and wash-basin. Tristan left the door open.

He spent the next several minutes with one ear to the bulk-head, tapping every panel in the cabin with his knuckles to be sure that none concealed a hollow space. Satisfied at last, he tested the lock on the door—even though he knew he'd never trust it.

Only then did he peel off his sweat-stained clothing and fill the washbasin. But he kept one eye on the reflector the whole time he washed.

They were two days out from Kaleo when Admiral Serege called him to a tiny conference room in the aft part of the ship. Tristan found Generals Pitesson and Choe also seated at the table when he came to the door, and he paused there, stomach suddenly taut under his ribs, until his father motioned him to the seat next to his own.

"General Pitesson will be our operational commander in the Issel system," Serege said, "so I've asked him to in-brief you, Tris. But before he begins, I'm required to tell you that the information you are about to receive is classified Top Secret, as it is part of a Top Secret battle plan. You've been authorized to receive a temporary clearance, which will grant you access to the information essential for the accomplishment of your mission, and which will terminate at the completion of this operation. You must not discuss any aspect of this information with anyone but those of us now in this room, except for your commanding officer and your teammates, and only then within a secured area such as this one. Violation or abuse of this trust is punishable under military law. Is there any part of what I've just said that is unclear to you in any way?"

The implications of the question left Tristan's mouth dry, made his heart rate speed up, but he looked his father in the eye and said, "No, sir."

"Good." The admiral placed a memory pad and stylus in front of him then and said, "Your signature verifies that you understand."

Tristan glanced up once as he took the stylus, and Serege gave him a slight nod. He signed the pad.

General Pitesson took the pad when he finished, slipped it into the flat pouch on his lap, and removed a folder. "I should probably begin, Tristan," he said, "by bringing you up to date on what's been going on over the last few months." He leaned forward, interlocking his hands on the table. "Shortly after you departed for Kaleo, the masuki made another slaving raid against Issel. They've made a total of five raids now, and the number of people abducted has reached about one hundred eighty-three thousand. They're not occupying the planet—the situation seems to be more a state of siege—but Issel isn't in a position to offer any substantial resistance and the masuki are growing bolder, both on the planet and in their operations within Isselan space.

"Further, we've learned that a masuk fleet composed mostly of transport vessels—the type used for shipping slaves—is en route to the Issel system, so timing has become a critical factor. If those people are removed from the Issel system, the chances of recovering them are practically zero. That means our forces will have to initiate the operation before the Assistance Agreement is actually signed.

"Because of that," Pitesson said, "most of the Unified space force created under the Issel Assistance Agreement is already in position in the Issel system, and in another few days the resupply, tender, and hospital ships will also be in place."

"Those two Isselan cabinet ministers would have strokes if they learned that," murmured General Choe with the barest suggestion of a smile.

Pitesson expressed agreement with a slight nod and continued, "By the time we reach Sostis two days from now, the Spherzah ship *UWS Shadow* will be prepared to launch. It's a cloakable troop ship which carries infiltration craft, and it will provide transport to the Issel system for the Ulibari and Anchenko Spherzah detachments, the latter of which you have been assigned to as a civilian scout."

The Anchenko Detachment! Tristan's tension eased somewhat. But Pitesson was removing a drawing from his folder, which he placed on the table before them. Tristan recognized it at once: a map of the terrarium cave system on Issel II, which he'd drawn during the debriefings months before.

"Key to this operation's success will be our ability to seize and control the command post on Issel Two." Pitesson indicated the dot on the map that represented the administrative complex. "There will be two Spherzah teams assigned to that mission. The primary team will be inserted through an abandoned mine complex at one location, and the backup team, to which you're assigned, Tristan, will go in through another." He looked up. "This is where your familiarity with the caverns will come in, as you will have to travel through the cave system to reach the command post."

Tristan shifted forward in his chair. "Sir, those closed mines are sealed off from the rest of the cave system," he said. "They aren't pressurized. They're like—being on the surface."

"We know that," Pitesson said. "That's why you'll all be wearing pressure suits when you infiltrate, and you'll stay in them until you've reached and secured the command post."

Images of caverns as great and craggy as canyons and lined with turquoise lichens rose up in Tristan's memory. The thought of traveling them in a pressure suit made him want to shudder. He suppressed the urge, fixing his full attention on the general.

"Should the primary team encounter difficulties," Pitesson was saying, "it will fall to your team to either cause a diversion, drawing the pressure off of the primaries, or to go on in and take the command post yourselves. That decision will be made by the team leaders if it becomes necessary, but both teams must be prepared for either contingency."

"Yes, sir," Tristan said. And then, "What will we do there?"

"Your part in that mission will be completed when you get there," the general said. "You can lie low and let the rest of the team do its job—unless they need you for an extra hand with something. You should also try to get some rest, because once the space battle is over and Issel Two has been secured, the rescue teams will be sent in."

"Rescue teams?" Tristan furrowed his brow.

"Spherzah intelligence has confirmed that the people who were abducted from Issel are being held at the active mines which surround the command complex," Pitesson said.

"Which ones, sir?" Tristan asked. "There are ninety-three working mines."

"Activity has been observed at all of them," Pitesson said. "Your second mission will be to guide the rescue teams out to them, where they will liberate the hostages and evacuate them to waiting hospital ships." He swept a hand across Tristan's map. "Because of the distances involved and, again, the necessity of traveling through the cave system, we expect this to take several days to accomplish."

Several days in the caves. Tristan's stomach tightened up. "Sir, the working mines all have their own landing bays," he said. "I flew out of one at Malin Point. Why can't the rescue teams go in there?"

"Because we expect that the mines will still be under masuk control and defended against outside attack," the general said. "Breaching sealed bay doors in a spaceborne assault could too easily result in the death of the people we're trying to rescue. With any resistance from the masuki, it would also be very costly in terms of Spherzah lives."

"Oh." Tristan lowered his eyes, feeling foolish, and more

than a little ashamed of his anxiety about the caverns.

But General Pitesson didn't seem to notice. "The masuk factor is our greatest cause for concern with this mission," he said, "because there is no available intelligence on how many there may be at each of the mines, how much they may use the cave system for their own movement from place to place, or even how heavily they may be armed. We expect the situation at each mine to be different.

"Nor do we fully know what to expect when it comes to the hostages themselves. We're anticipating injuries and disease as a result of hunger and poor sanitary conditions, but there may be other problems as well, including psychological ones. There's as much potential for danger there as on the command-post mission, so every team member—yourself included, Tristan—will be heavily armed."

Pitesson looked directly at him then. "While aboard the *Shadow*, you'll also be expected to work closely with the intelligence folks. All they've had to use for mission planning are the sketches you did during your debriefings. Any additional details you can give them on the layout of the mines, conditions in the caves, or how masuki work may mean the difference between success and failure."

Tristan met the general's eyes. Saw the grimness in them and swallowed. "Yes, sir," he said. But the import of the responsibility he had accepted settled like a weight on his chest, so heavy that he could barely breathe.

The weight hadn't lifted by the time he stretched out in his berth, long after the ship's lights had dimmed for the "night" watch. Tristan lay for a long time listening to the regular thrum of the engines, aware of every footfall, of every muffled voice in the passage, despite the echo through his mind of everything General Pitesson had said.

He didn't realize that he'd even fallen asleep until a slight acceleration of the engines' thrumming, a slight shift of the ship's gravity, snapped him back into wakefulness. He listened for a moment. The acceleration was continuing; the ship must be approaching its second lightskip. He reached for the berth's safety webbing, drew it taut over his body and secured it. Then he closed his eyes and focused his whole attention on breathing, on keeping every muscle relaxed.

He was expecting the 'skip siren when it came; he didn't jump, didn't tense. As its pitch rose, as the pressure increased, he concentrated on drawing one breath at a time.

The sensation was like being shoved bodily through a bulkhead. For a moment it robbed him of breath, wrenched at his stomach, but then he was through, lying on his back in the berth with air rushing into his lungs.

He lay still while the siren wound down and stopped echoing through the passage outside his cabin. Lay still while his breathing steadied and the nausea passed and his limbs ceased their shaking. Then he moved cautiously, lifting one hand enough to loosen the safety webbing a little.

He didn't sleep again. General Pitesson's briefing was back, echoing through his mind.

The Issel II cave system.

He'd been sick the last time he'd gone through those caves, just beginning to recover from a flogging that had bruised his kidneys and broken several ribs. He'd barely been able to walk, but his rescuers couldn't allow him to stop—not for very long, at least. They were being pursued.

He turned onto his side at the memory of the ache through his back. His whole body was taut, his palms clammy with cold sweat.

He glanced at the timepanel on the bulkhead. It said 0543, standard time. He sat up, sighing. Sat for some minutes before he could stand. Then he stepped out into the passage and tapped at his father's cabin door.

He knocked once more when there was no response, and then touched the OPEN button and peered inside, calling "Sir?"

Admiral Serege's berth was empty.

Tristan found him standing in the center of the common area in the horseback stance, the microreader he wore suspended from the cord around his neck cradled in his hands.

He looked up from the 'reader when Tristan paused at the hatchway, then he closed it and straightened and moved toward him. "Are you all right, son?"

Tristan sighed. "I don't know, sir." He paused, sighed again, turned his face away. "When you came for me on Kaleo and asked if I was ready, I thought I was. But—" He hesitated. Shrugged. "I keep thinking about everything General Pitesson said yesterday, and—now I don't know if I'm ready or not. I don't feel like I am."

Serege put a hand on his shoulder, gripped it hard. "No one ever feels ready for his first mission, Tris. I certainly didn't. But there's only so much your *ishku* can teach you, only so long that he can drill you, before you have to start applying it. That's where the greatest learning comes."

He paused, then said, "I chose Fathi Tonaso to teach you because I knew he'd drill into you the things you'd need to make it back. I knew he'd do that because I taught him years ago, and I knew that he used my methods in his own teaching."

Tristan stared. "*Your* methods, sir?" He tried to imagine the admiral pitching pebbles at Tonaso, or attacking him in the dark of a latrine, or making him march up a mountainside with an empty belly and an empty canteen and an awkward duffle on his shoulder.

Serege seemed to know what he was thinking; he smiled. "My *ishku* trained me that way, too," he said. "He knew that a little pain goes a long way in impressing Spherzah candidates with the seriousness of what they're undertaking. You've learned the value of vigilance and obedience, and those will do more to insure your safe accomplishment of the mission than anything else Tonaso could've taught you."

That was true, Tristan knew, but—"It's not that, sir," he said. He hesitated, ducking his head. "It's—I don't know if I can—go back through those caves again."

The admiral said nothing to that, and Tristan didn't dare glance up. He swallowed dryness. "I haven't had any nightmares about—killing b'Anar Id Pa'an—for a long time," he said. "For the last few nights they've—been about going back through those caves—where Governor Renier's men hunted us. I—don't know if—I can do it, sir."

The silence stretched on for several seconds after that, until Tristan felt compelled to look up.

His father's features were solemn when he did. His father's hand came back to his shoulder. "Come here, son," he said, and guided Tristan toward the bench that ran the length of the bulkhead. He opened his microreader again as they seated themselves, and said, "I came across a passage in my reading a little while ago that I think might help you." He scrolled the display up once, twice, then said, "Here it is," and began to read:

" 'When you go up to battle in my name and for my cause, I will go with you; I will go before you and behind you. I will be beside you in the dark valleys and on the high mountains and over the great waters. I will be to you as your sword and your shield, for I will protect and defend you. I will make the weak and the humble to be strong and courageous, to do mighty works, for I am mightier than all they who will come against you, and you will triumph in me.' "

"What is that?" Tristan asked when the admiral had finished, and indicated the microreader in his hand.

"It's called *The Law of the Prophets*." His father closed the 'reader carefully. "It's the instructions and promises given by God."

Tristan studied him for a moment, remembering a classmate at Aeire City who had said that all Topawans were religious fanatics. His classmate had made that seem bad, even something to be feared, but Tristan had never found anything fearful in his parents' religion.

"I've heard that before," he said at last. "Mum had a 'reader like that on Ganwold for a while, until there was a flood that washed away a lot of our belongings. She used to read to me when I was small. . . . May I look at it?"

"I'd like you to keep it," his father said. And he removed the cord from about his own neck and put it over Tristan's head. "Read from it every day," he said. "It's as important to strengthen your soul with truth as it is to strengthen your body with exercise."

Tristan scrolled through the text for a few moments, pausing once or twice to read something that caught his eye, until his father said, "There's one more thing I'd like to give you, Tris."

He looked up then. "What's that, sir?"

"My blessing."

The concept was no stranger to him than the passage of scripture had been, though he'd never experienced it before. "I'd like that," he said.

"Listen carefully then," the admiral said, "so you can remember." And he stood, and placed his right hand on Tristan's head, and bowed his own.

"Tristan Lujanic Serege," he said, "in the name of our God and with the authority passed on to me in this same manner by those who came before me, I assure you that you are prepared to accept the mission to which you have been called."

His voice was quiet, as it was when he gave thanks before meals, but it bore an authority that Tristan would only have expected to hear on the bridge of a ship during battle. It sent a shiver through him, like a pulse of pure energy rippling from his head to his feet.

"You've been taught well," his father said, "not only by your instructor on Kaleo but also by your mother and the companions you had during your childhood on Ganwold. Remember and draw on their lessons, too, and I promise you that you will be able to accomplish whatever you may be called upon to do, capable in body, mind, and soul.

"I promise you wisdom to know what actions to take and when to take them, even to guidance at the very moment you need it. Use this only for good, to help your team and those you're being sent to rescue. I promise you that the anxieties which you feel will not overwhelm you or prevent you from carrying out your duties. I promise you that you will not be alone. I, as your father, will be with you in mind and soul; and the One who created this universe, whose literal child you are also, will be with you, to be your defense in times of danger and your peace in times of fear. He above all can be trusted, and I promise you this in His name."

Admiral Serege's voice fell silent; his hand lifted from Tristan's head. Tristan raised his eyes to his father's face.

Serege smiled, extended a hand to draw him to his feet, and wrapped both arms around him in a tight paternal hug. "You'll be all right, son," he said, close to Tristan's ear.

The inner calm that had come with his father's blessing remained until the courier docked at Qarat Military Station. But Tristan's stomach tightened a little as the shuttle dropped toward Sostis, and Ramiscal City came into view between the midwinter snow clouds.

In a few hours he would be aboard another shuttle, leaving Herbrun Field for Shinchang Station and the *Shadow*.

Leaving Sostis for Issel.

He turned away from the viewport with a shudder.

A squad of security personnel and the executive officer from the Anchenko Detachment were waiting when the shuttle touched down. The exec handed Tristan a tan envelope. "Your orders," he said. "We need to get you over to Deployment Processing right away."

"Yes, sir." Tristan's mouth was dry. He glanced over at his father.

"Reg will help you through Deployment Processing and take you to the boarding area," the admiral said. "I have some duties of my own to take care of right now, but your mother and I will be there in time to see you off."

Tristan nodded acknowledgment—it was all he could manage—and followed the lieutenant named Reg.

The next three and a half hours were spent crisscrossing all over Herbrun Field, beginning with the barber who shaved the back and sides of his head and left only a one-centimeter thatch of sand-colored hair on top, "for helmet padding," he said. Then it was on to the quartermaster and supply buildings, where uniforms and weapons and gear were issued and signed for; to the base clinic for a series of immunizations and to turn in snips of his hair to the DNA Identification Office; to Training Certification; to Payroll; to the JAG Office to sign a will; to the Security Office to verify his clearances; and at last to Transportation to confirm his seat on the shuttle and his berth on the *Shadow*. "That's it," Reg said finally, looking over the checklist with its stamps and seals and signatures. He sounded relieved. "You've just got time to change into uniform before we need to head for the boarding gate."

The boarding area was mostly empty when Tristan came in with Reg, but his parents were there, as his father had promised. A wave of self-consciousness washed over him when he knew they'd spotted him, self-consciousness about his shaved head and his awkwardness in his stiff new boots. But Admiral Serege looked proud.

His mother was biting her lip. She'd done that the day she'd seen him off to Kaleo, too, and Tristan remembered her reaction when she'd learned of the Defense Directorate's request for him.

"Where are their heads?" she demanded. "In decaying orbits? Don't they have any idea what Tristan's already been through? How could you even allow them to consider it, Lujan?"

"I told them it would be completely up to Tristan," his father had said, "and that I'd back him up fully, no matter what he decided. He made the decision himself."

"Did you, Tris?" His mother had studied him, anxious. "You didn't let them pressure you into this, did you?"

"No, Mum." He shook his head. "I went outside to think about it, by myself, and I thought about that time we talked about it at dinner. You said that the Isselans were victims, too, remember? But they didn't have any hope of being rescued, and you said you thought we should help them. And I thought about how I felt when I saw—b'Anar Id Pa'an—holding you in the cave, and—I knew that I had to do it."

She'd looked stunned at that, for a moment. She swallowed hard. And then she had wrapped her arms about him and held him tightly and wept.

That had been four months ago. There were no tears today, but Tristan saw that same maternal love, mingled with her fear for him, in her eyes. Still, she managed a smile, looking him over. "Pulou would've been appalled at that haircut!" she said. Then, taking his shorn head between her hands as a gan mother would, she added more quietly, "But he would've approved of why you're doing this."

She studied him silently for another several seconds before she finally slipped her arms around him and pulled him close. "I'm so proud of you, Tris!" she whispered. "I love you so much! Please, please be careful!"

"I will, Mum." It was all he could get out, so he ducked his head to touch his forehead to hers, as gan children did to express their affection.

And then he turned to his father.

"I'm proud of you, too, son," the admiral said, and hugged him. "I always have been. You'll do fine out there."

He couldn't keep himself from looking back once as he strode up the boarding ramp.

The only "private" cabins aboard the *Shadow* were in "officer country," where four officers shared each two-meter-by-two-meter space in twelve-hour shifts. The troops were assigned to long open bays with stacked berths and minimal stowage space. The *Shadow* was plainly designed to transport the maximum number of troops and equipment to the war zone.

Tristan's bay, when he found it, was as crowded as a tsigi nest, but filled with the buzz of subdued human voices rather than the buzz of wings. He located his berth, an upper one, by its number on the bulkhead but had to wait until the soldier who had the lower berth finished stowing his gear in order to get to his own locker. That young man, like the others who brushed past him while he waited, fixed him with cold, appraising eyes and then moved away without speaking to him.

He was stuffing folded uniforms into their compartment

when he sensed someone behind him. He turned just as she reached out to touch his arm. "Kersce!" he said.

"Tristan!"

She didn't comment on his haircut; her head was shaved the same way. But it made her green eyes seem larger, Tristan thought, and her smile wider. He studied her for a moment, trying to think of something else to say, but she solved his dilemma for him.

"Walked off any good cliffs lately?"

"You mean rappelling?" He grinned. "Not since I did it with you." He hesitated, then asked, "Have you been on this ship before? How do you find your way around?"

"Easy," she said. "Tell you what, when I get my gear stowed, I'll take you on a tour."

"Fine." Tristan nodded, and watched as she turned away, to learn where her berth was.

He was latching his locker shut when he realized someone else was coming up behind him. There was a tap on his shoulder—a hard tap, not Kersce's touch. He turned around—

—and found himself face-to-face with a stocky lieutenant: towheaded, jut-jawed, with angry eyes. SLADSKY, his name patch said. The one who had set speed records at rappelling, Tristan remembered.

"Tristan Serege," Sladsky said.

Tristan held his ground. "Yes sir."

"Civilian scout." Sladsky sneered it.

"Yes sir," said Tristan.

"I don't have any use for any civilian," said Sladsky. He paused to lean close, and Tristan heard sudden silence up and down the bunking bay. He could feel everyone's eyes on them—no, on *him*. Could almost feel them holding their breath as they listened.

"I know who you are," Sladsky said in his face, "and I know where you've come from. I've heard about your nightmares and your flashbacks, and I don't want you on my team. I think you're a walking liability. But the big guys say I have to take you, so I have to take you—but you won't get any chances to screw up my mission. The first time you do *anything* that puts it or the lives of my team in jeopardy—the first time you do so much as *twitch*—you're dead, kid. Doesn't make any difference to me who your old man is; if you threaten our mission or my team's lives, I'll kill you myself, do you hear me?"

Tristan didn't let his gaze waver from those slate-blue eyes, though he felt half a hundred gazes fixed on his own. He snapped out, "Yes sir."

"What was that, Serege?" Sladsky leaned closer still. "I couldn't hear you!"

"Yes *sir!*" Tristan said again.

Sladsky said, "Hmph," and turned around and strode away, and Tristan stood still in the silence of the others' stares.

TWENTY–ONE

Tristan was setting his dinner tray down on the long chow-hall table when the call came over the address system: "Now hear this! Now hear this! Edelgard and Sladsky teams, you will don full combat gear and report for your premission briefing in twenty minutes. I say again, Edelgard and Sladsky teams, you have twenty minutes to don full combat gear and report for your premission briefing."

Tristan froze, still on his feet, and looked across at his team leader.

Sladsky, his first bite halfway to his mouth, shot a swift glance around at his team as he set down his utensil and stood.

They were almost out the door by the time the announcement ended, their dinner trays left untouched on the table and the eyes of everyone else in the room fixed on their backs. Kersce, jogging up the passage beside Tristan, said, "This is it!"

The *Shadow* had reached the beacons marking the border of Issel's planetary space only fifteen hours before. The ship-wide announcement had put everyone on a sort of alert status, had started a mental countdown that didn't have a set end.

That not knowing had been the worst part. It had burdened Tristan with a dread anticipation, had wakened him during his sleep shift with his heart hammering hard against the insides of his ribs. Loping up the passage with his teammates now, he felt an odd sense of relief that the waiting was over.

During its flight out from Sostis, *Shadow*'s Spherzah force of 150 had been split into twelve-hour shifts. At any given time, half of the teams were on sleep shift while the other half prepared for combat. Duty shifts were filled with inspecting and maintaining gear, reviewing the daily intelligence files, and drilling in hand-to-hand combat in the common area, which served as both dojo and chow hall.

Lieutenant Edelgard's people, summoned from their sleep shift, were already unstowing their gear when Sladsky's team entered the suiting area. They dressed in silence, brows drawn together and mouths pressed tight, their full attention given to their preparations.

Reaching his own locker, Tristan stripped off his shipboard uniform, hung it up on its hook. On his chest, under his shirt, lay his father's microreader. He picked up its cord, began to pull it off over his head—

He hesitated.

Left the microreader around his neck.

He pulled the pressure-suit undergarment from his locker, shook it out, tugged it on. It was one piece from hood to feet, made of black-and-gray mottled thermal material. Lacking pockets and patches, except for his name tape, it fit like a bulky second skin, an insurance against extreme temperatures and the pressure suit's chafing. He fastened it up the front and turned to the pressure suit.

Although armored, it wasn't as heavy as he had expected it to be. Still, donning it made him feel that he was climbing into the gutted carcass of some hard-shelled animal. He shoved feet and legs into it first and secured its boots at his insteps and ankles. Then came the urinal attachment, like an external catheter applied through the fly of the thermal suit. With that in place, he pushed his head and shoulders up through the torso until his head emerged through the collar ring for the helmet. He tested life-support and radio lines, tested the drinking tube that drew from four water flasks snapped into the suit under its upper body armor. Finally, he pushed his arms into the sleeves and his hands into the gloves and double-sealed the suit's front.

His equipment vest and backpack were next, but he didn't don those until Lieutenant Sladsky had inspected his suit's seals and connections. Sladsky poked here, tugged there, and gave a stiff nod as he slapped two spare rifle powercells into Tristan's gloved hand. Snatching up his bubble helmet, Tristan followed his teammates up the passage.

Commander Amion and General Pitesson, the latter also clad in a pressure suit, were waiting in the intelligence section when they filed in. Lieutenant Palahotai, the intelligence officer Tristan had worked with over the past two weeks, motioned them up close around a holotable in the center of the compartment. There was barely enough room for them all, even after some shuffling and shifting.

Palahotai waited until the door to the corridor behind them was closed before he said, "This premission briefing is classified Top Secret, everyone." And he swept their suited circle with his gaze as he switched on the holotable.

The image it projected was an enlargement of the Issel II cave-system map Tristan had drawn during his debriefings. "Your orders," Palahotai said, "are to capture and secure the military command post on Issel Two." He touched a marker in the center of the map. "This is vital to the success of the Unified campaign, as it will deny the enemy its use for the command and control of their forces and shift that control, as well as the management of our own forces, to General Pitesson, the Unified Worlds field commander."

Palahotai touched an abandoned mine marker about five kilometers north of the headquarters complex and looked up. "Lieutenant Edelgard, your team will go in here. Your primary mission will be to capture the command post. Lieutenant Sladsky, your team will be responsible for getting General Pitesson there. You'll go in over here." And he pointed to a second abandoned mine marker, eleven kilometers to the southeast.

Both team leaders nodded, and Palahotai touched a cue button at the edge of the table. The cavern system was replaced by a corresponding picture of the moon's surface, from which projected a forest of inverted red cones.

"The cones," said Palahotai, "show coverage by early warning and tracking systems to an altitude of ten kilometers. Both of your ingress routes come through this coverage, so you'll have to go in cloaked. We believe that all antispacecraft weapons in this area are fully operational."

There were a few exchanged glances at that, but the lieutenant touched the cue again. The cone projections vanished, leaving only ragged red circles on the surface where projected bluffs and broken hills blocked the sensors' reach. "This shows the sensor net at surface level," he said. "Your landing sites, here and here"—he touched two untinted areas—"are terrain-masked, so you can uncloak once you're down behind the elevated terrain. The specific coordinates have been entered on your pods' navigation chips.

"Once down, you'll have to shift power from cloaking to your acoustic and magnetic scanners and laser bores, to locate and penetrate the tunnels nearest the surface. We suspect those tunnels may still contain power cables and pipes, which will make them easy for the sensors to find."

"Aren't those tunnels pressurized?" asked Lieutenant Edelgard.

Palahotai looked at Tristan. "You're the resident expert, Tris. What do you know about that?"

Fourteen pairs of eyes fixed on his face. His mouth turned suddenly dry, but he said, "The abandoned mine complexes aren't pressurized; Governor Renier said it'd cost too much. They're sealed off from the caves with triple-shield doors, like air locks."

"So you can get into the cave system without depressurizing everything?" said Sladsky.

Tristan nodded. "Yes sir."

"What about the caves themselves?" asked Edelgard.

Tristan's mouth felt drier still. "They're pressurized," he

said, and gripped the table's edge as he described walls like a canyon's covered with blue lichens. He could almost feel the humid heat produced by the misting system and the floating lights, could almost hear the creak of the plastic grating underfoot. "The governor said they were trying to grow edible plants in some of the side caves," he finished.

General Pitesson and Commander Amion exchanged glances at that. "Sounds like he was preparing for a siege," said Pitesson.

More questions followed, about maintenance tunnels and shield doors and alarm systems, and Tristan told them everything he knew.

"What about getting into the command post?" asked Edelgard.

Lieutenant Palahotai touched the cue, filling the holotable with a cutaway view of the headquarters complex, and Tristan leaned over it, pointing. "The command post is here, at the end of this hallway. You can get into it from the emergency stairs, here; they go down to the tunnels. At the other end of the hall, down by Communications and Operations Planning, is the main lift. That goes down to the tunnels, too, but the masuki probably use it. I don't know if they know about the emergency stairs."

"Where are there shield doors?" asked Sladsky.

"At every door that opens into the lift or stairs," Tristan said. "That's how Nemec kept the governor's security men from coming after us when we escaped down these stairs over here; he sealed the doors on every level." He tapped a stairway shaft on the far side of the display.

"Nemec?" Commander Amion looked up at him. "Do you mean Lieutenant Commander Ajimir Nemec, Tristan?"

"Yes, sir," Tristan said—and saw that everyone was eyeing him again. He swallowed. "I think—he's dead. A shield door came down—out at Malin Point mine—when we were trying to get to the shuttles, and—it trapped him inside the passage."

"He's still listed as missing," Amion said. He hesitated for a moment. Then he motioned with one hand and said, "Go on about the shield doors."

Tristan pointed out their locations, every one that he could remember. "They seal by themselves in an emergency," he said, "but they have manual triggers as well."

Lieutenant Edelgard nodded, studying the map. "Good."

And Lieutenant Palahotai went on with his briefing. "You will remain in your pressure suits until you're set up in the CP," he said, "to insure against accidental depressurization, poison gases or lack of oxygen in the mines, or use of gas by the masuki.

"All team-to-team communications while in the caves will be encrypted and will utilize frequency hopping, but keep your comms down to the minimum necessary to coordinate your attack. Your teams' call signs are Blade One and Blade Two.

"You'll use concussion grenades when you go in; it'll probably take two or three for an area the size of the CP. They'll give you about three seconds to clean house. All masuki are to be eliminated; any humans still in there are POWs. Got that?" Palahotai looked around the circle.

Everyone nodded, and he said, "Once the CP is cleared, the computer programmers will go to work. You people have two tasks: Establish comms with both our fleet and the enemy's, and reconfigure all the Isselan ships' firing solutions. Within planetary space, their weapon systems are capable of being overridden and controlled from the CP—one of Renier's insurances against a military coup, I suspect." He shot a tight smile around the circle and touched the holotable's cue, replacing the map with a chart. "Here are the specified frequencies and enable codes. When you finish with the computer programming, you'll turn the show over to General Pitesson. He'll take it from there."

There was another nod, and Palahotai said, "You should expect to be sealed into the command post for two to three standard days, but you've got provisions for five, just in case. Once the space battle is over, the next wave of Spherzah will go in to mop up and secure the rest of the headquarters complex. At the same time, communications will be opened with the government on Issel and arrangements made for the repatriation of its people. Those of you who will be involved in the actual rescues from the mines will receive another detailed briefing before beginning that operation. Are there any questions?''

There were a few, which Palahotai answered before they filed out into the corridor and headed toward the launch deck.

The infiltration pods, designed to carry six-member teams in full combat gear, lay snugged into two long rows of launch tubes in the *Shadow*'s ventral hull. In order to squeeze seven troops into a pod, backpacks and equipment vests had to be removed and stowed under acceleration benches. Except for Sladsky in the pilot's position, communicating with Launch Control in clipped sentences, everyone stowed their gear and secured their helmets and buckled in without speaking. Tristan noted their narrowed eyes and taut jaws as he fastened his own straps.

Next to Sladsky in the copilot's position was Chief Petty Officer Caddesi. At thirty-eight standard years, he was old for an operative; he'd been a Spherzah almost as long as Tristan had been alive. Then there was Neveshir Shankil, the team's computer-programming and communications specialist, as black as she was brilliant; and Piro Espino, the explosives technician from Yan who was better known as Pyro; and General Pitesson, no more a Spherzah than Tristan but a veteran of the War of Resistance; and Kersce, the sensors operator, her features set in a way Tristan had never seen before.

"Four seconds to launch!" Sladsky's voice came through Tristan's earphones. ". . . Three . . . two . . . one . . ."

The launch shoved him back into his bench, robbed him of breath. He clenched his teeth, closed his eyes until the pressure eased. Then he looked forward, through the cockpit canopy.

The view was slightly fuzzy—the effect of being under cloaking, Tristan knew—but there was no mistaking the orb that hung before them. Half of its surface lay hidden in nighttime shadow, the rest was shrouded with swirls of clouds.

Issel.

It had been a year and a half since he'd first seen that world, but the memories it conjured hadn't faded. He shuddered.

The flight was almost seven standard hours. They passed mostly in silence, everyone absorbed with his or her own private thoughts.

As they circled the planet on approach to Issel II, Caddesi finally said, "Traffic monitor shows a large number of ships in the vicinity of the moon. Got about thirty of them right now."

"Target practice for the Unified fleet," said Sladsky.

In another few minutes the nearest ships became visible, cast into silhouette against the moon. "That's an Isselan spacecraft carrier," said General Pitesson. "Probably the *Adamaman*."

They eyed it in silence until Sladsky said, "Initiating approach and landing program. Keep an eye on that warning receiver, copilot. We're entering the early warning net . . . now."

The pod settled steadily toward Issel II, dropping until red lights flashing at the tops of towers and the metallic domes of shuttle bays stood out against the dark rock of the surface. The warning receiver showed only a routine scan pattern by enemy systems, but Tristan's stomach clenched up anyway.

The pod banked around and braking thrusters fired. It slid over the surface as its momentum ebbed, until a final firing of thrusters brought it to rest in the shadow of a small butte.

Sladsky shut down the engines. Waited for their thermal signature to be decreased by cooling before he shut off cloaking, too. Everyone eyed the warning receiver, but it didn't give so much as a blip. "Power over to scanners," Sladsky said at last. "What've we got, Sensors?"

Kersce's scanners revealed a tunnel intersection fifty meters below the surface, barely twelve meters west of the pod. A high-power laser bore, pulled from an equipment hold in the outer hull, made short work of creating a vertical shaft. "Best way down will be by rappel," said Sladsky, standing on its rim. "There're ropes in the packs. Let's get our gear out of the pod and get moving."

They anchored the lines around a boulder, clipped carabiners into rings on their pressure suits. "I'll go in first," Sladsky said, "then you, scout." He jabbed a gloved finger toward Tristan. "You'll do your looking around while the rest lower the gear and get down there. Cad, you bring up the rear."

Caddesi nodded, and Sladsky flicked on his helmet light.

Watching as the lieutenant disappeared down the shaft, Tristan felt a sudden chill. He'd climbed down a manhole on Issel II before. That one had had metal rungs, not ropes, and bearing part of his weight with his arms had shot pain like lightning bolts through fractured ribs and tortured muscles. Halfway down, his foot had slipped and—

He started at the light flashing back up the hole, at Sladsky's voice sharp in his earphones: "Off rappel! Come on, scout!"

"Just like Lost Prospector Canyon!" Kersce said, grinning at him as she snapped the lines into his carabiners.

It wasn't like the canyon at all. The shaft was too close to lean back into the harness, so the start would have to be executed in a crouch with a couple of short steps. Then it would be straight down the rope. Inside his gloves, Tristan's hands were slick with sweat. He took his lower lip in his teeth as he backed up to the edge.

Something slapped softly against his chest.

His father's microreader.

Words from one frame glowed within his mind, as if across a screen before his eyes: *I will go with you; I will go before you and behind you. I will be beside you in the dark valleys.*

And, *He will be with you,* his father had said in his blessing, *to be your defense in times of danger and your peace in times of fear.*

He was over the lip. He let out his breath. Let back his braking hand on the rope.

Thirty seconds later his boots touched the bottom.

"Off rappel!" he said, and turned toward Sladsky.

The lieutenant eyed him, fists planted on his hips. "What took you so long? Stop for lunch?"

"No sir," Tristan said.

Sladsky snorted. "I need to know three things, scout: any indications that we've been detected, confirmation that this is the right location, and whether or not we can get into the cave system from here."

"Yes sir." Tristan reached up to switch on his own helmet light, played it over gray walls and low ceiling.

There were markings on the walls where the tunnels met, done in fading glowpaint. He brushed the layered dust away, tracing the characters with a gloved finger until he could make out the words. "This is the right place," he said, and read the markings to Sladsky:

← SHUTTLE LEVEL
← UTILITY PLANT E-4
TERRARIUM ACCESS →

Caddesi pulled in the rope when everyone was down, and they all shrugged back into packs and equipment vests and unslung their energy rifles. Tristan glanced at the heading projected in the lower left corner of his faceplate like a head-up display. Two hundred seventy-eight degrees. "This way," he said, and set off down the tunnel at a fast jog.

The tunnel sloped steeply down, made a switchback turn after half a kilometer, and they found themselves facing a shield door. It had no manual controls on their side, just the pressure sensor that would trigger the door in an emergency. "It has an alarm, too," Tristan said. "All the shield doors near the surface do."

"It's probably tied into the automatic trigger," said Kersce, "so any pressure fluctuation sufficient to fire the door would set off the alarm as well." She reached for a front pocket in her equipment vest and produced a plastic case no larger than a microreader. It contained needle-nose pliers, neat coils of wire, and a small powered screwdriver.

Pressure-suit gloves notwithstanding, she had the cover off the sensor in seconds. She eyed its components and nodded. "There's the alarm." She traded screwdriver for pliers. A couple of quick tugs at two wires disconnected it. "Now the door . . ."

The rest took up cover positions as she went to work, their helmet lights off, their energy rifles leveled.

Silent in its vacuum, the shield door slid open. Slowly. Ponderously.

It revealed only an empty space, like an air lock, with a second shield door on the far side. When the first door closed behind them, Kersce hot-wired the second one, too, then equalized the pressure in the air lock with that of the tunnel beyond.

The third shield door had a manual trigger. Kersce tugged, but its metal seemed welded shut by years of disuse. Sladsky tried it himself. Nothing budged. So, signaling the team to take cover, he took two running steps and leaped, slamming the trigger with a swift karate kick.

The shield door shrieked open, a scream of steel against steel that rang for several seconds afterward.

They froze, waiting, watching from the blackness of the air lock. Crouched behind his rifle, Tristan realized that his jaw ached, his teeth were locked so hard.

Nothing moved in the tunnel beyond. Kersce slipped around the door frame, lifeform sensor in one hand, rifle set to fire in the other. After several moments, she beckoned.

The tunnel went on for another kilometer, slanting down the whole way, before it opened into the cavern. Weapons still poised, they emerged warily, blinking at the sudden brightness in that moment before their faceplates darkened. Mist shrouded the boulders and floor and curled around their boots, and Tristan wrinkled his nose, remembering its musty odor. He couldn't smell it this time; his pressure suit blocked it out.

He checked the atmosphere and pressure readings at the right periphery of his faceplate, checked the heading at its left.

He was motioning the others to follow when a voice crackled in his headset:

"Blade One to Blade Two, we've got quite a bit of business around here—about four hundred customers. Think you could open up a new attraction at your end?"

"Coming right up," Sladsky said. He turned to Tristan. "What's the closest mine complex and how far away is it?"

"Thrax Port is closest. It's two kilometers from here." Tristan pointed. "This way."

"All right. What would it take to shut down the power in the complex?"

"There are generators in the utility plants," Tristan said. "You get to them through the maintenance tunnels."

"Good," Sladsky said. "Let's go."

They covered the distance, at a jog, in a quarter of an hour, and found the tunnel access to Thrax Port mine where the plastic walkway led into a side cave. The shield door had a cipher lock, but Kersce pulled out her hot-wire kit again.

"The new combination is forty-two fifty-eight," she said when she finished. "Just don't tell any pursuers!"

"Got it." Sladsky glanced around. "Scout and Pyro, you're with me. The rest of you wait here with General Pitesson." He nodded at the field commander.

The access beyond the shield door was a stairwell. Tristan eyed its metal steps and swallowed, remembering the stairs he'd made his way down months before. Every step had sent pain through his right side, had left him shaking. He resisted the urge to rub where the ache had been. Let his hand brush across his chest instead, where the microreader lay under his pressure suit.

I will be beside you on the high mountains. . . .

"Well, scout?" he heard.

He looked at Sladsky. "The stairs will be noisy," he said, "and there'll be another shield door at the top."

"We can fix the door," said Sladsky. "And we'll take the stairs real easy. Let's move."

Stalking skill and boot soles designed to silence footfalls

cut out most of the metal stairs' ring. The rest was lost under the throb of compressors. Audible even at the bottom of the stairwell, the mechanical pulse crescendoed as they climbed, until the stairwell seemed to echo with it. By the time they reached the platform at the door, they could hear the shriek and whoosh of ancient valves as well.

The door had a manual control. Tristan and Espino crouched, rifles ready, as Sladsky punched the trigger.

The shield door shrieked open. . . .

A shape at the desk in the dim room beyond leaped to his feet, twisting toward them—

—and two bright bursts of energy slammed him backward into the wall. He slumped to the floor and lay still.

Tristan swallowed hard.

The office had an open doorway opposite, into a passage, and a closed one to the left marked UTILITY PLANT L-7.

"Scout, watch the passage!" said Sladsky. "Pyro, over here!" He jerked a thumb at the utility plant.

"That's alarmed!" Tristan warned, flattening himself to the wall by the passage door.

Sladsky pulled a sensor from his web belt, ran it around the door frame. "Yeah, it is." He played the sensor over the wall, back and forth. Paused two meters away from the door. "Lots of power conduits and pipes, but I'm reading a clear space right here. We'll just cut our own door." Clipping the sensor to his belt, he swung his rifle down, adjusted its setting. "Put it on continuous burn-through, Pyro. Cut across the top and down the left; I'll do the right side and bottom."

They hadn't quite finished when a shadow blocked the dull light at the end of the passage.

"Somebody's coming!" said Tristan.

Sladsky's response through his headset was almost a hiss. "If he comes in here or detects us, scout, take him out!"

The shape strode up the passage. Tristan pressed himself back, willing the unyielding wall to conceal him. Silently, he swung his rifle around. . . .

The masuk paused outside the doorway. Stood there for

the space of several heartbeats, so close that Tristan could see his nose wrinkle as he sniffed.

Tristan held his breath. Curled his finger around the rifle's trigger.

The masuk drew his lips back from his teeth—but then he strode on up the passage. Tristan let his breath out in a rush.

He glanced around once, for a moment, at the sound of his teammates' grunting and panting. Saw them shoving aside the stone block they'd cut out, saw Espino bending down to duck through the hole. Turning back to his post, he heard Sladsky say, "Don't take out life support; they're holding humans here, remember. All we want to do is turn off the lights, maybe give 'em a few fireworks. Make it look like a massive short circuit or something."

When he glanced back again, Espino was gone and Sladsky was crouched near the hole.

And there were voices coming back down the passage. Loud masuk voices, rising over the thunk and the scream of compressors. Tristan put his back to the wall again, signaled to Sladsky. The lieutenant froze, rifle leveled.

They stopped outside the office: the masuk who had come up the corridor earlier and three more for backup. Those three stepped inside. One crossed at once to the corpse behind the desk and dropped down on his haunches.

Tristan watched, barely breathing, as the masuk searched his dead cohort. When his hand found the burn wounds, he stiffened, wrenched around—

Sladsky's shot caught him in the midsection, hurled him backward. The other two wheeled, pulling knives from their belts. Tristan held down his trigger, sprayed them both with his fire—and then twisted, rifle barrel swinging up, when the fourth masuk sprang through the door.

Red energy ripped through his chest, sent him crashing down over the others, but his bellow reverberated from the walls.

Sladsky swore. "The whole mine probably heard that! Finish it up, Pyro! Get moving!"

Gloved hands appeared at the lip of the hole; a helmet emerged, scratched and dusty.

Bootfalls rumbled like thunder in the passage, rolling closer.

"Help him out, scout!" Sladsky shouted, taking his place at the door.

Tristan reached for rings on Espino's shoulders and pulled. Espino's backpack jammed against the hole's upper rim. Tristan pushed him down onto his chest so his pack cleared, and Espino shoved himself free.

"Move! Move!" Sladsky waved them toward the stairwell's shield door with his rifle barrel.

They dove through. Crouched down, one on each side. Both fixed rifle sights on the door to the passage.

Sladsky leaped headlong for the shield door as the first masuk barreled in, shooting. The shots went wild, bursting on door frame and wall. One seared past Tristan's ear, another nearly creased his left side. Teeth clenched, he fired back, covering Sladsky.

He didn't see Espino suddenly slump back against the stair rail, just heard his strangled scream through his own earphones. Heard him start to gulp and gasp as if his air had been abruptly cut off. "Pyro?" Tristan said.

Sladsky rolled through the shield door; Tristan put a bolt through its control box. The door slammed down, sealing them off from their pursuers, shaking the stair platform.

"Pyro!" Sladsky said. Coming up on his knees, he lunged for his teammate.

Espino sagged against the rail, his torso heaving, his black eyes wide with shock behind his helmet's faceplate. He coughed every time he exhaled, spraying the inside of the faceplate with the frothy blood that burbled from his nose and mouth. Each desperate effort to draw one more breath was accompanied by a rattle. The noise of it raked through Tristan's headset.

A moment's search revealed the bolt's entry point. Blackened slag marked the left side of Espino's pressure suit, where the armored plates met. A chance bolt had found the chink there, had penetrated his rib cage. Blood bubbled from the wound, too, with every breath.

Tristan had seen an injury like this once before: a gan hunter caught through the ribs by a peimu's horn. His mother had taught him after that how to seal a sucking chest wound, how to keep the victim's lung from collapsing. But he'd never actually had to do it.

He had to try now. "Put him on his left side!" he said, shouldering Sladsky away. "That way gravity can help him breathe." He turned Espino over as he spoke, and told Sladsky, "Start opening up his suit. We have to get to the wound!"

Espino's olive skin was already darkening from oxygen deficiency, and his eyes showed confusion and fear. They locked on Tristan's, pain-filled and pleading, as Tristan straightened.

He swallowed hard. Fumbled his medkit from its pouch in his equipment vest. "Keep breathing, Pyro!" he whispered. "Just keep breathing! I know what to do. Just hold on!"

Sladsky opened the pressure suit's outer seal the whole length of Espino's torso. He groped with heavy, quivering gloves for the inner seal, panting behind his own faceplate when he had to restrain the other's struggling.

Tristan pulled a gauze pad, ten centimeters square, and a tube of burn salve from his medkit. Awkward in his gloves, he squirted the salve onto the pad, still in its plastic wrap, and smeared it with one finger. It would be enough to make a seal.

As he bent over his teammate once more, Espino's choking gulps gave way to gurgles. His thrashing slackened; his face turned ash gray and his lips purple behind his faceplate. Tristan shook his shoulder. "Keep breathing, Pyro!" he panted. "Keep breathing!"

Espino only shuddered. His body went rigid for a long second, then limp. His eyes fixed.

Tristan swallowed again, dry-mouthed. "He's stopped breathing!"

Sladsky reached into the opened pressure suit, under its collar, and pressed a hand to Espino's carotid artery. "Heart's in fibrillation," he said.

"Start compressions!" Tristan rolled Espino onto his back—felt his own heart racing against his ribs. He realized he was shaking with urgency. Locking his hands together, he centered them on his teammate's chest.

Sladsky gripped his shoulder, pulled him away. "It's too late, scout. Forget it," he said. "There's nothing more we can do. Besides, there isn't time; Edelgard's team is waiting on us." He reached for Tristan's medkit, began to fish through it. "Let's give him some morphesyne so he'll be more comfortable and seal his suit back up. If we succeed at this mission, we'll come back for his body. If we fail, it won't matter."

Tristan forced himself not to look back as they rose a few moments later. Forced himself not to look at the blood on his gloves.

They took each short flight of stairs in three leaps, heedless of their clanging this time. "Blade Two to Blade One," Sladsky called through his headset, "be ready to move on my order!"

"Roger that!" Edelgard answered.

"Do these mines have more than one way into the cave system, scout?" Sladsky asked next.

"Some do," Tristan said.

"What about this one?"

He hesitated, uncertain. "Unknown, sir," he said.

Rejoining the rest of the team, Sladsky said, "We lost Pyro. The masuki know we're here, so let's move it out. Comms, see if you can find a frequency to listen in on."

Neveshir Shankil nodded. "I've been scanning, sir," she said. "Nothing significant while you were gone." She tapped a tiny button on her helmet, over her right ear. Jogging beside her, Tristan saw her wince behind her faceplate, tap the button again several times, furrow her brow. "I'm picking up something new," she said in a moment. "They're sending a squad down through Firnis to hunt us; apparently this one's sealed off."

"Scout," said Sladsky, "where's this Firnis mine complex?"

Tristan swallowed. "Right where we're heading, sir. About a kilometer and a half up ahead."

"Getting close, sir," Shankil said after some minutes.

Sladsky looked around, pointed at a side cave off to the left. "In there. If they don't come looking, we let 'em go by. If they do, we take 'em out."

Though not lighted as the main cavern was, the side cave must have had some utilitarian value: Plastic walkway grating had been laid heading into it. That grating revealed no trace of their diversion.

Sladsky led them in for some distance, helmet light on, rifle ready. Led them around a sharp corner and down a short, steep slope—into another lighted chamber.

It was nearly as large as the main cave, but this one wasn't lined with lichens. Its ragged walls were bare brown stone, streaked where water trickled from the ceiling, and its whole length was filled with rows of planters set up on waist-high racks. Fronds and leaves and vines of several kinds spilled over the planters' sides and stretched for the floating lights.

"One of the experimental gardens," said Pitesson softly.

Sladsky looked it over. "This'll be—" he began, but Shankil cut him off:

"They're entering the side cave!"

"Cut the lights, Cad!" Sladsky gestured at a power switch set in the wall above the NCO's head. "Everybody down and against the wall, helmet lights off! Make sure you all know where everyone is and don't move. If they come down this far, they're fair game."

They waited in darkness, pressed up to the walls on either side of the entry. Listened as the crunch of boots on plastic grating drowned out the steady sounds of dripping water.

A palm light played on the wall facing the corner. Swung around it. Shot down its shaft into the chamber.

Tristan locked his teeth. Curled his finger about his rifle trigger.

A brief exchange, mostly in grunts, ensued at the top of the entry. There was a pause. Then the palm light turned away and the boots withdrew up the walkway.

No one seemed to breathe for several seconds. Then Sladsky said, "Comms?"

"They're heading on down the main cavern," said Shankil.

"But they may have posted a guard." Sladsky eased himself off of the wall. "Sensors?"

Kersce slipped her lifeform sensor out of a vest pocket, flicked it on—

—and twisted around, facing the chamber. "Lights up!"

The whole team spun about, rifles leveled; the lights flared up, blue-white.

A man stood between two rows of planters, a man who certainly hadn't been there moments before. He stood with arms open and palms up to show that he was weaponless. He was thin, dirty, bearded, and as dark of skin as the cave had been a heartbeat earlier.

Tristan lowered his rifle. "Nemec!"

"You know who he is, scout?" It was Sladsky, suspicious.

"Yes! Yes, it's Nemec!" Tristan punched the external comms button at his pressure suit's neck and said again, "Nemec? I—I thought you were dead!"

"Tristan?" The man took a cautious step forward, arms still outstretched, eyeing the others' rifles. He saw the patches on their shoulders, too, and said, "With a Spherzah team on Issel Two?" And his eyes, with their dangerous glint, narrowed.

Pitesson, still on internal comms only, said, "Tell him we'll explain later." Then he nodded to Sladsky. "Carry on, Lieutenant."

"Yes sir." Sladsky turned to Tristan. "Until we can confirm who he is and what he's doing here, he's under guard, scout. *Your* guard, got that?"

"Yes sir," said Tristan.

"Good," Sladsky said. "Then let's move."

TWENTY–TWO

"Blade One to Blade Two, where are you?" the question crackled through Tristan's earphones. "It's time for dinner!"

"I'm taking a walk in the park," Sladsky answered, "but I'm heading home right now."

"It's about time!" Tristan heard. "Don't get hit crossing the skimway; the traffic's pretty heavy. You should probably use the bridge."

"Right." Sladsky gave a tight smile behind his faceplate. "Last one home has to put out the dogs!"

Switching back to internal comms, he glanced around at his team. "Everybody get that? Edelgard's in position. There're a lot of masuki in the tunnels, so stay sharp. And we'll have to use the lift."

They all nodded. Tristan's palms were suddenly damp and his mouth dry again. Glancing sideways at Nemec, he said, "Lots of masuki in the tunnels. Stay sharp."

The most concealed way out of the cavern was up through a manhole in a side cave. A manhole with rungs up its side. The same one he'd once fallen down.

He locked his teeth as he reached for the first rung. Heaved himself up.

The microreader slapped against his chest.

I will be with you. . . .

He mouthed the words over and over, with every rung,

until Sladsky thrust a hand down into the hole and caught him by the wrist and pulled him out.

Nine or ten meters away, the cross-tunnel intersected the main one. Tristan dropped to hands and knees and then to his belly, to reduce his silhouette as much as possible when he peered out into the tunnel.

It had dim lights set at regular intervals next to the low ceiling, and its glowpaint was distinct, pointing out the direction to Utility Plant 6 and Terrarium Main Access. But the only cover would be other intersections.

He ducked back, sitting up, at the sudden sound of footfalls from the direction of the lift. "Masuki!" he hissed into his pickup.

Behind him, the others froze around the manhole.

He brought his rifle around as the footfalls came closer. Braced his back against the wall. Took his lower lip between his teeth.

The masuki thundered past the intersection: six or seven of them, heading toward the terrarium access. All were armed with energy rifles.

So, the masuki were still searching the cave system for them.

"Which way from here?" Sladsky asked, coming up behind him.

"Left," Tristan said. "But there isn't much cover—just the intersections—and I think more masuki will be coming down in the lift."

Sladsky nodded acknowledgment. "All right," he told the others, "we'll have to spread out a little. Move from intersection to intersection; that's all the cover there is. Unless you're detected, let any masuki in the tunnel go by. Let's go!"

It was a process of dash and duck, dash and duck. Twice before they got there, the lift disgorged handfuls of masuk troops, and Tristan, shoulder pressed to a side-tunnel wall to shield Nemec behind himself, held his breath as they charged by.

The lift was descending with another load when they

reached it. Sladsky signaled them flat to the walls on either side. "Let them all get clear of the lift," he said, "and then—no survivors."

The lift stopped with a squeak and a bump. Doors hissed open. Boots rang on its metal floor. Tristan, teeth clenched, couched his rifle.

The masuk in charge spotted them when he strode into the tunnel. He swung down his weapon, barked a warning.

The tunnel lit up with crisscrossing red energy. It glanced off of walls, seared into stone, created a pall of bitter smoke. The masuki staggered in the cross fire, shooting blindly at shadows. A wild burst smashed into the wall above Tristan's helmet, sent down a shower of stone chips. He kept shooting until the bellowing ended and the last masuk lay still on the floor.

"Move!" Sladsky said, panting. He waved his team into the lift. "Let's get going!"

Its doors closed. Sladsky punched for the command-post level, and the lift jolted upward.

"Kersce, Cad," Sladsky said, "stand by with the grenades. Scout and Comms, stay back with the general and him." He jerked a thumb at Nemec. Touching the comm button on his helmet, he said, "Blade One, we're crossing the bridge! We'll be at your front door in—ten seconds!"

"Roger!" came the reply.

Braced against side walls, the team raised its rifles.

The lift bounced to a halt; its double doors parted.

The masuk guard in the front office turned, jerked a side arm out of his sash—and dropped it when two energy bursts pierced his chest.

"Go!" Sladsky shouted. "Clean out Operations and Comms! I'm sealing this end!"

They lunged out of the lift. Behind them, the shield door came down with a crash.

An explosion shook the corridor. Two more followed in quick succession, like near misses by lightning; there were flashes and ear-shattering bangs. Tristan, guarding Pitesson and Nemec in the front office, glimpsed more pressure-suited shapes through the smoke: Edelgard's team, bursting in from the emergency stairs. He heard volleys of shots, several shouts, a few masuk roars.

It was over in minutes. As the shooting subsided, Tristan heard through his headset, "That's it for round one. Scout and company, time to come in for dinner!"

By the time he entered the command post, the smoke was already starting to thin and Kersce was testing the internal atmosphere with a small sensor. Two of Edelgard's people worked over a third on the floor: an injury, apparently serious.

"What do we do with these?" asked Caddesi, nudging a hirsute corpse with the toe of his boot.

Sladsky, his armor smudged and carbon-scored, looked around briefly. "Take them down to Operations; we won't be using that. And then seal the door! Scout"—he motioned at Tristan—"give Cad an assist."

They and a couple of Edelgard's team dragged dead masuki down the tiled corridor. Laid them out side by side on the floor. There were twenty-three altogether. Tristan tried not to look at their faces.

Shankil and Edelgard were bent over control banks when he returned to the command post. Both had discarded their pressure suits, freeing their hands to fly over keyboards, dials, switches, and to reach into compact component boxes. Their mouths were pursed, their brows drawn together with concentration.

Then Shankil swiveled round in her chair and tapped at her headset. "General, fire-control computers are programmed and ready," she said, "and comms are now open to the Unified fleet."

"Thank you." Pitesson nodded. "Tie in all Unified fleet attack frequencies and hail the Isselan carrier *Adamaman*."

"Yes sir." There was a pause, and then, "'s'Agat Id Du'ul, captain of the *Adamaman*, is responding, sir."

"Put him on visual," said Pitesson.

The center screen on the command post's far wall crackled

with a wave of static, then cleared. A masuk face, four times larger than life, leered out of it.

Tristan recoiled.

Pitesson did not. "Captain s'Agat Id Du'ul," he said, "I am General Ande Pitesson of Mythos, hailing you from the command post on Issel Two. As field commander of the Unified Worlds fleet, I order you to surrender."

Id Du'ul appeared shocked at first. Then he threw back his head with a roar of laughter. "Surrender to *what*, General? How can you, from a command post on a moon, force *me* to surrender?"

Pitesson looked Id Du'ul directly in the eye. "Unified fleet, uncloak on my order," he said. And then, "Execute!"

With a flicker, the command post's left screen lit up like a midsummer night's sky. But the points of light filling it, enveloping Issel and both of her moons, were not stars.

They were warships.

Id Du'ul's expression changed. He bared his teeth in a snarl. "There is no honor in surrender! We will fight you to the death!" He twisted around in his command chair. "All combat ships into attack formation! Upload penetrator torpedoes and stand by to fire on my mark!"

On the tracking screen at the right, symbols for masuk-controlled Isselan ships moved into position against the Unified task force.

Shankil and Edelgard hunched over the control boards, tracking, recalculating, reprogramming.

On the center screen, Id Du'ul ordered, "Fire!"

Bright blips on the tracking screen showed the masuk ships' weapons firing. Dotted lines traced the torpedoes' flight paths. Tristan watched, breath stopped in his throat, as those flight paths arced away from the targets Id Du'ul had intended and began to converge. . . .

Id Du'ul's own tactical display must have shown the same tracks. A warning siren went off; red lights flashed on the bridge. Id Du'ul leaped to his feet. "This is treachery!" he roared.

The *Adamaman*'s symbol suddenly flared with a hit. And then a second. And a third. Then three more, all together.

The center screen erupted with the bright light of explosions. Its brilliance enveloped the *Adamaman*'s bridge, engulfing Id Du'ul. The screen flickered for a moment, flashed once more—then went blank.

Every gaze in the command post was fixed on it.

"Comms," General Pitesson said across the silence, "hail the Unified fleet. Upload weapon systems and put fire control on active to execute on my order."

"Yes sir," said Shankil.

"Then hail the captain of the masuk second ship." Pitesson's face and voice were impassive, but his eyes, Tristan saw, blazed with controlled fire.

"Captain r'Agmah Si'irit of the battleship *Subedar* is responding, sir," Shankil said after a moment.

"On screen."

Another masuk face appeared where Id Du'ul's had been; Si'irit bared his fangs at the sight of his opponent. "You will not seize our weapons again, human!" he said. "My weapons officers have full control."

Pitesson ignored Si'irit's challenge. "Your ships are surrounded and outnumbered," he said, "but they do not have to be destroyed as your flagship was. I offer you a second chance to surrender."

"Never." Si'irit leaned toward the screen. "I and my people will die before we will surrender."

Pitesson held his gaze for a long moment. "Very well," he said. "Unified fleet, open fire."

Tristan left the command post only when he realized he was swaying where he stood. By then the tracking screen was mostly cleared of masuk-controlled ships; the battle was nearly over. He turned away, reaching out to a console to steady himself.

The communications room up the corridor had been designated as quarters. There was space on the floor to lay sleeping cocoons and a door in back to a latrine.

Nemec, stretched out on a mat at one side, turned his head when Tristan came in.

Tristan saw him but didn't speak. He just shrugged off his backpack and equipment vest, let them thunk to the floor. Fumbled with the seals of his pressure suit.

He crawled out of the pressure suit's torso, removed the urinal attachment, sat down to shove the suit off of his legs.

He started at the sight of the sear marks on the suit: one along the right shoulder, another across the left hip. The firefight at the utility plant, he knew. He thought of Espino— could see his wide eyes again in his mind—and swallowed. Thought how easily it could have been himself.

I will be to you as your sword and your shield, he suddenly heard over the tumult of his thoughts. *I will protect and defend you.*

He touched the microreader on his chest, beneath his thermal suit. He could almost feel his father's hand upon his head. He released a shaky breath.

He needed to eat. He'd lost track of the hours since he'd set down that tray on the table on *Shadow*—the meal he hadn't gotten to eat. He reached for his backpack, for the pouch where the ration packs were. Pulled one out. Then, feeling Nemec still watching, he pulled out another and asked, "Want something to eat?"

"Thanks," Nemec said, sitting up. "After all those months on nothing but green plants grown in caves, even a ration pack sounds good!"

Tristan handed one over. Tore open his own.

Someone's voice in the corridor brought his gaze up. He didn't see who it was going by. Saw only the sealed door facing the comms room. The door to Operations.

Twenty-three dead masuki laid out on the floor.

He'd tried hard not to look at their faces. Had tried harder not to look at their blast wounds.

He turned his face away from the door.

They all burned through his mind like the bright bolts that had killed them: the one at the desk in the utility plant, the ones who had barreled in after, the ones coming out of the lift. He saw all their shocked faces, all their energy-riddled bodies.

His stomach rolled under his ribs. When he looked down again, he was shaking; the ration pack rattled in his hands. Suddenly weak, he leaned his head back on the wall and closed his eyes.

"It all just caught up with you, didn't it?" said Nemec.

"What?" Tristan opened his eyes.

"All the killing," said Nemec, "and all the close calls—the things you can't think about while the adrenaline is going, while you're doing the job. It all catches up with you afterward."

Tristan studied him for a moment, feeling pale.

"It's all right," Nemec said. "It means you're still human. It's the ones that aren't affected who are cause for concern."

Perhaps that was right, Tristan thought, but knowing it did nothing to stop his hands from shaking or ease the queasiness in his stomach. He closed his eyes again. Swallowed. He was sweating.

And the hardest part of his mission had yet to be done.

TWENTY—THREE

"I'd really like you to attend the ceremony with me tomorrow, Darcie."

The unexpected request brought Darcie's vision up from her dinner plate. "Luj, you know I have that micropathology exam to take within the next five days," she said. "I need time to prepare for it. Besides, I don't have anything appropriate to wear."

Lujan smiled at that. "You're probably the only woman in the galaxy who can say that truthfully. . . . The blue suit you wore to Governor Gisha's dinner would be appropriate."

"Governor Gisha's dinner." The memory of that evening still made Darcie's hand tighten on her utensil.

"That was six or seven months ago and you haven't worn it since," Lujan pointed out. "Of course, there's still time to order something new if you'd prefer."

She shook her head. "I'd really prefer not to go. It isn't a matter of what to wear as much as it is how uncomfortable I am at these things."

He reached across the table then and laid his hand over hers. "I'm uncomfortable about this one myself," he said. "You know I have been all along. But now the Triune has asked me to stand as one of the witnesses to the sealing. I'd like to have you there to remind me of why it's so important that we go through with this."

The seriousness of his words took her slightly by surprise.

She looked into his face. Saw the gravity in it, the urgency in his eyes. She turned her hand over under his and gave it a small squeeze. "All right," she said quietly. "I'll go."

She wore the suit Lujan had suggested. It was sapphire blue, tailored and refined, with a simple long-sleeved white blouse. And she drew back her hair and fastened it with a clasp so that most of its length cascaded in loose curls down her back.

"You're beautiful," Lujan said when she emerged from their bedroom with her heavy coat over her arm, and he pressed a kiss to the back of her neck as he helped her put it on.

He told her that often enough—sometimes even when she felt anything but beautiful—but the light in his eyes at the moment was almost ardent. She couldn't help smiling. "You're pretty breathtaking yourself!"

He chuckled at that. "I feel pretty pompous in this, actually."

He wore his ceremonial grays. The fabric was so dark it appeared almost black, lending sharp contrast to the silver braid of his rank on the sleeves and the rows of medals on his chest.

A squad of policemen was waiting for them on the rooftop, their own skimmers running, when Lujan's rose on the lift from the parking level. They flanked it like wingmen on a combat mission as the driver banked it around to head down the fjord.

They came in over the city. Looking down as they approached the Unified Worlds Tower, Darcie glimpsed the people in the street at its base: a mass of them with banners and hand flares, pressed together against the bitter midwinter cold and swaying to the rhythm of chants she couldn't hear. The protests had been covered in the newscasts ever since she'd arrived back on Sostis with Lujan, but somehow they had never seemed so massive on the holovid. "My word!" she whispered.

The Ramiscal City Law Department had taken the protests

seriously from the very beginning, she knew. Security had been increased around the Flag Officers' Residential Complex months ago; and ever since the death threats began, no one in the Defense Directorate had been allowed to go anywhere without two or three police escorts. Every bomb and death threat was thoroughly investigated and the perpetrators prosecuted to the full extent of the law.

That knowledge should have been reassuring, Darcie thought; but the very fact that the officials were giving the matter such serious attention was enough to make her wonder if there was more to it than even the media claimed.

The driver set the skimmer down on one of the Tower's upper-level landing pads, and another police squad immediately dashed outside to surround it, all facing outward with energy rifles readied. A doorman with a riot shield reached for Darcie's hatch; he raised the shield to cover her as she stepped out of the skimmer.

The only thing that resembled an attack was a sharp gust of wind and the roar of the protesters' chants, reverberating up between the neighboring buildings until the words were lost in the echoes. But the note of anger in the shouts was clear. Hustled into the building by the man with the shield, Darcie released a breath of relief when the closing doors shut out the noise. She gratefully accepted Lujan's proffered arm.

The chamber where the sealing of the Agreement was to take place lay on a lower level; a lift carried them swiftly down and disgorged them into a lobby milling with people in uniforms and ministerial robes. There were only two entrances into the chamber itself, Darcie noticed, and police guards were already posted at each. Beyond them, people in the blazers of various newsnets could be seen moving about as they set up and tested their equipment.

Darcie had met many of the people in the lobby before, but some were familiar only from their appearances on the newscasts. She bowed, clasped hands, kissed cheeks—whatever was expected under the social customs of each individual to whom Lujan introduced her. Having to remember which greeting was to be used in which instance always left her anxious for such socials to end.

"Admiral Serege," someone said at Lujan's shoulder.

He turned, and Darcie found herself looking into the grave features of a middle-aged black man wearing the robes of an Isselan cabinet member. Lujan said, "Minister Borith."

"I trust that our final amendments were received in time by Document Preparation?" the minister asked.

"Yes," Lujan said. "My executive officer hand-delivered them."

"I've not seen the final document," Borith said. "I will not place my seal on a document that I have not had opportunity to review in its entirety."

"The Agreement will be read from the podium prior to the actual sealing," said Lujan, and Darcie could hear the tautness in his tone. "Your Ambassador Pegaush will read it. You'll have the opportunity then to either accept or reject it."

Borith inclined his head briefly at that, and then arched a sparse brow in Darcie's direction.

"This is my mate, Captain Darcie Dartmuth," Lujan said. "Darcie, Nioro Enn Borith, Issel's minister of planetary defense."

She made a polite nod of acknowledgment, and when Borith excused himself and moved off a few moments later, Lujan caught her eye. He didn't have to say anything; she knew what he was thinking. She had listened to him talk about the minister often enough. Slipping him a slight smile, she said, "I see what you mean about him being distrustful. But I don't think he's the one you need to be concerned about, Luj."

No handbags or ceremonial weapons were permitted past the guards at the chamber doors; such items were identified and shelved. And police troops stood all along the side walls, from the newsnets' gallery in the rear to the platform at the front.

"They're not taking any chances, are they?" Darcie said as Lujan escorted her to her seat.

It was in the fourth row from the front, between the head of Topawa's delegation to the Unified Worlds and Lujan's exec, Captain Jiron. Close enough that she would be able to see the signatories' faces as they burned their seals into the document.

The reading by Ambassador Pegaush took less than five minutes, including the amendments—a surprisingly concise document, Darcie thought, considering that it had taken six months and probably twice that many drafts to make it mutually acceptable. She saw Lujan, seated in the first row, turn his head to speak to Borith, watched as Borith, brows furrowed, listened and then nodded.

"The Agreement for the Provision of Military Assistance to the World Government of Issel by the Unified Worlds will now be sealed," the ambassador said, "certifying it as a legal and binding contract between the aforementioned powers. Signatory for the Unified Worlds will be the Honorable Pite Hanesson of Mythos, member of the Unified Worlds' Triune, witnessed by His Lordship Hampton Istvan, minister of interplanetary relations of Issel. Signatory for the World Government of Issel will be His Lordship Nioro Enn Borith, minister of planetary defense of Issel, witnessed by Fleet Admiral Lujan Ansellic Serege, commander-in-chief of the Unified Worlds' Spherzah Force."

They rose to take their places on the platform as he spoke: Borith and Hanesson seated at its table, Lujan and Istvan standing on either side, a couple of meters away from them. Darcie saw how Lujan swept the chamber with his gaze as he moved to his position, just as he had surveyed the area around the Tower's landing pad before the skimmer touched down, and the crowded lobby before he'd let her step out of the lift. It was a habit ingrained by long years of field experience, she knew, and one that had probably saved his life any number of times. She saw the tautness of his jaw and tried to catch his eye with hers so she could mouth "Relax!" to him, but his vision seemed fixed at the rear of the room.

A page came forward, presented the signatories with laser

styluses from a flat case, and withdrew. A hush settled over the chamber as the signers lifted their hands.

Darcie didn't see or hear whatever it was that happened at the back of the room, but Lujan suddenly shouted, "Get *down!*" and twisted around to lunge for Minister Borith.

There was no flash. No explosion. Not so much as a warning hum. Lujan simply convulsed in his headlong leap, his back arching, his face contorting as if he'd been struck by lightning. Darcie heard the crack as his head hit the table. Saw Hanesson slump forward, and Istvan and Pegaush collapse where they stood.

Before she could even gasp, she was on the floor, too, Jiron's hand hard on her arm. From the back of the chamber came the shout, "For Na Shiv!" and the sounds of a struggle. She raised her head just enough to look toward the platform.

A swarm of police guards was already there, crouched behind the draped table so that only the tops of their heads were visible. Bent over something on the floor.

Darcie wrenched her arm from Jiron's hold—

He pushed at her shoulder. "Stay down!"

She shoved his arm away. "I was a combat surgeon! There're injuries! I've got to get up there!" Struggling to get free of him, scrambling up from hands and knees, she dashed for the platform, staying low.

A policeman moved toward her as she reached the platform steps, his energy rifle held across his body like a barrier. "I was a combat surgeon!" she said again. His white, tense face relaxed a little; he extended a hand, pulled her up onto the platform.

She looked around quickly for Lujan first. Couldn't spot him among the shapes stretched on the floor or the police troops knotted around each of them. Saw only the police captain speaking urgently into his hand radio. Calling for help, she hoped.

And then, "There's no pulse!" she heard, almost at her feet. She looked down, into the unconscious face of Minister Borith and the sweat-beaded one of a young police trooper.

It was like being back on the trauma deck of *Venture* during the War of Resistance. Darcie dropped to her knees and leaned close to Borith's face to listen for breathing, to watch for his chest to rise. She lifted his jaw to open his airway when she heard nothing. The pallor of his gums suggested cyanosis. Sealing her mouth over his, she gave him two long, full breaths and then felt for a carotid pulse.

Nothing. If his heart *was* still beating, it was very weak. "Certified at CPR?" she asked the young trooper.

"A couple of years ago," he stammered.

"Okay." She ripped open Borith's ministerial robe, probed for his sternum, positioned the heels of her hands on his chest, one atop the other. "Give him one breath for every five compressions. Lift his jaw the way I did when you breathe for him. Let's go!"

She had to use her whole weight to compress Borith's chest the necessary four to five centimeters.

". . . three–one thousand, four–one thousand, five–one thousand," she counted half aloud, and paused, shooting a look at the trooper.

He lifted Borith's jaw, bent over him—and terse voices just to her right caught her attention:

"Stabilize the C-spine before you turn him! There might be an injury!"

"Okay, got it. Together, now—"

"Move back! Give 'em some room!"

The knot of policemen shifted back as she began counting out the next five compressions and she caught a glimpse of the victim between their boots.

Lujan!

Her own heart seemed to stop for a split second; she lost count of the compressions.

"Ma'am!" said the young policeman.

She stopped, shaken. Stared while he breathed for Borith.

Lujan's face was ash gray and smudged with a little dark blood, which had oozed from his nose and a gash on his forehead. She watched a policeman check for breathing and pulse, saw him administer emergency breaths and motion a counterpart to start CPR. She bit her lip as she began the next set of compressions.

Borith's chest rose on its own under her hands. And fell. And rose. She shifted, reaching to his throat to feel his pulse.

He stirred and opened his eyes. Blinked up at her and the policeman as if through a haze. "What happened?" he asked. His voice was a rasp, his face gray with its pallor.

"Looked like—an assassination attempt," said the policeman.

"What?" Borith tried to move but Darcie held him down with a hand on his shoulder. He winced instead. "—Pain in my chest—!"

"That's to be expected," Darcie said. "My arms feel a little shaky, too."

He stared up at her, eyes widening at the sudden realization of what she meant.

"You're out of immediate danger," she assured him, "but you're in shock; just lie still now." And she patted his shoulder.

The room was warm, and his ministerial robe was heavy enough, once she drew it back over his chest, that she doubted spreading her suit jacket over him would make any difference. She used it for padding instead when she propped up his feet on a tipped-over chair.

And then she turned to look back toward Lujan.

They had stopped giving him chest compressions, but two or three policemen still knelt around him, their features creased with tension as they waited to relieve the man giving him breaths. His fingers and fingernails were still blue but he had a blood pressure now: The forehead laceration was streaming blood. There was no sign yet of returning consciousness. Darcie swallowed hard and whispered his name.

A shout from the chamber door jerked her vision away from Lujan. She peered over the signing table—and was startled to see that the chamber had been completely cleared. A double handful of paramedics charged unimpeded down the aisle, nudging their repulsor sleds along with them.

She shifted away from Borith, giving him a quiet, "You'll be all right," and another pat on the shoulder when a couple of medics dropped down beside him. Hands suddenly cold, she moved toward Lujan.

The two medics who took over on him didn't waste a single motion. Lip caught between her teeth, Darcie watched as they braced his cervical spine, then slid him onto their med sled. The hands that supported his head smeared blood over the left side of his face.

Dark blood. His breaths were too shallow, too weak; he was growing cyanotic again. ". . . have to intubate," she heard the team leader say.

He gave Lujan two full breaths first; intubating would be more difficult with his neck braced, Darcie knew. She found herself holding her own breath until the tube was in place in his throat and secured, and the ventilator, set at low pressure and synchronized to assist his weak respirations, dispersed the grayness from his skin.

His ceremonial tunic and shirt had been ripped open by the police who'd begun CPR. The paramedics cut the tunic's front panels off and one pushed the pieces behind him, out of his way. Darcie stooped to pick them up, rolled them into a bundle—hugged the bundle hard to her chest as they tore away the rest of Lujan's shirt.

They slapped silvery ECG monitor transmitters all over his chest, and in a minute the man at the monitor said, "Blood pressure is seventy-eight over twenty, pulse is one-twenty-four and erratic."

The team leader nodded. "Start an IV, normal saline with one bolus LH."

LH. Lidosynth hydrochloride, Darcie knew. She remembered it from the trauma deck of *Venture*. Had used it more than once to stabilize cardiac rhythms.

The second man was pushing a large-bore intracath into his patient's right arm when Lujan went into a seizure, a violent shaking caused by the rapid, rhythmic contracting and relaxing of the muscles of his arms and legs. The jerking left the intracath in the medic's hand, and he gripped Lujan's arm when it began to bleed.

That was when Darcie glimpsed the deep burns on the tips of Lujan's fingers. She checked his other hand, found burns there, too. Exit burns, like those caused by an electrocution injury.

The seizure lasted only thirty seconds or so, but when it subsided, the team leader said, "That could happen again anytime. Get that IV going!"

Kneeling near Lujan's head, Darcie shoved a loose strand of hair out of her eyes and watched the other place a new intracath, in Lujan's left arm this time. She watched while he added the drug, and eyed the ECG monitor beside him. Her own racing heartbeat made her whole body shake.

The team leader glanced up at her as he placed a dressing over the scalp laceration. "You're his mate?"

"Yes." She nodded.

"You'd better come with us," he said, and then nodded in response to a voice in his earpiece. "Roger that, Base." He glanced at the ECG monitor, then at his partner. "Let's transport."

Darcie stepped back when they switched on the med sled's repulsors—and a hand touched her arm. She twisted around.

It was Jiron.

"I'm going with him," she said, as if he might try to stop her.

He didn't. He just nodded, white-faced himself. "I'll meet you there after I pick up Heazel."

The ambulance shuttles had been forced to set down on the VIP pad at the top of the Tower because of the mobs in the streets. One shot up with a roar as Darcie followed Lujan's sled out of the lift and into the wind that raced over the roof. Laden with ice particles, it nearly took her breath and she realized only then that her heavy coat was still checked in the lobby.

A second ambulance was firing its thrusters now, raising

billows of vapor. Covering her ears with her hands, Darcie dashed toward the third, after Lujan's medics.

They shoved Lujan's sled aboard first, locked it into the rack on the right, then pulled Borith's sled in, too, and locked it down on the left. Hunkering close beside Lujan, Darcie saw the minister turn his head under his oxygen mask. Saw his convulsive swallow as his vision fixed on Lujan's bloodied face, and reached out to touch his shoulder, to offer him assurance despite her own horror.

The rear hatch slammed down; the thrusters fired. The abrupt G-force of launch nearly shoved Darcie down onto Lujan's bared chest. She braced herself over him, her face so close to his that she could hear the rush of air through the endotracheal tube. She pushed herself back as the pressure let up, her heart beating hard, her breath coming in gasps.

"Who's his regular physician?" the medic beside her asked over the thrum of the engines. "We need to contact him."

"Doctor Moses," said Darcie. Her words came as if she'd been running. "It's—Doctor Libby Moses. She's—assistant to the chief of surgery—at Winthancom Military Medical Center."

"Good," the medic said. "That's where we're going."

Lujan had another seizure en route, a brief one as before, but no less violent. And there were still no signs of returning consciousness.

Barely six minutes after its liftoff, the ambulance banked into a gradual descent. Darcie swallowed against the pressure in her ears as it spiraled down, down, then leveled out. She felt a bump, a settling. The rear hatch flew open and the medics moved—fast. Snatching up the shreds of Lujan's ceremonial tunic, which she had dropped on the deck during launch, she followed.

The trauma wing's landing area and main corridor were a mob of police uniforms. Whole squads stood guard outside two or three trauma bays, their rifles at the ready, while their officers, crackling radios clutched in their hands, strode up and down with grim duty etched on their faces.

"Coming through! Coming through!" Lujan's lead medic shouted. He had to shove two or three policemen out of his way, and Darcie dodged around them, sticking close to the sled.

As the paramedics guided the sled into a brightly lit bay, a woman in a med tech's uniform caught Darcie by the shoulders and held her fast. "I'm sorry," she said. "You can't go in there."

Darcie tried to pull free. "But I'm a—" she began. She was panting, her pulse racing with adrenaline. "He's my mate!" She strained to see around the other woman's shoulder. Caught one brief glimpse of Lujan's face as the doors closed. "Let me go!" she gasped, and tried to push the other away.

The woman held on, offering a sympathetic expression but shaking her head. "There's a waiting area up the corridor," she said. "It would be best to go there."

It was some minutes before Darcie stopped resisting, until the adrenaline rush subsided. It left her feeling weak and shaky.

". . . all right now?" she heard the other woman ask, as if from a distance. She nodded, and the woman let go of her.

In another moment she found herself alone in the chaos of the corridor.

She stood still then, feeling suddenly numb. In shock, she realized in a detached kind of way. She swayed—and reflexively steadied herself—when someone brushed past her.

Then a voice from her left broke over the hubbub, rising clear and sharp on a note of rage: "I *knew* it would end in something like this! I told him so over and over again! . . ."

The words jerked her head up, snapped her out of her numbness.

Five or six men stood in a knot a few meters away. All wore gold bandoliers, gold crests on their tunics, and faces as rigid as masks.

The Isselan Embassy staff.

As Darcie eyed them, a doctor approached, and one of the

speaker's comrades signaled him to silence with a hand on his arm. They all turned.

The doctor hesitated. "Gentlemen, I'm very sorry," he said. He spread his hands. "There was nothing we could do. The holoscans show almost complete cauterization of the brain stems. Minister Istvan and Ambassador Pegaush both died instantly, as did Pite Hanesson of the Triune. The two who survived probably did so only because they were moving out of the direct line of fire."

Cauterization of the brain stem? Darcie stiffened. Only an electromagnetic weapon could do something like that!

Two or three of the Isselans bowed their heads. The others' expressions grew darker still, eyes narrowing, mouths compressing into thin, tight lines. Their dialogue, now subdued, blended back into the murmur around them.

Cauterization of the brain stem. Darcie gnawed her lower lip. She hadn't heard of an injury like that since the Resistance.

"Acting Ambassador Eraut," she heard someone call. She looked up.

It was one of the police captains. He strode up to the Isselans, to the late ambassador's second-in-charge, his radio in one hand, a display plate in the other. "I've got a background report on the guy," he said, and held out the plate. "There's not much. Name's Rahm Guavis, age thirty-eight standard years, employed by InterStar News Network since thirty-three-oh-two. He's got no prior police record, no family onworld, no known affiliations with criminal or terrorist groups of any kind. Pretty much keeps to himself. There's only one noteworthy thing about him." The officer scrolled up the display with a touch. "He's not a citizen of Sostis. Not a citizen of any of the Unified Worlds, in fact. He's been here on work or education permits ever since he arrived here in his late teens."

"From where?" asked the Isselan.

"From Na Shiv." The officer's features were grim. "He was deported from there and eventually came here."

"But what of his weapon?"

"He built it himself," said the policeman. "He has an advanced degree in electromagnetic sciences and applications. Looks like it was based on an old Isselan design"—he emphasized Isselan—"except that he gave it a tighter focus. It all fit inside his press holocorder. The lab's still trying to figure out how he pulled so much energy out of two standard holocorder powercells!"

The Isselans looked shocked. "That's impossible!" one of them said. "Electromagnetic weapons were outlawed at the end of the War of Resistance!"

"By the Unified Worlds," said the police captain. "*Your* government didn't ban them until thirty-two-eighty-eight...."

An electromagnetic weapon.

Darcie turned away, not wanting to hear any more. As a combat surgeon, she'd done autopsies on soldiers found dead without a mark on their bodies—except exit burns. Some had died of cardiac arrest, their hearts' regulatory P-waves evidently overridden by an EM pulse. Others, like Istvan, Pegaush, and Hanesson, had suffered massive damage to the brain stem.

Or to other parts of the brain.

The hardest cases had been the ones who'd lived. The ones whose injuries had reduced them to little more than infants. Or the ones who had never awakened from their comas.

The thought of Lujan like that turned her cold. "No!" she whispered. "Please, no!"

She had to get away from that spot, as if distancing herself from the talk and the thoughts would prevent them from becoming reality. Clutching the torn tunic close, she strode up the corridor.

It was cordoned off beyond the waiting area by a police line with more rifles, more radios. But the waiting area itself was practically empty. She crossed to a chair in its corner and sank into it, shaking.

It was some time before she looked down at the panels of fabric sprawled over her lap.

The medals on one panel lay in a tangled mass: heavy discs and wreaths and stars of bronze and silver and platinum, suspended from their varicolored ribbons and spot-welded together by the EM pulse. She didn't even recognize them all. She began to sort them out, trying to smooth and straighten them with trembling fingers.

She remembered the Aerospace Combat Medal. It designated an ace, and the tiny stars pinned to its blue and gold ribbon declared Lujan an ace five times over.

She knew the platinum wreath on the crimson ribbon, too. The Liberty Bought with Blood Medal, for injuries received in the line of duty.

Lujan had received his first one at Yan when his fighter, disabled in the Dominion Station attack, had burst into flames as it entered *Venture's* recovery ramp. His gloves had been charred, his hands blistered with second-degree burns from beating out the fire in his cockpit. He'd been rather embarrassed about getting the medal for something he considered so minor.

She touched the three clusters on its ribbon.

The second Blood Medal had been given at Tohh, when Mordan Renier's treachery had nearly cost Lujan his life in a supposed training mishap. The third and fourth ones she could only guess at, after seeing the scars that twisted around his upper right arm and the ones that crossed his abdomen. He'd only said, "You don't want to know, Darce," when she'd asked about them. She'd had to question Libby to find out how his arm had been so badly mangled, and then she learned that he'd nearly died of an allergic reaction to the cell cultures they had tried to use to reconstruct it.

She stroked the platinum wreath with her fingertip.

"Darcie?" The word was little more than a squeak.

She hadn't heard, hadn't seen Heazel and Jiron come up. When she touched Heazel's gaze with her own, the other woman promptly lapsed into tears.

Rising, Darcie gathered her into her arms. "He's a strong man," she said. "He'll make it, Heazel."

"I know that. I know," Heazel said between sobs. "I should be the one telling you that!"

Darcie managed a dim smile, drawing her to the chair next to her own. "I may need to hear it from you later on."

"He has more reason to live now than he's ever had, since he has you and Tristan back," Heazel said.

Darcie didn't say anything to that, and Heazel, twisting up a handkerchief in her lap, went on, "You two were always in his heart. It was always 'Darcie used to do this,' or 'Tristan used to do that,' and he always just seemed so—lonely." She shook her head a little, as if recalling it. "So Jiron and I sort of adopted him into our family."

She hesitated. "When he had to come back from Topawa alone that first time a few months ago, we invited him to dinner, and I asked him how all of you were doing. He said he hadn't been so happy since you two were first joined, and—I could tell that he was, Darcie. He finally seemed—complete. Fulfilled." Heazel looked up. "He—said he would have given up his admiralty for you."

Complete? Fulfilled? Give up his admiralty for me? Darcie felt a pang through her heart, recalling the argument they'd had the night before his report to the Assembly, the others they'd had before and after that—her attempt even yesterday to beg off attending the sealing with him! She shook her head, lowering her eyes. They stung with tears. "It hasn't been as nice for him as it's seemed," she said, and tried to swallow the constriction in her throat. "I've been very selfish sometimes, trying to readjust to all of this, and worrying about Tris. I've been impatient, I've been demanding, I haven't always been there for him—"

"Stop that!" said Heazel. She wrapped an arm about Darcie. "You're here for him now. He's never needed you as much as he needs you right now."

They both lifted their heads when Jiron strolled up. He'd been walking the corridor, pausing here and there to talk to a police officer or to someone on the hospital staff, and now he stopped in front of their chairs and dropped to his heels. "They just took Minister Borith up to the VIP suite," he said.

"He'll be hospitalized for several days, but they say he'll be all right."

Darcie felt a rush of genuine relief. "I'm glad," she said.

And Jiron looked her in the eye. "The admiral will be all right, too." He hesitated, a suggestion of a smile touching his mouth as he shot a quick glance at Heazel. "He survived those stuffed eggs, after all!"

"Oh, Jiron!" Heazel rolled her eyes.

"Eggs?" Darcie straightened a little. "But Lujan *hates* eggs!"

Heazel was bright red. "I didn't know that when he held his first command function. The staff officers' mates organized it all, and when I was assigned to do hors d'oeuvres, I made stuffed eggs."

Darcie could almost guess what was coming. "Oh, no!" she said, a faint smile tugging at the corners of her mouth.

"Oh, yes!" said Heazel. "I was nervous about it all, anyway—Jiron had just been selected as exec and I wanted to make a good impression for him to his new boss—but I'd never attended a command-level social before. So I reviewed the Unified Worlds protocol, and one point it made was that refreshments are always offered to the highest-ranking individual first.

"So that evening, when I brought out that tray of stuffed eggs, I set a direct course across the room for the admiral. He was talking with two or three of the guests right then, and he paused when I held out the tray. He looked from the eggs to me, and back to the eggs, and finally he said 'Thank you' and took one. He just sort of held it while I served the others—probably wondering the whole time how he could get rid of it!—and then he seemed to realize that the others weren't supposed to eat until he did."

"So he ate it?" Darcie asked, incredulous.

"Manfully!" said Heazel. "I actually offered him a second!"

Darcie couldn't help smiling. "What did he do?"

"He just said, 'Not right now, thanks,' so I went on my way." Heazel's smile still looked embarrassed. "It wasn't until we were clearing up afterward that someone told me how he feels about eggs—and then I was absolutely mortified! I was sure he'd choose a new exec or something!"

The mental image of Lujan, always the diplomat, eating that stuffed egg without so much as a grimace made Darcie laugh. Made her laugh until the tears rolled down her cheeks.

And then her breath caught, and the laughter turned to sobs.

She wept until she was weak.

She didn't realize that she had dozed off until someone called her name. Then her head jerked up from Heazel's shoulder and she blinked.

Doctor Moses, clad in her surgical scrub suit and looking weary, knelt in front of her. She was flanked by a lanky young man in similar clothing. "How—?" Darcie began. She couldn't finish the question.

Libby laid a hand over hers—the one that was curled around Lujan's Blood Medal. "He's out of surgery, Darcie," she said, "but there're some things we need to talk about."

The young man stepped forward then, extending his hand. "I'm Doctor Berron Gavril, neurosurgeon and attending physician. Please come to my office, Captain Dartmuth."

Darcie glanced from Gavril to Moses and back. "All right," she said. Softly. Heazel gave her hand a squeeze as she stood.

The corridor was calmer now; most of the policemen were gone. The lighting was dimmer, too. Darcie felt a hollowness in her stomach as she walked, half numb, between the doctors, and she wondered how long it had been since she'd last eaten. She glanced at a timepanel on the corridor wall. 0447. The surgery had taken over thirteen standard hours.

None of them spoke until the office door was closed and they were seated. Then Gavril touched a button beside the holoscreen on the wall and said, "Play preop diagnostic holoscan from Trauma Bay Four, patient name Serege, Lujan."

A ripple of light crossed the holoscreen, and then an image appeared: a skull and its attached cervical spine. Also visible were nasogastric and endotracheal tubes, running down beside the vertebrae.

Darcie spotted the damage at once: The fourth cervical vertebra was shattered. Her breath caught in a tiny gasp.

"Hyperextension of the neck," Libby said. "There's some soft-tissue trauma to the cervical area as well."

"He hit his head on the table when he fell," Darcie whispered.

Libby nodded. "That could do it. . . . Delete skeletal structures and magnify spinal cord."

The skull and spinal column disappeared; the brain and milky cord were enlarged on the holoscreen.

The cord hadn't been severed but the crushing damage was extensive. Darcie took her lower lip between her teeth.

"There's more," Doctor Gavril said after a few seconds. "My greatest concern is the EM damage to the brain itself." He hesitated. "Forward to brain-stem 'scans."

On the holoscreen, the spinal cord vanished and was replaced by the structures of the brain stem.

He let Darcie study the series of images that followed without trying to explain them; he knew that she knew what they meant.

The EM pulse had left a series of lesions, much like those caused by an electrocution injury. Probably because Lujan had been in motion, Darcie thought, which hadn't allowed the pulse sufficient focus for complete destruction. It had miraculously left the pons and medulla oblongata unscathed, seeming instead to have struck randomly at the cranial nerves that radiated from them.

The optic tract appeared to have taken the brunt of the pulse; it was completely burned away, from the optic chiasma to the retinas of both eyes. The third and fourth pairs of cranial nerves had been skipped, but the fifth pair had been hit. So had the seventh; and the eighth pair was burned all the way through, as were the cochleas of both ears. The left member of the ninth nerve pair had also been burned, but the pulse seemed to have spent itself by then; that damage appeared minor by comparison.

And those were only the noticeable burns, Darcie knew. Great enough magnification of the holoscan would doubtless reveal a multitude of microscopic lesions throughout the cerebrum.

The likely outcome of it all milled around in her mind: loss of sight, of hearing, of equilibrium; loss of motor control of mouth and facial muscles; random memory loss; quadriplegia. . . .

With almost no apparent injury to any of the association areas of his brain, Lujan could well be left as little more than a cognizant mind trapped within a nearly useless body.

Blinking back sudden tears at the thought, Darcie looked over at Libby. She couldn't speak; her throat was too tight for sound.

As if reading her mind, Libby shook her head. "This doesn't necessarily mean that Lujan is condemned to spend the rest of his life in near-total disability," she said. "Most of the time we were in surgery was spent repairing the damage to the spinal cord, and we've already started him on a regimen of regeneration drugs. Neurosurgical techniques and regen drugs have both continued to improve since the War of Resistance." Libby's tone was reassuring. "With time and therapy, Lujan has a good chance of overcoming the quadriplegia."

"I wish I could be as optimistic about the cranial nerve injuries," Doctor Gavril said after a brief silence. He eyed the brain-stem images on the holoscreen once more and shook his head. "I don't think his intellectual capacity has been damaged, but without sight, hearing, or an ability to speak, still having a functioning mind may almost be more of a curse than a blessing.

"In most cases, we would surgically implant a neural-cell culture. With gene stimulation for differentiation and growth, that would rebuild the damaged nerves. It's usually very successful. But the admiral has a severe allergy to derived-cell cultures."

Darcie exchanged a glance with Libby. "I know that," she said. "Aren't there any alternatives?"

Gavril considered for a long while. "There are some—electronic implants, for example—but none that would fully restore what he's lost," he said at last. "At this point the outlook for restoring the cranial nerves appears very bleak. We won't know for certain how extensive the damage is until he regains consciousness—"

He suddenly cut himself off. Hesitated. Said more quietly then, "*If* he regains consciousness. There's a strong possibility with injuries this severe that he won't. They also put him at risk from a number of life-threatening complications. We're assembling the most advanced team of neurologists and therapists available in the Unified Worlds and we'll give him every chance we possibly can, Captain, but it may not be enough. I'm very sorry."

Darcie only nodded a little. "I understand," she said after a moment, and let her head droop.

Her gaze fell on her hands, white-fisted in her lap.

Fisted around Lujan's Blood Medal.

She opened her hands slowly. Studied the medal. Remembered what Libby had told her about Lujan's mangled arm. About the deep scars across his belly.

"He's a fighter," she whispered after a moment. "The fact that he even survived the surgery shows that he's not done with fighting yet. He'll give it all he has left."

"Minister Borith," said the voice on the intercom, "the visitors you've been expecting have arrived. Shall I send them on to your room?"

"Yes, please," Borith said.

He pushed himself stiffly up in the bed, wincing at the remaining soreness in his chest. At least his robe concealed the fading bruises and the cardiosensors stuck all over it.

As the door slid open, he glimpsed the guards outside, standing at attention for Acting Ambassador Eraut and Alois Ashforth of the Unified Worlds Triune and a handful of people from their respective staffs. Eraut crossed to the bed at once, his brows drawn together in an expression of gravity that bordered on apprehension.

"My lord," he said, keeping his voice low, "you must know that I am adamantly opposed to what you are about to do! How can you *possibly* trust this alliance after what happened three days ago? Ambassador Pegaush and Minister Istvan are dead—"

"So is Assemblyman Hanesson," said Borith, "and Admiral Serege is horribly injured." He shook his head. "The incident was not of the Unified Worlds' doing; I'm confident of that, Eraut. Particularly since it was Admiral Serege—my sworn enemy—and his mate who saved my life."

He saw how the acting ambassador swallowed at that, and straightened, and he said, "Yes, the cost has been great, Eraut, but great achievements always come at great cost. Do not reduce Istvan and Pegaush's death to meaninglessness. The cost will be greater still, to our motherworld, if we fail to act now on what we have gained."

"Yes, my lord," the younger man said, though he still didn't sound entirely persuaded.

Borith met his eyes. "Trust must begin somewhere, Eraut. Someone must take the first step." He looked across at Alois Ashforth of the Triune, carrying her narrow briefcase. He knew what it contained. "I'm willing to take that step," he said. "I wish to seal the Assistance Agreement, and I wish to do so without any further delay."

TWENTY-FOUR

The shuttle's hatch slammed closed. Tristan turned and ducked through the launch bay's arched doorway before its door came down as well, allowing the space dome to spiral open.

Lieutenant Thirup was waiting beyond the launch bay in the loading area. "One left," he sighed as Tristan joined him.

One mine left to liberate.

Malin Point.

Beyond the sealed bay door, the shuttle's engines roared to life. In a few moments it would lift off with another load of evacuees from the Alioto mine. There were still two to three hours before the troop shuttle would arrive with the last combat team.

Thirup glanced around, at Spherzah organizing and assisting the people still waiting for shuttles, at Spherzah on guard with their rifles readied. "Take a break, scout," he said, clapping a heavy gloved hand on Tristan's pressure-suited shoulder.

Tristan nodded in response, too weary to speak.

Every mine complex had management and shipping offices on the shuttle level, compact spaces the masuk invaders had claimed for their quarters. They had been ransacked and filthied but they were still a better choice for a bivouac than what lay below in the caves. Rifle balanced in his hands, Tristan warily entered a back room. Its lighting no longer worked, but the infrared scope on the rifle probed its dark corners and found no one there.

Allowing himself a sigh, Tristan laid his rifle down on a desk shoved up against one wall—from which he could snatch it up quickly if he had to—shrugged off equipment vest and backpack, and began to unfasten his pressure suit's double seals. He'd have two or three hours' relief from the suit, time to eat, to find a latrine, to wash his face, maybe even get a little sleep before he had to climb into it once more.

Leaving the suit on the floor like an abandoned chrysalis, he took up his rifle—then paused to scratch at the places where the thermal garment made his skin itch, up and down his sides and across as much of his back as he could reach with one hand. There were spots where the pressure suit had chafed, too, despite the thermal suit's padding, and those spots, at shoulders and elbows and insides of legs, were tender and raw when he touched them. He winced.

The itching eased, he nudged debris out of his way with his foot and settled himself carefully in a squat. Pressing his back to the wall, he balanced the rifle across his knees and closed his eyes.

He'd been in the caves for eight days now—over eleven days if one counted the time he'd spent sealed inside the command post. It felt more like eleven weeks.

Lieutenant Palahotai had given his second premission briefing over the command post's viewscreens via commlink from the *Shadow*, three days after the post's capture. By then, Isselan space and the rest of the governor's underground complex had been cleared of masuki and secured by Unified Worlds personnel. Operation Liberation was all that remained to be done.

Palahotai had begun by projecting the cave-system map on the center screen. "In order to accomplish this mission in a minimum amount of time," he said, "the caverns have been divided into three sectors, which will be worked simultaneously by separate Spherzah groups." A projected pointer marked each area as he spoke. "Lieutenant Manolis, you have the north sector; Lieutenant Jahmal, the northeast branch; and Lieutenant Thirup, the southwest sector, down here.

"Each of you will have four ten-member teams, which will rotate through your area of operations." A chart appeared on the right screen, and Palahotai said, "Prior experience with similar operations indicates that each mine can be liberated within six standard hours, including travel time from the CP, approach and positioning, defense suppression, attack, and mop-up. The remainder of the eighteen-hour combat shift will be spent doing triage, first aid and helping hostages to shuttles, and control of the criminals, before reporting back to the CP for six hours of sleep. Team leaders, who will remain in the area of operations, will be resupplied by their primary team each time it rotates in.

"Even if you are capable of moving faster, it is important that you do not do so, due to the logistics demands of giving medical care and transporting groups of three to six thousand people off the moon, from three different mine complexes, at one time."

Palahotai paused to bring up a mine-complex schematic on the left screen. "Now for the nitty-gritty," he said. "According to Lieutenant Commander Ajimir Nemec, who observed several mines during the months he spent in the caves, the masuk guard complement is approximately ten at each mine, but only one or two are likely to be on patrol in the actual prison area at any given time. The rest will most likely be up here"—he placed an arrow on the schematic—"in the shipping offices. Concussion grenades will be most effective there, with two riflemen moving simultaneously to eliminate masuki in the prison level. *All* masuki *will* be eliminated.

"The number of hostages in each compound ranges from about one thousand in some to over two thousand in others. Sanitary facilities are primitive at best, if existent at all, so we expect a high level of disease as well as widespread malnutrition, and injuries from acts of brutality, including rape and fighting. The possibility of psychological casualties among the prisoners is also very high.

"Therefore," Palahotai said, "all evacuees will be shuttled to hospital ships for decontamination and in-processing. Those with urgent medical needs will be admitted; the rest will be transported to receiving centers being set up on the planet. The first wave of hospital ships is already positioning itself in orbit around your moon. Comms frequencies and call signs will be as shown." A new chart appeared on the right screen, and Palahotai paused to allow the team leaders to study it.

"There is one exception to the evacuation procedure," he said, and his tone turned grim. "All criminal occupants of the mines will be shuttled, under heavy guard, directly to one of three security ships also waiting in orbit. You must consider these individuals as great a threat to the mission as the masuki themselves. Therefore, you are authorized to eliminate anyone who attempts any violent act or otherwise endangers fellow prisoners or rescue personnel. Is that understood?"

His audience in the command post murmured affirmatives, and Palahotai said, "At the time the headquarters facilities were secured, a message was released from the Mine Control Center to all mine complexes. It said, in effect, 'Having communications problems, take no action, please stand by,' and all communications between mines were shut down, to prevent word of your presence from spreading. Still, you must remain alert for masuk patrol activity in the tunnels and caverns and take out any masuki you encounter.

"On completion of this operation, all rescue personnel will report to the hospital ship *Mercy* for decontamination, medical and mission debriefings, and rest. Do any of you have any questions?"

No one did. Within an hour the three primary teams had suited up and were moving out into the caves.

Nothing Palahotai had said in his briefing had prepared Tristan for what they found at the first mine they freed. Sitting in the dark office, he shuddered at the images that came back, clear as holograms in his mind, of skeleton-thin people cower-

ing in the corners of the wire-mesh cell block, dazed eyes staring out of their hunger-gaunt faces. They were children and
elderly mostly, the ones who lacked size or physical force to
fight for the limited rations.

There were images of women, too, with torn clothing,
bruised bodies, distraught eyes, cringing away from his outstretched gloved hands, some weeping, others actually trying
to fight him off, all afraid they were going to be raped again.

There were images of an old man with gangrenous ulcers
on his legs; of two small boys with tear-streaked faces, their
skin and hair crusted with grime, who clung to him tightly as
he carried them out to an evacuation shuttle; of a woman they
found cradling her days-dead child in her arms, who
screamed, "Don't take away my baby!" when two pressure-
suited shapes reached down to lift her to her feet.

There were images of the criminals, most of them men,
who leered while they were searched and locked into re-
straints under the leveled rifles of the Spherzah. Their hardened eyes and bodies, not gaunt from lack of food, were more
telling than their colorless uniform coveralls. Watching as one
group was marched to a shuttle, Lieutenant Thirup had
shaken his head. "When the bottom five percent of a population seizes power," he muttered, "the other ninety-five percent
always suffers."

Hardest of all to dispel were the images of the people who
hadn't survived, the ones Tristan had helped to place in body
bags. Youngsters who had been trampled in rushes to get rations or succumbed to disease in the filthy enclosure. Victims
of starvation or their fellow prisoners' brutality.

Tristan opened his eyes to force their nameless faces from
his mind and tipped his head back against the rough stone
wall.

The situation had been the same at the second mine, and at
the third, and at the fourth. Like recurring nightmares, he
thought, except that each time the faces were different.

Then they had reached Thrax Port.

The only way in was by the same stairs and through the

same shield door that Tristan had closed with a rifle burst days before. But this time the utility plant provided no covering compressor noise. The combat team crept up the flight of stairs one wary step at a time.

Espino still lay on the platform where Tristan and Sladsky had left him. Tristan swallowed, seeing him there. But Thirup just pointed at two team members. "Take his body down to the first landing; we'll need the whole platform. We'll bring him out when we're done cleaning up here."

They'd had to rebuild the shield door's control box, splicing in wires and soldering new connections to make the door operational.

"It'll probably come open with a bang," Chief Petty Officer Ryoko cautioned when he finished.

"Right." Thirup nodded. "Sensors?"

"I've got seven lifeforms in the room," came the response. "Probable masuki."

"Looks like they know we're right here." Thirup detached a concussion grenade from his belt. "Riflemen, to your positions; everybody else take cover. Okay, Ryoko, *now!*"

Ryoko pressed his switch. The shield door slammed open.

Red energy lanced across the room, shot through the doorway. One of the riflemen went down, just in front of Tristan. He raised his own weapon, returned fire as Thirup rose up enough to hurl his grenade. They all ducked—

Its blast shook the stair platform. "Move!" Thirup shouted.

They lunged forward into the room, into the smoke. Infrared sights picked out masuki slumped in the corners; quick rifle bursts finished them off.

"There's more on the way, sir!" shouted Comms.

Bootfalls thundered along the passage. Palm lights cut wild swaths through its dark.

"Take cover!" said Thirup.

The masuki didn't come into the office; they took positions outside its door and fired into the settling smoke. Pressed up to one wall, Tristan heard one of his teammates yell, saw him crumple. Saw the team's medic drop down beside him.

"Need another grenade!" Thirup said.

Tristan yanked one off his own belt, slapped it into his team leader's gloved hand. Thirup pulled its pin, pitched it out into the passage.

Its bang stopped the shooting. Thirup led them out into the passage, riddling the stunned shapes on the floor with rifle fire. "Let's go," he said. "Sensors, up front; there'll probably be more of them. Stay sharp, everybody!"

Espino's explosion appeared to have shut off every light in the complex; the whole place was pitch-black. "Night visors on," Thirup said. "Rifle maglights only, and only for shooting."

They moved swiftly through the tunnels, rifles trained on every shadow that could shelter an enemy. Twice they exchanged fire with snipers, and the second time, Sensors was hit.

"It's not serious," the medic said when he'd tended to the wound and the firefight was over, "but he won't be walking out of here. He took the burst in the thigh."

Thirup slapped the lifeform detector into his palm a couple of times—then handed it to Tristan. "Take over, scout," he said.

"Yes, sir," said Tristan. His mouth was suddenly dry.

He took the point position with his heart racing hard. His hand shook, wrapped around the lifeform sensor.

I will go before and behind you, he heard in his mind. *I will be beside you in the dark valleys. . . .*

He let out a pent-up breath and made his way silently down the passage.

The shield door at its bottom had a manual control. Thirup motioned his team to take cover before he punched the trigger.

The shield door grated open.

"Sensors?" said Thirup.

The display in Tristan's hand should have lit up with readings from hundreds of humans, all crowded close together. Instead, it stayed blank. "Something's wrong," he said. "I'm not getting any readings at all."

"Are we in the right place?" Thirup asked. "Try the area sensor."

He did. The natural chamber they faced was over one hundred meters across, nearly fifty meters wide and thirty high, and the wire-mesh cell block itself stood out plainly in its center.

"We're in the right place," Tristan said, "but—there's nobody here. No masuki—no humans."

Thirup hesitated, considering. Then he said, "Palm lights on, but hold them wide. Let's have a look—but stay on your guard!"

They spread out. Advanced warily, rifles leveled. The life-form sensor stayed blank.

Palm lights played through the mesh of the cell block.

"They're all on the ground in there," someone said. The tone, even through Tristan's headset, sounded puzzled.

A few meters to his left and a little ahead of the rest, one of his teammates suddenly froze. "They're all *dead*," he said. "Three or four days, I'd say."

Everyone stopped and stared. Shocked.

Men, women, youths, children. All lay sprawled on the stone floor and over each other in a tangle of twisted limbs. Their bodies were marked with energy burns, their faces still bore expressions of terror, of panic.

It was several seconds before someone even whispered a profanity. Tristan turned his head away from the sight, swallowing down the gorge that rose in his throat.

A faint glow from the sensor gripped hard in his hand caught his eye. He looked at it in disbelief.

There were *three* faint lights.

"They're not all dead," he said, his voice shaky. "I'm getting three readouts, all really weak. One's this way and two"—he pointed—"are over there."

"Let's get them out," said Thirup.

It didn't take long to find them, using the sensor: an older woman, and a teenage boy and girl. All were severely dehydrated, and all were injured, so it took a good deal longer to remove them from beneath their fallen cell mates, whose bodies had shielded them from the slaughter.

By the time they'd been moved on improvised stretchers up to the shipping level to meet the medevac shuttle, all three survivors were conscious and partly coherent.

"What happened?" Lieutenant Thirup asked, crouching between two of the stretchers. "How did everyone die?"

The older woman stirred in her shroud of hypothermic sheet, and Tristan, kneeling near her head to hold up her IV bag, had to strain to make out her words.

"The lights went out," she said. Her voice was little more than a whisper. She swallowed, wet her lips. "All of the lights went out," she said again, "and then pretty soon we could hear the masuki up on the—" She raised a bony arm, motioned as if to indicate the overhead walkway, but the medic caught her hand and brought it back down to her side. "They went up there and they just began shooting," she said, "for no reason at all, just shooting and shooting, and everyone was running and screaming. . . ."

"It's all over now," the medic said comfortingly. He patted her shoulder and glared daggers at Thirup for asking. "You're safe now. It's all over."

Tristan felt suddenly weak. His stomach lurched under his ribs; his arm sagged, holding up the IV.

"Scout, get that back up there!" said the medic.

Tristan jerked his arm up. But his blood felt like ice in his veins, and all of it seemed to have drained from his face. "It was our fault," he whispered. He felt sick to his stomach.

The lieutenant peered at him through his faceplate, his brow puckered up. "What's that, scout?"

Tristan swallowed. Shook his head inside his helmet and ducked it away from the other's gaze. "We—shut down the lights the other day," he said, "to cause a distraction when Edelgard's team got pinned down. The masuki knew we were there. We made them do it."

Thirup's hand closed hard on his shoulder. "Let's get one thing straight, scout," he said. "What your team did was create a diversion that was necessary to accomplish the mission; you didn't *make* those dogfaces do anything! *Nobody* expected them to do something like this! Whatever the reason, it was completely *their own.* You got that?"

Tristan looked at him and didn't answer.

"You hear me, scout?" Thirup demanded.

He finally said, "Yes, sir," but he didn't really believe it.

They had loaded 1,225 body bags into the shuttles, including Espino's, and three wounded Spherzah as well as the prison survivors. When they were finished and Thirup called a rest break, Tristan had gone off to a dark, quiet room, tugged the helmet off his pressure suit, and heaved until he was strengthless.

"Scout!" Lieutenant Thirup's voice reached him from the outer office. "Troop shuttle's setting down! It's chow time!"

Tristan sighed deeply and shoved himself onto his feet, grimacing at the stiffness in his legs and back. He stretched a little, trying to relieve it, and made his way out to the loading area.

The launch-bay door was sliding open when he got there, the first troops ducking under it and striding toward them. Thirup, shed of his pressure suit, too, returned their team leader's wave and said, "Hey you guys, what's the word from topside?"

The other lieutenant grinned behind his faceplate. "The word is, you're running the logistics folks ragged! Every available shuttle is in the air. They've got two of 'em grounded for engine replacements, and the maintenance crews are working nonstop."

Tristan recognized the voice: It was Sladsky. He felt a new tension in his stomach.

He turned away from the talk when another pressure-suited figure approached him, carrying an extra pack. Kersce, he knew, even before he could make out her face inside the helmet; and he felt mild surprise at realizing how much he'd been anticipating her arrival.

She set the pack down at his feet and looked him up and down. "It's a good thing this is just about finished," she said. "You and Lieutenant Thirup look almost as bad as the people we're trying to rescue!"

He was about to protest when he glimpsed himself reflected in her faceplate. He barely recognized his own eyes, hollow and circled from too little sleep, or his haggard features, etched with lines of exhaustion and half-hidden by eleven days of whisker stubble. Still, there was no comparison with the images that rose unbidden in his mind. "I don't look *that* bad," he said seriously.

Kersce just smiled. Caught his arm and squeezed it with her awkward gloved hand. "Come on," she said. "I brought your provisions. I'll replenish your pressure suit while you eat."

He let her steer him away from the loading area, where the new team was assembling, but only after he'd shouldered the provision pack himself.

Dinner consisted of more combat rations: high-protein, low-fiber food bars that tasted like the plastic they'd been packaged in. Tristan sat on the desk in the darkened office, dangling his legs and chewing slowly and watching Kersce work over his suit on the floor.

In spite of her gloves, she replaced his nearly empty water flasks and oxygen canisters with filled ones and the urine reservoir with an empty one in a couple of minutes. "It's ready to go," she said, rising, and placed fresh powercells on the desktop beside him. "There's some new ammo, too."

"Thank you." Tristan reached for his weapon, ejected the spent powercell, shoved a new one into its slot.

Only one mine left, he reminded himself.

But this mine was Malin Point. Where Nemec had been lost. Where Pulou had been fatally wounded.

And Sladsky would be there, watching him.

The first time you do so much as twitch—you're dead, kid, he could hear Sladsky saying. *I'll kill you myself, do you hear me?*

Climbing back into his pressure suit, he found that his hands were shaking.

He'd been seriously ill when he'd come through this part of the cavern before, barely conscious most of the way. But the landmarks he scarcely thought he'd seen then stood out now as if he'd specifically marked them. He set his teeth, steeling himself against a barrage of bad memories.

He swallowed when he spotted the side cave, splitting off to the left. With Kersce at his shoulder, reading her sensor, he slipped forward, rifle ready in his hands.

The cave was dark, as it had been when he'd come here before. His heart thudded harder in his chest.

"All clear for at least one hundred meters," said Kersce beside him.

Tristan signaled "This way" to the others, and snapped down his night visor—

—and froze.

A body lay sprawled on the floor at his feet. A human body clad in a criminal's coverall, facedown in the dirt with an energy burn in the middle of its back.

Tristan jumped at the sound of a footstep behind him, jerked around as Thirup and Sladsky came up.

"What've we got here?" said Sladsky. "Another case like Thrax Port?"

"Nobody at Thrax Port managed to get out of the cell block," said Thirup, "and this guy's been dead a lot longer than that. I don't know." He prodded the body with the toe of his boot, turned it over.

Decomposition was well advanced, but it hadn't obliterated the name FOROS stamped on the coverall chest.

Thirup stepped over the corpse, glanced around. "Maybe there was a breakout," he said. "If so, this guy probably wasn't alone, so stay sharp. Maglights only." He nodded to Tristan. "Let's go, scout."

The tunnel made a corner and split into two, one going up, the other down. Pausing at the fork, Tristan heard machinery noise in the distance. He remembered the heat, the thump of the compressors, the throbbing ache in his right side.

He glanced over at Sladsky and forced back his fear.

"The right tunnel goes up to the utility plant," he said, pointing. His mouth was so dry that he choked, had to swallow. "The utility plant opens into the loading area. There's an automatic door at each end, and a shield door at the far end as well. The left tunnel goes down to the prison, and it has a shield door, too."

"Right." Thirup looked around. "Comms?"

"Not much going on, sir," said Comms. She tapped the button on her helmet, again and again, and then shook her head. "It's almost *too* quiet."

"I don't like it," said Thirup. "This feels too much like Thrax Port." He considered for a moment, surveying the team: ten of them, besides Tristan and himself. "Vinn and Caddesi," he said, "you two go on down with the riflemen, give them some backup. Take one of the lifeform sensors, keep the comm channel open—and watch your backs!" He paused. "That leaves eight of us to take the shipping level."

The tunnel's floor was a ramp. Tristan clenched his teeth, leaning into the climb. His heart was beating too hard and too fast; it made his breath come as if he were running. The machinery noise grew louder with each meter he advanced, until it made his head throb.

He had made it to the top of the ramp only because Weil and Pulou half-carried him. He stood panting between them while Nemec ran his sensor around the door. . . .

Tristan shook his head against the memory. Turned his thoughts instead to the words he'd read over and over on the microreader's screen: *I will go before you and behind you. . . . I will be to you as your sword and your shield, for I will protect and defend you. . . .*

And the words from his father's blessing: *I promise you that the anxieties which you feel will not overwhelm you or prevent you from carrying out your duties.*

He shifted his grip on his rifle, trying to quell his hands' shaking before Sladsky saw it.

The automatic door marked D-5 UTILITY PLANT had been blasted almost out of its track. Thirup examined it briefly, eyes narrowing. "Wonder if this has anything to do with the guy down in the cave?"

Tristan shook his head, swallowed hard. "No, sir. It happened when Nemec and I escaped from here before."

Nemec had sealed it to cut off their pursuers, to buy them some time, and Renier's security troops had blasted it open.

It wouldn't buy them any time now.

"Sensors?" said Thirup.

"No lifeforms here, sir," came Kersce's reply.

"Good. Stay sharp." Thirup stepped through the door, rifle readied. The team followed.

The passage was narrow and dim. It echoed with the shriek and thump of machinery. And it was hot. Very hot. Tristan's mouth burned. He found the drinking tube inside his helmet and drew a couple of quick, cooling swallows.

"What's it like out there?" Thirup said when they reached the door at the utility plant's end.

The layout burned vivid in Tristan's mind. "There are five landing bays, in a circle." He swallowed again to clear the tremor from his voice. "The one straight across from us has a lift that goes down to the prison level; they can bring in reinforcements that way."

That's what had happened before. He and the others had come out of the passage into a firefight.

"Then we'll try to close it down," Thirup said. "Sensors?"

"I've got twelve readings—maybe fourteen," Kersce said, "ranging all around the perimeter."

"Waiting for us." Thirup's features hardened behind his faceplate. "What's the area scan look like?"

"Pretty much like the others," said Kersce. "Lots of shuttle-support equipment in the loading area for cover."

"All right. We'll have to use four grenades, since they're all spread out. Then stay low and move fast. Scout, you and

Doc"—Thirup jerked a thumb toward the medic—"cover us from here. Got it?"

Tristan nodded; his mouth was too dry to answer.

I will make the weak and the humble to be strong and courageous, to do mighty works, he heard at the back of his mind.

He let out a breath. Pressed himself back to the wall as four of the others pulled out grenades.

Thirup waved the automatic door open—

Red energy seared across the shipping level, shot through the door; Comms reeled and collapsed.

Four grenades lit up the loading area.

"Go!" Thirup yelled. "Move it!"

His teammates leaped forward, firing. Tristan, crouched at the door frame, curled his finger around his rifle's trigger.

A ribbon of light sizzled over his head. He squeezed off several shots in the direction it came from.

The whole loading area seemed filled with lightning. White flashes and red showed Spherzah concealed behind starter carts and ore chutes. Tristan watched as they made their way forward. Pinned down their adversaries with his own fire.

"Medic!" someone yelled over the melee.

Doc straightened beside the suited shape stretched out on the floor. Grabbing his medkit, he sprang into the smoke, staying low.

Tracers arced after him. Tristan turned his fire on their source.

"Behind you!" he heard.

He wrenched around, rifle leveled.

Bootfalls rang up the passage behind him, barely audible over the thump of compressors. The approaching shapes were just shadows. Large shadows!

Masuk reinforcements!

He couldn't see how many there were in the dimness; his rifle scope showed four, maybe five. He aimed into the group, squeezed the trigger.

The lead masuk went down; the rest dove for cover, returning his fire.

A burst smashed the wall close beside Tristan's helmet; flying stone fragments struck his faceplate. Another burst flashed off his armored right arm.

He fired again and again. Stole a glance, between rounds, at his teamate lying still on the stone two meters away and the shield door less than one meter behind him. Wondered at his chances of pulling the other through—and whether they'd even be safer on the other side.

A bright bolt shattered on the door's trigger; the pressure shield slammed down like a multiton ax.

"Scout!" he heard someone yell through his headset.

This is exactly what happened to Nemec. The thought crossed his mind in a detached sort of way.

An energy bolt grazing the armor plate over his belly snapped him back to the moment. Two masuki, crouched somewhere in the dark, were still shooting. He wedged himself into his corner, tried to make himself smaller. And kept shooting back.

—Until one of his rounds hit his nearest foe's weapon. The force of its explosion threw Tristan to the floor.

He lifted his head, his lip smarting, his mouth tasting of blood. The passage was silent, the smoke and the dust already starting to settle. He shifted just enough to peer through his rifle's infrared scope.

It picked out five masuk corpses in the passage, half incinerated by the blast and already starting to cool.

He pushed himself up slowly, shaking, sweat streaming down his face—and wondered who had warned him to look back.

Something seemed to touch his head, a sensation like a hand placed upon it, and his father's words echoed in his mind: *I promise you wisdom to know what actions to take and when to take them, even to guidance at the very moment you need it. . . . You will not be alone.*

Tristan reached for the microreader lying on his chest. Touched it, through armor and plastic and thermal suit, and looked upward.

He was gaining his feet when he heard the scuff of a step on the stone in the passage. He swung his rifle around. . . .

"Scout, you still with us?"

Sladsky's voice.

Tristan lowered his rifle. "Yes, sir."

Sladsky paused in the passage. Played his palm light over the remains at his feet, then over Tristan's scorched suit, and grunted. "Guess I won't have to kill you after all; it looks like you almost did that yourself." He glanced around again. Shook his head inside his helmet. "Not bad for a civilian." And he looked Tristan full in the face. "Get your schooling, Serege, and put in your time in the service, and I'll write your recommendation for the Spherzah myself. I'll take you on my team anytime."

The prisoners' faces were pale ovals in the near dark, ovals with eyes that looked up and turned toward them at the crunch of their boots on the stone, and then studied them with uncertainty: some fearful, some with a glimmer of hope. It had been the same at every mine they had freed.

"It's all right," Lieutenant Thirup said first, holding out both hands with his empty palms up. "We're here to free you. We're here to send you home."

A few of the prisoners gained their feet as they approached, and one made his way at once toward the mesh gate. His hair was long, his face bearded, his clothing as filthy as those of every other person in the compound, but there was authority in his bearing—even in the way he eyed them through the wire. "Who are you?" he demanded.

Their palm lights' beams picked out braid down the seams of his trousers, tarnished silver epaulets on his shoulders, and a patch over his breast pocket that bore the name OCHAKAS.

Tristan saw how Thirup drew himself up. "Unified

Worlds Spherzah, sir. Acting under the mandate of the Agreement for the Provision of Military Assistance to the World Government of Issel."

"Spherzah!" Ochakas said the word as if it tasted bitter on his tongue. He studied them all, his jaw working.

Thirup stayed respectful but firm. "Sir, we have evacuation shuttles coming in. Those with injuries or illness will be given first priority. After that we can take you out in groups of fifty. The more cooperation you give us, the quicker we can get you all out of here."

Ochakas held his gaze hard for a moment, then nodded. "Of course." Turning away, he motioned to a handful of others. "Siador, Tradoc," he said, "let's move everyone who needs medical attention up front to the gate."

All of the evacuees were gone now. Even General Ochakas, who'd been among the last to leave. Standing guard in the loading area with his rifle ready, Tristan had watched as Ochakas moved among the people waiting for shuttles and relayed Thirup's orders through his staffers. He hadn't let the general out of his view for a moment. The sight of that uniform sent tension through his gut and fanned his smoldering suspicions.

But the general, taking his leave at last, had paused on the rescue shuttle's ramp to look into their visored faces. "I never would have believed I'd ever be glad to see one of the Spherzah," he said. "I believe I have a few years of distrust to unlearn."

Thinking about it now, Tristan ducked his head.

"Shuttle's coming in!" someone shouted across the shipping area.

Tristan sighed, shifted his rifle to the crook of his arm, and scooped up his pack.

"Tired?" asked Kersce beside him.

"Yeah," he admitted. "Bone tired." But somehow it felt good.

He filed with the others up the shuttle's short ramp, stowed his rifle and gear in their racks, and strapped himself in.

He was asleep before the shuttle lifted off.

EPILOGUE

Tristan woke what seemed only moments later with someone shaking his shoulder. "C'mon, sleepy head, we've docked," he heard, as if from a distance. "It's time to wake up!"

It took a few moments to force his eyes open, another few to make them focus. Still groggy, he shoved himself stiffly to his feet. Looked around at his companions as he collected his pack and rifle. They appeared no more awake than himself. Stumbling into line in the narrow aisle, he followed them out through the docking lock.

The bright lighting of the corridor he stepped into made him blink; the volume of the words ringing from an unseen speaker made him wince: "You are now entering the quarantine deck. Please proceed to decontamination booths as directed by the attendant."

Personnel in sterile suits just inside the hatch relieved them of weapons and gear; another sterile-suited figure directed them, one to the left, the next to the right, into tiny rooms lining both sides of the corridor.

Still more asleep than awake, Tristan started when his booth's door came down, closing him in. "Please hold your arms out from your sides and turn around slowly for ultraviolet sterilization of suit exterior," a synthesized voice requested. He complied.

More directions followed once the UV lights switched off:

"Please remove pressure suit and thermal garment and deposit them in the decontamination chute in front of you." And then, "Stand with legs wide apart, arms extended from sides, and eyes and mouth closed for disinfectant spray."

The solution had a sharp smell that made him wrinkle his nose. It burned on the raw spots where his pressure suit had rubbed. Tristan gritted his teeth.

The water shower that came after the decontaminant was warm, relaxing. Tristan scrubbed himself, glad to be rid of twelve days' worth of grime, but somewhat surprised at how thin he'd become. He ruffled through his bristly hair and whiskers with both hands as warm air dried him off.

"Please proceed to the next room for medical evaluation," said the synthesized voice, and the booth's back wall slid aside.

Tristan stepped through it into a second space no larger than the first, but this one was equipped with holoscan antennae, a vital-signs sensor panel, and rows of numbered drawers on one bulkhead. He placed his right hand on the sensor panel, stated name and ID number as directed, and waited, nearly drifting into sleep on his feet, while the antennae made a full body 'scan.

Something brushing his right wrist made him open his eyes. He looked down in time to see a robot arm shaped like a pincer retracting into its slot on the sensor panel; a plastic band imbedded with medical-data microchips had been secured about his wrist.

"Serege, Tristan," said the synthesized voice. "All vital signs are within normal ranges. You are now free of external contaminants but you have traces of internal alien bacteria in respiratory and digestive systems. Quarantine procedures will apply until cleared by your attending physician. Please put on the clothing found in drawer number eight and then exit to your right. An attendant will escort you to your cubicle."

The drawer held loose trousers and a tunic, like a surgical suit, and cloth shoes like moccasins. Tristan struggled into them, feeling inordinately awkward, and shuffled through the door into another white passage, where someone else in a sterile suit waited. It was all beginning to feel like a repetitious, sterile dream, he thought.

"Tristan Serege?" the man said.

He nodded.

"This way, please." A gloved hand took his elbow, guided him down the corridor.

He couldn't remember later how he got to the cubicle. Remembered only pausing at the doorway and nodding wordlessly as his guide pointed out the head in the back corner and the cabinet in the bulkhead through which his meals would be delivered by pneumatic tube. It looked like his sickbay cubicle aboard *Destrier*, where he'd recovered half of forever ago. But what it looked like didn't really matter; it had a bed. Tristan flung himself down, full length; he never even felt his head hit the pillow.

He spent the next day and a half mostly sleeping and eating. The meals prescribed by his doctor were bland, but after twelve days on rations, even the minimal variety was welcome.

He roused enough once to shower again, more thoroughly this time, and then applied beard foam from a dispenser. But the whiskerless face that looked back from the reflector when he finished still held a hint of strangeness. He cocked his head, trying to figure it out.

It was his eyes, he decided at last. They seemed older. Deeper, somehow.

He was only beginning to feel coherent, after two full days of rest and recuperation, when the intercom on the bulkhead begged his attention with a series of chirps. He rolled over to reach for its SPEAK button. "Tristan Serege," he said.

"Good," a male voice rattled back. "Serege, you're scheduled to meet with your debriefing team at fourteen-hundred hours today. An attendant will escort you to the conference room. Understood?"

A debriefing.

Tristan sat up. Swallowed. "Yes sir," he said.

The team was waiting when he arrived at the conference room: his doctor, the psychologist, an intelligence officer, all clad in sterile suits and seated around a table. Only the intelligence man was unfamiliar; he rose, introduced himself, extended his hand. Tristan clasped it briefly, feeling weak, and accepted the chair to which he was pointed.

The debriefing was conducted as a casual conversation. He answered questions about masuki and mines, shield doors and snipers, filling in as much detail as he could. Feeling the others' eyes fixed on him the whole time, he rarely raised his vision from the tabletop.

After four hours, his vision blurred over and the questions no longer made sense. "I can't do this any longer," he said, rubbing at his eyes with one hand. "I—need to sleep again."

"Yes, you do." The doctor reached over, gave his shoulder a squeeze. "Go back to bed. We'll continue tomorrow."

The debriefings continued for four days in a row, and there were as many questions about what he was feeling as there were about the mission itself.

He had just returned to his room on the fourth day, feeling desperately in need of a nap after a particularly grueling session, when a medical attendant came to his door. "Commander Amion of the Anchenko Detachment is aboard the *Mercy*," the man said. "He's asked to speak with you."

"With *me?*" Tristan blinked. "What about?"

"I don't know. Follow me, please."

He followed. Not to the conference room this time, but to a small office near the deck chapel. The attendant left him there, at the open door.

Commander Amion wasn't alone, Tristan saw. With him were the chaplain from the *Shadow* and the psychologist who had attended all of his debriefings. He furrowed his brow, puzzled, but had enough presence of mind to come to attention. "Serege reporting as ordered, sir," he said.

"At ease, Tristan," Amion said. "Come in, please." With a gesture, he offered the chair between his own and the chaplain's, and when Tristan was seated, he said, "I'm sorry that I have to bring you some very bad news from Sostis."

"Sir?" Tristan said.

Amion interlocked his hands between his knees. "There was a terrorist incident at the sealing of the Isselan Assistance Agreement. The signatories and their witnesses were fired on with an electromagnetic weapon. One of the victims was your father. The message we received said that he was in critical condition with extensive damage to his central nervous system. There was some question as to whether or not he would live."

The shock was like nothing Tristan could ever remember feeling before. Like a blow that robbed him of breath and left him reeling. He shook his head vehemently, unable to speak. When the words came at last, they were accusing: "That can't be right! It *can't*! You must have heard wrong!"

"I wish I had," Amion said quietly. "I *hoped* I had. I asked for a hardcopy of the transmission and I read it through carefully."

Tristan just stared for a long space, seeing nothing. "Is he—still alive?" he asked finally.

"We don't know." Amion shook his head now. "We've received no further word since that message; we're in a communications-silence zone here."

"Oh." It was a mere breath.

"I've initiated orders for your immediate release from duty on humanitarian grounds," Amion said. "The *Mercy* will be leaving the Issel system for Sostis in two days and I've arranged for you to remain on board and go home with the casualties. Customs and quarantine personnel at Shinchang Station will be notified before you arrive, to get you through without any snags."

Tristan nodded automatically and let his head droop. Emotions raced through him as if swept by a wind, fleeting, fragmented, without any order. There was nothing to grasp at, nothing solid to hold to, just wave after wave of overwhelming confusion. He shook his head again.

Beside him, Amion leaned forward and looked down at

his hands. "There are very few people I respect as much as I do Admiral Serege," he said, then paused. "By the time he was promoted to captain, he was already being considered for eventual high-level positions, and he was offered the command of any Spherzah detachment he wanted. He chose Anchenko.

"A lot of his colleagues, thinking he'd chosen it just because it was his home region, tried to talk him out of it." Amion glanced up. "Anchenko didn't have the reputation then that it does now. It was the assignment nobody wanted—where the marginally competent were sent. It was a remote tour in a harsh environment on an underdeveloped colony world. Performance ratings were poor and morale was low. Even some of his superiors questioned his choice, but when they asked him why, he said, 'Because that's where the most work needs to be done.'

"He went in and ran that place with a titanium fist. He was a strict disciplinarian; he insisted on no less than the best out of everybody, from his command staff to the lowliest grunt. And everybody hated his guts—this upstart captain who was younger than some of his troops!

"The initial resentment didn't last very long." Amion favored Tristan with a wan smile. "Whether it was war games in the desert or dirty, heavy civil-disaster duty, he was always out there sweating along with his people. He *showed* them how to accomplish the mission. He led personally. He took time to talk to them one on one. He admitted his mistakes—not that he made very many—and accepted advice and suggestions from the old heads. He looked out for his people, and he dished out praise freely and publicly when it was due. Inside of six standard months there wasn't a soul in the unit who wouldn't have followed him on the most impossible mission. I know that," Amion said, "because I was one of those souls.

"By the end of his four-year tour there, the Anchenko Detachment's performance ratings had gone from the absolute lowest to among the highest in the whole Spherzah force, and we were unbeatable in the annual skills competitions. When your father was made chief commander, Anchenko adopted the motto 'The Admiral's Own.' Only the best get billets there now—which is why we were selected for this mission."

Amion looked down again. Stayed silent for a space. Shook his head once more and said, "He's a strong man, Tristan. No matter what happens, don't you ever forget that. And don't count him out yet."

Tristan's throat was so tight that it actually hurt. "I won't, sir," he said.

He returned to his room a little later with all thoughts of sleeping forgotten. The emotions he'd felt earlier were now mingled with memories: the stranger's face in the sterile-suit bubble telling him, "I'm very thankful to have you back," and his own stubborn reply: "No you're not." The shock in the admiral's eyes when Tristan had once demanded of him, "How many people did you have to assassinate to make admiral?" The shadow seated on the foot of his bed, offering to help him carry a peimu called Guilt. The figure standing, arms folded, on the bank while he fought with a stream salamander. The glint of tears on the admiral's face, the sorrow that had drawn out his own confession, the muscled arm that had supported him while he wept. The sure, solid hand placed on his head . . .

The rush through his mind made him restless. He paced. Five steps up and five back, the length of his cubicle. He felt helpless. Lost. Empty. And never before, even as a hostage on Issel, had he felt so alone.

Something slid against his chest as he walked, under his tunic. He stopped. Caught at the cord with both hands and pulled it out where he could see it.

His father's microreader. His father's gift. More than anything else Tristan could think of, it represented everything his father was. He studied it, held it there in his hands for several minutes, while his emotions collided and crashed, increasing the ache in his heart.

—Until the ache was swallowed up in sudden anger. He hurled the 'reader onto the berth. "You told me you'd always be there when I needed you!" he said. "I need you *right now!*

Where are you *right now?* Why did you leave me like this? Why did you do this to me?"

A cautious rap at his door cut him off. Made him freeze. He realized only then that he'd been shouting.

"Tristan?" he heard. "Tris, it's Kersce. May I come in?"

He hesitated. Then he crossed to the door in two strides.

She stood there, obviously shaken. Studied his tormented face. "They told us about—the admiral," she said, "and—I thought you might—need someone."

He didn't say anything. He couldn't. He just motioned her in.

"I'm so sorry," she said.

He only nodded. Started pacing again. After a few moments he said, very quietly this time, "I used to make him angry a lot. I know I did, but he never showed it. Ever. I don't know how he did it.

"I was scared of him. I thought he'd be ashamed of me. I didn't even believe him when he told me he wasn't. I—didn't know if I *could* believe him.

"He kept telling me he'd be there for me whenever I needed him. I didn't even *want* to need him—but he was there anyway. Even down on Issel Two the other day. And now—"

His voice broke; his breath caught. He turned away from Kersce, embarrassed.

He didn't hear her step up behind him, just felt her arms slip around his waist. She didn't say anything, just held him. And finally he stopped fighting it. He turned and wrapped his arms around her, too, and wept.

That memory was two weeks old now. Clad in a shipboard uniform instead of his patient's pajamas, Tristan stood in the patients' dayroom, watching via holovid as *Mercy* slid up to her berth in Shinchang Station. His mouth was dry, his palms damp. He couldn't remember ever having spent a longer two weeks in his life.

An attendant came to the dayroom's doorway. "Tristan

Serege?" she said. "Your shuttle to the surface is waiting. Come with me, please."

He scooped up his duffle and followed.

An aide waited at the mouth of the boarding tube, a folder of forms and orders clutched in his hand. "Tristan?" he said. "Everything's in order. We can get you on your way without delay."

He spent the shuttle flight to the surface staring out the viewport by his seat, his mind a millrace of memories and feelings and fears. As Herbrun Field came into view through a break in the late winter clouds, his heart accelerated, racing against his ribs, and his palms grew damp with cold sweat.

His legs felt weak when he disembarked from the shuttle. Flanked by its crew, he hunched his shoulders under his uniform coat and crossed toward the landing bay's arched entry. He looked around, chewing his lip.

The first face he saw was his mother's. Her features looked weary, but she still tried to smile as she swallowed him up in her arms. "Tris!" she said, hugging him, and then, as she stepped back, "Are you all right? You've lost weight." She searched his eyes with her own.

He'd already regained most of what he had lost. "I'm fine," he assured her. Hesitated. Swallowed. "How is—?"

He choked. Couldn't finish the question.

"Your father?" His mother squeezed his hand. "He'll be relieved to know that you're home. We can go directly to the hospital, if you'd like."

"Yes," Tristan said.

He listened, jaw taut, as his mother described his father's injuries. Scarcely noticed the last winter snow still covering the landscape beyond the skimmer's canopy.

"He—looks different—than he did when you left," Darcie said. "They performed a tracheostomy to assist his respiration a few days after the incident, and the tube is still in place in his throat; don't let that startle you.

"He's lost a quite a bit of weight, too. We're giving him

food by mouth now—thick liquids mostly—but due to the cranial-nerve injuries, most of his facial muscles are slack, so eating is very slow and difficult.

"He lost his hearing and sight, and some recent memory, too," Darcie said, "but he's responding well to the regen drugs. He has most sensation back; he can feel you take his hand and tell whether your hand is warm or cold. He's still very weak, but he's beginning to regain some motor control—he can move his arms and legs on the bed a little. Libby expects he'll be walking again—with assistance, of course—in less than a year."

She sighed, then said, "Yesterday they performed the first of several microelectronic implant surgeries. They had to wait until he'd regained enough strength to go through it. The implants bypass the burned auditory nerve and will allow him to hear—not perfectly, but well enough. When he's healed sufficiently, they'll do the same thing for his optical nerves to restore some form of sight."

Tristan only nodded; it was all the response he could muster.

"His doctors are allowing him a few days to recover before they activate the implants' processor and begin auditory therapy," his mother said, "so we're still communicating with him by a tactile pad; but he'll understand if you key in the words slowly."

Walking down the hospital corridor toward Critical Care a few minutes later, Tristan felt as shaky as he had upon leaving the shuttle, awash with bittersweet anticipation.

A pair of police guards posted at the door of the admiral's room eyed Tristan and his uniform as he and his mother approached. Darcie pressed her hand to the identification scanner one of them produced and then said, "This is our son, Tristan, just back from the Issel system."

The guard made an ID scan of Tristan's hand, too. "Good to have you home," he said, and stepped aside to let them both pass.

When the door slid open, Tristan froze on the threshold.

Admiral Serege lay on his back in a fluid suspension bed, his head encased in curafoam bandaging so that he seemed to be wearing a close-fitting white helmet. Slack facial muscles allowed his mouth to sag open a little, and a narrow tube emerged from an opening in his throat. He appeared to be asleep; his eyes were closed, perhaps held shut by the small silver discs at their outer corners.

Tristan's throat constricted; he tore his vision away from his father's face, swallowing hard.

His mother scanned the vital-signs monitor on the wall above the bed, then checked the tactile pad placed on the admiral's upper chest. Apparently satisfied, she turned to a small keyboard on the bedside cabinet and began to tap out a message.

The admiral opened his eyes. Seemed to look directly at her for a moment, then began to blink: a deliberate effort, though it seemed erratic, starting and stopping and starting again.

Tristan recognized it in a moment: a dot code that Tonaso had taught him. ". . . feel better," he read—evidently in response to what his mother had written.

Darcie patted her mate's shoulder. "Good," she tapped out, and then, "Tris is here, love."

The admiral's mouth worked a little, as if he were trying to speak, but the tracheostomy didn't allow any sound. His right hand moved slightly at his side.

Darcie picked up that hand and then reached for Tristan's. She placed them together, one in the other.

Tristan closed his hand tightly about his father's: the hand that, barely two months before, had been placed with such power upon his head. The fingers were warm but strengthless now, unable even to wrap about his own.

Tristan's throat tightened again at that. It was some moments before he reached out with his free hand. "I'm home, Father," he wrote. "Finally." He tapped it out in dot code on his father's chest. "I'll be here whenever you need me."

ABOUT THE AUTHOR

Originally from Smithfield, Utah, Diann Thornley now lives in Ohio, where she was stationed during her active-duty career in the U.S. Air Force. She has also lived in Texas and the Republic of Korea, courtesy of the Air Force. Now a member of the Air Force Reserves, she is still fascinated with high-performance aircraft (both U.S. and foreign) and anything related to medicine. She has completed her third novel for Tor books and is currently working on a fourth, also set in the Unified Worlds universe. Her short fiction has been published in *The Leading Edge* magazine and in a 1993 anthology entitled *Washed by a Wave of Wind*.